CW00983400

May you follow your
path towards harmony,
Maria Pelengin

The Veils Of Illusion

A Novel

(An Allegory: Mind, Body, Spirit)

By
Maria Pelengaris

authorHOUSE™

1663 LIBERTY DRIVE, SUITE 200
BLOOMINGTON, INDIANA 47403
(800) 839-8640
WWW.AUTHORHOUSE.COM

First published by AuthorHouse 11/14/05

ISBN: 1-4208-8486-7 (sc)

Printed in the United States of America
Bloomington, Indiana

This book is printed on acid-free paper.

Dedications

This book is dedicated to my father.
Although you did not live to see this,
you are always with me.

Also, for my beloved mother.

With special love and thanks to D. K Lingham,
without whose support and guidance this book
would not have come to fruition.

With thanks to artist Jacquelyn Lemley Owens for
the beautiful cover image "virgo".

Contents

Part One
Awakening

Chapter One
The Cage

Sophia sat cross-legged on the floor of the Cage, her long dark hair hanging loosely around her rather pale drawn face. She felt older than her twenty-seven years. Her big brown eyes looked longingly out through the bars of the Cage that had entrapped her for so long. How she longed to be free, to feel alive . . . . . 'Whatever that means,' she said quietly to herself.

Just then, as the rumblings of her soul got louder, Sophia found herself uttering an impassioned plea:

'Here I sit inside my Cage
In the midst of a forest clearing,
Intriguing sounds of nature all around me
Whetting my appetite, arousing my senses
For I could explore this fascinating jungle
Of colour and sounds,
If it were not for this Cage.

If only I could get out!
If only I could find the key!
Why would anyone want to trap me?

I start to pace up and down my Cage
Feeling the anger begin to seethe in me.
I grip the bars with my bare hands
And start to shake them violently,
'Let me out,' I scream,
'I want to be free!'

Then falling to the ground,
I hang my head in despair.
About to give up
I suddenly look up
At the door of the Cage,
Only to find that there is no lock
And there is no key to be found . . . . .'

In disbelief, Sophia slowly got up from the floor and opened the Cage door. As she took her first steps outside, she felt very strange and somewhat dazed by her new-found freedom.

Sophia had wanted to escape from the restrictions in her life for so long, that now she had found her way out of the Cage, she felt lost. For she had spent most of her time on the inside looking out, waiting and hoping that someone would come to rescue her. But every time someone came along they were never quite "right" so she had decided that it was probably just as well to stay where she was. Somewhere deep inside, however, Sophia had questioned the validity of her assumptions, and as time moved on she had started to wonder whether she would always be looking outside of herself, for someone or something to rescue her. She had started to fear that she would be waiting forever.

Yet now it seemed she had managed to free herself purely by chance! "So how," Sophia wondered, "has this all come about?" As her mind preoccupied itself with such thoughts, she wandered around the forest clearing aimlessly.

Suddenly a man's voice said, 'Ah, so you finally broke out of your Cage. Well it was about time, miss! I've seen you in there for quite sometime now.'

Sophia was startled by the presence of this stranger, who was standing only a few yards away from her, and by the nature of his message.

'Well I hope you were enjoying the show!' she responded defensively. 'Watching me struggle, were you? Why on earth didn't you try to get me out?' For she could not believe that this man had not helped her.

'Because the time was not right,' he replied, nonplussed by Sophia's anger.

'And I suppose the right time is now, is it?' she continued, rather sarcastically. Then, seeing that there was no response, she said, 'Well?! Why is it the right time?'

The man seemed to soften his posture a little before delivering his answer. 'Because you had to discover for yourself that your feelings of entrapment were self-imposed. Only then could you see that there was a way to get out. I could have come and held the door open for you but if you were not ready to come out, then you wouldn't have.'

Sophia was stunned by his words. She had always thought of herself as a woman who was dynamic and independent; a woman who made her own choices. Yet here was someone she had never met before, behaving as if he knew her better than she knew herself. Her anger began to resurface.

'You don't know what you're talking about! Of course this wasn't self-imposed! What do you take me for? I do what I want, when I want!'

'Then why have you been looking out, hoping for someone to come along and rescue you? Rescue you from what?' the man replied indignantly, so sure was he of

Sophia's predicament.

She didn't like what he had said one bit, yet he had her stumped. Sophia clenched her jaw and fists in frustration, for she didn't know how to reply to this man, and she was too afraid to face the prospect of there being any truth in what he was saying. She walked a few paces away from him, trying to think, trying to comprehend what was happening to her. It was all so confusing.

Yes, it was true that Sophia had often been looking for something else or someone else to change her life, but every time "it" came along she never felt that it was quite right. Or perhaps it was at first, but after a while everything would be the same again; a burst of life, eventually followed by a return to an insidious feeling of deadness within her. At other times, there were ongoing feelings of tension, frustration and resentment; just so many negative thoughts and feelings that Sophia did not care to acknowledge – not now and not before. They had all been blotted out as best as they could, only to be replaced by ensuing feelings of guilt followed eventually by more deadness.

Suddenly the man spoke again. 'Yes, you have been round the round-a-bout a few times haven't you?' he said matter-of-factly. 'But welcome to the next step of your journey.'

It seemed to Sophia as if this rather impertinent and intrusive man had read her mind. It made her feel even more uncomfortable, but it also had the effect of bringing her back to the present moment with a jolt. 'Do you mind?!' she retorted. 'I think you're being very rude. Who are you to tell me about myself? I've just met you – what do you know about me?'

Sophia was very much on the defensive, trying to make a feeble attempt to protect her feelings from what she saw as an attack. Yet still she remained standing there, although now her arms were clasped tightly across her chest and her stare was averted away from the direction of the man. The tension began to rise as Sophia continued to stand in the same spot, not wanting to stay but not wanting to leave. A state of inertia gripped her, the result of these two opposing forces within her. And then with sudden sharpness of clarity, Sophia knew that she needed to look at these two forces within her. But how? She could not battle with them alone – she needed help – except she had never known how to ask for help.

"And to ask for help from a man," she thought to herself, "this man?!"

For Sophia had spent most of her life managing on her own in the Outside World. It was difficult to know exactly why this was, but it seemed that she had a strong need to prove to herself and the world, that she could get by without any outside help. Yes, she had sometimes asked for practical help, a bit of advice or "muscle" here and there – but not raw emotional help or support. That would be, in Sophia's mind, like giving in to a rather distasteful image: that of the submissive woman. Yet here in this strange forest of colour and sounds, Sophia was faced with a possible life-changing dilemma:

"Do I walk away and go into the forest on my own with no map, no compass and no idea of where I am or where I'm going, but with my pride intact?" she contemplated to herself. "Or do I swallow my pride and try to converse with this man, who I don't necessarily like, but who nevertheless is here and knows the forest?"

There was of course one more option, which Sophia could hardly bring herself to even consider, and that was to go back into the Cage. The Cage, which stood for all that was restricted and limited in her life - in her mind, body and soul. Sophia had lived in this Cage for so long without fully realising it. And when she had realised that her world had become too small and suffocating, she assumed it was "others" who restricted her, and therefore "they" who were at fault and had to change. It was "they" who held the key to her freedom; it was "they" who trapped her. The rest of the time, Sophia had simply accepted these restrictions as part of her life. "For isn't it just the same with everyone? Well, most people anyway," she had often thought, thus deciding to try to make the most of what she had. And that, for the most part, was what Sophia had done. Until now.

She stopped and looked back at the open Cage. 'So, was this the prison that I created?' she said quietly, not really wanting to hear the answer. But she did know that she was not about to choose to go back into the Cage.

Whilst a multitude of thoughts ran through her mind, Sophia's body posture had changed without her realising. Instead of the rigid and defensive stance - arms tightly crossed as if to provide the necessary armour for her upper body and its insides - her shoulders and head had now fallen somewhat, and her arms rested upon her abdomen. Seemingly oblivious to the presence of the man, Sophia's new stance seemed to display a need for nurturing and comfort rather than one of keeping the world at bay. In its unspoken way, Sophia's body had answered the dilemma she was facing: It was telling her that she needed more love and care in her life, that she needed to let go and accept some help.

Gradually, Sophia became more conscious of herself and of the presence of the man. She felt as if her inner vulnerability was being exposed, as though she was standing naked for all to see and to humiliate. As she lifted up her head to face the man, she felt that he could have represented the whole world at that point. She expected him to be smirking at her, or something similar at any rate. Yet at this very moment, Sophia was passed caring. She didn't feel as if she had much of a choice in her current predicament, and this in itself gave her an unbelievable sense of relief. For she had finally come to the point where she didn't have the will or energy to keep fighting.

'What am I fighting for anyway?' she suddenly said aloud, without looking at the man who stood in silence. 'I mean, I don't actually care what you or anyone thinks!' Sophia sounded rather majestic in her announcement, if not a little unfair. But, to her, she had made a very significant discovery, which she was now about to enlighten her companion with:

'You see,' she began, 'it's not like when you get into a strop with someone, and then say – "I don't care what you think". That's different because underneath - if we really cared to admit it - what we are really saying is that we do care, but we're damned if we're going to show it, or give others the pleasure of knowing how we feel!' Sophia suddenly seemed to be in her element, pausing momentarily before continuing. 'Well, this "I don't care"- that I'm feeling now - is different. I'm not just saying it for the sake of saying it. I truly believe it! I've finally given up the fight, you see, and somehow I feel a sense of peace. Do you know what I mean?'

For the first time she looked directly at the man, though not necessarily wanting a reply from him. She saw that he was not smirking, nor was he looking at her in a patronisingly sympathetic manner or anything else that could be construed as offensive. In fact, Sophia could not describe how he was looking at her, except that it was exactly how she would wish him to look at her. She couldn't describe it, because it was nothing like she had ever known. "Yes, that's it," she suddenly thought to herself, "it's a knowing look. As if he knows my pain underneath these well rehearsed defences."

In silence she turned away, realising that this was something she had always yearned for. To have someone or something just to be there, without expectation or demand; a guardian angel of sorts, who was not going to judge, scorn or give advice when she didn't want it or need it. Tears began to fall down Sophia's face. It seemed that in such a short space of time her emotions had see-sawed from one extreme to another, something she was most unused to in her life. Yet it was the very attempt to keep everything under control, that had made her life feel like a prison. It was only now that she had stepped out of her Cage, that Sophia was so glaringly aware of how much she had relied on her conscious rational mind to direct her life, her goals, her decisions, in order for her to maintain a sense of control. And there was nothing terribly wrong with that in itself, except that it had ended up being an end in itself!

'And what's the point of that?' Sophia asked out loud, as she turned her tear-strained face back towards the man. 'I mean, why be so fearful of the unknown, of things we don't have much control over? Emotions, whims, fantasies; this is the stuff that makes us feel alive, isn't it?! If so much in life feels like it is under control for fear that it will be out-of-control, then aren't we just continually trying to tame a wild beast that we fear will burst out of its cage and create catastrophe and havoc?'

So much emotion was being expressed with her newly forming beliefs and in the questioning of her old ones, that the man who had patiently waited with her, did not think of interrupting. This was a new experience in itself for Sophia – to be listened to - and it allowed her to spring forth those murmurs from the "beast" she felt had been contained deep within her.

'No, we are "civilised" human beings, aren't we?' she said, sarcastically. 'We don't have wild beasts to tame. We are the ones who show to the Outside World, how civilised and rational and reasonable we are. We've kept our "beasts" in the Cage where they belong, haven't we?' Sophia pointed over to the Cage, before looking back at the man. 'But these "beasts" are still part of us, somewhere in that deep dark underworld, make no mistake! And the mere fact that we find them so abhorrent, has led us to convince ourselves that they don't exist at all. No, those dark forces only exist in the more "undesirables" of people!'

With these new insights, Sophia was clearly angry at what she saw as the extreme hypocrisy of the world in which she had been living. But more than that, she was angry at what it had done to her; at what she had let it do to her. She started to pace back and forth, as if still restricted in her movements by the Cage. Finally she stopped pacing, her anger having somewhat abated, and let out a heavily laden sigh. Looking down at the ground, Sophia spoke her next words with heart-felt sincerity:

'I'm beginning to feel that I have killed off half of myself. I have been so scared of that "beast" and of what others might think of it, that I have become half a person – a reasonable, rational, helpful, in-control person. Not bad, I suppose, but I have felt so rigid and lifeless at times.'

She lifted her head and for the first time addressed the man directly, in a more open and friendly way; 'But now I am going to find out what I really want in this lifetime. So, please . . . . . which way shall I go then? To get out of this forest, I mean?'

The man grinned, then simply replied, 'Follow me.'

'Oh, by the way, what's your name?'

'Bob.'

Sophia scuttled after him. 'My name's Sophia.'

'I know,' was the quick yet familiar response.

Sophia thought about asking him how he knew, but decided instead to direct her energy towards a more worthwhile cause.

"I think this is going to be a long journey," she thought to herself.

Chapter Two
The Crossroads

B ob was a trustworthy person. He had lived and worked within the surrounds of the ancient forest for so long now that he knew it like the back of his hand. He saw himself as a kind of "policeman of the woods", a duty he took very seriously, and one which had seen him direct many people safely on their way. Such was his want to focus entirely on the task at hand, that most people who met him found his ways a little strange. Bob did not much care about that; as long as these same people found their way safely out of the forest, it would be enough for him.

Sophia followed swiftly behind Bob, away from the clearing and through a section of the forest. She could see he was a man of relatively few words, intent on performing his task with as few distractions as possible. Hence, Sophia was not able to appreciate with any real purpose the natural wonders of the forest and its inhabitants. There was undoubtedly a sense of urgency in his strides, and at times Sophia struggled to keep up with him. She wondered where on earth they were going, feeling both a sense of anxiety and excitement at the newness of it all. But Sophia was concentrating so much on keeping up with Bob, that she hadn't realised he had stopped. Onwards she hurried, all the time looking down at the ground so as not to trip up on any obstacle in her path. Her dark hair was matted with sweat, and her vision was becoming increasingly blurred. Sophia knew she could not go on anymore.

Stumbling to the ground, she gasped for air, her heart pounding so hard that it was the only sound she could hear and the only sensation she could feel. She lay on her side for several minutes until her breathing returned to something resembling normality. Then, she slowly pulled herself up to a sitting position and looked around her.

'Bob! Are you there?' She waited for a reply but none came. 'BOOoob!' she shouted. 'WHERE ARE YOU?'

Feelings of panic began to take hold, as Sophia realised that she was on her own. Getting to her feet, she dragged her heavy limbs in the same direction as before. She couldn't believe that Bob would do this to her. She felt as though she had left one cage for another. All she could do now was to keep going. This time though, she kept her eyes peeled ahead of her, in the desperate hope of finding her way out of the forest.

Then she saw it: the edge of the forest. Suddenly, Sophia felt a new surge of energy, which helped her to move with greater ease towards it. Perhaps Bob had shown her the right way after all, she thought to herself, as she approached it.

Standing at the edge of the forest, Sophia saw the large expanse of grey sky above, and the large open space of bare level terrain below. The sudden brightness made her squint. There was still no sign of Bob, which she found to be very odd, but she could only assume once again that he had completed his task of pointing her in the right direction.

'So, now what?' she sighed, as her eyes skimmed the horizon.

This, however, was not that fruitful a past-time because Sophia was rather short-sighted, so could not be sure of any object beyond about twenty feet - unless of course it was a very large object! Then there was the greyness of the sky, which did not help much in terms of visibility. In fact, there was no defining object or entity within her immediate vicinity that indicated to Sophia where she should go.

Then, as if to prevent a further downward slide in her spirits, she started to walk. 'Come on then, old girl. There must be something out there.'

Sophia walked for about an hour in what was a fairly straight line. The ground was pretty solid making it good for brisk walking, but its grey-brown colour with nothing else to interrupt the monotony, offered little inspiration or joy to the proceedings. Eventually though, Sophia was to come across something of great significance. For in the distance, she saw what appeared to be a Crossroads.

As she approached the Crossroads, more details became visible to her. There was a weather-vane located at the centre of the intersection, and an old woman sitting by the side of it. Sophia slowed down the pace of her steps as she approached. The old woman seemed to be in a world of her own, not flinching at the sound of Sophia's footsteps. She wore a headscarf of blue and white, as she looked dreamily into the distance from under its rim. Sophia had got to within a dozen feet of the woman, before deciding to stop and wait. Suddenly she felt awkward, as if she was intruding upon someone else's space, even though this clearly was public domain.

Sophia decided to retreat a few steps. She sat down by the roadside with her back facing the old woman. She needed time to think. Her options seemed very similar to the situation she had faced with Bob: To ask for help, or go it alone. She found herself starting to feel like she was being tested somehow. "Yet why make such a big deal out of it?" she wondered to herself. "Well, that's easy," was her lightning reply to herself, "I'm not used to asking for help, am I? Pathetic really!" Sophia sighed heavily, not realising how loud it was.

'My, that's a heavy sigh for one so young,' the old woman suddenly said.

Sophia's head shot round to see that the woman was smiling at her, though her eyes were closed.

'Oh, I don't feel so young,' replied Sophia.

'But you are, my dear.'

Sophia smiled back at the old woman, not quite sure how to continue the interaction.

"What am I supposed to say to her?" Sophia thought to herself. "Can you tell which way to go please, even though you don't know me or anything about me?"

There was no doubt that she was caught in what was fast becoming a familiar trap, yet she could no longer use her old tools and techniques to help her out of this one. This was unknown territory for Sophia.

Then, as if to answer the never-ending conflicts in Sophia's head, the old woman began to recite a verse of poetry to Sophia:

'Why am I still standing at the Crossroads?
When will I know it is time to move on?
Which will be my chosen path?
And how will I know?

Yet each time I ask myself this,
I hear a wise voice in my head, saying:
"You will know when the time is right."

Yes, it is my impatience that blinds me,
For I feel I've wasted time as it is.
Such contradictions all around to be seen,
And I've never been good at standing still.

So, perhaps this is one lesson I have to learn.
To act recklessly now would just leave more wreckage,
And there's enough deadwood in my lifetime,
For me to clear through.'

Sophia had listened to every word intently, and the words had both comforted her and frightened her. This woman seemed to know her, really know her. In fact she seemed to know Sophia better than Sophia knew herself! How could that be? She had only just met her! Sophia was starting to find this journey rather surreal, if not plain cryptic. The people she had encountered thus far were unlike any she had known before in her life, and she was finding that she didn't know how to interact with them. How was Sophia to respond to what she had just heard? Yet she felt rude not saying anything, because there was little doubt that the words were meant especially for her.

A fidgety, awkward Sophia got to her feet as quietly as she could. 'Thank you', she said, before wandering by the roadside aimlessly.

The old woman remained silent, still looking dreamily into the distance as if she belonged to another world; a special world. But it was not long before Sophia started to feel agitated, pacing up and down as she had done inside and outside the Cage. She found herself repeating a line from the old woman's poem:

'It is my impatience that blinds me'.

As much as she didn't want to believe it, Sophia knew that she had to put her faith in something or someone other than herself, and it seemed that the lesson now was: to be still.

The two women sat in their different places for quite some time. Neither looked at the other or spoke, yet in their inner worlds they were miles apart. For the old woman sat in peaceful contentment in the centre of the Crossroads, untroubled by decisions concerning directions or anything else. She could have been there for eternity, in contrast to the younger woman who struggled to contain her impatience and agitation. But struggle Sophia did, using her older companion as a visual guide and model of tranquillity. And eventually, Sophia did calm her physical state of being, down to a more tolerable level.

The old woman's voice then entered the silence; 'It is time for you to make a decision as to which way you are to go. It is time to make your choice.'

Sophia was surprised by suddenly hearing the woman's voice, but not by the sentiment expressed. 'I know,' she whispered. 'I have waited here for a while until I felt calmer, so that my decision would not be based on reckless impulse - as you said in your poem.'

The old woman smiled in acknowledgement. 'Then you need to make your first steps, for I believe that you already know which road to take, even if it is the one that scares you most.'

Sophia got to her feet, starting to feel more nervous on hearing these words. For in truth, she didn't really understand them. She stepped onto the road and walked towards the centre of the Crossroads, looking up at the weather vane and its four directions. All the while, the old woman did not look directly at her but continued to look into the distance.

'Actually, I don't know which way to go,' Sophia said, anxiously. 'I'm not sure whether it matters much? I expect there'll be a testing time ahead no matter which direction I choose?' Then, revealing her lack of conviction in her own words, she added, 'I don't suppose you could point me in the right direction, could you? I mean, if there is a right direction?'

The old woman did not speak but let out a little chuckle, which left Sophia with no doubts as to her answer.

'No, I didn't think so,' Sophia sighed. 'Worth a try though, don't you think?'

Again, there was no reply. Sophia was beginning to wonder why she didn't just choose a direction and walk! What was holding her back? Particularly as it was clear that she wasn't going to get an affirmative response. With this in mind, she decided to be honest about her reasons for deliberating.

'Okay,' she began, taking a deep breath. 'I guess I would like to have a crystal ball, or a wise person like yourself, to tell me what lies ahead. I know that's not possible but what if I was to go down one road, to the East say, and find that there's a big black hole, what do I do then? I'd have to come all the way back again, exhausted and demoralised, with very little inclination to set off again! You see, I don't feel I have much energy left as it is. To be honest, I'm finding this all very hard . . . . in fact, it scares me.'

Sophia was surprised at her own honesty. Yet it was this honesty that prompted the old woman to speak:

'Yes, my dear, I can see that you are weary and rather downhearted. But is that not why you are here at this Crossroads? Everything is a paradox, you see; when you think you have all the answers, that is when you are most blind. Then, when you realise there is much you do not know and are searching for answers, that is when you are in fact more seeing, more knowing of yourself.'

'I suppose so,' Sophia sighed. She was glad to hear

the old woman's voice, but remained as confused as ever.

Looking down at the ground for a while, Sophia was able to maintain a somewhat peaceful silence. Slowly it began to sink in that she needed to accept her predicament rather than to try to force it; she needed to accept that she didn't know all the answers, and that by doing this she would allow the answers to come to her - eventually. Or at least that was the theory.

Sophia decided to set herself the task of making up her mind which direction to walk in, and then to stick to it. 'Okay then,' she said forthrightly, 'I will make a decision! North, South, East, or West? Let me see? . . . . . North reminds me of colder climates and darkness, so I won't go that way . . . . . South on the other hand feels warmer to me, so maybe I could go that way . . . . . East is towards the sun . . . yes, I like the idea of that.'

As she got into the swing of it, Sophia began to feel a touch of excitement. She was already making progress, no matter how gradual or arbitrary the decision making process seemed to be. Suddenly it came to her:

'That's it!' she said triumphantly. 'I'll go West! For that is the direction the sun takes as it moves across the sky. So, I'm going to follow the sun!'

Sophia walked over to the start of the West Road. She looked and felt much lighter already. At last she was going to expend some of her energy in pursuing her path, rather than wasting it on the internal conflicts in her mind.

Before heading off, she looked over at the old woman, and said, 'Thank you for listening, it's been more helpful than I thought, just knowing someone's there. And it's true that with your help I eventually came to a decision myself. Of course, now I can't blame you if things go wrong!' Sophia laughed heartily.

The old woman finally looked directly at Sophia, and smiled. 'Good luck, my dear. You have chosen well.'

It was only then that Sophia realised her companion was blind.

Sophia had been walking along the West Road for about an hour. The sun was high in the sky on what was a particularly warm day, and Sophia was longing for shelter and rest. In the distance, she could see a sparsely wooded area, and was determined to get to it as soon as she could.

When she got there, she gratefully sat down in the shade of one of the trees, and before long was fast asleep. She wasn't sure how long she had been there, but something suddenly jolted her out of her deep sleep. It felt as if something had touched her face. Quickly, Sophia looked around her to make sure that no one was there, and when satisfied that that was the case she got to her feet.

'I must have been dreaming,' she said, feeling a little dazed. 'But then, this whole journey feels a bit like a dream.'

The sun was still fairly high in the sky, but now a pleasant breeze blew through the wood. Sophia felt surprisingly peaceful, not to mention pleased with her choice of direction. She wondered whether to stay a while longer, or to go further on into the woods. As she stretched her arms above her head, one of her hands touched a branch, and in an instant a bird swooped down in front of her swiftly followed by another. A startled Sophia sprinted several feet away from the tree, cursing in her defence. The two birds circled the tree for a while, before eventually coming to rest on one of the branches. It was only then that Sophia realised there was a nest in the tree, and that the birds were obviously protecting their young. She hadn't been dreaming after all – something had touched her face!

Sophia grinned up at the birds. 'I get the message! This is your tree, and you don't want any outsiders invading your space. I'm really sorry little birds . . . . . I think I'll take it as a sign to move on!'

And with that, she headed off into the heart of the open woods, not entirely realising the amount of truth in her words. For this was just the start of many signs and messages that would come Sophia's way, as part of the learning of the West Road.

By now, the sky was interspersed with clouds of grey and white. Increasingly uncomfortable with the occurrences taking place, Sophia started to swim back towards the bank. But before she could make any ground, the same voice sounded with the same message:

'TO BE TRULY FREE YOU HAVE TO FACE YOURSELF.'

It seemed to be pulling her back into the main body of water.

This time Sophia responded. 'I don't understand what you mean! Who are you?' she said anxiously.

She stopped moving and tried to be as quiet as she could, in the hope that she would hear or see something. For it was a nice voice, a kind voice, and she wanted to understand its message. But there was an almost eerie silence as clouds began to gather around Sophia. They descended at an amazingly rapid rate, until there was no clear division between sky and sea. Sophia became almost paralysed by what was happening, and it was not long before the bank disappeared from view. The misty clouds twisted and swirled into different shapes and patterns, whilst Sophia looked on in disbelief.

And then . . . . gradually the clouds began to disperse, leaving a gap through which Sophia could see the figure of a woman ahead in the distance. Like Sophia, the woman was immersed in the water up to her shoulders, but she was looking out across the sea seemingly unaware of Sophia's presence. Sophia tried to get her attention by calling out to her, but there was no response. It was as if Sophia was looking through a one-way mirror, whereby she could see and hear the other person, but the other person could not see or hear her.

Suddenly the woman began to speak, and with such a commanding tone and sense of purpose, that Sophia could not help but be her captive audience:

'I had to look to see,
That which I did not wish to see.
The need that I had abandoned in me,
Cast deep in the ocean of thoughts,
Where no ships pass through day or night.
For ships will not come to rescue in calm waters.

Yet under calm waters a storm began to brew,
And like the hurricanes in our natural world,
There was nothing I could do.
For it threatened to bring to the surface,
The "me" I had buried down below.'

Sophia felt moved upon hearing this - as if the woman's sentiments somehow reflected something deep within Sophia herself. But who was this woman at sea? Where had she come from? And what was she in relation to Sophia? Sophia was contemplating whether to try to swim a little nearer to her, when suddenly the waters surrounding the woman started to swell. As the previously calm waters became rougher, Sophia quickly realised that the words she had just heard were now beginning to play themselves out.

The woman began to struggle against the rising waves as they jostled her one way and then another. She cried out to the culprit below the surface of the sea:

'GO AWAY! You are causing too much commotion, can't you see? The sea was calm before you started to shout and scream! You're going to drag me down with you, until we are both blocked from other people's view.'

Then, a distressed voice rumbled from the depths of the sea, up to the surface:

'Is that all you care about? What you look like to others? WHAT ABOUT ME? No-one can see me, not even you!'

'But who are you?' the woman above the water replied frantically. 'I don't recognise you.'

The voice underneath the water persisted:

'Then let me tell you. But you will have to bring me closer to you, otherwise you won't be able to hear.'

The woman above the water began to plead:

'I can't come down there, I've told you that! For then we will both be lost from this world.'

Then the voice from the depths of the sea began to sound more pained and resigned to its fate, saying:

'I am already lost from your world. Yet for all the time you've been up there, no ship has passed to offer you help.'

The woman above the water was clearly thrown by these words, as she struggled to maintain her upright position:

'But I . . I have no need for anyone's help. My waters are calm, it is y-yours that are not,' she said, desperately trying to discourage the voice from below the water.

But the voice of opposition would not be discouraged and so continued unabated:

'But we both share the same body of water, do we not? If I dare to move or speak, the ripples impact on you also. And if I do not move or speak, then I am but trapped in this underwater world. And YOU, . . . YOU exist in a world of lifeless calm! Is that what you want?'

By now, the continuous rising and falling of the waves brought about by the voice underneath the water, was beginning to drain the energy of the woman above the water.

'I don't know if it's what I want,' the woman above the water replied tiredly. 'But it's what I know.'

'So you are afraid of what you do not know?' the voice underneath continued to persist.

'I didn't say that!' shouted the woman above in desperation. 'How can I be afraid when I never need help? It is others who need help, and I who help them!'

'Then why won't you help ME?' cried the voice from underneath the water, determined not to let go of the woman above.

'Because if I help you, you won't go away,' replied the woman above in angry tones. 'You will be up here with me, rather than down there where I can't see you.'

The woman above the water was now also agitating the water by thrashing about with her arms and legs, trying in vain to get rid of the voice below.

The voice underneath the water was gripped with anguish: 'Why do you hate me so? Why am I such a burden to you?'

Suddenly, to the great surprise of the woman above the water, it delivered its parting message:

'Now I will try to be more silent, so that your waters slowly calm. For I would rather remain alone and unseen, than to be seen and hated - to be scorned by all those up there who you hold in such high esteem. Here, at least it is only I who can hold myself in esteem. All I have is my honesty, my truth, me.'

And then the voice from below the water was gone, and the sea became still once more.

Sophia was so engrossed in all she had just seen and heard that she began to feel emotionally and physically drained herself. For although she was at a distance, she had nevertheless been close enough to be affected by the roughness of the sea. Sophia had found herself at first to be worried about the woman above the water, but then her heartstrings were pulled by the cries of the voice from under the sea. Sophia couldn't help but feel pained by the abandonment of the person who was hidden below the surface.

Sophia wasn't sure what to do. For she could still see the woman above the water in the distance looking out across the sea. The woman seemed unaware of Sophia's presence like before. Sophia tried to call out to the woman, but there was no response. She wondered whether to make her way back, for she was starting to feel a chill build up inside her. Yet she also felt she would be abandoning the woman in the distance, if she just swam away from her. What was Sophia to do? What was the meaning of all this?

As if to answer Sophia's dilemma, the woman in the distance began to speak once again. Her voice no longer had its previous commanding sound, this time softer and more sad in nature. Nevertheless, Sophia could hear every word with the clarity of someone speaking right next to her. The woman was speaking to the voice underneath the water:

'I guess I always knew you were down there
But I never dared to look,
Not too closely anyway.
And although I did not like the stormy seas
That your rumblings brought,
At least I knew I was in a sea!

For I could feel the ebb and flow of the water
Under my feet and touching my body.
I could feel myself because of what was touching me,
And I was touched by your honesty,
As pure as any water I may drink from a stream.

More perfect than the face I show to the world,
Knowing that it is what "they" want to see,
Rather than that which is the true me.
In truth I know that I have been afraid,
Afraid that ships would pass and not notice me,
If I was not the "me" they wanted to see.

So that is why I left you down there
When I can see now that you are the one,
The one who speaks the truth.
And if all I have done is dismiss you,
Tell me why you still ask help from someone like me?'

Silence then returned to the proceedings, but it was a silence filled with emotion, as the woman above the water waited to hear from the voice below. Suddenly the woman couldn't bear to think that she might never hear from the voice below the sea again. And she had never felt more alone than she did now.

The woman above the water suddenly felt the sea begin to gently swirl around her, touching her body with the gentleness and ease which only the fluidity of water could bring. The woman's spirits rose, as she heard the lost voice from underneath the water, say:

'I always hoped that one day you would hear me. I have had to live in hope. You see, that is my reality.'

The woman above the water began to cry:

'You've touched me deeply. This ocean could be filled with my tears. And how strong you are compared to me.'

'And you are more in need than you care to admit,' returned the voice from underneath. 'You worry that ships will not see you and that you will be left alone, yet they only see you from the distant horizon. They never come close because they can see you are not in need. As you have said: "ships do not come to rescue in calm waters."'

'But why should they only come close in order to rescue?' asked the woman above the water. 'That is what I do not understand! Why not just come close to see me?'

It was now the voice from below, which brought a sense of calmness and balance, for it knew that it had finally managed to engage the protagonist of the show - the one who showed her face to the Outside World. And the voice underneath the water wanted to help the woman above. So she continued:

'It seems as though you want ships to come close to you, but you don't want them to see you too closely! How can that be?' The voice underneath the water let out a quiet ripple of laughter.

The woman above the water was a little perturbed at first to hear the laughter, but it wasn't long before she too saw the funny side of her predicament. In fact, she was rather relieved to have a lighter note entering into the equation. She began chuckling in unison with the voice underneath the water, whilst the sun suddenly appeared from behind a cloud.

'And I also see a disparity,' the woman above the water said to the voice underneath. 'You are the honest and wise one, who is not afraid to speak the truth, yet I keep you hidden far beneath me for fear that it is you who will not be liked. I like you more than I like me! Yet I want others to see ME! How can THAT be?'

The laughter had stopped now, as the voice underneath the water shared its own wisdom with the woman above the water, before finally departing:

'Because, people are afraid of their own inner truths. You must not worry too much about others' truths; they are not yours to worry too much about! Worry instead about your own. Worry instead about me. Help me, for I am part of you.'

In the distance, Sophia watched whilst the clouds blew away as rapidly as they had appeared. The chill had gone away and now the sun beat down strongly upon Sophia's face, her eyes squinting to see what was happening with the woman above the water. Putting her hand up to shield her eyes, Sophia saw that the woman was gently swimming towards her. When the woman had got closer, she stopped swimming and looked directly at Sophia, smiling. Sophia could not believe her eyes. For the woman looked exactly like her!

Suddenly, the sun's rays flashed across Sophia's eyes, momentarily blinding her. Then when her vision was restored, Sophia saw that the woman above the water had disappeared . . . .

At that same moment, Sophia awoke from her sleep. She was very confused at first, and then astonished to discover that she was floating in the middle of a large lake. She splashed her eyes with the cool water and shook her head to make sure she was actually awake. Everything around her seemed the same as when she had first entered the lake, but Sophia herself felt different. All she wanted to do now was to get out of the water. So wasting no more time, she swam as fast as her body would take her towards the bank, before any more strange dreams could take hold of her.

Chapter Four
The Illusion

Sophia heaved herself up on to the bank as if carrying the weight of the world upon her shoulders. She was indeed very shaken and confused by what she had just experienced, albeit in a dream. For the dream had been so vivid and so profound in the nature of its message, that Sophia felt almost overwhelmed by it. Suddenly all she wanted to do was hide away in a cocoon; shut everything and everyone off; make the world go away. But for now, she would curl up her dripping wet body as tightly as she could and cry quietly into the ground beneath her. For the world would not go away.

Instead, Sophia heard a voice that sounded vaguely familiar to her. It said:

'So now you are going to create another cage for yourself when you have just broken out of one!'

Soft and gentle in tone, Sophia recognised it as the old man's voice she had first heard in her dream. She lifted her heavy head to see a man sitting on a rock somewhere between the nearest tree and the edge of the water. He was indeed advanced in years, dressed in black and resting his hands on a cane. To Sophia he looked like the archetypal hermit of centuries gone by.

'And what will you do in your cocoon?' he continued.

'I don't know, I don't care!' Sophia answered back, as she buried her head within the slightly built frame of her body.

The elderly man could hear her snivels. 'I can see you are in pain, my child,' he said kindly. 'To have time on your own may be a good thing, but not if you always cry alone. You must listen to the messages that have come to you through your dream, even if you do not fully understand them. Your child spirit, whose voice spoke from the bottom of the sea, is speaking to you now through your tears – she does not want you to leave her there any longer. You will, in time Sophia, know great joy too through her, but first you need to learn to ask for help. Otherwise, the child's cries will bring overwhelming waves that may drown you. Remember what happened in your dream?'

Sophia began to tremble at the sound of his words. How could he see into her thoughts, enter her dreams? It was all too much for someone so normally level headed to comprehend.

'But I don't know what happened in the dream!' she exclaimed. 'I mean . . . . wasn't it an illusion? And what's this thing about a child? I don't know anything about a child!' Sophia held her head in her hands as her body heaved in tearful convulsions of pain and fear. 'What is happening to me? I'm s-so c-confused . . . . I u-used to help other people, b-be s-strong for them. That is the real me, isn't it?'

She awaited a reassuring reply that didn't come. She could not bring herself to look at the wise old man, or to loosen the tight posture she had placed her body in. Yet somehow Sophia eventually managed to find the words which would lead the wise old man to impart some more of his wisdom upon her:

'I don't know how to ask for help. Not really,' she said in a quiet voice. 'Not help for me personally.'

'What are you frightened of, my child?'

'Rejection, I suppose,' Sophia answered spontaneously.

Her body was more still now, and she had uncurled it a little. She lifted her head slightly to look towards the old man, and then continued her confession:

'I am afraid that if others see my dark side - the side I don't like - then they won't want to know me . . . . I guess it's like the woman who was above the water in my dream.'

'Yes, my child,' the wise old man said with quiet enthusiasm. 'There are indeed two sides; it is called duality. Let us consider what just happened in your dream: the woman above the water is the one you most recognise - it is the one you like most and you feel others like too. Therefore, you identify so much with this person that you begin to believe it is who you are. And as you saw in your dream, as long as there are not too many waves, everything stays just as it is. The illusion is intact.'

He paused for a while, concerned not to overburden Sophia with his words. Sophia began to sit up. She felt drained and dizzy, yet willing to hear more. So the wise old man continued:

'Sometimes in life, things happen to disturb the status quo and it is then that you discover the side of yourself that is hidden under the ocean; it is the Unconscious, or your Shadow, if you prefer.'

'No I don't prefer anything!' Sophia retaliated, before quickly moderating her response, 'I mean, I thought I was pretty "together" and independent, yet now I don't feel I know who or what I am. I thought I was good at helping others, at helping them to see their problems with more clarity, when it now seems that I don't even know my own problems let alone how to help myself!'

Sophia could feel the weight of despondency begin to descend upon her. Sensing this, the wise old man altered his approach accordingly:

'Yes, you have helped many people, my dear. And you have helped them so well because you saw the wounded and neglected child within them. You have cared with compassion and insight that can never be learned in an academic institution. But the rest of your life needs to be dedicated to yourself, and to your own child within. The rest will follow, Sophia. The rest will follow.'

Sophia had fallen asleep again, but it was not long before the cold eventually woke her up. It was starting to get dark and she realised that she had fallen asleep in her wet underwear. Managing to prise open her heavy eyelids, her head feeling like it was badly hung-over, Sophia tried to make out where she was. She wondered whether she had been dreaming, this time about an old man wearing black and resting on a cane. The West Road was playing funny tricks on her mind, she decided. But what was real and tangible to Sophia, was the blanket that now covered her.

'Did you have a good sleep?' the familiar, kind voice suddenly said. 'I hope you don't mind my covering you with the blanket, but you looked rather cold and exposed.'

The black cloak of the wise old man now came into Sophia's view, as he approached her. 'N-no, I-I a-am v-very g-grateful,' she said shivering.

The wise old man slowly bent down and placed a large steaming mug by Sophia's side. 'Drink this, my child. It will take away the chill more than any other remedy I know of. I've made a fire near the tree over there,' he said, pointing. 'So if you would like to come and join me when you are ready, I'll spend a little more time with you before I go on my way. Oh, and your clothes are drying by the fire.'

'Th-thank y-you,' Sophia replied, her hand coming out from under the blanket and making its way towards the hot mug.

Sophia sat opposite the wise old man with her blanket wrapped around her shoulders for extra protection and insulation. A gentle fire burned between them. Suddenly Sophia felt very shy in front of this man who had been very kind to her, more kind than she was used to. Yet she had also experienced enough on this journey to know that no small talk or unnecessary conversation would be entered into by her learned companion. So she tried to think of what she could ask him; something that might help her on her journey. But what could she ask him? To Sophia, it would be like asking the way out of a maze, except she didn't even know whether that was what she wanted.

She looked over at the old man and saw that he was sitting in a most peaceful and relaxed posture. He had a white wispy beard and pale blue eyes that looked into the fire and far beyond. "He's probably not even aware of my presence," Sophia thought to herself.

Nevertheless, she found herself asking him: 'Do you live in the woods?'

The faraway eyes drifted back. 'I am here now,' he answered, with a sweet smile.

Silence returned, but suddenly Sophia knew what she wanted to ask. 'In my dream,' she said eagerly, 'yours was the first voice I heard. I'm sure you said: "To truly be free you have to face yourself."' She paused before asking her question. 'But how do I face myself?'

The old man looked at her attentively before answering, 'You must find your way to the Centre Point.'

'Where is that?' Sophia asked excitedly.

'You will know when you find it, my child.'

'What do you mean?' insisted Sophia. For although she was trying not to sound too frustrated or demanding, she was struggling with what she felt to be impossible odds. And she could not contain her mounting anxiety, whilst her companion remained so calm and silent.

'But why do I have to do it all myself?!' she asked, frantically. 'I thought the whole point was for me to ask for help, rather than do everything myself!'

This time the wise old man responded. 'You do not have to do it all by yourself, my child. You will find teachers and guides all the way along your path.'

Sophia seemed to visibly relax as she heard these comforting words. Indeed, if she had only thought about it she would have seen that she had already met and been helped by such people.

The wise old man continued: 'You will be given messages and clues to help you also, but you must be open to receiving them. And when you feel lost and despairing, you must go somewhere very quiet and still within yourself, and ask for help. For if you truly seek help, the Universe will always answer you. But remember, Sophia, although it will be your inner child that feels vulnerable and will ask for help, you yourself are still an adult and will have to learn how to moderate your child's behaviour.'

In the ensuing silence, Sophia felt a mixture of relief and confusion. She nodded and smiled awkwardly at the wise old man, who did not seem ruffled at all by her questions. Instead he sat peacefully for a little while longer before gesturing to speak. When he did, his oratory tones conveyed to Sophia a depth of meaning and insight that was powerful:

'What thoughts lurk in the Unconscious mind?
Repressed but not dismissed,

Somewhere in the tunnel of time.
But, alas, to your soul do not be too unkind,
Do not let your fears, hopes and wishes
Be impossible to find.
For then you are in danger of losing your inner self,
Of meeting the hopes of others,
Of anyone but yourself.
And only in the midst of night
Will there be no need to fear,
When the shadows in your footsteps
Have finally disappeared.
For even a tormented soul
Imprisoned inside a human cage,
Should not underestimate those latent powers
Which can eventually enrage,
By one day revealing to the world
And more especially to you,
No more to live a lie
But to be to yourself forever true.'

Sophia was dumbstruck. But something had happened to her. It was as if this wise old man had spoken to her very soul, and in doing so had awakened it from its slumber.

'I had best be on my way now,' he said, slowly getting to his feet. Then addressing Sophia directly he held out an item towards her. 'I have something for you, Sophia'.

A slightly dejected looking Sophia looked up from the fire and saw that the wise old man was holding up a brown cloth sack.

'I thought this might help you along your way,' he explained. 'It looks heavier than it is'.

Sophia got up, her blanket still wrapped around her, and went over to receive her gift. She thanked the wise old man warmly. The opening at the top of the sack was tied with string and there was a rope cord running through the inside of the sack, which looped around the outside, thus providing a type of shoulder strap. Curious to see what was inside the sack, Sophia began to untie the string.

'Save that for a later time, my child,' the wise old man interrupted. 'It is of greater importance that you see the ancient site which lies along this path. It has a powerful story to tell.'

Sophia's eyes lit up. 'How wonderful! I love ancient sites.'

'Good! Your clothes have now dried,' he pointed with his staff towards Sophia's clothes, which were lying next to the now dying fire, 'so once you have dressed, we will make our way there.'

Sophia followed his instructions in silence. She placed the sack on the ground and went over to pick up her dry clothes. Then she found a nearby tree, behind which she dressed herself as quickly as she could.

'I'm ready,' she announced, coming out from behind the tree. Then, skipping over to her sack, she picked it up and pulled it up over her right shoulder.

'Let us then proceed,' the wise old man smiled.

So on their way they went, the student following her wise teacher into the ancient forest, excited in her anticipation of what was to await her. There was a spring in her step as she left behind her the large body of water, and headed towards the more solid nature of earthly structures. What type of site would it be? A temple? An amphitheatre? Perhaps a castle? All these things, Sophia wondered, as they went deeper and deeper into the forest.

'We are almost there,' said the wise old man, who was now rather out of breath and leaning more and more heavily upon his cane. 'Over there, look! Beyond the trees!' he panted, managing to raise his cane a few feet to point in the same direction.

Sophia looked beyond the trees and saw that there was an open space, but she could not see an ancient structure. Not wanting to jump to conclusions, she decided to wait until they reached the site before saying anything.

What Sophia eventually saw, however, rendered her speechless. Not because of its beauty or untold splendour, nor because of its magnitude and strength, but rather because of its lack of any structure at all! For Sophia found herself looking upon a small field with large pieces of rock strewn across it, and no way of telling what might have once been there before.

'You look disappointed, my child,' the wise old man interrupted her thoughts. 'Were you expecting something else?'

For a moment, Sophia wondered whether she was being teased. Putting her sack on to the ground, she replied, 'I suppose I was expecting something else - when you said it was an ancient site, I mean.'

'But it is an ancient site!' he retorted. 'However, the most important thing is the story behind it – these are the lessons of the West Road.'

With that, the old man walked over to one of the pieces of rock and sat down. Almost immediately it seemed as if he had become part of another world, an ancient world to which he had once belonged, and now he wanted to impart a story of great importance upon his student.

'Come, my dear,' he beckoned. 'Take a seat and let me tell you the Story of the Tower.'

Sophia was now intrigued. She found herself a place on the grass next to a large rock, which she leant against, and waited for her teacher to begin:

The Story of the Tower

The Tower shone its Light for the world to see,
Standing strong and proud as if to say;
'Come to me,
And I will guide you along your path,
I will give you the love that you need.'

And so they came, one by one
Some in awe and some in pain
And some who did not believe
At first.
Yet they also, in time, could not help but be
Touched by the Light that would still shine
In their darkest hours.

Others took a glimpse from afar
Only to turn away and take another path.
Yet still the Tower stood strong and proud,
Its Light shining even brighter,
For now it could see all the good it could do.

And so more people came
To take some of the Light,
Til smiles dawned on their weary faces
Or at least a little pain drained from their eyes.

But the brightness of the Light also cast
Darker shadows which it could not see,
And in the shadows lurked those
Who scorned the Light
And wanted to see it fade.
They would throw stones at the Tower
Or try to stand in the Light's way,
They would seek to turn people away,
Yet still more came.

Til soon the Light flickered and dimmed,
For it could not take the strain
Of all the people in need
And all those who wanted to break
The Tower.

Pieces of rock began to fall away
From the Tower which once stood strong and proud,
And there were those who became angry
At what they saw,
For they wanted the Tower to remain strong for them
And to be guided and comforted by the Light.

There were others still who were glad
At what they saw,
For they wanted their own light to shine instead.

Still more pieces of rock fell away
From the Tower's face,
Until the Light had almost burned itself out.

Finally the Tower had succumbed
To what it could see as its fate.

Alas, the Tower was no longer a tower,
And only the remnants of its shell would remain.

After the Story of the Tower had been told, Sophia's heart felt heavy. She felt as if the stones and pieces of rock strewn on the ground were remnants of a person destroyed under untold pressure and strain.

'What are you thinking?' asked the wise old man. 'You look saddened by this fable.'

'Yes,' Sophia replied in a quiet voice, not looking up at him. For she did not want him to see that she was crying.

There was something about the story which reminded Sophia of herself; not so grand or majestic perhaps, but nevertheless an aspect that was familiar. And for what seemed like an age, Sophia sat in silence against her chosen rock with her head buried in her knees. She had realised by now that she was on this journey to learn about herself, but that it was a type of learning unlike any other. She could never tell, for example, at any given moment what was going to suddenly reach in and touch the deep well of emotion that existed within her. The very moment she felt calmer and more in control of these powerful aspects of human nature, something or someone would come along and let her know otherwise.

'Control!' Sophia finally looked up from her burrow and addressed the wise old man, who had his eyes closed. 'Now that's a thing, isn't it? We all want to be in such control - control of our emotions, our thoughts, our behaviour. And if we can't do that, we do it to others, don't we?'

She was conscious of saying the word "we" when really she meant herself, but Sophia didn't want to feel alone in her inadequacies. The wise old man had opened his eyes to see the face of one who was craving comfort.

'There are many people who have come this way, my child,' he said softly. 'Not all, however, have heard the Story of the Tower. There are some who do not even pause here, they simply pass through.'

Sophia felt greatly comforted by the sound of his voice. It seemed to encourage her to know more and to accept more easily the role of the student. 'Why is that?' she asked. 'I mean, is there any difference between those who pause here, and those who don't?'

'There are many differences between all those who walk this path,' he explained. 'The one thing you all have in common is that you have chosen to come this way, but that is all. Whatever happens along this path is ultimately unique to each individual, for no two individuals have lived the same life even if they have grown up in the same family. You, Sophia, have paused at this particular place because something within you felt drawn to it. The Story of the Tower touched you deeply because it touched on something deep within you; something you alone recognised as familiar, even though you did not consciously realise it.'

'So those who just pass through,' Sophia attempted to clarify, 'don't recognise it as familiar to their own individual experiences, you mean? Whereas other situations they come across may trigger something in them.'

'Yes, that is indeed true,' agreed her teacher. 'It is however also true that others may pass through because they are not yet ready to face something in themselves. It is in fact too deeply buried for them to access.'

Sophia was now bright and alert, her posture straight and upright much to the pleasure of her wise teacher, who had also become somewhat revived himself. He eagerly awaited her next question, which did not take long to arrive.

'So what happens to them then?' she asked. 'The people who just pass through? Shouldn't they stay and face things, rather than escape? Otherwise they are just avoiding things, aren't they?'

The wise old man paused a little as he prepared to express his wisdom in the best way he could. 'It may be the avoidance you speak of,' he began, 'but this is not a competition, my child. To come along this path that you have chosen is not about winning a race or getting to the winning post at the end. That is the stuff of ego's – the side of human nature that seeks to gain status and to accumulate possessions for its own sake, and its own sake alone. Defences – like the walls of the Tower - are there to guard and protect the ego. This path of the West Road is about the truth which is hidden behind those defences.

You see, Sophia, one can only be exposed to as much truth as one can take. Otherwise it can be overwhelming...'

His voice trailed off as he looked upon the rubble scattered across the field. And for a moment Sophia wondered whether the Story of the Tower reflected a time in his own life.

'Yes,' a more thoughtful Sophia responded, 'I think I know what you mean.'

After a short time spent in contemplation, the wise old man began to take his leave. 'And now, my child, I really must be on my way.'

As he got to his feet, Sophia could see that he was saddened. Yet she was even more concerned by her own feelings of fear at the thought of him leaving her. She remained firmly rooted to the spot, unable to bid him farewell.

The wise old man came over to where Sophia sat. As she felt the palm of his hand upon her head, she fought to stem the flow of her tears.

'Do not be afraid, Sophia. Keep going along your path and you will reach the Centre Point, however long it takes.' Then removing his hand, he made his way back in the direction of the lake.

As Sophia watched him go she tried to call after him in an attempt to thank him, but every time she tried nothing seemed to come out of her mouth. She recalled this only ever happening to her in bad dreams, and now how she wished she would wake up instead of watching the wise old man leave.

Chapter Five
Into The Forest

S ophia was drawn to the darkness and shelter of the forest. She did not question this or fight it, for the urge to hide herself away now seemed to be the over-riding force in action.

Sitting against the thick solid trunk of an oak tree, she opened the cloth sack for the first time. The largest single object was that of a rolled-up sleeping bag, whose thick soft interior of feathers would provide warmth and protection on the coldest of nights. Sophia found herself wondering whether the wise old man had already known of her forthcoming plight, and had been helping her to prepare for it. She pulled out the remaining items from the bottom of the sack: a notepad and pencil, bread, a canteen of water and several paper bags containing a variety of fruit, berries and nuts. She thought it a rather strange collection of assortments, yet at the same time found this in itself to be endearing.

Sophia broke off a piece of bread, then drank it down with some water before heading off to find a place to sleep for the night. It was late summer, so the ground was still fairly dry and the days were long. "Too long," Sophia thought, as she walked despondently through the multitude of trees. Each foot seemed to become heavier with each step, and all she wanted to do was sleep. Eventually she came across a small stream, which trickled elegantly as it meandered its way through the forest. A more perfect spot she would not find, not just from a perspective of nature but from one of sheer necessity: the supply of water. Sophia lay her bag down against a nearby tree, whose distinctly shaped trunk provided a little hideaway of sorts. Nestling into her sleeping bag, she closed her eyes to the world, and slept.

Sophia spent many days and weeks in the forest seeking no human contact, having only the birds in the trees and the occasional squirrel who chose to venture near her, as her distant companions. She sought no conversation of words with any living being, no longer wishing to hear any message of any kind. For that would need her attention, and even if she decided not to listen it would still require some effort on her behalf; expenditure of energy which Sophia did not feel she had. Sometimes she would summon the energy to go for a short walk, usually alongside the stream so as not to get lost, yet she would once again retreat if the light of the sun became too bright. She needed the branches and leaves of the trees to filter out the glare of the sunlight, which she found to be searing and overpowering in nature. For the light within Sophia had all but gone out. She was merely existing, going through the motions of survival, nothing more. Gone was the emotional nature of her being, on first exiting the Cage - the volatile anger, the tears of vulnerability – and in its place were numbness and emotional detachment.

Sophia had detached herself from the Outside World and all things external to her, but more worryingly she had also become unreachable to herself. It seemed that her body and mind had shut themselves down in order to defend against the onslaughts of her life;

telling her that they could take no more pain, no more rejection, no more abandonment. And so, Sophia would remain in her cocoon for however long she needed to be. There was really no other choice.

One day when she was out walking through the forest, Sophia came across a small pond of water with rocks and twigs strewn in different parts of it. On one side of the pond there was a tree trunk lying on its side. The day was grey and overcast, the ground damp from the recent autumn rains, and the light wind brought with it a chill signalling that the forthcoming winter would soon be on its way. Sophia found a spot on the tree trunk to sit. Resting her face in her hands, she felt the all-encompassing nature of darkness descend upon her. When once she would have yearned for the large open expanse of a bright sky in which to run and play, now it was hard for her to believe that such a time had ever existed, and even harder for her to imagine that brighter days would be hers again. Lost in this dark lonely forest Sophia did not have the will to find her way out.

When she lifted her face up from her hands, Sophia saw that there were some narrow streams of light, which cut through the trees and struck the water in different places. It seemed that this very separation of light into distinct parts had a particular meaning for Sophia. Perhaps it was that she could now look upon this light and actually see it without being overwhelmed by it. Sophia found herself looking intently at this natural phenomenon before her, and was touched by it.

'It's perfect,' she said softly. 'The perfection of the Universe'.

These things had of course existed before today, had always existed, yet somehow Sophia had not seen or felt their beauty in the same way; there was a depth to her senses that she had not known until now. It meant that she was fully and completely experiencing the moment, and in doing so she felt a stronger connection with the

Earth, with the Universe. In this one mesmerising moment Sophia felt that she was part of something much greater, that she was truly sharing the world with every other living creature and creation. And for that fleeting moment Sophia no longer felt alone or afraid.

Then suddenly the streams of light were gone, as clouds concealed them from view, and Sophia felt herself coming out of her reverie. It was as if the sun and clouds had conspired to tell her that it was time to come out of her daydream. Feeling a little lighter, she looked around her slowly and caught sight of a frog sitting on the other side of the pond. She watched the frog for quite some time fascinated by its stillness, and smiled at the thought of their similarities. There they both were, sitting motionless and silent, on opposite sides of the pond.

'Hello, little fella,' she grinned. 'You and I have something in common, don't we?'

It was the first time in a long while that Sophia found herself smiling – a spontaneous, unforced smile – and one that brought with it nothing less than a small wonder. For however small it was, it brought her a sense of hope and that was something to build on.

Sophia's mind drifted back to the memory of the stone remnants of the Tower; how they had lain there as scattered debris, where once the very same stones had been joined together and built upon to create one solid structure; a structure which, no doubt, had purpose and beauty despite its underlying flaws. What was its purpose now, she wondered? Was it there solely to remind those who came upon it, the dangers that can be involved when one goes to the extreme of giving their all; like the fated Tower whose light had always been directed outwards?

And so, as she sat alone in the middle of the forest with winter approaching, Sophia questioned her own purpose. 'What am I supposed to do now?' she asked aloud, to anyone or anything in the Universe who might hear her.

There was no answer, no sign, nothing. 'That's it!' she suddenly knew the answer to her own question. 'Nothing! I am supposed to do nothing. I have no purpose now but to just let things be. I have no energy or will to do anything anyway. I am so very tired.'

She looked back at the frog. It was still sitting in the same place as before. Sophia found this comforting. Then she made a decision: She would move from her tree trunk when the frog moved.

And so they remained as they were, Sophia's mind wrought with thoughts of everything and anything, the frog calm and peaceful in its stillness. How Sophia wished she could know such peace and tranquillity. She found herself wondering whether she actually looked calm and peaceful on the outside. "After all, isn't that what most people go by - outward attributes and behaviour?" She thought about how most people's behaviour belied what they really thought or felt. "Is this mainly to protect themselves from others, or others from themselves?" she asked herself. "On the one hand, most people would seem to want honesty, but how much honesty would they be able to hear about themselves? It is indeed a brave man or woman who can look at themselves openly and honestly."

Eventually, Sophia's mind went back once more to the wise old man and his story. For he had brought her attention to the limitations of individuals, when he spoke of those people who simply pass through the scattered debris without stopping. If this indicated that Sophia had shown courage in stopping, then it was not using criteria generally used in the day-to-day running of the Outside World. "No, the world that I'm used to is divided into those who cope and succeed within the parameters set by society, and those who do not; the archetypal winners and losers."

Sophia looked over at the frog once again, and said, 'When I look at you, Mr Frog, your very stillness makes me think of the constant "doing" which has taken up most of my life. At the time, of course, it seemed like the only thing to do, but now I'm beginning to see how unhealthy it all was.' She let out a deep sigh before continuing to state her monologue of thoughts:

'It's just that it always seems that what a person "does" makes up such a large proportion of what he or she "is". I mean, the most important feature of a person seems to be what they do for a living, not what they are like as a person . . . . . . and just think of that expression – "do for a living"! What does that mean? . . . . . If someone asks, "Who are you?", we say our name, where we are from, we may talk about where we live, what we do, our family-'

Sophia suddenly held her head in her hands. For in truth, she did not know how to answer the question, "Who are you?" anymore.

It now seemed that the days and weeks of numbness and detachment had finally given way to an overflow of mental turmoil and confusion. Difficult as this was, it nevertheless revealed the first signs of life within Sophia. As she dug her fingers into her scalp, trying to alleviate the throbbing and aching of her head, Sophia decided to lie down and hope that sleep would come to her. Opening her cloth sack, she pulled out the sleeping bag and curled up inside it. Then looking over at the frog, she said, 'Sorry, Mr Frog. I can't stay awake any longer.' And in an instant she was asleep.

When Sophia awoke, it was to almost total darkness. She heard the same noises of the night forest that she had heard on many occasions before. They did not scare her, so familiar had they become. However, for the first time since entering the forest, Sophia found herself wanting some contact with another human being. She wanted some friendship, some guidance, some warmth; warmth that came not from the sun, but from the light that shone from within another human soul.

A voice then sounded within her; 'Remember what the wise old man said: the Universe will always answer those who truly seek help.'

Sophia answered softly out loud, 'Yes, I will make my move when it is light.'

It had been light for sometime now, yet Sophia had not moved. She always felt worse in the mornings, like a car engine on a cold morning that didn't want to start.

'Come on, old girl,' she told herself, 'put one leg in front of the other and start walking. It doesn't matter if you only walk for ten minutes.'

Wearily, she packed up her sleeping bag and started to walk. 'Oh! What about Mr Frog?' she stopped and turned around to see that he was no longer there. 'Aghh, you beat me to it. Never mind - remember that this journey is not a competition. Bye, Mr Frog.'

Along the way, Sophia stopped at intervals to rest and sometimes eat. There was no doubt that part of her tiredness and weakness was due to the loss of weight she had experienced on her journey. Yet even if she had been surrounded by an abundance of food, the fact was that Sophia did not actually want to eat. Her appetite for food had disappeared along with her appetite for life itself. Still, she forced herself to eat something each day, however small.

Sophia had followed the example of the squirrels, the rabbits and the birds that she had lived amongst, for they had found a fair supply of nuts and berries to keep them happy. Sophia did not know what kind of nuts or berries they were, but they were the very same ones she had received from the wise old man, so she trusted that they were safe enough for her to eat. He had, it seemed, been helping Sophia even though he was not there.

When Sophia could walk no further, she found a place to rest for the remainder of the day. Sitting back against a tree, she drank what was left in her canteen and closed her eyes. Her breathing was heavy and laboured, and her heartbeat pounded loudly in her ears. She felt like an old woman. When her body had finally calmed itself and returned to a state resembling normality, it was then that Sophia heard a rhythmic thudding sound in the distance. Its sound, however, did not belong to the sounds of the forest.

The distant thudding stopped. Sophia waited expectantly. Then it started again - the same thudding sound, the same rhythm. "What was it?" she wondered. Curious to know who or what was making these sounds, Sophia decided to go and find out. Getting to her feet, she forced her tired body onwards. In the distance there seemed to be an open space, for she could see the increase in light. She had to reach it. As she staggered through the forest towards it, all she could hear were the overpowering sounds of her laboured breathing. She panted and gasped for air, feeling as if her heart was going to explode inside her chest. Then finally her legs gave way and she collapsed to the ground. The open space was only a few yards away. But Sophia could no longer hear the thudding sound; either it had stopped or she had journeyed further away from it. Punching the ground in frustration, she cried out in despair, 'Where's all the help and guidance I was told about? The help that I would find along the way? In the end I have to do it all myself!'

By now she had broken down into tears, her pain expressed in her spoken plea: 'I need some help, can't you see?'

Sophia had fallen asleep on the spot where she had landed. It was around midday when she awoke, the autumn sun shining high in the sky on what was an unusually hot day. The light breeze blew some of the fallen leaves along the ground and the birds' song somehow sounded sweeter than ever. Sophia closed her eyes and listened to these pleasant sounds of Nature, at the same time taking in a few deep breaths. Suddenly she found herself remembering something that the wise old man had said:

'. . . . When you feel lost and despairing, you must go somewhere very quiet and still within yourself, and ask for help, ... If you truly seek help, the Universe will always answer you. . . . .'

Sophia had spent many weeks in near total silence. Inside she had felt numb and empty - like a computer that had shut down - but now, for the first time, she wanted to fill the void inside her; not with just anything, but with something meaningful. So, as she lay there on the ground she let her body become more relaxed and her mind more aware of her breathing, until her mind began to calm. Sounds and images from the world around entered her mind and body, leaving her feeling strangely intoxicated and a little disorientated. Yet in this disorientated state of mind, Sophia felt more calm and relaxed; she felt the beginnings of warmth and light stir within her. She felt in touch with something much greater than herself; something all encompassing but intangible; something nurturing and loving. More than that, she could not say. And as it began to fill the void inside her, tears gently forced their way from under her closed eyelids.

Sophia lay there for a while longer before sitting up. Suddenly she had an idea, more than an idea really; an urge to write. Was this what people called inspiration? she wondered. She quickly pulled the almost forgotten notepad and pencil from her bag, and found herself writing verses. The words seemed to come upon the breeze:

THE LIGHT

How wonderful it feels to be lying here
Touching Nature's hand
Feeling the warmth of the sun,
The strength the Universe holds
I am beginning to understand.

The wind is blowing through the trees
And blowing through my hair,
Yet only this morning I was tense and afraid,
Trying to control my future and present
My intuition, alas, betrayed.

The sun moves further in the sky
And distant voices become more distant.
I listen instead to the voice deep inside,
The voice which has remained silent for so long,
And I feel I could stay here all day
Gaining more of your strength
Feeling I could do no wrong.

I close my eyes to the world around me,
This time is for me alone
And I open my mind, body and soul
To a world I barely know.
A world of wonder and love
Of true and marvellous creation,
Mysterious and unseen
Yet my trust in you is beginning to grow.

For the world around me believes
In that which is proven and shown,
In the worship of the constant and the tangible
Which sometimes seems so cold,
Like a lifeless, hollow cavity.

The light of the sun is slowly dying
As I lie here on my own,
Yet I have felt at one with another world,
A higher power, my guiding light.
Then no matter that the sun no longer touches me
As the night begins to unfurl,
For how wonderful it is to know
You are the constant in my life.

Chapter Six
The Wood Chopper

The following day Sophia ventured towards the open space. It was a large clearing covered with lush grass, on the other side of which was the start of another forest; perhaps it was all part of the same forest, except that the trees looked different to Sophia. She decided to walk across to the other side of the clearing, and then along the edge of the forest in the direction from left to right. The rhythmic thudding sound she had heard the previous day was no longer evident, and although she was disappointed she did not feel quite so desperate to locate its source. Whatever it had been, it had at least served the purpose of luring Sophia out of the woods.

There was no doubt that Sophia felt encouraged by her recent experience of tranquillity and inspiration, even if it had been all too fleeting. When she read back what she had written, she wasn't sure where the words had come from or even what she had meant by some of them. To write of such things as "higher powers" and "guiding lights" was an alien concept to Sophia, yet there was no denying that she had believed these words to be true. And now she had to place her trust in them.

As she strolled along the edge of the forest, Sophia spoke some of the words she had written:

'Trying to control my present and future
My intuition, alas, betrayed.'

It was that word "control" coming up again that bothered Sophia; the use of the conscious rational mind to plan ahead, to work out solutions, to seek guarantees and assurances; the world of routines, budgets, and expected behaviour. The list went predictably onwards. That, perhaps, was the crux of it for Sophia: that everything in her life had felt so predictable. And every time she had questioned this, she had told herself that there was nothing terribly wrong with it and that things could be a lot worse. End of subject! But of course it had not gone away. She had been trying to convince herself of a truth that was not her own truth.

Other lines from her verses suddenly came into Sophia's head, as if to reinforce her thoughts. She spoke them aloud as she continued her walk:

'I listen instead to the voice deep inside me,
The voice which has remained silent for so long.'

And her mind thought sadly of the woman at sea who had not listened to the voice below. Sophia could see now that it had been a reflection of herself, and the inner realisation of this was proving to be rather painful. For now she was here on this journey with no map to guide her, and no guarantee as to where she was heading or of what lay ahead. Yet difficult though this was, it also brought with it the potential for excitement and exploration, freedom and inspiration, and perhaps most surprisingly to Sophia the awareness of her own creativity.

Sophia's body was starting to droop and she felt incredibly thirsty. Lost in her thoughts, she had walked further than she had intended. Then suddenly, the rhythmic thudding sound returned. This time it was much louder than before so that Sophia knew instantly what it was.

'A wood chopper!' she exclaimed in excitement. 'Perhaps I'm being guided after all!'

Ahead in the distance there was a figure standing between two trees. The figure had short brown hair, was not very tall, and was wearing jeans and a lumberjack shirt. "Very appropriate," thought Sophia, as she slowly edged her way forward. She could not see anyone else around, just this solitary figure raising an axe aloft, then swinging it down with substantial force and precision, onto a large block of wood. Sophia started to feel a little uneasy. Although she wanted to believe in the guidance she was being given, she also knew that ultimately she had a choice in deciding what to do. After all, there were still dangers that existed in the everyday world. She had to think quickly. "What's your gut feeling?" she asked herself, stepping back into the forest to conceal herself from view. Closing her eyes, she waited to see if an answer came to her, but in the end she wasn't sure one way or the other. Finally, she took a deep breath and decided to go for it.

When she got to within a few yards of the Wood Chopper, her heart began to thump so loudly against her chest, that she could almost hear it above the sound of the axe striking the wood. The Wood Chopper was, however, still unaware of Sophia's presence, having had his back towards her all the while. Now was the time for Sophia to make her move:

She took a deep breath, and said, 'Hello there.' Her voice came out in a feeble and barely audible tone, certainly not loud enough for someone chopping wood to hear. Sophia took another deep breath, and called out again, this time louder; 'Hello there!'

The Wood Chopper halted in mid-action, then spun around, clutching the axe as if ready for attack. Sophia was startled, not only from this response but also because she realised that the Wood Chopper was in fact a woman.

'Surprised I'm a woman?' the Wood Chopper said, as if to read Sophia's thoughts.

'Oh,' Sophia was clearly embarrassed. 'Well, I...er, yes, I suppose I am. You see, I-'

'Don't worry about it. I'm used to it,' she said rather abruptly, whilst Sophia shifted awkwardly under her cold piercing stare.

'Don't look so scared,' the Wood Chopper said, a little softer now. 'I won't bite.' She wiped her brow with the sleeve of her shirt, and tossed the axe on the ground behind her. 'There! Is that better?'

Sophia smiled. 'Yes, I suppose it is.'

'You suppose a lot then?'

'What?'

But before Sophia had the chance to think, the woodchopper cut in with; 'You should watch those suppositions, you know.'

There was no doubting that this woman had a sharp mind and a sharp manner to go alongside the blade of her axe, and Sophia was at a loss as to know what to do or say next. She had only just found her way out of the forest and was not ready for such a brusque encounter; its only effect was to make her want to retreat back to the protection of the forest.

Yet as if to reassure her, the Wood Chopper said, 'Here, do you want something to drink? You look like you could do with something.'

Sophia managed to make brief eye contact with her. 'Thanks, that would be great.'

'Take a pew,' the Wood Chopper pointed over to a nearby log, before going off to fetch some water.

Sophia was grateful for such small mercies. On her return, the Wood Chopper brought back a large wooden bowl filled with water and handed it to Sophia. Taking it with both hands, Sophia thanked her profusely and then proceeded to down the entire contents of the bowl. The Wood Chopper grinned to herself as she went over to a nearby tree and sat down in a tired heap.

'So, how long have you been in the forest?' she asked Sophia. Her voice had an almost expressionless monotone sound to it. Yet, there was something about her that seemed pained to Sophia.

'I'm not sure really,' Sophia answered. 'Months probably.' She looked down at the ground, suddenly feeling sad.

'It's tough going, alright!' acknowledged the Wood Chopper. 'I've seen quite a few people come this way, and some don't fare too well.'

Sophia looked up. She was interested in what she had just heard; comforted to know that others had come this way before her, but also wary of finding out what had happened to them.

'How long have you been here then?' Sophia asked the Wood Chopper.

'A long time. Years probably.'

'Really!' Sophia was startled. 'But why? Why have you stayed here so long? Haven't you ever wanted to move on?'

The Wood Chopper glared at Sophia, as if viewing her comments as insults to her way of life. 'I don't see it as any of your business as to the why's and wherefore's of my being here. I'm here because I want to be here and I'll move on when I'm good and ready.'

A tense silence filled the air. Sophia felt like an outspoken child being told off. She had not intended to be arrogant or patronising – if that is what she had been - as she genuinely wanted to know about the Wood Chopper's experiences. Instead she had achieved quite the opposite, the Wood Chopper having sought to defend herself against what she felt to be an unwelcome attack or intrusion. Yet underneath Sophia was a little scared to know that someone who appeared so strong was living in such a restricted and sheltered way. And she wanted to believe that the road ahead would get easier.

Sophia finally broke the awkward silence; 'I'm sorry. I really didn't mean to offend you.'

'Well, I guess you've got a point,' the Wood Chopper was more generous in her response than Sophia had expected. 'I'm not used to such directness, that's all.' She showed no expression, though it seemed clear to Sophia that she had become preoccupied with her thoughts.

The light had now dimmed as dusk began to set in. Suddenly the Wood Chopper got up from the ground, picked up her axe and said, 'I'm going to turn in now. I'll see you in the morning – if you're still here that is.'

Then off she went into the depths of the forest, Sophia having bid her farewell. Left contemplating what to do, it did not take too long for Sophia to decide to stay for a while – at least for the next day – in the company of this rather strange yet intriguing woman.

It was a beautiful morning. The sun had been up for an hour or two, the birds were singing so joyfully, and Sophia was finding it difficult to remain asleep. Her mind was busy thinking about the coming day and what it would bring with her new acquaintance. She allowed herself a smile as she realised that this was the first time in a long while that she had not dreaded the coming of a new day.

Eventually she decided to get up. Her legs ached and wobbled as she tried to stand up, the effects of so much walking over the previous two days. As she leant against the nearest tree for support, an image came into her mind which made her chuckle: that of a newborn foal struggling to stand up on its own. Sophia, it seemed, was discovering the more humorous side of herself; her child spirit was coming alive again, and it felt good. Once she had steadied herself, she wandered over to a pile of chopped wood. In fact there were several piles consisting of pieces of wood cut to almost the same size. The woodchopper did indeed show perfectionist qualities, Sophia thought to herself, wondering what she did with all this wood. Were there other people she mingled with and supplied wood to?

After an hour or so had gone by, there was still no sign of the Wood Chopper, and Sophia was starting to feel a little edgy. As she began to automatically worry that the Wood Chopper would not turn up, her emotions fluctuated from those of concern about the welfare of her absent acquaintance, to ones of irritation with her. She could feel herself on the verge of becoming consumed by such emotions, which she knew would ultimately lead her into a downward spiral of negativity that had been so familiar to her in the past. But today Sophia did not follow this route.

'Never mind,' she told herself, 'it is still early, not even noon yet.'

Instead she tried to occupy herself by going for short strolls and having short talks with her special friends; the squirrels, the birds and the rabbits. Then she sat on the grass in the clearing, closed her eyes and felt the sun on her face. She focused inward, on her breathing, on herself. Yes indeed, Sophia felt she had achieved something on this day.

Yet there was still no sign of the Wood Chopper, and now there were only about two hours left of daylight. Sophia began to feel angry. After all she had waited patiently all day for the Wood Chopper who had not bothered to turn up even when she had said she would. Sophia thought about the conversation they had had on the previous day; had her directness pushed the Wood Chopper away? But what then of the Wood Chopper's sharpness, surely that had been more than a match for Sophia's so-called directness? Yet whatever the reason for her non-appearance, it did not prevent Sophia from feeling dejected. Once again she had been left to her own devices – like the woman at sea, like the crumbling Tower.

Sophia could feel her defences of anger go up in an attempt to dampen her feelings of rejection and ensuing unworthiness. Deep inside she knew that this was futile, for like the woman at sea it no longer worked; the painful emotions below the surface were too strong to be kept at bay any longer, they needed to be heard. And like the broken Tower, Sophia no longer had defences of fortitude to speak of.

On this West Road she was going to have to find a way to heal her broken and fragmented self - like the wise old man had told her - for if she did not, the fragile structures she was just beginning to build, would break down once more. So, as disappointed as she was not to have seen the Wood Chopper again, Sophia packed her sleeping bag and headed off to find another place to rest for the night.

Over the next few days she moved onwards covering around a mile a day. Each day was pretty much the same; she kept to the edge of the forest during daylight, going into the forest at night, and not encountering or hearing another human being. But somehow the knowledge that she was moving forward gave her a small sense of achievement.

Eventually though, even this sense of achievement began to disappear and along with it, any lingering feelings of hope. No, on this particular day, Sophia could not take any more. She went deep into the forest, and screamed at the top of her lungs. She kicked and punched the trunk of a tree until her knuckles throbbed with pain and the skin began to break and bleed. She shouted and cried out in despair:

'WHAT . . AM . . I . . SUPPOSED . . TO . . DO?!! TELL . . ME . . PLEEEEEASE!'

With heaving sobs she fell to her knees, her heart throbbing in pain, until she felt that it too would break. The internalised build-up of emotions had finally erupted, and with a power that was driving Sophia to the edge. She was frightened by the power they had over her. Sophia was now the woman at sea who was close to drowning in a storm; she was on the edge of recklessness and destruction. These powerful forces came from within her, yet she felt as if there were two separate entities in battle with each other: One part of her was trying to keep some control over the other part of her that was out of control. Was this part of her the angry screaming needy child that the wise old man had warned her about? 'You must learn to moderate your child's behaviour . . . . . for you yourself are still an adult,' he had said.

But she couldn't. For Sophia felt out of control and was terrified of what she would do in this state. Her body was shaking in convulsions as she felt a tidal wave coming over her, and there was no way for her to hold it back. Yet in the midst of this tidal wave, Sophia somehow found herself wrapping her arms around a tree and holding on to it for dear life. She dug her fingers into the bark with all her might, pressing her face against its rough surface, finding the physical sensation of pain easier to deal with than the mental and emotional pain. This strong and solid earthly structure, which had stood here for hundreds of years, was at that moment Sophia's saviour. It was her strength now that she had none, and it was helping her to centre herself in her unbalanced state. It was her temporary foundation, keeping her rooted to the ground.

And eventually - how long it was impossible to say - the overwhelming forces which had risen up within Sophia, began to subside. Thereafter, she lay her exhausted body down to rest.

A man's voice infiltrated her dreaming mind; loud abrupt tones conveying a sense of urgency. Sophia's eyes opened to make out blurred images of a figure leaning over her.

'Are you alright, miss?!' pleaded the man.

Her sight somewhat restored, Sophia could make out a middle-aged man who was now trying to help her to sit up. A container of sorts was placed to her lips. She felt the cool sensation of water in her mouth, and then started to cough and splutter as it hit her gag reflex. Once this episode had subsided, the man placed the beaker of water in Sophia's hands, urging her to drink it.

'Why, you're the one who was in that Cage!' he said in amazement.

Sophia had already recognised the man as Bob, but couldn't bring herself to respond in any way.

'I hardly recognised you,' he continued unabated. 'You look a bit worse for wear, I must say.'

Again, there was no response as Sophia concentrated instead on trying to force out every last drop of water in the beaker. Bob immediately refilled the beaker, which was still clasped firmly in her hands, whilst he tried not to show his shock at seeing her like this.

'I was worried when I heard all that shouting and screaming.' For the first time, Bob conveyed his obvious concern and it resulted in Sophia finally looking up from her beaker, registering some form of connection with him.

'When I saw you lying there, I thought you were a gonna!' he said shaking his head.

Sophia found herself forcing a grin at his choice of words. 'That's not so far from the truth, you know,' she finally said.

'It will get better. You just need time. You'll see,' Bob tried to reassure her.

He was not used to being in this role and consequently felt very awkward, but Sophia was grateful for such simple words and small acts of mercy. She had, it seemed, received support from a most unlikely source and was beginning to think that perhaps the Universe was listening after all. Suddenly she found herself saying:

'Trust the beating heart
Of the Greatest Unknown
You will ever know.'

'What's that you said?' Bob enquired.

Sophia smiled at him, able to see more clearly than before the good qualities that he possessed and that he had not been able to show before. Perhaps she was helping him too?

'Oh nothing, I don't know really,' she replied. 'Can you lead me out of this place? I think I need a change of scenery.'

'That's more like it, my girl,' he said, getting to his feet enthusiastically. 'You need some colour to your cheeks. You're not looking too good.'

As Sophia tried to get to her feet, she lost her balance.

'Here, let me help you out of here,' Bob intervened offering his arm for her to lean on.

'Thanks,' she replied taking his arm gratefully.

Bob led Sophia out of the forest and onto an empty roadside. Although downhearted and very tremulous, Sophia was relieved to finally be out of the forest. She was also relieved to have stopped walking, and wasted no time in collapsing onto a nearby piece of grass. It seemed that these days she never ceased to feel weak and depleted in energy; it seemed to be her constant state of being.

Bob quickly got round to the business of refreshments, extracting several sandwiches and a canteen of water from his rucksack. Sophia was lying on her side breathing heavily, her eyes open and staring straight ahead though not seeing anything in particular.

'Come on, girl,' Bob said, going over to Sophia. 'You need to eat more than I do!'

Sophia responded in an almost robotic manner, silently sitting up and taking a sandwich, no expression in her face or eyes. Even when she thanked Bob, her voice was bereft of any expression or emotion. Yet she did eat - and she ate like a wild hungry animal. Bob decided in turn not to eat, but to keep his sandwiches aside for Sophia to have later. He watched as her intake of food seemed to visibly revive his travel companion; a light began to flicker in Sophia's dark eyes, and a hint of colour returned to her pallid cheeks. She glanced over at him and smiled briefly, before looking away again.

'So, have you got any stories to tell me?' Bob asked chirpily. 'About your travels, I mean?'

'Not really.' It was Sophia's turn to be abrupt, not wishing to talk about anything she considered personal.

'You're very cagey, aren't you?' he quipped. Then, when there was no response, he said, 'Get it? Cagey?'

Sophia smirked at him, then felt annoyed with herself for being so uncharitable. She took a deep breath to try to calm her nerves, which felt so raw that almost anything seemed to agitate them. She thought of something she could say to break the awkward silence, something that was not directly about herself.

'Actually, I met a woman who was chopping wood,' she said. 'Do you know her?'

'Oh yes,' Bob relied immediately. 'It's difficult not to really. She makes enough racket so as not to miss her!'

'I take it you don't much care for her,' Sophia asserted rather bravely.

Her older companion looked a little embarrassed, as if surprised that she had not gone along with his views. 'I wouldn't say that. I mean, I don't know her that well, do I?'

Then, after a brief pause, he continued; 'She's been there for ages - but she's a bit funny if you ask me. I'm not sure I'd trust her with that axe – she's probably one of those women who hate men!'

Sophia found herself feeling agitated again. All these assumptions made on face value, she thought to herself, deciding that there was little point in pursuing the conversation. For it seemed that Bob had already made up his mind about the Wood Chopper. Yet why, she wondered, was she defending someone who had indeed behaved rather rudely towards her? Wouldn't it be more understandable if she just went along with Bob and condemned the Wood Chopper for the upset she had caused her? The truth was that Sophia had seen something in the Wood Chopper that reminded her of herself:

vulnerability, something which Sophia had found almost impossible to show in her own life.

'Are you ready to get going yet?' Bob started to stand up. 'We don't want it to get too late.'

'Okay,' Sophia responded gloomily, 'although I wouldn't really say that I'm ready.'

She struggled to her feet, looking at the level gravel road ahead. 'Which way are we going anyway?' she asked.

Sophia's heart sank when she heard the reply.

Chapter Seven

The Mountain Road

'We're going up the Mountain Road,' Bob answered, as he started walking along the road. 'It's not far. Come on!'

Sophia dragged her feet as she struggled to follow him. She was starting to feel panicky because she knew that she was pushing her body beyond its capability. Her heart was already pounding, which was as much to do with her high anxiety levels as it was to do with her physical exertion. She didn't want to show signs of weakness but if she continued to go along with something she knew to be wrong for her, than wasn't she back to where she was before? The crumbling Tower? The struggling woman at sea? Surely Sophia needed to learn these lessons and try something different.

She stopped walking. 'I'm sorry,' she panted. 'I . . can't . . .go . . any . . further.'

Bob, who was walking up ahead, looked around to see Sophia crumpled in a heap on the side of the road. He made his way back towards her. 'Look, I know you're tired but it's getting late and I need to get back home before it's dark.'

'Well I'm sorry to disappoint you, but I cannot walk any further,' Sophia was adamant. 'Look, you don't have to stay with me if you don't want to – you can go! It's up to you!'

She realised of course that she was taking a risk in calling his bluff. Why couldn't she just say that she appreciated his having stayed with her and having showed her the way forward? Why couldn't she just ask him to stay rather than tell him to go? In the end, it was simply because she did not want to risk him saying 'no'; she did not want to experience another rejection.

Bob looked a little taken aback by her outburst, but also amused. 'Cor, you're a feisty one aren't you? Nearly bit me head off!'

There was no doubt that Sophia felt relieved that he had not just walked off. She stayed silent though, not wanting to push it any further.

'Okay then,' Bob said, 'how about you getting some sleep, and me going home for the night? I'll come back first thing tomorrow morning, and then we'll carry on.'

'That would be great,' Sophia was thankful. 'I think I'll sleep like a log. Thanks, Bob.' She managed to smile at him.

Bob placed the leftover sandwiches and remaining water by Sophia's side, and then bid her farewell before heading back towards the forest.

'You will come back, won't you?!' Sophia called after him, thinking back to the Wood Chopper's disappearance.

'Why, are you missing me already?' he answered with a cheeky grin. Then seeing the look of worry on Sophia's weary face, he said more seriously; 'Don't worry, I'll be here first thing.'

Sophia had fallen asleep almost as soon as she had laid down in her warm sleeping bag. She had slept so deeply that when she woke the following day, it took her quite a while to get her bearings. The daylight seemed so bright even though the sky was grey. "Where are all the trees?" she wondered. "And why am I lying by the side of a road?" This was of course the first time that she had not slept in the forest. Slowly, certain images started to come back into her mind, like pieces of a jigsaw puzzle, to eventually reveal the whole picture.

She sat up, her head feeling very groggy, and looked around her. Up ahead, the road veered off to the right behind a hill, so that it was impossible to see how much further the road went. As far as she knew, no one had passed in either direction whilst she had been lying there; this was indeed a very quiet road. Sophia looked up to the sky to try to make out what time of day it was, but the sun was well and truly hidden behind a thick blanket of cloud, which seemed to be darkening by the minute. It looked like it was about to rain, as Sophia lay back down and hid her head inside the sleeping bag.

She was starting to feel anxious at the thought of Bob not coming back. She hated feeling so dependent on others – she was not used to it – and it left her feeling powerless. But more than this, she hated those others for letting her down, for leaving her in this position. Sophia felt as if she was being punished, or tested to the point of extreme, without really knowing why. For it seemed that every time she thought she was learning something – about herself or about the world in which she inhabited – she was knocked down again. This whole journey felt like an endurance test to Sophia, and nothing more. And now, once again, she was starting to give up. She longed to go to sleep and not wake up; she wanted infinite peace to descend upon her, to engulf her worn out body and mind, and to take her away from this life on Earth; this life which she was finding so difficult to live.

Her eyes started to sting with pain as tears formed in them, and a tremendous feeling of fear had developed inside her soul. Sophia closed her eyes to pray, her small voice uttering words to convey the deepest darkest emotions she had ever known:

'Please, dear God, dear Higher Power . . . . whoever you are . . . . don't leave me here. Help me, I can't make it alone. Please . . . help . . . me.'

'Miss, wake up! It's raining.'

Sophia looked out from her sleeping bag to find Bob standing over her. 'You came back!' she shrieked, her thrilled tones seeming to startle him. 'Thankyou, thankyou!'

'What's all this then?' Bob retorted. 'I said I would, didn't I? Now come on – let's get some shelter under that tree.'

Sophia scrambled to her feet. The spark of life had come back to her just as she thought it would go out.

The rain was heavy as they stood under the canopy of a medium-sized tree. Almost immediately, Sophia went to sit down against the trunk, her legs visibly shaking as she bent them. She felt so much older than her years.

'Cor, you're in a bad way, aren't you?' Bob opened his rucksack. 'Here! You'd better eat something before you waste away. Gotta get some meat on your bones, girl.'

He took some more sandwiches from his bag and thrust them towards her. He had also brought with him some home-made soup in a sealed container, the warmth of which brought the hint of a smile to Sophia's face. She was grateful for the presence of this man whom she hardly knew, but who in his direct uncomplicated manner had given her a much needed sense of stability. She was touched by the basic human kindness that existed beneath his no-messing exterior. It was this kindness which had been fundamental to her very survival.

The rain had all but stopped now, leaving behind it a wonderful sense of freshness that only Nature could bring.

'Right Miss, I think we should get a move on,' said Bob, hurriedly getting his things together.

Sophia felt a little drowsy from the food she had eaten, but nonetheless had been expecting the inevitable. 'Yes, I know,' she replied, slowly getting to her feet.

And so without further ado, they went on their way along the Mountain Road. Once they had passed the point where the road curved to the right behind the hill, Sophia saw for the first time the ascent of the road as it wound its way up the mountain. Her heart filled with dread, but she kept telling herself that she was still moving forward, and that that was all she could do. In fact, she had to stop and rest every few hundred yards, which Bob was very good about. Despite what he might have felt, he did not pressurise her to go beyond her capabilities. On one of their longer stops, they shared refreshments and conversation:

'Oh, you know that woman you were talking about yesterday,' Bob said, 'the one who chops wood? Well, I bumped into her. Funny that!'

'Really!'

'Yes. I told her that we were going up the Mountain Road today, and she said to wish you luck – that you were braver than she.'

'What do you mean?' Sophia said in anxious confusion. 'Has she been up this road before? What happened? Why is no one else walking up this road?'

'Hold your horses!' Bob's firm tones instantly halted Sophia's spiralling anxiety levels. 'I don't know much about her. All I know is that she has been up here before but for some reason turned round and went back down again.'

'But why?' insisted Sophia. 'What's up here? You're scaring me, Bob!'

'Look, Sophia, there's no need to feel so scared,' Bob was equally insistent. 'Everyone's different. Some carry on and keep going, others don't. I've seen all sorts since I've been here, believe me!'

'But what about you? Why are you still here?'

'Because this is what I do. I help people along their way, and along this road. But I can't sort out their lives for them, they've got to do that themselves.'

'Yes, I know that,' Sophia said irritably. 'I'm not expecting you to.'

There followed a pause in conversation. Sophia was starting to feel angry, for she didn't understand why things were so difficult; this journey had become like an army assault course to her. "And for what?" she asked herself. As far as she was concerned, she was not trying to be a martyr pursuing some unknown glory single-handedly, yet when she asked for help she felt as if she was asking for so much. At this moment, Sophia felt like a sulky child who had retreated into an angry silence.

Meanwhile, an unperturbed Bob carried on with his eating. In sharp contrast Sophia felt as if she would choke on the piece of bread that was now trying to make its way down her gullet. It almost stuck like a piece of cement; a rock that blocked all in its pathway, so that nothing could flow between the inner and outer entities.

That is how Sophia saw her life, as she sat halfway up the Mountain Road: a wall had been built around her to protect her from outside forces, from potential threats to her inner structures and to protect her flawed ego - until eventually nothing was able to permeate her mind or body, good or bad. This she understood now, all too clearly. And to this end she had tried, on this journey, to be open to other possibilities. Yet she felt neither happier nor more relieved as a result. In fact, she felt worse than ever. For all the faults and imbalances of her previous way of life, she would have gladly changed places with it now; go back to the way things were; go back to the time of the Tower.

But Sophia could not go back. Alas, there was no Tower to go back to. And so, as she looked down the Mountain Road and thought of the ruins she had left behind her, she turned instead to look in the opposite direction. She saw the uphill climb that faced her and the unknown future it led to, and the most overwhelming feelings of panic and terror began to surge within her. They surged forth with a power that threatened to destroy and demolish any obstacle in their path, Sophia's fragile structure struggling ferociously to contain such primal forces. She looked down at her body to see it shaking violently. An internal earthquake had it seemed taken hold, radiating destructive energy from her core outwards. And the power of these natural forces was such that Sophia was certain she would be demolished and disappear into oblivion. She could not fight this one.

Sophia looked straight ahead of her, to the edge of the road. She decided then and there that she would run towards it and project herself off the side of the road, into the body of the mountain. Then it would be over - the pain, the struggle, the terror, the emptiness - all of it, obliterated once and for all. There was still a force within her pulling her back from the edge, but Sophia easily resisted it. She wanted to go. Suddenly she was on her feet and running as fast as her depleted body could go, towards the edge of the mountain and towards oblivion.

'LET GO OF ME!' she screamed. 'GET OFF ME!'

Sophia lashed out with all the strength she had left in her, trying to break free from Bob's clutches, but he would not let her go. Eventually the last drops of energy drained away from her, and she gave in. Bob led her away from the edge of the road, not daring to loosen his grip. When they had crossed to the other side, he finally spoke:

'Promise me, Sophia, that you will never do that again!' He looked directly into her eyes, still gripping her arms tightly. 'I'm damn well gonna get you to the top of this road, if I have to carry you myself.'

Sophia saw the look of shock on his pale face, and perhaps for this reason alone she agreed to his wishes. She was so tired that at that moment she could have fallen asleep standing on her feet. Bob helped her into her sleeping bag and soon after she descended into the world of sleep.

Over the next few days Bob and Sophia made their ascent, stopping to rest and to eat and drink at frequent intervals along the way. Sophia did not experience again such overwhelming intensity of internal destructive forces. Instead this was replaced by a lower grade level of anxiety and vulnerability, which seemed to be present during her waking hours and within her night time dreams. On each day that she woke, she prayed that the weight of gloom and dread be lifted from her, but each day was much the same as the next. In the end she had to be content with the knowledge that she was making progress on her journey, regardless of the poor state of her mind and body. Sophia hung on to this belief by the finest of threads – it was all she had.

When they eventually reached the top of the Mountain Road, Sophia felt no great sense of achievement, just a sense of relief. For at least she could now look down upon the landscape she had climbed, rather than upwards at a winding road. Yet the main thought that occupied her mind was the impending departure of Bob. She knew that he would go back to his home and that she would have to go on alone. She was frightened of this, as she was frightened of most things.

'I suppose you have to go now?' Sophia said sadly, having grown rather fond of this man whom she had come to depend upon.

As she went to hug him, Bob spoke to her with sentiment unexpressed before:

'Don't worry Sophia,' he said gently. 'Things will get better. You'll see.'

Then he placed some coins into her hand, and was gone.

Chapter Eight
The Sibyl From The Land Of The Shadows

Sophia looked down into the valley below. She could see a small town whose inhabitants seemed to be going about their daily business in much the same way as she had seen in other towns before. But Sophia had been out of contact with such a world for so long now, that the thought of venturing into the town below seemed extremely daunting.

As she sat down on the hillside, she thought once again of the broken and fragmented structure of the Tower. She wondered if and how it would be rebuilt, for not all collapsed or damaged buildings were re-built – some were simply left to rot and decay. Closing her eyes, Sophia felt her sinking heart fill her soul with the utmost fear and dread. Again she wanted to run back to the forest and hide forever.

The tears that now welled up in Sophia's eyes began to force their way out from beneath her eyelids. She felt as though her body and mind were so fragile that the smallest of knocks threatened to dismantle them; that the smallest of touches would leave severe bruising.

'This is the Land of the Shadows,' a voice suddenly said. It was a woman's voice, and one which exuded great command.

Sophia opened her eyes and looked up to see a beautiful woman standing in front of her. It was a mystical image, a vision, which left Sophia mesmerised. For the woman was dressed in flowing robes made of the finest golden textures; her dark hair was placed up above her head, and her eyes though almost black in colour radiated an almost penetrating warmth. All in all, she looked to be the archetypal image of a Greek or Egyptian goddess. Sophia was so mesmerised that she could not speak, instead just letting the tears roll silently down her cheeks. And at that moment she felt the most intense craving for affection.

'I am the Sibyl from the Land of the Shadows,' the woman finally said.

Sophia continued to gaze at her in awe without responding. She did not know what to say, for in her ignorance she did not know what the woman meant, and she did not want to ask. But the woman did not seem to mind Sophia's silence; her smile put Sophia at ease, as if to say that it was all right. But more than this, Sophia began to feel a sense of peace and tranquillity; a feeling she had only ever experienced at the time she had felt compelled to write the verses of "The Light". It seemed that the very presence of this magical woman had transformed Sophia's state of heart and mind into an altogether different state of being.

The woman of mystery spoke once again, this time elaborating a little as to her identity:

'I am a Prophetess, a Seer. But I prefer the name Sibyl. Perhaps it sounds less grand – to others, you see.'

'Oh, so that's what you meant,' Sophia said nervously. 'How amazing!'

Suddenly Sophia felt like a young child, mesmerised by the magical, and believing the unbelievable. For she did not feel the slightest need to question or challenge such a fantastic idea. She just believed – in the way that children do. Yet now she also began to feel embarrassed when she realised that she had been staring at the Sibyl. Sophia felt herself blush in her new found state of self-consciousness, whilst the Sibyl in contrast did not flinch. How majestically assured she appeared to be, and not merely in a superficial way; more an inner serenity, which radiated outward until it enveloped her physical frame and beyond.

'Are you normally this quiet?' the Sibyl enquired, though not unkindly.

Sophia looked down with a sheepish smile, for she liked the Sibyl's gentle directness. Eventually she managed to find an answer:

'Not usually. In fact I used to be quite a talker. I don't seem to know what to say these days, it's all so confusing.'

'Are you frightened, my dear?'

Sophia looked up at the Sibyl, but was unable to maintain eye contact. She knew that the Sibyl could see right through her, see things that she herself could not see, and so Sophia did not answer the question. Instead the Sibyl spoke:

'I know that it feels as though you are all alone at this time of great need, but you must try to believe that you are not alone in this magnificent Universe – what we sometimes call the Greatest Unknown. You must know that everything is as it is.'

Sophia thought for a moment about what the Sibyl had said, and slowly began to realise that she was right. For whenever Sophia had felt despairing and most in need, someone had appeared bringing solace and comfort to her. At times it had been Sophia herself who had seen something that brought comfort - the frog, the sunlight through the trees, the strength of a tree. Yes, she could see that despite feeling alone for most of the time, she was not alone in this great and magnificent Universe. And now the Sibyl from the Land of the Shadows had appeared to her.

'What is the Land of the Shadows?' asked Sophia.

'I did wonder when you were going to ask,' replied the Sibyl. 'Usually people can't wait to find out, then when they do, they often don't want to know – or else they don't want to believe it has anything to do with them. I must admit, I am rather relieved to come across someone with a different response. I was getting quite disillusioned with the human form, I can tell you!'

Sophia grinned shyly, finding the Sibyl rather amusing. How refreshing it was, thought Sophia, to be with someone who obviously had an important position and role, and yet although serious and dedicated, was also light-hearted and amusing as well. "What a wonderful combination," she thought.

'Well, in answer to your question about the Land of the Shadows,' the Sibyl said, turning to face the valley, 'look over there.'

She was pointing to a slope on the other side of the valley, beyond the small town. Sophia got to her feet and went over to where the Sibyl was standing. Looking into the distance all she could see, being a little short- sighted, was a blurred image. She squinted to try to get a clearer picture but in truth she did not know what she was looking for. She wondered whether the Sibyl could see how much she was straining to get a clearer image, and was just about to come clean about her short-sightedness, when suddenly she saw it. A fleeting image it was, but nonetheless it left Sophia feeling flabbergasted. For the hillside yonder was littered with shadows shaped in the human form, some moving and some stationary. These were not shadows cast by the sun, for the sun was not shining on this particular day.

It was then that the Sibyl told Sophia about how each of the shadows belonged to someone living in the Valley Town, but that each person either did not know of their shadow's existence or else they chose to ignore its presence. Either way it meant that there existed two separate "communities": One community consisted of those in the human physical form, each with their own personality, status and role, and which the Sibyl called the "community of egos". The other community was made up of the darker, or hidden, aspects of each person, aspects that they preferred not to show or acknowledge and so cast aside; this was sometimes called their unconscious side. Both sides, however - the ego and the shadow - belonged to each and every individual. It was another example of duality, which Sophia had first heard about from the wise old man.

'But as you can see,' continued the Sibyl, suddenly sounding a little sad, 'the Shadows do not go away, they simply cast their darkness across the Earth.'

In the ensuing silence, Sophia went back to where she had left her bag and sat down. Her head felt strangely bombarded by the images she had just seen and by the explanations she had just heard. Her mind automatically went back to an earlier time on the journey when she had fallen asleep in the lake. She had dreamt the most vivid of dreams, about a woman above the water and the one below. There had been talk then of the shadow side, of the unconscious, of the hidden aspects of herself. Later Sophia had talked with the wise old man about her fear of showing that side of herself, and her fear of rejection, and she remembered his words . . . . .

. . . .'To truly be free, you have to face yourself'.

Did this mean that she had to face her Shadow? Did Sophia also have a Shadow on the other side of the valley, along with all the others?

Closing her eyes, Sophia tried to block out some of the information that was starting to overwhelm her. Her stomach felt knotted up with fear, her face grimacing at the physical discomfort it was causing.

'You look in pain,' said the Sibyl, who had now come over to where Sophia sat.

Sophia looked up at her. 'My digestive system feels all knotted up,' she explained. 'I've been getting this quite a lot, it's very uncomfortable.'

'What do you find difficult to digest?' asked the Sibyl.

It was a clever probing question, thought Sophia, but one she found difficult to answer. 'I don't know,' she grimaced, not entirely sure whether she was being honest.

Then suddenly Sophia did something that she hadn't done before - she asked the Sibyl what she thought: 'What do you think it is that I can't digest?'

The Sibyl smiled. 'I cannot say what it is specifically. These are things that you will come to know as long as you are open to the answers. But it does seem as if you are holding on too tightly to something and are afraid of letting it go.'

Sophia listened attentively to the answer the Sibyl had given. She thought about how simple it was yet how profound it was too. It seemed to Sophia as if the straightforward and uncomplicated nature of the Sibyl's wisdom served to cut straight through to the core of Sophia, and to challenge her to face her own fears. For Sophia knew that she was hanging on to the past, to the life she had known before she had commenced this journey, and to that which was most familiar to her; all because she feared the unknown. She feared it to such an extent, that it almost rendered her paralysed.

Sophia began to shake, as once again an avalanche of fears and other suppressed emotions forced their way up through her body, like a trapped animal trying to get out of its cage. As the convulsions took hold, she tried to gain some control of her body by pulling her knees up to her chest and clasping her arms tightly around them. By now she was unaware of her surroundings, having become immersed in her own world of mental and emotional chaos. It was then that she became aware of a gentle presence around her, a gentle force of warmth and comfort embracing her body.

'It is time to let go,' the Sibyl said softly, as she held Sophia in her arms.

And slowly her mind and body let go of some of the anguish, until the shaking stopped and her body became still. It was then that the Sibyl released herself from the embrace and stood up.

'Rest now, Sophia,' she said. 'Tomorrow will soon be upon us and there is much to do.'

Then the Sibyl was gone, and almost as quickly Sophia fell into a deep sleep.

When Sophia awoke the next day, she saw that the Sibyl was already present. Sophia wondered whether the Sibyl had slept at all – whether in fact she needed any sleep – for there was indeed something about her that seemed from another world altogether. The blissful serenity that emanated from her, reinforced to Sophia that the Sibyl couldn't have been further away from her on the serenity scale if she had tried. This did not necessarily trouble Sophia in any way, because more than anything she knew she needed the comforting containment of the Sibyl's presence. And now that the Sibyl had arrived, Sophia wondered what the coming day would bring.

They began to walk down the hillside towards the Valley Town below, the sun shining brightly upon the spring day. Somehow the prospect of visiting the town and its people did not seem quite so daunting to Sophia today. This of course was largely due to the presence of the Sibyl, for no longer did Sophia feel so alone and afraid. She had found in the Sibyl both the nurturing love of the maternal, and the perceptive guidance of the wise old woman. Sophia felt that in such magnificent company she would not only survive, but she could eventually thrive as well; it would be all right after all.

Yet just before they had reached the bottom of the hill, the Sibyl stopped and turned to face Sophia. 'From here I go no further,' she said to an astonished Sophia. 'But you must venture into the Valley Town, and find your way.'

The colour drained from Sophia's already pale face. She felt as though she had been hit with a sledgehammer, unable to comprehend what was being said to her. The Sibyl went over to her and touching her arm said:

'Remember, Sophia, I am with you. You are never truly alone. Just use your powers of visualisation if you need to see me, or call to me if you need help; listen and be receptive, and the wisdom of the Universe will be yours.'

But Sophia did not want to listen. She did not wish to hear about the Universe and its wisdom; all she wanted was for the Sibyl to stay with her.

'NO! I'm not going there. Why should I?' Sophia took her arm away, before storming back up the hill. She felt like a child being left by its mother on the first day of school, not wanting to take her first steps alone in the Outside World, and not understanding why she had to.

Sophia stopped halfway up the hill and sat down without looking back down towards the Sibyl; she was angry with her, she was frightened, and she was distraught. She also felt rather foolish. And then she remembered the wise old man warning her to learn to moderate her own child's behaviour; that although it was important to listen to the child, she should not let it take over. In all honesty Sophia did not care about this, because as far as she was concerned people kept leaving her anyway, so why bother trying to moderate her behaviour? To what end?

As Sophia continued to sit alone on the hillside, she wondered what the Sibyl was doing. She had, of course, been hoping beyond hope that the Sibyl would come after her and put her arms around her like she had done before; that she would console Sophia and tell her that everything would be all right. Deep down, though, Sophia knew that this was not going to happen. So when she finally brought herself to look back down the hill, she expected the Sibyl to be standing in the same place. But alas this was not so, for the Sibyl wasn't there at all. Sophia got to her feet and peered into the distance for as far as her eyes could see. She went back down the hill, frantically looking around her, yet it seemed that the Sibyl had disappeared just as effortlessly as she had first appeared.

'Why are you punishing me so?!' Sophia cried out uncontrollably. 'It's not fair . . . . I don't deserve this!'

Then she looked up into the sky, and shouted, 'WHAT DO YOU WANT FROM ME?'

And when Sophia had drained herself of all her resources, she went to sit by the side of the road that led into the Valley Town. She sat there for hours, frozen to the spot, whilst the occasional person passed silently by.

As the night sky descended, Sophia found herself delving into her bag for her notepad and pencil. She opened the notepad to see before her the verses of "The Light" that she had written in the forest. But she had no wish to read such enlightened words, not now when she felt so consumed by pain. Instead, she turned to a blank page and from somewhere within her frozen motionless frame, there flowed a stream of thoughts and emotions, which yearned to express themselves in the form of the written word.

Sophia wrote a piece from her heart:

"WHERE DID YOU GO?"

We were walking along the same road,
Unsure of where it would lead,
But what are adventures if not to contain the unknown?

Yet suddenly I looked around
And you weren't there!
You said you would not walk with me anymore,
You said that we could talk instead.
But how could we, with such distance in between?
For now I could not hear you like before.

I was a lost child looking for someone to find me,
To lead me back to safety,
Or take me further along the road.
I sat with my head in my hands,
And asked the heavens:

'What have I done?

I thought you said this was the way to go,

Did I mishear?

What did I get so wrong?

For now I am lost and don't know what to believe,

Did I see the light, to find that it was a mirage?

Or did I run before I could walk,

Too fast for my own good?

I really thought I understood,

Yet now my friend has gone.

Please show me what I need to see,

Don't leave me here alone,

Surely that's not what you meant for me'.

I waited a while looking down the empty road,

The darkness setting in,

As was the fear in my soul.

In the dusk a man's voice served as a timely intrusion. 'What is this romance with the written word?' he asked.

Sophia looked up to see a middle-aged, dark skinned man of slight build and greying hair; his face was kind, his eyes almost obsidian black. Sophia quickly shut her notepad. She managed a half-smile, but there was little warmth in it.

'You look cold out here,' the man said with concern in his voice.

'I'm alright,' Sophia replied curtly.

She hoped it would discourage the man from staying, but instead he persisted; 'I do not expect you to trust me, or to like me. Why should you? But I do know that you are new to this town and that staying out here in the dark and cold would be perilous.'

Sophia did not reply. She knew that he was right of course, and in all honesty she didn't really want to sit by the side of the road all night, but neither did she wish to converse with anyone. The dark skinned man however was still standing by her on the roadside.

'Look!' Sophia snapped. 'You don't have to stay in order to persuade me to move from here. I'll be alright on my own - it's what I'm most used to anyway.'

'So, someone has done you a misfortune. You feel let down and rejected,' he stated, at the same time making it sound like a question.

Sophia looked directly up at him, and said, 'I don't mean to be rude, but I really don't want a counselling session! I just want to be left alone.'

Although she knew she had been rude, the man did not appear to be offended in the least. But he did not move either. At this point Sophia could feel herself getting angry.

'For goodness sake, what do you want?!' she snapped, in exasperation. 'Why are you still standing there? Are you trying to provoke me or something?'

Sophia was surprised at herself for speaking so candidly. However, it still did not deter the man.

'I am just concerned for your welfare, that is all,' he answered calmly.

Yet the more calm he remained, the more irritated Sophia became. She got to her feet, suddenly wincing when she realised how stiff her limbs had become.

'Concerned!' she exclaimed. 'You don't even know me. Why should you be concerned about my welfare? What's your game?'

Sophia did not know what was going to come out of her mouth next. The man in contrast remained nonplussed.

'I do not have a game,' he replied. 'I simply do what I feel is right. Nothing more, nothing less.'

'Oh, I can't be bothered with this!'

Sophia grabbed her bag and stormed off along the road that led into the town. She did not glance back to see what the man was doing. In fact, she felt a certain kind of relief at not caring or worrying about someone else's welfare. This time, she decided that she was going to focus on herself and what she needed.

Chapter Nine
The Valley Town

It was dark by the time Sophia entered the Valley Town. She walked into the first establishment she saw that was likely to sell food and drink; it was a bar. She was surprised at her forthright behaviour, never having found it easy to go into such places on her own in the past. This time, however, she had not thought about it – she had just got on with it. It seemed that her feelings of anger and irritation by the roadside had propelled Sophia to overcome the blocks that had been constructed by her fear.

The bar was dimly lit and warm. Sophia was grateful for this. Without pausing to look around, she made her way straight to a barstool and sat down. Her head felt dizzy and her limbs trembled from the cold and lack of nourishment. All she could focus on was finding something to eat and drink. From somewhere in the bottom of her bag, she retrieved the coins that Bob had given to her. She had never seen coins like these before; they were gold and silver in colour and of different sizes, but they did not have any motif or information written on them. Sophia was at a loss as to the value of them.

The barman finally came over to her, and she was sure that he had a look of surprise on his face when he saw her. Wasting no time, Sophia asked the barman whether they served food; he informed her that they had only soup and bread rolls left over from earlier on in the day. Sophia gratefully accepted whatever they had, but when he told her how much it cost, once again she was at a loss as to what this meant. Opening her hand, she showed the barman the coins she had.

'I'm new to this town,' she said, 'so I don't know the money system yet.'

He seemed to look surprised when he saw the coins in her hands, but not as surprised as Sophia when he only took one of them. Furthermore, he brought her back some change in the form of smaller coins. Sophia smiled broadly to herself at this piece of good fortune. She realised of course that the barman could have taken advantage of her ignorance if he had so wished, and once again she was grateful that he had chosen not to. Suddenly it seemed that there were several things for Sophia to feel grateful for, so when the barman placed a bowl of piping hot soup in front of her, she felt temporarily uplifted.

'Thanks Bob,' she said softly under her breath, before delving into her food. As she broke off a piece of the bread roll she suddenly became aware of how dirty her hands were. She had become used to feeling dirty after the time she had spent in the forest, and in a way it had brought her a new found sense of freedom in not having to worry about what she looked like. Yet now, looking down at the dirt marks imprinted on the bread, Sophia found herself wondering what she looked like to others. Glancing quickly around her, she saw that there were a few people dotted here and there; she caught someone's glance and was convinced that they were making comments about her. Turning back to her food, Sophia decided to eat up as fast as she could and then leave.

As she got herself ready to leave, the barman approached her and said, 'Is there anything else I can help you with?'

Feeling rather more self-conscious than before, Sophia was about to say 'no' when she changed her mind. 'Well, actually, do you know a place I could stay for a few nights?' she asked. 'With the money I've got, I mean?'

'Yes, there's a cheap hotel just a bit further along this street. It's called the Shadows Inn.'

'Thanks very much,' replied a weary Sophia, as she lifted her bag over her shoulder.

She then bid him good night before heading off in search of the hotel.

Sophia's hotel room at the Shadows Inn was basic; a small bed, a small window, a small washbasin - but it was her sanctuary. The money had ensured that she could afford to stay for up to three months if she wanted to - with enough left over for food and perhaps some extras! She now knew why the barman had looked so surprised when he had seen the coins in her hand.

Sophia was shocked by the reflection she could now see as she looked into the mirror that hung above the washbasin. She let out a gasp at the sight of a face she did not recognise. For she had a look of wildness in her face, her dark eyes staring out from under an umbrella of matted hair, and her face was streaked with lines of dirt. But the single most distressing thing to Sophia was her stark loss of weight; her cheeks were sunken in and they had a sick, unhealthy pallor to them. As she looked down at the rest of her body, she knew that there was just more of the same, and was glad that there was no full-length mirror in the room to reinforce her fallen state.

Sophia lay on her bed and cried. And when her tears had run dry, she went to the bathroom down the hallway and lay in a warm bath for what seemed like an age. The warm smooth texture of the water caressed and cleansed her body like nothing else could, and this too made her cry. Eventually she started to feel cold, and so she lifted herself out of the water and then watched as the dirt stained water slowly drained away.

When she returned to her room, Sophia got straight into bed and quickly went into a deep sleep.

Over the coming week, Sophia sometimes slept for whole days. At other times she would sit by her window for hours and watch the people of the Valley Town go about their daily business. When she did venture out it was just to buy food and drink, which she invariably took back to her hotel room to consume, for she was still rather wary of people and she felt too self-conscious about her appearance.

One day she decided to purchase some scissors and a headscarf. Then on returning to her room, Sophia started to cut off great clumps of her hair; this was the only way she could see to untangle it. She then tried to even out the length of her hair as best she could, but she knew that it still had a very tufted appearance to it. Her hair was now above shoulder-length, shorter than she could ever remember, but she felt a considerable amount of relief at what she had done. It seemed such a simple thing but in fact Sophia had never had the courage in the past to have her hair cut short. Now that she had cut it, she felt that she had allowed herself a new freedom of choice; the choice of how to wear her hair.

Sophia had many goes at trying her headscarf on, for never having worn one before she wasn't sure how to put it on. She tried folding the headscarf in different ways, but whatever she did she felt she looked either like a nun or an old woman. In the end she found some humour in the whole procedure and decided that it didn't much matter how she wore it.

During the second week, Sophia began to feel restless. This feeling of restlessness conflicted with her almost perpetual feelings of tiredness and weakness, and as a result she was left in another state of confusion:

Should she stay in relative comfort for a while longer here in the Valley Town, building up her stamina and strength, before carrying on with this difficult journey she had started? Or should she leave now, in her eagerness to continue moving and to face her own truths, by trying to find the Centre Point?

She kept telling herself that there was always the option of giving it all up and going back, but each time this thought crossed her mind she found herself uttering the words; 'You haven't come all this way to go back to what you already know.'

From wherever these words came, they represented an internal force to be reckoned with. It was an inner voice, an inner spirit, that somehow would not allow her to give up. It reminded Sophia of her dream in the lake; when the voice below the sea would no longer remain silent. Or the powerful words from the wise old man's oration that came to her now:

'Do not underestimate those latent powers
That can eventually enrage,
By one day revealing to the world
And more especially to you,
No more to live a lie
But to be to yourself forever true.'

Sophia knew instinctively that she could not go back again.

This of course did not stop her from struggling to cope with the immense tension that had built up within her. For there was still so much she didn't understand, so much that she still feared, and so much that still pained her.

Sophia began to pace up and down her room in an attempt to dissipate some of the mounting tension. Back and forth she went, like a pendulum swinging, oscillating around the same central point. Her mind was racing, filled with thoughts of everything and anything, but in the end it was all a meaningless jumble. Suddenly she interrupted her pacing to look out of the window – why, she did not know. And yet the answer seemed to present itself to her almost immediately: the dark skinned man, whom she had met on the edge of the town, was walking past the hotel at that very moment. Sophia could not believe it; perhaps this was another glimpse into the workings of the Universe, of the Greatest Unknown. For the belief in mere coincidence was not, she had decided, going to help her on this journey.

Sophia dashed out of the room, down the stairs, and out through the front door of the hotel. Turning to her right, she caught sight of the man as he continued to walk along the street. He walked amongst various people yet there was something about him that seemed different from the rest; somehow he seemed lighter and less burdened by the passage of life. As Sophia caught up to him, she began to walk at a slower pace, suddenly hesitant about approaching him. She felt embarrassed, ashamed even, by the curt behaviour she had shown towards him. Why should he want anything to do with her, just because she had now decided that he might be of help to her? Although Sophia felt her motives to be somewhat suspect, she thought that if she did not take a chance when it was presenting itself to her, she would remain in the same position; she would continue to pace up and down in her room, remaining within the restrictions of yet another cage.

The dark skinned man was still in her sights but was now further away. Then he turned the corner and was out of view. Sophia could feel herself starting to panic, for if she left it any longer the moment would be gone; her chance would have passed. She started to run. When she got to the corner she prayed that he would still be in sight. To her amazement he had stopped to look in a shop window a little further down the street. Finally she approached him, taking some deep breaths in an attempt to control her rapid heartbeat.

'Hello there!' she panted.

He looked around, as if he knew straight away that it was he who was being addressed. His face broke into a smile and he bowed his head slightly as a means of acknowledgement. Sophia was greatly relieved.

Still out of breath, she said, 'I saw you passing by . . . . . . the hotel I've been staying at . . . . . . the Shadows Inn . . . . . . so I thought I'd come . . . . and say hello.'

'Hello then,' he offered his hand to Sophia. 'I am Victor, and I am pleased to meet you – again.'

'I'm Sophia,' she replied, taking his hand. 'It's nice to meet you too.' There was a brief pause before she continued. 'Actually, I wanted to apologise . . . . . . for my behaviour towards you. I was extremely rude.'

'Apology accepted,' Victor said warmly. 'I could see that you were having a difficult time. I do not take such things personally.'

'Oh, I'm glad. Thank you for being so understanding.'

A silence followed, during which Sophia did not know what say or do. Instead, it was Victor who spoke:

'Would you like to have some tea with me? There is a rather pleasant Teahouse across the street that I often frequent. I think you might like it.'

Sophia grinned, nodding in response to his invitation. There was something about this man, she thought to herself - his grace perhaps, or his eyes, that seemed to hold you in the moment but which seemed to be far away at the same time – and whatever it was, she felt instinctively that he would somehow help her along her way.

Sophia followed Victor across the street and into the Teahouse, where he greeted a member of staff in his usual polite manner. She then followed him as he went straight through to a small courtyard at the back of the Teahouse. The courtyard caught the sun during the afternoon, and Sophia thought the setting most pleasant. The blossom trees displayed the most glorious shades of pink against the blue sky above, now that the season of spring was well upon them, and Sophia could feel the rays of sun impart some warmth as they touched her skin.

When the tea arrived, Victor took the initiative of pouring it. Sophia in turn savoured the taste of each sip she took, in what was the perfect setting for afternoon tea. They sat in silence for a while. Victor seemed to be a man of few words, and Sophia had succumbed more and more to the solace of silence.

Suddenly she felt his hand gently touch hers, the friendly physical connection bringing her out of her reverie. Her sad tired eyes met his, whereupon they filled with tears, yet this time Sophia managed to hold back the tide. Instead the shallow pools of water remained in fragile suspension.

Victor took his hand away gently, as if knowing the art of perfect timing, and smiled warmly. 'More tea?' he asked.

'Yes please,' smiled Sophia.

Victor got up and went inside the Teahouse to order the tea. On returning, he seemed rather more upbeat in mood: 'It is all very well being a courageous warrior, but even courageous warriors have to attend to their basic needs!'

At that moment a waitress arrived and placed at their table a plate of pastries and sandwiches.

'Oh my goodness!' exclaimed Sophia. 'What a feast.'

She sat looking at the food whilst her companion made the first move and picked up a sandwich.

'Well? What are you waiting for?' he said. 'You need this more than I do.'

Sophia smiled in acknowledgement before tucking in. At first she revelled in such delights, but then each mouthful seemed to turn into a solid lump which had to force its way down. She was immediately reminded of her encounter with the Sibyl; when she had asked Sophia what it was that she couldn't digest.

'What is the matter, my dear?' Victor looked concerned.

'I don't know exactly,' replied Sophia, holding the top of her chest. 'It won't go down. It's painful.'

'Yes, rejection is painful, isn't it?'

Sophia was startled by his words, and did not know how to respond; it seemed as if he knew her pain already. She simply closed her eyes and waited until the lump in her throat had finally reached her stomach.

When she opened her eyes, Sophia looked towards Victor and asked, 'How did you know?'

'It does not matter, Sophia, how I know,' he said softly. 'The important thing is that you are not alone with it. That is why I am here at this time.'

'Yes, but how do I know that?' she protested. 'I've been told that before! And then when I dare to trust it, the same thing keeps happening – when I feel I'm drowning in grief, I'm still being punished!'

Victor paused for a short while before saying what he had to say: 'The Sibyl filled your heart with hope and love, like the blissful and divine union of mother and child, or the innocent love of new lovers.'

Sophia could not speak. What could she say that would not seem but a wasteful interruption of the flow of wisdom? What could she say that he did not know already? Sophia conceded that it was she who did not know; that it was time for her to listen, time for her to take in that which was being given – as if they were also gifts being placed at her table, alongside the tea and the cakes.

But Victor did not continue to speak, and Sophia was waiting for his next word. Perhaps he only offered his thoughts when prompted, she wondered. She felt she had to know more.

'Do you know the Sibyl well, then?' she asked nervously.

'As much as anyone, I would say,' he responded. 'We go back a long way, you could say.' Then he grinned, almost dreamily, and said, 'Indeed, over many centuries.'

It was at this moment that Sophia found herself feeling a tinge of anger. "So Victor and the Sibyl know each other well," she thought to herself. She started to wonder whether this was all a game to them, whether they were testing her, playing with her mind and her emotions. "All the while, they seem to be all-knowing and in control, whilst leaving me on tender hooks," Sophia decided to herself. She felt like a starving dog waiting for scraps to be thrown – one minute being offered treats and the next, nothing! She was continually being hooked emotionally, and didn't know how to unhook herself. Yes, she had managed to be on her own in the forest, away from all humanity, but there was only so long that she could survive that.

Sophia suddenly felt on the edge of paranoia. Were the Sibyl and Victor accomplices, well rehearsed in luring strangers when they were at their most vulnerable? Did they appear just at the point when others were at their most needy, when they were craving affection, all their defences having been hacked down by life's blows and rejections? For they never seemed to give anything away about themselves, all the time remaining in complete control, whilst luring naïve others into their cage. "Well," Sophia decided to herself, "I am not about to get caught in another trap!"

Glaring at Victor across the table, she said, 'You think you can buy me with all these goodies, do you? I can see what your game is . . . . you're both in it together, aren't you? You may be able to manipulate and control others, but you can't fool me! I was right the first time I walked away from you.'

Victor looked a little startled, but not unduly so. 'Alas,' he said, almost resigned, 'I see that I have become the demon in your eyes – and so suddenly. I feel saddened that that is all you see, but perhaps that is the way it has to be, for now.'

Sophia remained adamant that she had got it right, that she needed to take back some control. Yet even with the most forceful of outward conviction, deep inside she was confused and unsure of what was going on. "A clear thinking person" was how she had often been described by other people; someone who was not given to "irrational emotional outbursts" that she had often heard attributed to women, and someone who could see the wood and the trees. Now however, Sophia felt completely lost.

She got up from the table. 'I've got to go,' she said, as she left Victor sitting at the table with a plate of uneaten pastries.

She drifted out of the Teahouse in a daze. She had to find her way back to the hotel, to rest her troubled mind and body, for she was starting to doubt her own mind. All she had left that seemed real and could not be argued with, were her emotions and her physical symptoms. Her body was once again crying out for rest, and as she made her way towards the Shadows Inn she found herself remembering something that Victor had said:

'Even courageous warriors need to attend to their basic needs.'

Chapter Ten
Transition Of Mind

Sophia spent the next couple of days within the confines of her hotel. She slept, she ate and she bathed. Sometimes she would lie there wondering where the Sibyl and what had been the significance of meeting her. Sophia's thoughts would flit from perceiving the Sibyl and Victor as collaborators in mental and emotional manipulation, to seeing them as genuine people of great wisdom and intuition; as caring people who were not trying to "do" anything to Sophia but instead had good reasons for their actions. Depending on which web of thoughts she found herself entangled in, Sophia's emotional state would fluctuate from feeling hurt and angry, to feeling guilty and remorseful. To this end it seemed that the four walls of her hotel room were the container Sophia needed.

Indeed her mind seemed to gradually settle down into some form of equilibrium, and when it did Sophia was able to think in a more objective manner. She found herself wanting to believe in something greater then herself - otherwise she couldn't see the point to all she had gone through. What was the Greatest Unknown all about, she wondered. The term had come to her once very fleetingly when she was with Bob, and then the Sibyl had mentioned it to her up on the hillside. All the time Sophia was being asked to trust it, to believe in it, and now not only did she want to believe in the Greatest Unknown, she felt she needed to. And despite her doubts about the authenticity of the Sibyl, Sophia knew that she had seen the Shadows moving on the other side of the valley. Sophia knew that that was real.

As the days and weeks passed by, Sophia developed a fondness for the Valley Town; for its simplicity and predictability - the shops opening at the same time each morning, and the same familiar faces of shop trader and customer encountering one another. A short trip to the bakery or grocers was the extent of her interaction with other people, yet it provided Sophia with a much-needed sense of safety and stability. Her body was a little stronger now and her mind more settled, but her heart was still heavy. This was never more so than when she passed the Teahouse, which she had done on several occasions. She did not once, however, go in.

Today, Sophia walked a little further than the local shops. Taking a small picnic with her, she followed the road to the edge of the town and a little beyond. It was a particularly warm day, as the season of summer quickly approached, and Sophia found herself a nice spot of grass on which to lie. As she lay with the sun on her face, she realised that this was the first time since being in the courtyard of the Teahouse that she had felt the warmth of the sun upon her. And in her now calmer state of mind, she was able to think back to that time and to view it in a different way:

Sophia realised that she had been extremely sensitive - albeit for good reasons – to any external cues from others, unable to filter out those that were harmless or unimportant. In her vulnerable state, she had perceived almost everything as a potential threat from which to protect herself. Now she was able to see that perhaps those potential threats were imagined or simply misinterpreted. She was ready to accept that neither the Sibyl, nor Victor, were negative entities from which to protect herself.

At that moment, Sophia caught a glimpse in her mind's eye of the Sibyl in all her glory. For she was glorious. And she was graceful and serene, as Sophia had imagined a goddess to be. As Sophia let her mind drift in the sunshine, she found herself imagining the Sibyl existing over the centuries, as if she was in this world but not of it. Then Sophia tried to remember their last encounter just outside the Valley Town, and what the Sibyl had said to her before she disappeared – something that Sophia had not been able to hear at the time.

Suddenly Sophia opened her eyes and sat up. As if to emphasise her new found openness, she spoke aloud:

'The Sibyl said something about being with me even though I had to journey on my own . . . . to call her if I need her help . . . . . . something about visualising her . . . . .'

Sophia felt she had reached a turning point today, a willingness to ask for help and guidance, to listen and learn from those of higher wisdom. So, closing her eyes and letting her mind and body relax as much as she could, she tried to visualise an image of the Sibyl:

. . . . Into Sophia's mental picture came the Sibyl with gold flowing robes, as if gliding rather than walking. Then she stopped and stood still. She was standing alone at the bottom of the hillside. Then she stretched out her arms and beckoned for Sophia to go to her. Sophia now entered the picture and started to walk slowly towards her, all the time the Sibyl smiling warmly. Suddenly Sophia stopped, still several yards away from the Sibyl, and would not proceed any further. Still

the Sibyl continued to beckon to her, but Sophia remained motionless
. . . .

And then the image was gone.

Sophia opened her eyes. She had not been able to project the picture in her mind any further forward. It had remained frozen in that place, and in her mind.

At first Sophia felt rather disappointed, a little frustrated even, but soon she accepted that the frozen image reflected her own situation at this time. For she was, as the Sibyl had inferred, journeying on her own but at the same time she was not alone. The inner reflected the outer; and everything was all right, for now.

Sophia lay back in the sun and closed her eyes once again. She felt a feeling of warmth and of love gently rise from within her core until it filled her up. It was a feeling very similar to the experience she had had in the forest, when she had been compelled to write "The Light". It brought an overwhelming feeling of belonging, a feeling of being separate but together, of being glad to be alive in such a wonderful Universe . . . . and then its energy began to wane, and was gone.

When Sophia opened her eyes, she felt rather light-headed. Sitting up slowly, she looked around her and tried to adjust to her surroundings. She felt a little disorientated, as if she had been somewhere else temporarily whilst leaving her body behind. It was all rather confusing, yet Sophia was left feeling strangely uplifted. And at that moment she wondered whether she had been in touch with the Greatest Unknown.

So, in this rare optimistic frame of mind, Sophia gathered her things together and made her way back to the hotel, knowing that the time was approaching when she would leave the Valley Town.

There was, however, one thing she felt she had to do before continuing on her journey: revisit the Teahouse.

The following day Sophia awoke, but alas not with a feeling of optimism. Instead, an overwhelming feeling of heaviness had taken hold of her mind and body again. It seemed that the pendulum had swung once more, so that now the thought of journeying onward today filled Sophia with dread.

She pulled the covers over her face, closed her eyes and went back to sleep. She slept for much of the day and the following night, disturbing dreams interrupting her slumber at various intervals. How quickly the darkness had set in; how far away the hopes of yesterday now seemed. Sophia told herself that there was nothing else to do but to ride through the storm.

The next day seemed less dark and less frightening. Sophia knew that, from the moment she woke up. She was also aware of how hungry she was, enough in itself to push her outside to go in search of some nourishment.

Feeling as though she had survived a storm at sea and had been washed up the next day on the shore, Sophia found herself walking in the direction of the Teahouse.When she reached there she stood outside the Teahouse, hesitating to go in. Eventually she took a deep breath, opened the door and stepped inside. It was not very busy, perhaps due to the sudden cold spell, and Sophia was able to choose a small table in a discreet corner. She placed her order with the same waitress that had served her and Victor in the courtyard. Sitting there alone, she now wished she had not walked out on Victor, for in doing so she had rejected the one extended hand of friendship and kindness she had encountered in the Valley Town.

Whilst eating her toasted sandwich, Sophia thought back to her meeting with the wise old man of the forest. Once again she was reminded of his advice; to learn to moderate her child's behaviour. Yet it seemed that she had been unable to do this: the angry and frightened child had been more powerful than the adult. She wanted to listen to the child whom she had buried under the sea, but she couldn't seem to stop it from taking over at times. And when it did, Sophia did not like it very much; she wanted it to go away and to leave her alone.

She ordered more tea and another toasted sandwich. Then she took the opportunity of looking around her, and to her surprise the Teahouse was almost full. When the waitress arrived and was placing the order on the table, Sophia decided to ask her about Victor. She asked the waitress whether he had been there recently, describing his appearance as best she could. However, this was not necessary, as the waitress seemed to know who he was straight away.

'Oh yes, Victor,' she said. 'He's a regular in here.'

Sophia's face lit up. 'So you know him?'

'Well I wouldn't say that. He's a bit elusive, tends to keep himself to himself. He's been in this town for years but I don't think anyone really knows him.'

As the waitress was about to resume her duties, Sophia asked, 'Do you know when he might be in next?'

'Well, he comes in most days,' the waitress replied. 'In fact, that's him coming in now.' Then she went to attend to some other customers.

Sophia's heart was pounding, suddenly feeling terribly nervous at the prospect of seeing Victor again. Yet she also wanted to see him again; after all, that was why she had come back to the Teahouse. She could hardly look up as she heard the door open, her cheeks burning with embarrassment, for she did not know how he would respond to seeing her again.

Then she heard his voice say; 'Hello, Sophia.'

It was soft and comforting, and Sophia could hardly contain her relief. 'Victor!' she said joyfully, looking up at him. 'I was just asking about you.'

She could still feel the burning in her cheeks and knew that it must be visible to Victor. He smiled warmly though, not commenting, whilst Sophia continued on in embarrassment.

'Would you like to join me?' she asked, signalling to the chair facing her. 'The tea is very good here!'

Victor nodded in his unique way, as he obliged her and sat down.

'Victor, I want to apologise – again! - for my behaviour the last time we were here. It seems I make a habit of walking out on you.'

'It is quite alright, my dear,' he said gently. 'You must have had your reasons.'

Sophia could not believe how genuinely unaffected he seemed to be. Somehow, his reaction – or lack of it – seemed too reasonable, too measured, and Sophia did not understand this.

'Are you saying that it doesn't matter how I behave?' she asked him. 'You mean, I can be as rude as I like and you don't mind?' She wanted to understand.

'Of course there are always limits,' Victor grinned, 'and I would defend myself if I had to! But generally it does not come to that. You see, if you are disturbed by you own behaviour, than that is all that really matters. For only then will you be motivated to change it or to make amends . . . . . . as you are doing today.'

Sophia felt silenced by his words, not in the sense of retreating into herself, but rather a need to take in such wisdom and to understand it. During the silence, the waitress brought Victor his tea and pastry, and Sophia thought of some more questions to ask him.

'Victor,' she began, 'the waitress said that you've been in this town for years but that nobody really knows you. Is that true?'

Victor laughed without taking offence, his face lighting up and the whites of his eyes looking like candles glowing against his dark features. It was easy to become ever so slightly mesmerised without meaning to, and soon Sophia found herself laughing as well. And how perfectly wonderful it was to be laughing.

'I'm not sure why we're laughing,' she said, suddenly aware that several other customers were looking over at them.

'I'm not sure myself,' he replied, 'I just felt like laughing. Such a refreshing emotion, don't you think?'

Sophia nodded in agreement. 'Yes, in fact I'm really grateful for that laugh. I really needed it! It's made me feel much lighter.'

When the laughter had settled down, Sophia spoke a little more seriously. 'But are you being truthful with me, Victor, when you say that you don't know what made you laugh? It's just that you seem to know most things.'

Victor's face became more serious as he looked directly at Sophia and began to tell her insights of a more profound nature:

'It is true, Sophia, that I am in possession of wisdom concerning such things as the workings of the Universe, and of my part in it. But as it is much greater than I, I could never hope or wish to know most things – as you have suggested. For it is after all, the Greatest Unknown that we are talking about.'

He paused thoughtfully for a moment, leaving an intrigued Sophia waiting in anticipation for him to continue: 'Sometimes we do things, act in certain ways, thinking that we are in total control of our destinies,' he looked down at his teacup sadly. 'But the moment we start thinking this way, we start believing that we are greater than the Universe and its forces. Man then believes that his ego alone has ultimate control and power. That is a grave mistake but alas one that predominates.'

Sophia felt rather flummoxed by what Victor had said, but nevertheless she remembered the wise old man of the forest saying something about the ego, and then of course the Sibyl.

'I think I understand what you're saying,' she said a little unconvincingly.

Victor's face changed in response to her. He looked up and smiled. 'I am so sorry, my dear, I did not intend to go on. Sometimes I get carried away with my own preoccupations. Still, it seems that my spontaneous laughter was just the thing that you needed.'

'So, you knew what I needed without knowing it . . . . . . if you know what I mean?' Sophia giggled at her own playful comments.

'And now I can see that you, Sophia, are also very wise – without knowing it!' Victor joined in.

He looked briefly at the darkening sky outside. An unexpected clap of thunder sounded, which seemed to prompt him to say; 'Well, it seems that it is I who must be going this time.'

Suddenly Sophia felt a wave of anxiety sweep over her, at the thought of Victor disappearing and of not knowing if she would see him again.

'Please! Stay just a little longer,' she pleaded. 'I need to ask you something.'

'What is it, my dear?' he looked at Sophia with genuine concern.

'I wanted to ask you about the Land of the Shadows,' she found herself saying. 'You see, I've been in this town for quite a while now, much longer than I thought I would. And I've been thinking that I need to get going soon, but I'm still afraid of moving on.'

Although her nervousness was clearly visible, Sophia felt immense relief at being able to speak so honestly to someone. She took a deep breath and carried on with her confession:

'I feel as if I'm stuck and that every time I think about moving, I start to feel worse again. I don't want to go back but I don't want to stay here for much longer either – not to mention that I'm running out of money! Somehow I know that I need to journey to the Land of the Shadows – why else would I have met the Sibyl? And yet I feel daunted by it, by what I might find.'

'So it is your intuitive feeling that something foreboding awaits you if you journey that way?' Victor replied understandingly.

'Yes, I suppose so.' Sophia paused thoughtfully for a while, before deciding what else to say. 'But it's also about facing something that's unknown. I mean, I was frightened enough as it is to enter this town, even though I have lived in towns for most of my life. It's just that I feel so much weaker than I used to, more vulnerable I guess.'

'Not the tower of strength anymore?' Victor reiterated.

It was Sophia's turn to feel saddened by his words, and by the truth they conveyed. Her eyes filled with tears. For although she did not wish to be a tower of strength again, she had not been able to construct a replacement structure that was strong enough to withstand the outside forces of the human world. This saddened and frightened her more than anything. As she sat opposite her wise companion who would soon be departing, Sophia could feel these emotions bubbling beneath the surface. Yet, Victor seemed to temper her emotions with his words:

'Do not rush, my dear,' he said gently. 'It takes time to rebuild, and you need to make sure you have more secure foundations before you proceed. Otherwise you may collapse again.'

Sophia looked up at him. 'B-but I've b-been here so l-long,' she said. 'So much time is passing and I'm still here!'

Her distress was as apparent as Victor's calmness was containing. He reached over and touched her trembling hands. Then, looking into her eyes, he said, 'Listen, Sophia, you are doing extremely well. The Land of the Shadows will still be here, but you must be a little stronger before you journey there.'

'You're scaring me, Victor,' Sophia took her hand away. 'Is it that frightening there? Because I might as well give up now! What's the use of me trying anymore.'

'I hope you do not give up,' Victor tried to be reassuring. 'You have come so far, and there is much beauty that awaits you. It can be yours, Sophia, and such treasures are worth waiting for.'

Sophia was a little calmer now, having taken in every word that he had said and cherishing them. Then as Victor made his move to go, the tears that had filled Sophia's eyes spilled over and ran silently down her cheeks.

Before Victor left he leant towards her and said, 'When you get to the Land of the Shadows, there will be people to help guide you. As for your concern about the passing of time, remember Sophia: Time is never lost – it is in everything and anything.'

Sophia watched him go, wondering whether she would ever see him again, yet pleased that she had met him.

The waitress came over to the table bringing, Sophia assumed, the bill. She thought to herself that after paying for this, she would hardly have any money left. But before she had the chance to start worrying about her potential fate, the waitress smiled and said, 'Here's your change. Victor already paid the bill and told me to leave the change with you.'

Through her tear–stained face, Sophia could not help but smile. She accepted the change gratefully and thanked the waitress, before leaving the Teahouse and heading back to her hotel.

The money she had received from Victor was not an insignificant sum. It would ensure that she could stay for another few weeks at the Shadows Inn.

And so as more days and weeks passed by, Sophia accepted that her main task was to learn the art of patience and perseverance. For this would allow her to build up her physical and mental strength in preparation for the next stage of her journey.

By now summer had arrived, and the natural urge to go out into the warm sunshine began to take hold of Sophia. She went for strolls most days in the nearby countryside, often befriended by a bird or a squirrel. Sometimes she took bread or a few nuts with her to give to them, never having forgotten the time she had spent in the forest with the animals. They had become a great comfort to her at that time, and she had developed a great respect for them whilst they had all shared the same home on Mother Earth.

Today Sophia walked along the path that led to the river. It seemed to be quite a popular route, particularly on a sunny day, and some people went out on the river in boats and canoes. She found herself a place to sit, and she watched as people walked by. Some of the faces were by now familiar to her, and as they followed the path which aligned itself to the river, Sophia wondered where the path ultimately led. "Does it lead into the Land of the Shadows?" she asked herself, as she looked up towards the hillside upon which she had once seen the Shadows. Yet no matter how much she squinted and strained her eyes, she could not see any Shadows.

Sophia sighed deeply as she redirected her attention to her more immediate surroundings. More people walked by, some chatting and laughing, some silent, yet as she looked at them she could not help but wonder whether they knew about the Land of the Shadows. Had any of them been there? Had anyone met the Sibyl? Sophia even had the urge at times to go up to one of the passers-by and ask them, but she restrained herself in case they thought her mad. Instead her mind drifted to remembrances of the people she had already met along the way. She thought of the Wood Chopper and wondered if she was still in the same place, chopping wood throughout the day and retreating into the forest at night. She thought of Bob and smiled; his straightforward manner she had found to be rather liberating. She remembered something he had said about Sophia having been round the round-a-bout a few times.

'How difficult it is for us to hear the truth,' Sophia said quietly to herself. For she could see more clearly now that there were many undesirable patterns she had repeated in her life. Patterns that had ultimately restricted her life, that had kept her in the Cage from which she had seen no way out. The irony for Sophia was that on the surface she had been living what appeared to be a full and busy life, but below the surface she had not felt alive.

'Just like the wise old man said,' whispered Sophia,
'something like . . . . .
But alas to your soul do not be too unkind, Do not let your fears, hopes and wishes
Be impossible to find,
For then you are in danger of losing your inner self.'

She was surprised by how much she had remembered. It was as if the words were already imprinted in her memory and she could now just access them at will.

Somehow, on this particular summer's day, Sophia was able to see aspects of herself with more clarity than ever before, as though a veil had been lifted from her eyes. She could see that there were a whole host of internal restrictions she had placed upon herself, restrictions that had limited the way she had lived her life.

In an attempt to capture such clarity of thought as it presented itself to her, Sophia took out her notepad and jotted down some of her thoughts:

- What are these internal restrictions I have placed upon myself?
- Limiting beliefs, high expectations, guilty feelings, judgements, resentments, fears and whatever else one cares to throw into the melting pot.
- And who or what is responsible for what ends up in the melting pot?
- Is it all me? Have I been responsible for all that I've become? After all, as adults we are responsible for our own actions and behaviour, for the decisions we make in life. And if things turn out generally all right, we are quite happy to accept our own part in that success, aren't we?
- But what about when things are not so good - when life is a struggle yet others seem to have it easy? Where does the blame and responsibility lie then? Someone has to be guilty! Anger has to find its direction towards a culprit!
- It's just that in my case, the culprit has always been ME!

Sophia closed her notepad and lay back on the grass. For the first time she seemed to feel a genuine compassion for her own human nature. There was a kind of letting go, a release, as she no longer battled. She felt none of the impatience that she had recently battled with, only a strange stillness within her. Sophia could see that the pressure of time she had often felt, was just an illusion that she had created for herself. She didn't know how long this enlightened feeling would last, but at least for now she understood that her journey to the Land of the Shadows would happen when the time was right.

And so, the truth of Victor's words came ringing in her ears: 'Time is never lost,' she said aloud.

Sophia collected her things together in order to head back into town. As she stood up, she looked up towards the hillside, and knew that it was time for her to leave the Valley Town. She wanted to discover the mysteries that lay in the Land of the Shadows, whatever they were.

'And who knows – I might even see the Sibyl again!' she said, as she walked in the direction of her hotel for the last time.

Part Two
The Journey

Chapter Eleven
The Twenty One Steps

Sophia left the Shadows Inn the following morning, carrying her bag which contained the few items she possessed in life. Yet these were like trusted companions to her, and she felt comforted by their reliable presence.

As she walked through the familiar streets of the Valley Town, Sophia hesitated outside one of the shops. "Time to stock up on a few things," Sophia thought to herself, as she searched her pockets for the remaining coins she had. Somehow she knew instinctively that she would not have any need for money in the place that she was journeying to. So into the shop she went, and out she came with cartons of fruit juice, tins of food items such as beans and tuna, and a tin opener.

'Well, that's finally cleared me out,' she said, strapping the now considerably heavier bag across her back.

There was one shop, however, that Sophia had never had the courage to enter in all the time she had spent in the Valley Town. She had often wanted to go in, and sometimes she almost overcame the feelings of shame and embarrassment that held her back, but somehow she could never quite do it. And now that she had no money left, she felt a sense of regret at not having taken the plunge when she had the chance. The shop she was thinking about was a hairdressing salon.

Sophia stood outside the hairdressing salon for several moments, looking at the pictures of women with different hairstyles. She had not exposed her own head of hair to anyone since the day she had cut it off in her hotel room, preferring instead to keep the uneven jagged locks firmly hidden under her headscarf. She had tried to even out her hair as best as she could over the course of time, but in her eyes she still looked unacceptable. She did not want to have people staring at her, or making comments, but neither could she bring herself to have someone else cut her hair.

'Never mind, eh,' Sophia sighed. 'This is probably the least of my worries.'

She was about to move on when a woman's voice called to her: 'Can I help you?' The woman was standing at the entrance of the salon, about to go in.

'No, it's alright. Just looking,' Sophia smiled awkwardly.

'I work here, you see, and I've often seen you pass by and look in. We're very friendly in here, there's no need to worry,' the woman smiled warmly.

'No really, it's alright thankyou,' Sophia was blushing with embarrassment. 'Anyway, I don't have any money.'

Sophia started to walk away, when the woman called after her: 'I'll do your hair for free! Just a quick tidy up, won't take five minutes.'

Sophia stopped and turned around. 'Why?' she asked, in disbelief.

'Let's just say I've been there before! So are you coming in?'

Sophia felt that she simply could not refuse such an offer. So, she followed the woman sheepishly into the salon and then to a swivel chair next to a wash basin. There seemed to be so many mirrors in the salon that a very disconcerted Sophia did not know where to look. It was fairly quiet, only one or two customers, yet this did not stop Sophia from trembling with anxiety.

'Here, let me help you with that bag,' the woman said, which helped Sophia to focus on the task at hand. 'By the way, my name is Roseanna.'

Once Sophia had removed her bag, she replied, 'Thanks, my name is Sophia.'

Then she sat down in the swivel chair, whereupon Roseanna asked her to remove her headscarf. Sophia by now was visibly sweating, such was her fear of being exposed and ridiculed, and she could not bring herself to remove the headscarf.

'It's okay, Sophia,' Roseanna said, reassuringly. 'Let me do it.'

Carefully, Roseanna untied the knot at the back of Sophia's headscarf before slowly lifting it off her head to finally reveal Sophia's dark hair. 'There! It's really not so bad, is it?'

Sophia could see herself in one of the large mirrors fixed to the wall. She winced, not because she was particularly shocked by her reflection, but because she felt so exposed. In fact, Sophia felt that her hair did not look quite as bad as she had expected, but still she found it very hard to look at herself and so quickly averted her gaze. She was, it seemed, her own harshest critic.

'You're going to have to face yourself sometime!' said Roseanna, as she turned the swivel chair. 'Can you lean your head back for me, Sophia, so that I can wash your hair.'

Sophia silently obliged, and as the warm water began to seep through her hair and on to her scalp she felt an almost immediate calming effect. She closed her eyes and let her body relax into the moment, whilst the confident firm massage strokes of Roseanna's hands released the tension further. Yet the words Roseanna had said stuck in Sophia's mind:

'You're going to have to face yourself sometime.'

For they strongly resonated with the guiding words spoken by the wise old man of the forest:

'To truly be free, you have to face yourself.'

These were words that had stayed with Sophia all the way along her journey of the West Road.

'Lift your head now for me, Sophia,' the next instructions from Roseanna came.

Sophia felt the comforting softness of a towel being placed over her wet hair. Then Roseanna pushed Sophia in her chair over to a large mirror, and set about combing and cutting Sophia's hair with the swiftness and confidence of a much experienced hairdresser. Finally Roseanna blow-dried her hair for all of a minute, before announcing: 'There, all done! I told you it would only take five minutes.'

Sophia managed to glance at herself in the mirror, and for all her previous reservations she was rather pleased with the result. Her hair was much shorter than she was used to but now she felt she had some sort of hairstyle rather than just hair on her head.

'Well! What do you think?' asked Roseanna eagerly.

'Yes, I quite like it,' replied Sophia. 'Thanks Roseanna.'

As Roseanna brushed away the cut hair that had fallen onto Sophia's clothes, she said, 'So, are you leaving the Valley Town?'

'Yes, yes I am.' Sophia did not know what else to say.

'Where are you off to? Anywhere nice?'

'Well, er, I'm not sure yet. I mean I've never been there before.' Sophia could feel Roseanna looking at her, as she helped her out of the chair.

'Where is "there"?' Roseanna asked inquisitively.

Sophia felt embarrassed to tell her but decided to anyway. 'I'm trying to get to the Land of the Shadows.'

A broad grin appeared upon Roseanna's face, much to Sophia's surprise. 'Good for you, Sophia,' she said enthusiastically. 'You are a brave woman.'

'A lot of people seem to be telling me that. God knows what I'm letting myself in for! I don't even know how to get there.'

'Well, I think that it's great! Follow your intuition and you'll never go wrong.'

'Thanks Roseanna,' Sophia replied, sincerely. 'I really appreciate that.'

Roseanna helped Sophia on with her bag and then walked with her to the front door.

'By the way, Sophia,' she said pointing to the path that led to the river, 'if you walk along this path for about a mile, you will come to a small pathway that branches off to the right. There is no signpost, so don't worry that you've gone the wrong way. The path leads up the hillside - it's a bit steep in parts, but not too bad. Just before you reach the top of the hill, look out for some steps that lead underground – it's sign-posted so you shouldn't miss it! And good luck.'

As she lent forward to kiss Sophia's cheek, Sophia couldn't believe the good fortune she had already received on this day.

'Thankyou so much, Roseanna,' Sophia smiled. 'But how come you know where it is?'

Roseanna grinned and simply replied, 'Let's just say that I've been there before!'

Then she turned to go back into the salon, leaving Sophia to begin the next stage of her journey.

Sophia stopped when she got to the small pathway that branched off to the right. It was much quieter here, perhaps because the main path had veered away from the river, though Sophia wondered whether it was more to do with being close to the Land of the Shadows. She found a spot to sit on and removed her bag with great relief, before retrieving something to eat and drink.

Sitting on the grass, relaxing in the country air, Sophia thought of her most recent fateful encounter. She was so grateful for having met Roseanna; she felt a sense of freedom at no longer having to wear her headscarf; she felt more hopeful about her forthcoming venture into the Land of the Shadows, now that she had met someone who had actually been there. 'And Roseanna seems to be doing well,' Sophia reinforced to herself.

Now feeling somewhat full and sleepy, she lay back on the grass resting her head upon her bag, and closed her eyes. She decided she would rest for a while before continuing her walk up the hillside in search of the underground steps that Roseanna had spoken of.

Sophia was unable to resist the lure of sleep, and when she eventually woke it was due to a particularly large raindrop that had splattered upon her forehead. With a sudden jolt she opened her eyes and sat up. She shook her head, trying to offload the feeling of sluggishness that had accumulated during her slumber. Large grey clouds now enveloped the sky and the wind had picked up. Sophia felt a shudder run through her. It looked like there was about to be a heavy downpour, yet it did not appear to be raining at that moment. Somehow, it seemed that one solitary drop of rain had fallen upon the tiny space that Sophia occupied, as if to waken her and tell her that it was time to move. She thought once more of the Greatest Unknown, smiled a little sadly and said, 'Then it is time for me to go.'

Looking up in the direction of her destination, Sophia wondered what awaited her there. She felt that something deep inside her was driving her towards it, something stronger than the intellect of her mind, something stronger than the desires of her ego. Sophia could only conclude that it was the force of her spirit. She gathered her things together and started to walk up the narrow footpath.

The rain seemed to hold off as she made her ascent, and she was grateful for the moderate wind that blew against her face. For she could feel the heat rising in her body, forming a cold sweat that perspired from the pores of her skin. All the time she kept her eyes to the ground, seeing only the next step of her climb rather than what was further ahead. She decided that she would only look up when she needed to stop and rest. The path was rather rickety, which made Sophia's walk a little less monotonous if nothing else.

When she finally stopped to rest and drink some water, Sophia was surprised by how much ground she had covered; she guessed that she had climbed about two thirds of the way up the hillside. Indeed she had come to expect each stage of her journey to be difficult and testing, so that the relative ease of her current progress brought her a much needed sense of relief and encouragement. Now eager to get to the top of the hill, Sophia resumed her climb as soon as she had recovered her breath.

The narrow path however became steeper and less defined, so that Sophia was at times climbing upon rocks. She could feel the burning heat as it emanated from her body and became trapped between her skin and her clothing. Her breathing became more and more laboured as she gasped for breath, yet still she was determined to persevere with her mission and not stop until she reached her destination.

Suddenly the path seemed to disappear altogether and Sophia could only see rocks and bushes scattered in front of her. This forced her to cease her blind motion and to re-evaluate her position. She wiped the perspiration from her face with the sleeve of her shirt, before sitting down on a nearby mound of earth and grass. Removing her bag, Sophia loosened her shirt to allow the cool air in. Gradually her body returned to a calmer and cooler state, and when it did she was able to survey her surroundings more thoroughly.

Above her there was an assortment of trees that crowned the top of the hill; below her she could see the narrow path as it meandered its way up the hillside, only to disappear into the earth like the source of a mountain stream.

'So where are the underground steps Roseanna talked about?' Sophia asked aloud. She decided to stay put for a while, this being a good time to have some lunch. Then she would consider her next plan of action.

Whilst eating, Sophia noticed something out of the corner of her eye – something that moved. When she turned her head to look, her face broke into a joyous smile; for there, looking straight back at her, was a rabbit. It was peering over a small mound of earth like a meerkat, yet within a moment it had vanished back underground.

'Come on, Sophia,' she told herself, as she got up from her own mound. 'It's time to go underground!'

She walked over to where she had seen the rabbit and noticed that there were several rabbit holes dotted around. 'Hello, my friends,' she said as she walked past, careful not to disturb them too much. Then she climbed over another rock and noticed a particularly large mound of earth to her left. Sophia found herself being drawn to it. Her heart began to beat faster and her stomach tightened up a little.

She walked around the circumference of the mound, wondering what she would discover.

Then she saw it: the entrance to the Land of the Shadows. It was nothing grand or majestic – nothing in keeping with the serene grandeur of the Sibyl – just a tunnel with steps going down. Sophia felt her stomach turn at the prospect of descending into the darkness, for there were no lights that she could see. She noticed a sign hanging from just under the roof of the tunnel entrance, and decided to walk down a few steps so that she could see it more clearly.

It read: "THE TWENTY ONE STEPS"

'What does that mean?' Sophia mumbled to herself, as she sat down on one of the steps just under the sign. She was now sitting between one world and another, about to plunge into the unknown which looked to be a dark well of despair to Sophia. All she could see were images of herself walking along dark damp tunnels, clutching at the walls, terrified of suddenly falling down a hole or having rats crawling all over her. The possibilities were endless, but always horrific.

Sophia put her head in her hands, feeling so alone and abandoned. 'What am I going to do?' she said in anguish. 'I'm so frightened.'

It seemed that the voice of the child now spoke through her - just as the wise old man had said. Yet this time it was the emotion of the child within that Sophia felt, rather than the uncontrolled behaviour she had displayed before. Sophia could feel the depths of her child's anguish, could hear her cries, but alas did not seem able to help her. Sophia could not find it in her to comfort this vulnerable frightened child, for in truth she still wanted her to go away.

Closing her eyes, Sophia tried to let go of the tension in her mind and body. It was all she could think of to do. She inhaled a few deep breaths, breathing slowly out again each time, and gradually she began to feel less tense; her head became a little clearer, and she was more conscious of the light wind upon her face. She leant backwards, the bag on her back cushioning her body against the hard steps, and started to feel rather light-headed. In this almost dreamy state, she thought she heard someone say 'hello' - a soft gentle voice that sounded familiar, but which Sophia dismissed as only in her imagination. Yet soon she became aware of a presence, a strong sense that she was not on her own.

Sophia opened her eyes and sat up, but there did not appear to be anyone present. Her head still felt a little hazy but now she no longer felt so frightened. For she knew now more than ever before that she had no other mission, no other purpose, at this time than to seek her own salvation. And it was only at that precise moment, that Sophia suddenly grasped wholeheartedly the realisation that all other ego-pursuits were meaningless; that anything else she did would take her away from this one true path. Something had shifted in her that she could not explain. But it was only when this realisation had occurred that Sophia was able to see the "presence" she had previously felt so strongly.

A tall graceful figure emerged from the tunnel: it was the Sibyl. In an instant Sophia's heart filled with the love of a child, and she surged forward straight into the arms of the Sibyl. As the Sibyl's angelic frame engulfed her, Sophia felt the energy of the purest of love seep through her body, filling her with renewed life and love. Eventually the Sibyl withdrew her form and Sophia sat back down on the steps behind her.

'I am so glad that you made it here,' said the Sibyl, as she proceeded to sit next to Sophia. 'I was hopeful that you would, but I did not know how long it would take.'

Sophia could feel the coyness of her inner child become more prevalent in the presence of the Sibyl, but she managed to overcome it. 'I can't believe I am here!' she said. 'I stayed in the Valley Town for longer than I thought, most of the time too scared to leave.'

'Yet it is the courageous part of you, Sophia, that has got you here. Do not forget that.' Although the Sibyl's voice was gentle, it also conveyed a commanding tone as if to urge Sophia not to underplay this important side of her nature.

'Victor spoke to me about being a courageous warrior,' Sophia said, unconvinced. Then looking towards the Sibyl, she asked, 'What happens to other people on this journey – those who don't get this far?'

'Some stay in the Valley Town, whilst others go back,' offered the Sibyl.

'Like Roseanna,' Sophia stated. 'But why don't they get the help or guidance needed to take them further?'

There was a pause, before the Sibyl began to impart her words of wisdom:

'There is no point in helping those who do not seek help,' the Sibyl began. 'That would merely be an attempt to cajole or control another's thinking or behaviour. And it is not a game or competition, Sophia. You see, some people are simply not ready to take on board certain truths, either about themselves or about the Universe in which they live. Therefore they choose never to seek or accept help, or guidance, choosing instead to rely on the strength and resources of their ego-self to get by in this lifetime. This is neither right nor wrong – whatever you may think, Sophia. It is just as it is.

'Others, like yourself, realise somewhere deep inside that all is not right, that there is more to life than they are conscious of; that the depth and knowledge of the ego-self is very limited. They are the ones who seek help, sometimes even unconsciously, to find out about the hidden parts of themselves and about life itself. And it takes courage, Sophia, to do that.'

The Sibyl looked down towards the darkness of the tunnel which faced them, and concluded with: 'But the rewards are beyond imagination – certainly beyond the ego's imagination.'

Sophia tried to follow all that had been said. She felt that each lesson or piece of information, was like a piece of a large jigsaw puzzle, each piece giving the smallest of glimpses into a wonderful scene or landscape, but which seemed rather meaningless until the whole picture began to form. Yet as more of the picture was revealed, the easier it became to fit the remaining pieces into place.

Sophia decided to share a memory with the Sibyl. 'I remember Victor talking about ego's, and I must say I felt a bit confused at the time. But I think I'm beginning to understand a bit more now.'

Sophia paused thoughtfully for a moment, thinking about her meetings with Victor in the Teahouse. 'He said that he's known you for many years,' she half enquired.

'Yes, we do go back a long way, Victor and I. We help each other when the need arises.'

Sophia was surprised to hear of the Sibyl's need for help, but far from being disappointed she felt rather warmed by this honesty and openness. For if such wise people as the Sibyl and Victor could acknowledge and accept their own limitations and needs, then perhaps this was something for Sophia to aspire to rather than something to feel ashamed of. She found herself automatically wanting to share with the Sibyl aspects of herself that she would normally have felt too personal.

'After you disappeared,' Sophia said in a quiet voice, 'I felt so bereft and abandoned. I felt like a child who had lost its mother. I sat on the roadside for hours hoping that you would come back. That was when Victor came along. I had been writing about how I was feeling, and he said something quite beautiful – except that at the time I did not appreciate it!' Sophia's voice was somewhat louder now. 'He said: "what is this romance with the written word?"'

'Yes, that does sound like Victor. He is very poetic,' the Sibyl's smile conveyed her clear affection for her friend.

But Sophia was more concerned with the meaning of her own behaviour at that time. 'Yes, but all I could feel was rejection, and I just took it out on him. That's what surprises me I suppose, because usually if I feel hurt or angry I don't lose control. Not like I have done on this journey! I can't stand to see myself like that.'

The Sibyl was very quiet, whilst Sophia waited anxiously for a reply. Eventually it came:

'Listen Sophia,' the Sibyl took hold of Sophia's hands as she turned to face her. 'I know it has been painful and sometimes frightening for you, but this journey is about facing yourself – and that means the parts you don't like and don't wish to see. It is about facing your Shadow - the stranger you need to befriend in order to become whole. And it might be worth remembering, Sophia, that everybody has one!'

Sophia nodded without saying anything; she knew she needed to continue her journey until she had put into place as many of the pieces of the jigsaw puzzle as possible.

'Okay,' she suddenly said, looking up at the Sibyl. 'I'm ready to go down there.'

'Splendid! Then I will escort you some of the way.' As they made their way past the over-hanging sign, they crossed from daylight into darkness. It hit Sophia with such a force that she felt her heart skip a beat. She found herself clutching onto the Sibyl before they had even reached the bottom of the steps; hoping that soon her eyes would adjust to the darkness so that she would be able to see something – anything!

Suddenly they were at the bottom of the steps and were walking along level ground. Sophia strained her eyes to see something in the dark, but she could not see anything. All she could hear was the pounding of her heart against the walls of her chest.

Chapter Twelve
The Flame Carrier

Sophia and the Sibyl walked along a tunnel. Sophia gripped the Sibyl's arm tightly as they moved along the darkest of corridors beneath the surface of the earth. The air was musty and damp, and Sophia was finding it increasingly difficult to breathe the further they descended into the earth's body. It also seemed that the tunnel was beginning to narrow, for suddenly Sophia became aware of the left wall of the tunnel scraping against her arm. In the darkness she could not be sure of the accuracy of her perceptions, but she sensed that the tunnel was narrowing still further, closing in on her.

As she continued her forward momentum deeper into the abyss, Sophia began to feel very cold and it was not long before she started to lose sensation in the tips of her fingers and toes. Her breathing became more laboured and her teeth started to chatter uncontrollably, as the unrelenting cold and damp penetrated her skin. Soon Sophia could no longer feel her fingers at all.

And then suddenly, she collided head-on with granite rock. Letting out a cry of pain, Sophia clasped her face with both hands. It was only then that she realised the Sibyl was not with her anymore.

'SIBYL!' she screamed. 'WHERE . . . ARE . . . YOU?' But there was just stony silence.

The pain from the collision seared through her skull, distracting her somewhat from the emotional pain of her abandonment. Other physical symptoms now took hold; her body started to shake violently, whilst tears streamed down her bloody face. Feelings of terror seeped through Sophia's soul as she stared into the face of death. For deep in this well of nothingness, there was no light, no warmth, no comfort, and no salvation: there was only death.

Sophia sunk to her knees in surrender, wondering what she had done in her lifetime to deserve such torment, such punishment. Her head pounded, the taste of blood was in her mouth, and her body felt as cold and rigid as steel. Yet it was this very coldness that made Sophia decide to keep her body moving. And so she began to crawl along the floor of the tunnel in a futile attempt to force some warmth into her frozen limbs. She stayed close to the right wall of the tunnel, which seemed to have veered sharply to the left at the point where she had struck it. As she continued to crawl along the graduated descent of the tunnel, Sophia struggled to breathe in the diminishing levels of oxygen. Her eyes struggled to stay open, and her limbs began to seize up. Sophia had nothing left to give.

Finally she gave in and let her battered body fall the short distance to the ground. All that she was aware of was the sound of her own laboured breathing; all she had to wait for now, was for the last breath of her body to leave her. 'Please let it be quick,' Sophia managed to whisper.

She did not know how long she had been lying there with her eyes closed, but something made her open them suddenly. Something drew them to look in a certain direction, and despite Sophia's shifting state of consciousness, she thought she saw bright colours in the distance. Her heavy eyelids closed shut again as she drifted back to sleep momentarily, before she managed to open them once more. The same colours appeared: red, orange, and perhaps yellow. The colours wavered and interweaved with each other so that the image was never solid or stationary. Sophia wondered whether her mind was playing tricks on her in order to offer out false hope, in much the same way as a mirage in the desert. Yet every time she managed to prise open her eyes, she saw the same wavering colours of red, orange and yellow. Whatever it was, real or imagined, Sophia had to try to find out.

So with all the breath left in her body, Sophia dragged herself along the ground with her elbows, unable to make much use of her hands or her feet whose circulation seemed to have been all but cut off. It seemed to take her an age to get closer to the source of the vision, but still the vision remained. Sophia groaned in pain and gasped for air with every forward movement, until she was about twenty feet away from the image. She was beginning to make out what it was: A flame of fire!

Even in her near state of delirium, Sophia knew that this signified the existence of a source of oxygen. And it propelled her to crawl onward and complete the distance that remained between her and this precious source of life. The closer she came to it, the easier her breathing became and the warmer the air seemed to be. Such was Sophia's will to reach the source of the flame, that she somehow managed to increase the speed of her movement. She would not stop now until she had reached the flame and its bearer.

There, standing a few feet before her, was a cloaked figure dressed in black. The figure held aloft a torch whose flame roared with life, and whose light revealed the part of the tunnel that they both occupied. Sophia saw that the tunnel had widened again and that the cloaked figure stood at a point where the tunnel took another sharp turn to the left. She could not however make out the face of the cloaked figure, as it was concealed behind the large flame; all she could see was a black hood. Yet the figure did not seem malevolent to Sophia, who had managed to raise herself up on to her knees. And as she knelt before this silent figure, she felt as if she was almost praying to a god-like being for her salvation. Sophia had been stripped bare and was now merely a shell of her former self, yet this empty vessel that was bereft of all previous personality traits, with all its desires and need for status and material possessions, was now open to the potentialities of being filled with pure love and light.

The cloaked figure finally addressed the kneeling Sophia. The voice that spoke was female:

'I am the Flame Carrier. Do not be afraid, for I will lead you out of this darkness and on to the next stage of your journey.' Her voice was soft, almost feint. 'You have reached the darkest point and from here you will begin your ascent. There is still work to be done – of that there is no doubt – but rest assured that the deep emptiness you now feel in your soul, will gradually fill and be refilled in overflowing abundance.'

Sophia's eyes filled with tears at the sound of these words. Then the Flame Carrier held out her hand and beckoned to Sophia. 'Come with me, Sophia. Let us proceed out of this lifeless tunnel.'

And so she followed the Flame Carrier on her elbows and knees, along the ever-widening tunnel that twisted and turned, whilst warm air blew gently through. Her frozen limbs began to slowly thaw, and

Sophia could feel the physical pain of returning circulation as blood forced its way through her lifeless vessels. She grimaced but did not stop, her eyes never leaving the moving flame. Yet as the tunnel twisted once again, only to reveal another stretch of tunnel, Sophia wondered whether she would ever be able to make it out of there.

'Please!' she panted. 'I . . . . can't go . . . much . . . . further.'

'Come!' the Flame Carrier replied, without turning around or altering her pace. 'We are almost there.'

Sophia followed her command, wasting no more energy on words, and with one more twist in the tunnel they were suddenly out of it.

Sophia collapsed to the ground, her throat parched with thirst. She paid no mind to her surroundings, only craving water and rest. The next thing she knew, a jug of water was being brought to her and placed at her lips. And when Sophia had drunk as much as she could, she said 'thank you' without looking up to see who it was; she could barely keep her eyes open. Suddenly she felt someone lifting her up by the armpits, then another person lifting her legs. She was being carried into a room; she could hear people's voices around her . . . . . lights above her head . . . . now something soft beneath her body . . . . . . footsteps becoming fainter . . . . lights becoming dimmer . . . . . . and then silence.

Sophia opened her eyes to a dimly lit room. She was lying in bed, fully clothed, and could just make out the outline of a man. Everything was hazy, inside her head and outside, almost as if she had been drugged. Screwing her eyes up and then releasing them again, she tried to get a clearer picture, but the fog that hung over her would not lift.

'So you are Sophia!' The man slowly approached the end of Sophia's bed, his rich booming voice having the effect of jolting Sophia out of her drowsy state.

She could see him a little more clearly now; a thickset man of Mediterranean features, with a beaming smile.

'Yes,' Sophia replied with a rather feint voice. 'How did you know?'

'Believe me, when you have been here as long as I have, it is a great delight to know that someone new is coming to visit,' his face was animated with expression, his dark eyes sparkling within a round pleasant face.

Sophia could not help but grin at the extent of his warmth and friendliness, even though he had not answered her question, and somehow the bland and basic surroundings into which she had entered, were already shifting into something a little brighter.

'When you have rested some more,' the man continued, 'I will bring you something to eat. There is a bathroom on your right, with towels, fresh garments to wear, and so on. Okay Sophia?'

Sophia nodded, but as he walked over to the door she found herself asking, 'How long am I going to be here?'

The man stopped and turned around. 'You just got here and you're already wanting to leave!' He had a charming way of relieving any tension or awkwardness, without actually answering the questions put to him.

Sophia managed to smile, at the same time lifting herself up to a half-sitting position. The man pulled up a chair and placed it next to the bed before sitting down.

'I am Emil,' he said more softly, holding out his hand towards Sophia. 'Welcome to the Land of the Shadows.'

Sophia reciprocated, only then realising how much her limbs ached with pain and tiredness. She could feel her mind start to become overactive, wanting to ask Emil more questions, but at the same time her eyes were beginning to close. Suddenly she had fallen to sleep, and when her head eventually jolted her back awake, she saw that Emil was still seated by her bedside like a gentle centurion.

'Sleep now, Sophia,' he said gently. 'Do not worry about the passing of time.'

As she slid back down under the covers, Sophia replied in a half-asleep state, 'Yes, I know. Time is never lost.'

When Sophia awoke, the familiarity of her surroundings greeted her almost immediately; the basic features of her room were as rich in their comfort, as they were deficient in their outward charm. It was difficult to tell what time of day or night it was, because the light outside could barely be seen through the small gap that existed between the curtain and window opposite Sophia's bed.

She decided to go to the bathroom and run herself a hot bath, the thought of having a long soak sounding rather blissful. But as she got up from the bed, she was brought crashing back down again by a sudden attack of dizziness. Sophia was shocked by the fragility of her legs, which seemed to just buckle underneath her offering no resistance at all. Letting out a deep sigh, she waited for the dizziness to subside. Then, after a few minutes she tried to stand up again, this time more slowly and with her right hand resting on the back of the wooden chair placed next to the bed. Once this was achieved, Sophia began to walk the short distance to the bathroom. Her legs trembled all the way, so that when she had finally made it there she decided instead to settle for a quick wash and change of clothes.

The clothes Sophia tried on were cream-coloured; a loose fitting tunic and matching trousers, very much like those worn by martial artists, she thought. Sophia grinned in wry amusement at the incongruous comparison she had just made. Yet as she left her own dirty and well-worn clothes in the corner of the bathroom floor, she felt as though a small weight had been lifted from her.

When she had returned to her bed, Sophia was already out of breath. She did not however have the chance to dwell on this, as there was a sudden knock at the door. As soon as she called out in reply, the door opened and there stood Emil with a tray of food.

'Oh good!' his cheerful face beamed. 'You are awake. I have brought you some special delights from our kitchens to welcome you.'

Sophia smiled at him, at his kindness and at his warmth. After he had entered the room, Emil went over to a small wooden table next to the wall on Sophia's right, and put the tray down.

'Do you want some help over there?' Emil asked, when he saw Sophia struggling to get up from the bed.

But before she could answer, Emil was already by her side helping her to her feet. He towered above her, yet she did not feel overpowered. Neither did she see his help as intrusive, when once she perhaps would have, for now Sophia felt differently to anything she had felt before. And Emil was different to any man she had known before: She saw him as a protective fatherly figure without being authoritarian; friendly and welcoming but not overbearing; giving without forcing; and somehow knowing without being told. But perhaps more than anything, it was Sophia who was now more open and thus more able to see and to receive these qualities. Qualities that seemed to blend together, some coming to the fore when needed but never shutting off the others in case they needed to be called on at any time. "A fine balancing act," Sophia thought to herself, as she steadied herself to sit down at the table. Yet in no way did she see Emil's behaviour as an "act" or a list of perfected techniques, for this would be to miss the most important part of all: that these "techniques" were a part of Emil, they came from within him. He was simply being himself, his true Self.

Sophia thanked Emil for helping her over to the table, before she delved into the food in front of her. Emil sat down on the wooden chair placed on the other side of

the table, and waited silently until Sophia had eaten all she could.

'How long was I sleeping for?' Sophia enquired.

'Time is very important to you, isn't it Sophia?' Emil replied in a gentle manner, as if concerned by what he saw as an unhealthy interest in the subject.

'Am I? I've never really thought about it to be honest.'

Sophia could not help but be a little defensive, but she also knew that a defensive response would serve no useful purpose to her, and so she decided instead to let go a little, to be a bit more open and to think about what Emil had actually said to her.

'I suppose I am impatient at times,' Sophia said thoughtfully, looking down at her lap, 'and I get very frustrated when I think things aren't moving quickly enough.' She paused before looking up at Emil. 'It's as though I fear that I might fester too long if I stay in the same place.'

'To fester!' Emil seemed to seize this word with great exuberance, whilst Sophia waited in anticipation to see what he would do with it. Then he looked into Sophia's eyes and began to speak with a softness and sincerity that touched her deeply. 'Why, Sophia, must you see the opportunities that present themselves to you as merely a time to rot, to decay, to decompose like a dead flower in winter?'

The delivery of his words struck Sophia with the force of a thunderbolt, her chest suddenly felt as if it would crack with pain. She looked at Emil to see his eyes moisten with tears, and with this sight she could no longer contain her own hidden tears. As her chest heaved, it forced out the overflow of a saturated heart. For in truth, it was her heart that was the "dead flower" Emil had spoken of, and his sadness had spoken silently of its loss of life and the will to bloom once again. Yet once the tears had flowed there was a new found lightness, Sophia's heart no longer so sodden and weighed down. It was tiredness, instead, that overtook Sophia.

'Emil, I'm sorry but I can't keep my eyes open any longer,' she said.

'Yes, you must sleep as much as your body wishes you to,' Emil immediately got up to help Sophia back over to the bed.

Just before she closed her eyes to sleep, Sophia looked up at his warm eyes and wondered how it was possible to be as loving as he. 'Thank you, Emil. You are so kind.'

He touched her head gently and then made his way to the door. Before leaving the room, he said, 'Sophia, when you wake and wish to call me, I will be just outside. I am not far away.'

Chapter Thirteen
Moon Wisdom

When Sophia awoke, it was to the same dim light that encompassed her room. She noticed that the light was in fact coming from outside, as there were no lights inside the room. Yet the light outside never seemed to change, so that there was no indication as to when a day ended or when it began.

Sophia had, it would seem, entered a world that did not construct itself around the workings of the clock or the calendar. And thus it brought up the whole concept of time once again; of its meaning, its purpose, its usefulness. "Perhaps this is a place," Sophia thought to herself, "in which the pressures brought about by outside time constraints have been removed, leaving instead only the internal pressures we humans place on ourselves." It would undoubtedly help her to understand Emil's comments about time.

'Maybe time is of no importance in this world?' Sophia suddenly said aloud. 'Anyway, I don't think that time pressures will help my recovery. It will take as long as it takes.'

Already it seemed as if things were becoming a little clearer to Sophia, as if another thin veil had been lifted from her eyes. For she could see that the passing of time was of little significance as an entity in itself.

Slowly she got out of bed, and made her way over to the bathroom. Once there, she sat on the edge of the bath until she had regained her breath. Then she started to run herself a bath. She was grateful for the dim lighting - somehow anything brighter would have had the paradoxical effect of making her want to retreat under the bedclothes.

As Sophia lay back in the bath, the warm water against her skin felt divine. She closed her eyes to see images spontaneously appear in her mind; images of different places she had seen, and of people she had encountered along the way. She heard pieces of conversations and certain words of wisdom that had been imparted upon her. The images and conversations flowed and changed like those in a movie reel, making Sophia remember that there had been more encouraging and sunny encounters than she had thought. For the first time in what felt like an age Sophia laughed out loud, this time mostly at herself. She laughed at the memory of her first encounter with Victor, and how she had stormed off in anger; she laughed at the memory of first meeting with Bob, when she had got out of the Cage, and how she had snapped at him too. Then there was her impatience at the Crossroads, when she had wanted the old woman to tell her which way to go.

Sophia felt good at being able to laugh at herself - at the less desirable aspects of herself - and to accept these aspects as part of her own human nature, rather than something with which to beat herself. "What a revelation," thought Sophia, as she topped the bath up with hot water. "To not have to strive to be perfect!" For she could see quite clearly, in this dim light, that to strive for perfection only meant trying to be perfect in other people's eyes; and of course the reason for even attempting this almost impossible feat, was to be accepted, to belong, to avoid rejection.

'Back to that old chestnut,' said Sophia, as if to reaffirm her thoughts out loud. But she now understood that striving for perfection in order to avoid rejection, was an illusion: a creation of her ego mind. Indeed on her journey so far, it was at those very times when her behaviour had been less than perfect, that she had not been rejected! Victor and Bob were good examples of that. In fact, it was when Sophia had least expected it, when she hadn't done anything "wrong", that rejection had come; like her encounters with the Sibyl and the Wood Chopper. As she went over in her mind the encounters she had had with the Sibyl, Sophia somehow knew that what had happened then was not simply about rejection, but about a deeper learning. She was however yet to fully understand what this learning was about, and her heart was still pained by the thought of it.

The bath water had now cooled again, as had the brightness of Sophia's mood. After topping the bath up with hot water, she lay back again, closed her eyes and suddenly found herself thinking about the rather strange and unresolved meeting she had had with the Wood Chopper. Sophia had hardly known her, not even her name, yet the Wood Chopper had made a big impact on her. Perhaps it was something about the Wood Chopper's outward image of toughness and physical strength, which betrayed an underlying vulnerability; perhaps it was her aloneness and her determination to soldier on. Whatever it was, there was something about the Wood Chopper that reminded Sophia of herself. But it was only now, in this place called the Land of the Shadows, that Sophia could see this. It was only now, that she was ready to see it.

Sophia leant forward once again, this time to let the water out of the bath. As she climbed out, her mind was still on the Wood Chopper, wondering whether she was still chopping wood in the forest, or whether she had managed to break out of her own particular cage to venture up the Mountain Road again. Sophia grinned at the thought of an encounter between Bob and the Wood Chopper. But maybe Bob also needed to address his own negative perceptions and judgements about the Wood Chopper too, before he could help her to get to the top of the Mountain Road?

As Sophia made it back to her bed, she found herself hoping that they would both find a way to help each other. In the meantime, Sophia had to focus on herself.

The next time Sophia got out of bed, it was to go to the front door. She had decided that it was time to see what was outside her safe secluded space. She placed her hand cautiously upon the door handle and slowly turned it. Then suddenly she hesitated. Her heart had started to race at the mere prospect of stepping outside. Yet as this was the only way she would be able to call on Emil, she took a deep breath and pulled the door open.

Sophia stood in the doorway, neither inside or outside, and slowly began to take in the rather curious sight. The same half-light was now even more apparent, although she still did not know where it emanated from, and there was a quietness that felt almost eerie. A main street was lined either side by "houses", all single-storey and all the same in outward appearance. At that moment someone walked past Sophia, without seeming to notice her standing in the doorway. The person's head was hung down as if it was too heavy for their shoulders to carry. Baggy and shapeless clothes hung loosely from the person's bony frame, as their feet shuffled along the sandy gravel ground. Sophia could not tell if it was a man or woman. The image struck her with such a force that she immediately stepped back into the safety of her room and shut the door quickly behind her.

'What is to become of me here?' Sophia whispered, as she leant back against the door.

For she was beginning to fear that she would end her days here in the Land of the Shadows, and would indeed rot and decay despite the contradictory words of Emil. She looked down at her body dressed in the loose baggy clothing, and wondered whether she looked in any way like the person who had just passed her by in the doorway. Sophia had not looked at herself for quite a while in a mirror, and she had noticed that there were no mirrors in her room or in the bathroom.

'Maybe they don't want us to be freaked out by what we look like!' she said in distress, still leaning against the door.

Suddenly there was an assertive knock at the door, which almost made Sophia jump out of her skin.

'SOPHIA!' Emil's voice called. 'Are you alright!'

Quickly opening the door, a much relieved Sophia replied, 'Yes, I think so. Where were you? I couldn't see you!'

She stood aside to let Emil enter the room, then made her way to the edge of the bed to sit down.

'I am sorry, Sophia. I did not mean to cause you so much distress,' Emil's voice was full of concern. 'Sometimes I forget how afraid visitors are when they first arrive in this place.'

Sophia lifted up her heavy head to look at Emil, who was standing in the centre of the room. Upon seeing the level of sensitivity that so naturally exuded from him, Sophia felt the burden of her recent fear begin to disperse.

'It's alright, Emil,' she said. 'Please sit down, won't you. I'm just glad that you are here now. I was so frightened that I was going to be left here alone - just like when the Sibyl disappeared.'

Emil sat down on a nearby chair. He remained silent whilst Sophia got herself ready to ask him a risky question.

'Emil,' she paused for a lengthy moment. 'What is going to happen to me here?'

She waited for a response - any response - feeling unable to breathe until it came. "Why is he taking so long to answer?" she wondered. She could not even bring herself to look at Emil for fear that she would see something in his face that she did not wish to see. But the silence continued, until Sophia could not hold her breath any longer. Her lungs expelled with quite a force the air that had been trapped, and finally she summoned the courage to look at Emil. It was then that he spoke:

'What is it that you fear will happen to you here, Sophia?' he asked

Sophia grinned a little sarcastically at the fact that her question had been reflected straight back to her, instead of being answered directly by Emil. But she could also see that it was not being done in a way that implied rote learning on his part, or as a means to evade answering an awkward question. No, it was becoming clear to Sophia that it was done when it needed to be done; when the best form of learning required one to look inside oneself, knowing that the answers were there to be found. So, instead of reacting, or resisting this process, Sophia began to look inside herself for the answer to her own question. And it seemed that the actual process of stopping to think about the answer to her question, helped to calm her mind. In fact, thinking aloud calmed her even more:

'I suppose . . . . I fear . . . . that I'll never get out of here,' she began. 'That I'll remain here until . . . . . until I begin to decay-'

Her voice broke off as she realised that her fear of rotting or decaying was something that had surfaced before. 'I've said that before, haven't I?' she said, looking at Emil.

'And what did I say to you?' Emil smiled warmly.

'You said,' Sophia concentrated hard, 'something like . . . . . why did I see opportunities presented to me, as merely a time to rot . . . . .to fester! That was it!' Then she grinned at Emil as she said, 'Except you said it in such a beautifully poetic way.'

Emil smiled back in acknowledgement of what Sophia had said, but did not interrupt her flow of thought. Instead he waited until she was ready to speak again.

'You know, Emil, earlier on when I opened the door to see what was outside – and to find you – I was so shocked by this person I saw. They looked almost like a ghost . . . . . except they were alive, if you could call it that. This person seemed dead somehow, but still existing . . . . .' Her voice trailed off as the realisation of what she had said began to sink in.

'That is how you have felt, isn't it, Sophia?' Emil said gently. 'And you fear that you will remain that way forever.'

Sophia's head was lowered but she nodded in agreement. How she wanted him to tell her that everything would be all right. Of course she knew that he would not do so, but she waited for something – anything! And eventually it arrived:

'All I will say to you, Sophia, is that there are many people who leave this place eventually – some sooner than others – yet who can say how long it will take? For this depends on so many factors and it would be futile for me to try to list them. Different people, different factors.

'You, however, have already been courageous in getting to the Land of the Shadows. Let that courage take you further, Sophia, and at the pace only you can go.'

She lifted her head, feeling a sense of comfort from the words she had heard. 'Victor called me a courageous warrior. It was such a nice thing to say, even though I did not believe him.'

Sophia was beginning to tire of her own self-doubt and self-deprecation. It had become second nature to her, but she had never been so aware of its presence as she was now. It showed itself to her as a powerful example of her own entrapment. All the time she had been in her Cage, Sophia had remained largely unaware of the factors that had kept her trapped, and she was therefore impotent to do anything about them. Indeed she had known for quite some time that all was not "right" in her life, that a large part of her had felt a sense of deadness – the deadness she had seen so starkly in the stranger who had walked past her in the doorway. And now, she was finally beginning to see that this journey was her opportunity to become aware of these factors and to break free of them. Everybody she had met so far along the way had been helping her to become more aware of herself – to face herself! Yet only now could Sophia accept with greater openness, that such moments of awareness, of enlightenment, were indeed "opportunities" being presented to her. People had been there to encourage her to take another step along this West Road, but only when she herself was ready.

By now Sophia had become lost in her thoughts, but unlike previous times, it did not drain her energy. In fact, the slightest of glows had appeared upon her face, and her eyes had the beginnings of a sparkle. Emil observed this change with the look of a proud father.

'Tell me,' he said, his voice louder and more playful, 'what are you thinking?'

On hearing his voice, Sophia snapped out of her reverie and smiled. 'I just had a sense that things would turn out okay. As if things seemed to suddenly make sense.'

Emil clapped his hands together with genuine glee. 'Well done, Sophia!' Then standing up, he made his way to the door and said, 'To celebrate this moon wisdom, I will bring you some tea and cakes.'

Sophia laughed heartily, as she recalled her encounters with Victor in the Teahouse.

After some lengthy periods of sleep, interspersed with visits from Emil, the time finally came when Sophia felt ready to step outside her front door again. For she knew that she didn't have to do it all on her own, and in Emil she had an escort that she trusted.

Emil offered out his arm to Sophia as she stepped across the doorway. 'Let us commence the guided tour,' he said enthusiastically.

At first Sophia hesitated, suddenly feeling shaky in her exposed vulnerability, but then she took the remaining step towards Emil and gratefully accepted his arm. Only then did she notice how skeletal her arms looked next to his. Gasping in horror, Sophia stopped abruptly in her tracks.

'What is it?' Emil was clearly taken aback.

'L-look at m-me!' Sophia whispered with the voice of a frightened child. 'How did I get like this?'

She started to tremble with panic, believing that her biggest fear was about to be realised after all: that she would live in a state of decay, here in the half-light of the Land of the Shadows.

Yet it had not been long ago that Sophia's thoughts and insights supported something entirely different: that everything would turn out all right in the end. And so the pendulum of thoughts and emotions had swung sharply and convincingly in the opposing direction, leaving Sophia to clutch desperately on to Emil's arm as she tried to hold on to a more central position of relative calmness.

'Sophia!' Emil's voice was reassuring in its urgency. 'It takes time for the mind and body to heal and to restructure. That is why you are here. We are not here to trap you - we are here to help you. You must believe that!'

Sophia gradually began to feel calmer, and as she regained some of her composure she loosened her grip upon Emil's arm.

'Sorry Emil,' she said, feeling a little embarrassed. 'You must think me rather pathetic.'

They began to walk to their right, along the main street, and after they had walked for a few minutes Emil led Sophia over to a bench on the opposite side of the street. As they sat down, he said, 'Nobody who comes here could be considered pathetic, Sophia.'

Sophia remained silent, her eyes focused on the ground. Yet something drew her to look upwards, as if she could sense that something was there. Slowly, gradually, she lifted her head up, then further up, until she saw what had been there all along. It was the source of the half-light, and the sight made her gasp in true amazement. Sophia wondered how she had not noticed it before.

'Emil, it's incredible!' Sophia said, pointing up at the sky like an excited child. Her jaw dropped, for never before had she seen such a wondrous sight. The moon was so close and so immense in size, that she could actually see the contours of its surface; the craters, the mountains and the valleys. The moon displayed its "face" with pride, and in doing so emanated a light that was somehow more piercing and revealing than the direct light of the sun.

Emil had been observing the expressions of wonderment on Sophia's face, and only now did he decide to break his silence. 'Yes, She is indeed a magnificent body,' he agreed. 'She reflects to us Her true nature, and in doing so becomes whole. But She is only able to do so because the light of the sun shines on Her. What you see here, Sophia, is the most perfect example of masculine and feminine energies existing in balanced harmony.'

Sophia looked somewhat confused. 'I'm not sure what you mean.'

Her mind drifted back briefly to her talks with Victor in the Teahouse; when she didn't always follow what he was saying but nevertheless liked to listen to him. The difference now was that she wanted to understand this almost magical wisdom, rather than to simply feel frustrated because of her lack of comprehension.

In the ensuing silence Sophia continued to gaze in awe at the moon; at its wholeness and entirety.

In due course, Emil directed a question at the still mesmerised Sophia: 'What do you think and feel, Sophia, when you look at the moon?'

Sophia pondered a while over this question before answering. 'Well, it's mesmerising . . . . . magical . . . . . mysterious . . . . . and romantic!' she said, before adding, 'I suppose I feel fascinated by it – I mean, Her.'

Emil smiled, pleased in particular at her instinctive realisation of the moon's feminine nature. Sophia sensed this and was suddenly perturbed by it.

'So is this just about a romantic fantasy then? Female moon, and masculine sun?' The cynicism in her voice was clearly apparent.

She switched her attention suddenly away from the moon, being in no mood for an idealistic fairytale. She could not however deny the powerfully hypnotic effect of the moon, or doubt that the dreamer in her could have gazed at the moon for hours. It also seemed that Sophia's abrupt reaction did not deter Emil from continuing to reveal more words of intrigue.

'I suppose it does sound like a fairytale romance of sorts,' he began, 'but here in the Land of the Shadows we only deal with Reality, not fantasy. Those games of fantasy are left to the Outside World – for the ego minds to play.'

He paused, trying not to confuse Sophia with words, but Sophia was by now listening intently, waiting for Emil to say more. She did not have to wait long before he started to speak again:

'You see, Sophia, the Outside World is dominated by all that can be seen . . . . . scientific facts, appearances, results, actions. There is nothing wrong with each of these in themselves, but collectively it leaves a very imbalanced world; one in which we are blind to all that is hidden. Yet without that which is hidden, we are only half-alive . . . . .' he drifted off into his own reverie.

Sophia found her mind also drifting. For Emil's words had taken her back to an earlier time; a time when she had first become aware of a hidden power or force that existed in Nature all around her, and also within herself. In that brief period of time she had known herself to be part of something much greater, and she had felt a calmness that she had never known before. Such divine experiences Sophia had written about in her poem, "The Light", yet in all honesty she had felt the words to have come from somewhere else – or rather, from herself as well as from somewhere else.

There was so much that she didn't know, and indeed many questions still unanswered, many yet to be asked. But as she sat with Emil under the pale white light of the magnificent moon, Sophia trusted that such inner wisdom would come to her when the time was right. Emil in turn knew that the greatest lessons for Sophia to learn at this point in her journey were those related to herself, and that to face more truths Sophia would need to recover some more of her strength.

Emil stood up. 'Come, Sophia,' he said. 'We will walk a bit further, but then you need to rest and eat. Remember: balance in everything, balance is everything!'

Sophia smiled back at him as she slowly got to her feet. Emil then proceeded to gently lead her along the main street. As they walked, Sophia was struck by the intensity of the silence in the street.

'Why is it so quiet?' she whispered. 'Where is everyone?'

'Does it disturb you, Sophia?' Emil replied, once again choosing not to answer her question.

'No, not really. It just feels a bit weird to be the only people out and about.'

Sophia then started to chuckle, quickly covering her mouth with her hand in case her laughter disturbed the silence.

Emil was amused. 'What is it, Sophia?'

'Well, I was just thinking that when I was in the Valley Town, I spent a lot of time in my hotel room whilst other people were going about their day-to-day business. Now here I am, wanting other people to be around! I guess I never thought I would feel like that.'

'So, why do you think that is? What has changed?' Emil seemed determined for Sophia to understand her own observations about herself.

They walked in silence for a while, until Sophia felt ready to answer. 'Maybe it's because it feels different here . . . . . . safer.' She paused briefly, then said, 'Yes, that's it! I feel safer here. As if it's a kind of sanctuary where people don't have to pretend, or put on a front.'

She stopped suddenly. Emil followed suit, then turned to face her. Looking directly up at him, Sophia announced clearly and assertively:

'It's a place where there are no ego's!'

No other spoken words followed this, as Sophia and Emil passed by several abodes. The "houses" were built - like Sophia's - in the most simplistic of designs and structures; nothing decorative or aesthetically pleasing to the eye, just basic solid structures of brick, each house with one small window. They turned a corner to their right, to see the road ahead lined with the same single-storey brick houses. Further along however there was an overhead cover, which cast the street in near darkness. Sophia felt a twinge of foreboding come over her as they gradually approached the stretch of road that was drenched in shadow. Something suddenly caught her eye.

'What's that? Over there!' she said, pointing to one of the houses in the distance.

'Ah, yes!' Emil replied, answering her question for the first time. 'That is a flame, Sophia, in the Darkened Street.'

When the image had become clearer to Sophia, she noticed that she was trembling. 'It looks like the one that I saw when I was in the tunnels.'

Emil put his hand on her shoulder. 'Try not to worry too much, Sophia. You do not have to go back into those tunnels again. Remember what the Flame Carrier told you: this is where you start your ascent.'

Sophia looked up at him in surprise. 'How did you know that?' But she quickly realised that there was little point in asking Emil another question, and so she simply smiled at him.

They continued onward, their pace slowing down the closer they got to the Darkened Street, until they stood only a few steps away from it. Yet Sophia seemed determined to keep moving forward and to confront her fears. So with her next step the darkness came, and with it a sudden state of breathlessness that gripped Sophia, rendering her frozen to the spot. She could not see anything around her - not the houses, not the flame, and not Emil - for her mind and body had been taken over by the terror she had known in the total blackness of the tunnels.

Emil called to her; 'Sophia, Sophia! It's alright, I am with you.'

He kept repeating these words with increasing urgency, but he was not able to reach her. He shook her by the arms trying to bring her back to the present, but still he was not able to reach her. Then, delaying no further, he lifted her up with his bear-like hands, and carried her back across to the light. Looking directly into her eyes, his hands now clasping her upper arms, he almost pleaded; 'Sophia! It's alright – you are safe now!'

Suddenly Emil saw a flicker of recognition come into her eyes, a brief fleeting connection between them. He knew then that Sophia was on her way back, and his heart filled with joy and love. For he wanted Sophia to succeed in her quest, and he believed in his heart that she would. But he also knew that no matter how strong the human will or spirit was, it was not always enough to carry one through on its own. The spirit could indeed motivate and inspire one like nothing else; it could lead one along his or her true path. But the mind and body, one's physical form, had to progress and heal at its own much slower pace. It seemed to Emil that Sophia's spirit to overcome her fears and to progress along her path was admirably strong, but would be squandered if she did not listen to the needs of her mind and body.

Emil himself had lost sight of this principal in his eagerness to help Sophia along her path, and he felt most distressed and disturbed by this. But at this moment, more than anything he wanted Sophia to come back, and so he kept speaking to her, telling her his name and telling her that she was safe.

Gradually the flickers of connection between them grew, and eventually Sophia arrived back into the present moment. She was still trembling as she looked around her, then back at Emil, who was still holding her upper arms.

'My God! What happened?' she exclaimed. Then, in sudden realisation, 'I was in the tunnels again!'

'Sophia, thank God you are back!' Emil could not contain his glee as he leant forward to hug her.

At first she felt comforted by this, but it was not long before she was trying to push him away.

'You told me I wouldn't have to go back into those tunnels . . . . . I . . I trusted you!' Sophia was shouting and crying at the same time, her feelings of terror and fear having turned into anger. 'How could you lie to me? Just like the Sibyl who abandoned me in the darkness – I was so frightened I thought I was going to die . . . . . I wanted to die . . . . .' her voice trailed off into a well of tears.

Emil still held her. 'I am so sorry, Sophia,' he said with heartfelt tones. 'Please forgive me.'

Emil held Sophia until she had become more still.

'Let me escort you back to your home, Sophia,' he said softly. 'It really is time for you to rest.'

Chapter Fourteen
The Journey Back To The Darkened Street

M any days and weeks passed by as Sophia rested and recovered in the Land of the Shadows. Of course she could not tell the specific nature of the time that had passed, having to rely instead on her own internal rhythms, but somehow this seemed to have become quite natural to Sophia. It meant that she was learning to listen to her own body and its needs, rather than to watch an external clock and listen to the dictates of its constantly moving hands.

She regularly went for short walks along the main street, sometimes accompanied by Emil, who never seemed to broach the subject of the Darkened Street despite his many conversations with Sophia. Both knew, however, that Sophia would venture back to the Darkened Street when the time was right. And only Sophia would know when that would be.

She had started to write in her notepad again – the first time since she had left the Valley Town. The striking difference she noticed in herself was that back then her world seemed much more insular, as though she was the only person in it, whereas now others had entered into the frame. Now she wrote about her conversations with others, and the wisdoms she had learnt from them. All in all, Sophia was becoming a more open and receptive being. She had met one or two other people in the main street, although her interactions with them tended to be fairly brief and light in substance. But she was happy enough with this, knowing that her deeper conversations took place with Emil.

On one particular occasion, Sophia was eager to know more about the mysteries of the Land of the Shadows. 'Emil,' she enquired, 'why is this place called the Land of the Shadows? I mean, where are the Shadows? What do they look like?'

Emil pondered for a while, Sophia quickly realising that she would not be getting a straightforward reply. Not that she minded much these days. In fact, she rather liked the gentle debates that called on her to stretch her own mind and to gently exercise its latent powers. She had come to regard such exercises as the mind's equivalent of the body's physical exercise. But more than this, Sophia was responding to a new way of thinking; a new way of viewing the world around her and within her, and this newness was continuing to develop as a result of her conversations with Emil. Often a conversation would lead somewhere completely different to where it had started, so that she felt she was on a journey of adventure with the spoken word.

Sophia waited patiently until finally Emil spoke. 'First Sophia, tell me what the Land of the Shadows means to you so far. Then I will tell you a bit more.'

'Okay.' It was Sophia's turn to ponder - she was indeed learning the art of self-reflection. After a few moments she replied, 'I remember when I was standing on the side of the valley with the Sibyl, and I saw the most amazing sight over on the other side of the valley. Mind you, I don't think I would have seen them – the Shadows, that is – if they hadn't been pointed out to me by the Sibyl . . . . .'

Sophia's voice trailed off into the distance, her gaze now directed towards the full and ever present moon overhead. Emil however interceded to bring her back, lest her mind drift too far.

'Tell me,' he urged, 'about your meeting with the Sibyl.'

And so she opened her heart to Emil, with all the associated feelings of awkwardness and vulnerability. 'She left me when I needed her most,' Sophia said sorrowfully. 'Why did she abandon me like that, Emil? I just don't understand.' Then quietly and with more composure, she said, 'I hardly knew her, yet I loved her. What does it all mean?'

Emil touched her hand gently. 'The Sibyl left you because she knew it was time for you to face your Shadow. You see, Sophia, not everyone who journeys to the Valley can see the Shadows on the other side. But you could – that is why she came to you. I know it has been painful to see, but the truth is that the Sibyl wanted to help you to proceed along your journey. In time you will come to see this too.'

Emil was looking directly at Sophia, and when she in turn directed her gaze towards him, her eyes filled with tears. His words had helped her so much, and had also helped cause the view of her world to gradually change. As they sat quietly on their familiar bench, a comforting silence enveloped them.

Eventually Sophia's posture changed so that when she began to speak, she had assumed a more confident demeanour; 'Where is my Shadow then?'

'All in good time, Sophia, all in good time,' he smiled. 'Do not rush things.'

Sophia became frustrated. 'But why can't you tell me where it is? Is it so bad?'

'No, of course not. We all have a Shadow! But everyone's Shadow is different, just as everyone's personality is different. What I'm trying to say, Sophia, is that only you will know what your Shadow looks like, and where it is. I can help and support you, but I cannot just take you to meet your Shadow.'

Sophia's face dropped, all her confidence draining away like grains of sand slipping through her fingers. She looked up at the moon as if hoping to find within its reflected light some inspiration. Then quietly she said, 'You will know when you get there.'

'What's that?' Emil looked a little puzzled.

'A wise old man I met some time ago - rather like you really - told me about having to get to the Centre Point . . . . . to face myself. When I asked him where it was, he said that I would know when I got there.' Sophia grinned knowingly. 'I was really frustrated at the time – much more than I am now!' Then she asked her friend, 'That's progress, isn't it, Emil?'

'Yes, Sophia. That is great progress!' he responded in a booming voice.

Leaning towards her, Emil gave Sophia a big hug before escorting her back to her abode.

Eventually the time came when Sophia wanted to revisit the Darkened Street. Yet as she broached the subject with Emil, she noticed that he became a little uncomfortable.

Emil was remembering how distressed he had been the first time, when he feared that Sophia would not return from the darkness. Now it seemed the time had come for him to face his own fears, and somehow trust that Sophia would overcome hers. Emil decided on this occasion to share some of his concerns with Sophia, and as he did Sophia felt touched by his honesty.

'Don't worry, Emil,' she smiled warmly at him, 'I'm not rushing into this. I have thought a great deal about it, because I know of my tendency to rush into things! I used to get so annoyed and frustrated at not being told what I wanted to hear. I was like an angry child really.' Her face looked rather thoughtful and reflective as she recalled the earlier days of her journey. 'Anyway, I have learnt to be more patient and to listen to my body.'

'I am proud of you, Sophia,' Emil seemed to be genuinely humbled by her. 'You have worked so hard for your salvation and in searching for your own truth. I do trust that now is the right time for you to journey back to the Darkened Street.'

'For us to journey into the Darkened Street!' Sophia corrected him. 'We can help each other, Emil.'

He smiled at her, and thought of how far she had come. 'Yes, you are right, we must help each other. For it seems, Sophia, that I the teacher have become the student!'

They both laughed heartily as they made their way together towards the Darkened Street. As they were about to turn the corner that led off the main street, Sophia suddenly caught sight of something.

'My goodness, I don't believe it!' she cried, pointing across the street. 'The Wood Chopper!'

The figure she saw was no longer the physically imposing one she had seen on the edge of the forest; this person looked more frail and vulnerable, her clothes hanging loosely from her frame. Her hair had grown somewhat, yet there was no mistaking in Sophia's mind that this was the Wood Chopper. Sophia could not bring herself to go over to her, or to try to summon her attention. She was so shocked to see her after all this time, that she didn't know how to respond. In the end, Sophia knew intuitively that it was best not to go after her; that it was best to let the Wood Chopper go. The temptation of course was to go over to her, but like any temptation, Sophia had learnt that it would only steer her away from her true path; it would only divert her from the important goal she had set herself today.

So turning the corner, Sophia focused on the Darkened Street up ahead, and started to walk towards it. Emil silently followed her, but as they approached the Darkened Street, Sophia took his hand and together they stepped across into the darkness.

'Are you alright?' Emil whispered, without knowing why he was whispering.

'Yes, not too bad,' Sophia replied. 'But can we stop for a bit to see if my eyes adjust to the darkness. I can't see a thing!'

'That's a good idea,' Emil was still whispering, 'but it might also help if you look over to your right a little – there is a flame outside one of the houses in the distance.'

Sophia still held on to his hand as she turned her head slightly to the right. 'Where? I still can't see anything!'

'Don't worry, it will come. You'll see.'

'But how come you can see it and I can't?' Sophia almost sounded like a little girl, which amused Emil. She quickly followed this up with: 'Mind you, I am quite short-sighted too.'

She heard a chuckle. 'Are you laughing Emil?' Sophia nudged him playfully with her elbow.

When the light-hearted banter had ended, there they stood, almost rooted to the spot. This time, Sophia's voice took on a more serious tone:

'Emil, I still can't see anything. I feel as if I am blind. Why can't I see anything?'

Her hand gripped Emil's more tightly, for this was the only thing she could sense outside of herself. Sophia was not about to let it go just yet. Sensing the growing desperation within her, Emil sought a way to dissipate this negative energy.

'Let me explain something, Sophia,' he said assertively. 'The Land of the Shadows works very differently to the Outside World that you are more used to. Therefore, do not worry that you cannot see anything at the moment. The vision required here belongs to a different dimension; a higher dimension which touches deeper into the soul. The more you try to look with your two eyes, the more you will see only darkness. That is natural.'

'So what should I do?' Sophia enquired.

'Do nothing,' Emil replied softly. 'Just let go . . . . . and trust. Trust the Greatest Unknown, trust life itself. You are part of it – like a drop in an ocean. And it will carry you along if you let it.'

Sophia was silent for a while, contemplating his words, mesmerised by them. She wanted to trust what Emil had told her - indeed she did trust him - but it still felt as if she was being asked to jump off a high building and trust that she would be all right, when all she could see was a disastrous outcome! Emil was suggesting that she let these fearful visions go, and to jump anyway. Could she do it? Sophia felt on the verge of doing it but something still held her back.

Emil then spoke the words that would enable her to make up her mind:

'Sophia, if you should feel too frightened you can always go back. Just turn around and step back into the light.'

Without further hesitation, she let go of Emil's hand and walked several paces forward. Still the darkness remained, but an amazing thing happened to Sophia: She was no longer afraid. Onward she walked, at a slow and steady pace, knowing that at any time she could just turn around if she wanted to and go back. And then another amazing thing happened: She saw the flame of a torch lighting up a doorway.

'Emil!' she cried. Then suddenly realising the loudness of her voice in the silence, she lowered it a few decibels. 'I can see a doorway . . . . and the flame you were talking about!'

Emil appeared by her side, at which point Sophia no longer cared about keeping her voice down. 'EMIL! I can see you as well. This is incredible!'

She leapt forward and hugged him. It was Emil's turn to be surprised.

Sophia and Emil slowly approached the open doorway, Sophia's eyes continually drawn to the flame of the torch which was placed in a metal holder attached to the outside brick. She was transfixed by its brightness and its warmth; by its message of hope and love to souls bathed in darkness. Memories of her time spent in the tunnels came flooding back to her, and a lone tear began to roll down her cheek. Her throat began to feel hot and constricted. She raised her hand to her throat as if attempting to stop it from spewing forth the molten lava of emotion, which had lain dormant for so long. Emil put his arm around her. Sophia responded to his touch by resting her head upon his shoulder and letting more tears fall silently.

Through the open doorway Sophia could see a room very much like her own room. She remained in the doorway as Emil entered the room. There were no lights inside, so that Sophia was "blinded" for a while having gazed so long at the flame outside. But she could hear Emil talking to someone – a man who seemed to be in some pain.

'How are you today?' Emil asked. 'How is the pain?'

'It's very bad still-' the man let out a cry of pain.

'I'm just going to have a look, okay?' Emil said gently.

Sophia's eyes were by now beginning to adjust to the darker light of the room. She could make out the figure of a man lying on a bed in the middle of the room. She could see the large frame of Emil leaning over him, looking at different parts of his wounded body. Then Emil sat down beside the man and placed his hands gently over a part of his abdomen. He seemed to be performing some kind of healing, as far as Sophia could make out, but she couldn't see very clearly from where she stood. As quietly as possible she walked several paces towards the centre of the room until she was able to see more clearly.

The wounded man's face was full of anguish, his eyes closed, so that Sophia doubted whether he knew of her presence. She manoeuvred her position in order to see what Emil was doing, only to let out an unexpected gasp. For she was not prepared for what she saw: The man's abdomen and legs were covered in burns and scars, some of which were still open and raw. Sophia immediately covered her mouth with her hand, feeling angry with herself for exposing such a reaction.

'Who's there?' the wounded man suddenly opened his eyes.

'I-I am S-Sophia,' she answered awkwardly. 'I've come with Emil. I'm . . er . . pleased to . . er . . meet you.' She cringed at her response, wondering what Emil would think of it.

'Oh,' replied the stranger, sounding almost disappointed. He then closed his eyes without speaking any further.

Emil remained silent and deep in concentration as he continued to place his hands directly above the man's wounds. Sophia felt redundant, an observer of pain yet powerless to help. She did not know what she was supposed to learn from this. All she wanted to do at that moment was to get back to her own room. There would be time enough later for her to reflect on the experiences of this particular day.

Chapter Fifteen
The Lesson Of The Scroll

Over the next few days Sophia kept herself busy, writing down in her notepad a multitude of thoughts and feelings relating to her time spent in the Darkened Street. Images kept coming into her mind of the badly burnt man, lying alone in his pain. She wondered who, or what, was in the other houses along the Darkened Street. Were they empty? Was that why there was only one flame burning outside? Or did the other houses also contain burnt and wounded victims who could not fend for themselves? Were these the Shadows that Emil had spoken of, and if so, how did they relate to her?

"So many questions still to be answered," thought Sophia, as she closed her notepad. She let out a deep sigh.

Suddenly she recalled her sighting of the Wood Chopper in the main street. This was the first time since then that Sophia had thought about her. She was intrigued to know how the Wood Chopper had made it to the Land of the Shadows. Had the straight-talking Bob finally been able to help her get to the top of the Mountain Road? Sophia felt strangely uplifted in the knowledge that someone else she had known, albeit tenuously, had journeyed the same way as her and was continuing to do so.

Sophia got to her feet. She decided that she wanted to meet the Wood Chopper again. Of course there was some awkwardness about doing so because of what had happened when they had last met on the edge of the forest. But Sophia felt that an opportunity was now presenting itself to her, to help her resolve and overcome such past obstacles. Then she would be able to move forward unhindered. Besides, Sophia felt that they were bound to bump into each other eventually. So taking a deep breath, she opened her front door and stepped outside. As she closed the door behind her, she looked up at the magnificent moon and smiled; 'Wish me luck, my lady.'

She set off along the main street, aiming to retrace her steps back to the place where she had seen the Wood Chopper. She passed the same houses she had passed many times before with Emil, and she saw the same familiar faces. As she approached the section of the street where she had seen the Wood Chopper, Sophia's mood and demeanour changed with a suddenness that threw her. Her legs began to tremble, and the light confident air she had started off with was now replaced by a return of her old fearfulness. All that Sophia could think of was the memory of their last encounter in the forest; how she had finally mustered up the courage to approach the Wood Chopper, after spending so long in the forest alone, and how the Wood Chopper had cut her down again by not keeping her promise to come back the next day. Yet here Sophia was once again trying to approach the Wood Chopper, when the truth was that Sophia still felt a lot of negative feelings towards her. And so, what had seemed to Sophia like a good idea earlier on, now seemed like a foolish one.

As she stood on one side of the main street looking across to the other, Sophia felt overwhelmingly stupid. And the more she felt like this, the more she was convinced that other people were thinking it too. She decided to walk to the nearest bench which was on the other side of the street. She quickly sat down, somehow not feeling quite so conspicuous. "Why," she asked herself, "am I always looking for someone, or waiting for someone else to appear? And why, when I'm with them, do I always fear that they will go away?"

Sophia felt angry and frustrated, mostly with herself. For the painful truth was that she didn't want to need others as much as she did. And it was only at that very moment that she realised how much she had always denied this truth; she had always convinced herself that she did not need others.

An image of the crumbled Tower suddenly appeared in her mind, as if to reinforce the illusion she had created about herself: the illusion that she could cope with everything on her own; that she could give out to others in need, but did not need anything in return. The image of the Tower in her mind began to dissipate and suddenly another image appeared: Sophia could see herself back at the lake. In the image, she was crying. The voice beneath the water would not go away: it was the part of Sophia that was in need.

Sophia got up from her bench and started to walk back up the main street towards her room. For the light of the moon had reflected inner truths to her with such intensity, that she needed a little shelter from them.

Sophia slept for quite some time. When she woke, she had a long bath which helped soothe her. Then she took out her notepad and sat on her bed, contemplating what to write. But she could not seem to write anything. Her head felt in a kind of daze, though this was not particularly unpleasant - more like being lost in a daydream.

Suddenly her eyes caught sight of a roll of paper sticking out of her bag on the floor next to the table. She thought it very strange that she hadn't noticed it there before. Jumping up from her bed, she went over to investigate. She pulled out what appeared to be a rolled-up scroll. Totally intrigued by it, Sophia carefully unrolled it as if she was slowly untying the ribbons on a precious gift. The Scroll revealed a verse:

THE INCUBATION PERIOD

This is the time to heal,
The time to conceal
Oneself from the Outside
World.
Time to go within
And not be afraid
To face
The Unknown.

There is a Stranger you do not know,
Yet must.
The Stranger will guide you to places
You would rather not see,
For you would rather not be
The things he says you are,
The things you said
You would never be.

Befriend the Stranger
And his power ceases to be
The potent force
That has been unknown to you,
Until now.

Know his power to be yours
Instead,
And you will learn to lose
Your fear of it,
And of others too.

Then you will know
The time of healing to have truly begun,
And slowly will it propel you
To venture back to the Outside World
Where your living can be done.

At the bottom of the Scroll it was signed: "The Sibyl of the Land of the Shadows".

Sophia's eyes filled with tears. For she knew that she was holding something sacred in her hands - a tangible gift of wisdom and love from the Sibyl.

There was a knock at the door, which made Sophia jump. Expecting it to be Emil, she leapt across to the door and opened it. She was about to show Emil the Scroll, when she suddenly stopped dead in her tracks. For standing in front of her was none other than the Wood Chopper. The two women stood facing each other, neither able to say anything. It seemed like an age, but no doubt it was only a few seconds. Sophia finally found her voice and invited her visitor in. Then, pulling out one of the two chairs in her room, she gestured to her guest; 'Please, sit down.'

As the Wood Chopper shuffled over to the chair silently, Sophia sat down on the edge of her bed and placed the Scroll behind her, out of sight.

'Well, I must say this is quite a shock,' Sophia said, hardly able to look directly at the woman sitting opposite her. 'How did you know I was here?'

It was, however, the Wood Chopper who was finding it even harder to look at Sophia. The Wood Chopper slowly lifted her head; her eyes were sunken, her cheeks hollow, and her once solid frame was now almost skeletal. Sophia found herself feeling immense sadness for this woman, whose name she still did not know.

The Wood Chopper began to speak in a rather feint voice, as if she had almost used up her energy in finding Sophia's abode:

'I saw you the other day with Emil. I asked him about you and he seemed to think you wouldn't mind me visiting.'

'Oh, well, no! No, of course not,' Sophia replied rather nervously. 'It's just that I didn't realise you knew Emil.'

'I didn't. I just met him today when he came to visit me. A kind of welcome I suppose. I then remembered that I'd seen him with you a while before. It was quite easy really, because he looks rather different to the rest of us – well most of us anyway.' She looked down at her body, draped in loose clothing, in order to reinforce her point. 'You're looking better though – since the last time we met.'

'Am I?' said a surprised Sophia. 'In what way?' For she genuinely did not know how she looked.

'Yeah, I know! There are no mirrors here, are there?' agreed the Wood Chopper. 'Maybe it's a way of somehow getting us to ask each other for a reflection, so to speak.' She paused, and then answered Sophia's question: 'I would say you look healthier – stronger, I suppose. When I saw you in the forest, I thought you would be blown over by the wind! And there was I with this heavy axe!' She managed a smile, although it did not mask the pain as convincingly as it had once done.

Sophia smiled in response. 'By the way, I am Sophia.'

'Yes, Emil told me. I'm Jan.' She held her hand out towards Sophia. There was a firmness in her handshake; a symbolic remnant from her past.

Sophia wanted to ask Jan all sorts of questions, for she was intrigued by her, though she did not know why exactly. Perhaps it was that they seemed so different to each other; in their appearance, in their manner, and in their behaviour. Yet there was also something about Jan that felt very familiar to Sophia - something that she couldn't put her finger on.

'Well, I'd better make a move,' said Jan, 'before it gets dark.'

'Oh, but it doesn't get dark here!' Sophia responded enthusiastically. 'It's always the same half-light. The moon-' Suddenly she noticed the grin that had appeared upon Jan's face, and realised that she was being teased.   'Oh you nasty . . . ' Sophia stopped herself from going any further, immediately covering her mouth with her hand, embarrassed by her spontaneous outburst.

Sheepishly, she glanced over at Jan in order to monitor her response. Yet far from being annoyed or upset, Jan looked rather amused.

Lowering her hand from her mouth, Sophia said, 'Sorry about that.'

Jan burst out laughing, her face transforming momentarily into that of a joyful child. Sophia could do nothing else but laugh along with her.

'Well, that broke the ice, didn't it?' Jan said, after recovering. 'Anyway, I like someone who speaks their mind.'

Then she made to get up from her chair. 'Nice to meet you, Sophia. Again!'

Suddenly Sophia did not want her to go. 'Must you go so soon?' she said tentatively. 'I was just getting into our chat.'

'Yes,' replied Jan. 'You see, I get extremely exhausted these days. Not surprising really, considering what I've been through to get here!'

As Jan made her way over to the front door, Sophia got up from the edge of the bed to see her out. Jan opened the door and stepped outside. She turned to say goodbye. 'Come and visit me if you want. I'm just down the street, turn left, the house opposite the bench. I'm in most of the time . . . . . sleeping!' Jan smiled tiredly, before slowly making her way home.

'Thanks for coming by,' Sophia shouted after her, hoping that Jan would not disappear as she had done before in the forest.

Chapter Sixteen
The Story Of The Mirrors (Part One)

As time went on, Sophia tended to spend more time outside her room. To her, this signified an outward sign of her overall improvement. She liked to sit on a nearby bench and study the moon, each time noticing new features and formations upon its surface. She loved the fact that it was constant and ever present, yet was always moving and changing. Sophia would write about such paradoxes in her notepad, having become particularly interested in such phenomena.

Her body felt stronger now and she made sure that she went for a daily walk. On two occasions she stopped by to visit Jan. Both visits were fairly brief, as it was clear to Sophia that her acquaintance was still very weak. Still, she was pleased that she had someone to visit when she felt like coming out of her solitude. Of course Sophia looked forward to Emil's visits, but these seemed to have become less frequent as Sophia had become stronger and more comfortable in her environment. And she did indeed feel quite at home in the Land of the Shadows. She felt that she was healing at her own pace, and more importantly than anything, she felt safe here.

This feeling of safety, however, was beginning to worry Sophia a little. For how long could she stay here in the Land of the Shadows? She wondered whether she would ever feel like going back to the Outside World, and that if she didn't, would she be forced to leave? These questions, as well as many previously unanswered ones, were starting to play more and more on Sophia's mind. She felt she needed more answers in order to balance out this growing accumulation of questions. Looking back through her notepad, she found some of her earlier questions; they would have to wait until the next time she saw Emil.

Emil found Sophia sitting on the bench nearest her room. She looked deep in thought.

'May I join you?' Emil asked softly.

Sophia broke out of her reverie immediately. 'Emil! Oh, how glad I am to see you,' she said, moving quickly along the bench to make space for him. 'I've missed you.'

Emil smiled warmly and sat down beside her. 'Thank you for your kind words, Sophia. It is a shame I am not able to see as much of you these days, but perhaps it is because of this fact that I look forward to our meetings even more than before. If that is possible!'

'You are so charming, Emil. Do you know that?' Sophia smiled warmly in turn at her beloved friend and mentor. 'Actually, Emil, there have been quite a few things on my mind lately and I was wondering if you could help me . . . . . so many questions, you see . . . . going round and round.' She held her head, finding it hard to focus.

'What is it, Sophia? Tell me, and I will help you if I can,' Emil touched her arm gently.

Sophia looked up at him with sad eyes. 'Well . . . . how do people get out of here? I mean . . . . when the time comes for me to leave, how will I know? Will I just be told to go, or . . . . or do people stay here forever?' She was now trembling a little. 'I guess I'm too scared to stay, and too scared to go!'

Emil was not phased by what he had heard. 'This is a sign of your increasing strength, Sophia. The fact that you are thinking of the options in front of you means you are thinking of your future. There was a time when you saw no future at all.'

'Somehow you always know how to say exactly the right thing.'

'It is only the truth.'

'I know, Emil,' she said tearfully. 'I know you only speak the truth. That is why I trust you so.'

'But in answer to your other questions, Sophia, I can tell you that there are some – though relatively few – who stay here indefinitely. Alas, they are unable to find their back to the Outside World. But most do go back – one way or another.'

'What do you mean?' asked Sophia.

'Do not look so worried. This is not meant to scare you. What I meant was that there are different ways of getting back to the Outside World, and people tend to find their own way. Just like they do in getting here.'

'Do you mean that not everyone comes down the Twenty One Steps, and through the tunnels? That there are other ways?' Sophia looked alarmed at what she had heard.

'Yes,' Emil confirmed, 'there are other ways, Sophia.'

A period of silence followed, as Sophia tried to decide what she thought about it all. More than anything, she just wanted things to be clearer and more straightforward. She felt as if she was trying to put into place pieces of a jigsaw puzzle, but that just as she started to see the whole picture, the picture changed.

'What are you thinking?' asked Emil.

'To be honest Emil, I'm just feeling frustrated. I mean, it drives me mad sometimes – not knowing . . . . . not knowing . . . .' Sophia clutched her head tightly, unable to finish her sentence.

'Not knowing what?' Emil persevered.

'Just not knowing what I want to know!' She stood up and began to pace up and down. 'Don't you ever get annoyed about anything?' she asked Emil, who was sitting calmly.

'Sometimes,' replied Emil, 'though not often these days. I have lived my days of anger and frustration, believe me Sophia, but thankfully I have evolved over the years . . . . many years. This is where I am now, doing what I do, for however long I need to.'

Sophia listened with interest but was still insistent. 'But don't you ever want to know more, like how long you might be here or what you might want to do next?'

'I think, Sophia, that it is not I whom you should be addressing these questions to.' Emil paused for a moment before continuing. 'You have a lively spirit, Sophia - one that searches for the Truth. The flame within you is now beginning to burn more brightly and wants to show you the way. So, you must see the frustration you are feeling now, as positive. For it says that you want to follow your spirit. Embrace this, Sophia, and you can't ultimately go wrong.'

Sophia had stopped pacing. This man, whom she had come to rely on and trust, seemed to have an almost tranquillising and hypnotic effect on her. And it was as irresistible as the moon.

'I don't know what I would have done without you Emil,' she said tenderly, looking down at her feet.

'Thank you,' Emil smiled. 'But remember that a teacher can only help those who wish to learn. And you have been such a good student.'

Sophia, feeling rather humbled in Emil's presence, went back to sit down beside him. She glanced at her notepad lying at the end of the bench.

'You know,' she began, 'I had so many questions to ask you – I wrote them down in case I forgot them – but they don't seem as important now.'

'I think it is important that you ask them,' he encouraged her.

Sophia stretched across and picked up the notepad. Opening it, she browsed through the pages to see if anything jumped out at her.

'Oh yes, here is one that I've puzzled over for ages,' she finally announced. 'Why are there no mirrors in any of the rooms – well, the rooms I've seen anyway?'

Emil looked lovingly up at the moon, and smiled knowingly. 'Oh, but there are mirrors here, Sophia. Plenty of mirrors! It's just that they are a different kind of mirror to the ones you are used to in the Outside World.'

Looking very puzzled, Sophia followed his gaze up to the moon. 'You mean the moon?' she asked.

Emil lowered his eyes to look at Sophia. 'What I mean is that the mirrors here come in the form of other people, or situations. We see ourselves in other people; and the parts we see are aspects that we hide from ourselves – the parts we don't want to see. For example, our defects, our weaknesses, our fears, even our beauty – anything and everything.

'The mirrors you are used to, Sophia, are ones that reflect what is on the outside. Here in the Land of the Shadows we focus on what is on the inside, so we need a different type of mirror altogether – ones that reflect what is on the inside. We have no need here for the 2-dimensional mirror on walls. They would only act as a distraction.'

Emil seemed determined for Sophia to understand the different workings of her new surroundings; to let go of the limited vision that existed in the Outside World; and to replace her old perspectives with new ones. And in many ways Sophia wanted to do this also. What seemed to stop her, however, was her fear of not knowing the outcome. She always wanted to know more about something before she made a decision – what was usually called an "informed decision". This philosophy certainly had its place in the Outside World, but Sophia had grown tired of always trying to do the "right" thing. "Isn't that," she now asked herself, "how I ended up living within the restrictions of the Cage in the first place?"

In contrast, when Sophia had followed Emil's advice in the Darkened Street and had just let go and trusted, she had seen a different world. She had seen the flame instead of the darkness.

Emil seemed to be in tune with her thoughts, for he suddenly said, 'Remember when we were in the Darkened Street?'

Sophia nodded in amazement.

'At first you did not see the flame,' he continued, 'but eventually you did. When you let go of your fear, you allowed room for the flame of hope to burn within you. What I am saying, Sophia, is that the flame exists within you anyway, and that the outside flame reflected that back to you. It was a mirror that allowed you to see a part of yourself.'

Sophia was mesmerised, baffled and excited all at the same time. Suddenly she thought of Jan, and said,

'I've just remembered something that Jan said a little while ago. She suggested that the absence of mirrors – wall-mirrors, that is – was to make us ask each other for a reflection.'

'Ah yes, that is good,' responded Emil. 'Very good! Indeed that is another type of mirror we use here, for other people can often see things in us that we are blind to. Most of the time, is it not true, we do not want to listen to others – even those who we know love us! Who are they, we say, to tell us about ourselves? What do they know?'

Sophia chuckled to herself, as she recognised this reaction in herself. 'Well, I suppose it's because people often assume they know better – that they know what's best for us, but they don't really!'

'Of course, of course,' agreed Emil. 'That is also true. And it can be extremely confusing if one was to listen to all that came his or her way!' He raised his hands, as if to demonstrate his feelings of dismay with the Outside World, a gesture that amused Sophia. Then he continued; 'That is why one has to learn the art of discernment: how to decide what is of little use to us, and what is of benefit to us. That is the only way for us to keep on the right track - the one that will ultimately lead us to the Centre Point, to our true Self.

'It is not always straightforward – you know that Sophia – but even if you stray off your path, the quality of discernment will help guide you back. It is greatly helped by periods of solitude, of quiet reflection – what we would call an Incubation Period.'

'That's what I wanted to ask you!' Sophia cried out excitedly. 'About the Scroll! Except there's so much to take in . . . my head's starting to hurt.'

'Then this is a time for discernment. What do you feel is of most use to you now?'

Sophia was rubbing her aching head, though not in distress. 'I think I need to go back to my room for a while, and give myself time to take in what we've been talking about. Do you mind, Emil?'

'Of course not!' he laughed. 'You are just demonstrating the art of discernment.'

Then they both stood up and embraced, before going their separate ways.

Chapter Seventeen
The Story Of The Mirrors (Part Two)

Sophia continued to spend most of her time in solitude, but it was a different type of solitude to the one she had known deep in the heart of the forest. Her mind was becoming more alive and receptive to the information that came her way, and her heart was awakening to each new experience. Above all, she was learning to live again, perhaps even live for the first time.

Today Sophia decided to look at the Sibyl's Scroll again. It did not matter that she was yet to fully understand its message, for Sophia had come to accept that she would know such clarity when the time was right.

"Befriend the Stranger", was the line she focused on.

'Who is the Stranger?' she asked herself out loud, thinking that the Stranger sounded rather daunting in the Scroll's verse. Yet the verse also seemed to be saying that this was the way back to the Outside World:

'Where your living can be done,' Sophia read aloud the last line.

She was already starting to feel unnerved by the Scroll's message. She had first thought to put it up on her wall so that it was always visible to her, but at that moment she decided against it. Instead, she rolled it back up and put it in her bag. For the truth was that Sophia did not really want to go back to the Outside World. Not yet anyway. She felt safer here, in this place of learning without competition, without ego's. How Sophia wished that this world could be transported somehow into the Outside World.

She decided to leave her room and go for her daily walk. Today her limbs felt heavy and her head a little foggy. She thought about visiting Jan but didn't feel up to seeing anyone. No, she would keep walking and hope that her limbs would start to feel lighter and her head clearer. Sophia decided to walk a different way this time; she walked down a side road that led off the main street, making sure she was heading in a direction away from the Darkened Street. Yet as she walked further and further away from the Darkened Street, it suddenly dawned on her who the Stranger might be.

"Could it be the man I met with Emil . . . . . the badly burnt man?" Sophia's heart quickened along with her strides, until she had all but exhausted herself and had to slow down. She could see an open space at the end of the narrow side road, so made her way towards it.

When she got there, she saw that it was a large open square with a round wooden platform in the centre. And as with all the structures in the Land of the Shadows, there was nothing elaborate or decorative about the scene or setting. Its striking feature was its bold simplicity, and Sophia was fascinated with her new discovery.

'A circle within a square,' she found herself saying, without placing any particular significance to such words.

She then noticed that there were some wooden benches positioned at equal distances around the outside of the Square. She decided to go and sit down on one of them. Although she felt tired, her head was beginning to clear, and she found herself thinking about the perfect geometry of the place.

'It all seems so symmetrical,' she said quietly, 'and looking down on it all is the magnificence and wholeness of the moon.'

Sophia sat for a while, alone in the empty Square, just looking up at the moon.

'Hello, miss,' a man's voice called.

Sophia almost fell off her bench. 'My goodness, you almost scared me to death!' she panted, looking at the young man standing in front of her.

'Sorry miss, I didn't realise you hadn't seen me,' he said politely.

Sophia was immediately struck by the young man's attire; he was wearing a flat cap, charcoal-grey baggy trousers with braces, and a bright red cotton shirt. She rather liked it, especially because it was so different to what everyone else wore in the Land of the Shadows.

'It's alright,' Sophia said in reassurance, 'I'm very easily startled these days. I was looking at this marvellous stage. It is a stage, isn't it?'

'Yes. In fact we will be performing a play later on. You are most welcome to come.'

He handed Sophia a leaflet. She felt a rush of excitement at the thought of seeing a live play.

'Oh, how wonderful!' she exclaimed. 'I'd love to see it. I didn't realise that this was here – Emil never told me.'

'That's usual, miss,' the young man explained. 'It's only those people who find this place themselves who know it's here. That way they come of their own free will. We'd ask that you don't tell anyone else yourself, if that's alright?'

'I see,' Sophia said quietly, having been reminded that there was a reason for everything. 'No, no, of course I don't mind.'

She looked down at the leaflet in her hand. It said:

"THE MIRRORS"
A PLAY

One performance only
To be presented
by
Our special guest:

The Sibyl of the Land of the Shadows

Sophia gasped. 'I don't believe it! I was just reading the Scroll that the Sibyl gave me – and now she's going to be here. And Emil was explaining to me about mirrors the other day! It's just so amazing how everything fits into place at exactly the right time. I mean, if I had found this place a week ago, I wouldn't have known about the Scroll and I wouldn't have asked Emil about mirrors.'

She sat in disbelief, feeling a sense of wonderment, until she realised that the young man was no longer there. She looked around her but there was no sign of him. He had disappeared as suddenly as he had appeared. But at least Sophia held in her hand, tangible proof of his appearance and of her visit to the Square.

Sophia sat waiting in anticipation for the forthcoming events to take place; she didn't want to move away from the Square in case she missed anything. Closing her eyes for a moment, Sophia almost immediately fell asleep.

When she woke, it was to sounds stirring in the Square, for several people had started to drift in. All she could hear was the sound of feet shuffling along the gravel ground; there was no sound of people talking, because each person seemed to be on their own. It was not that they seemed particularly comfortable or confident on their own; "Far from it," thought Sophia. "In fact they look as awkward and nervous as I feel."

As a few more people trickled into the Square, they all seemed to find their own spot away from each other, whilst focusing their attention on the empty stage in the centre. Sophia suddenly became aware of her own position; she was the only one sitting on the outside of the Square. It made her feel different, but not the feeling of difference that came from a sense of uniqueness and individuality. It was a feeling of difference that came from a sense of exclusion. 'I don't belong,' she whispered.

Sitting alone within this strange setting, Sophia felt her heart pierced by the sharpest of images that now lay before her. Suddenly she understood with greater clarity the concept of the 3-dimensional mirrors, of which Emil had spoken. For just as the image of the fallen Tower had reflected to her aspects of her former self, the images of the people in the Square now reflected to Sophia her sense of aloneness and her deep craving for a sense of belonging.

Sophia's mind went back to her time in the lake, when she had had the most vivid and profound dream in which she was watching a "play" of sorts being performed in the water. The dream had been providing Sophia with messages from her unconscious – messages which she had sought to protect herself from at the time. For she had remained hidden in the forest, trying to defend herself from the associated emotional pain. But it was only now, sitting in this Square, that Sophia started to experience the full and painful realisation that she had abandoned her inner child – symbolised by the voice that spoke from beneath the waves.

Sophia could now feel that same pain beginning to surface again, and as it did it came with the force of big rolling waves that rose up through her body until her head was swimming and her throat was beginning to choke from the flood. As she began to lose sight of her surroundings, Sophia remained frozen to the bench until she felt the waves beginning to subside. She felt a strong urge within her to move forward, to leave the illusory safety of her bench, and to stand amongst the people within the Square. So rather than wait for the waves to rise again, Sophia got to her feet. Tremulously, she put one foot in front of the other, her child spirit leading her further into the Square and nearer to the central stage. She could sense that something was about to happen.

Suddenly, a loud boom resonated throughout the Square. Not for the first time Sophia almost jumped out of her skin, and when she looked around her it seemed that others were also looking ruffled by the unexpected loudness of the noise. Yet this simple sudden vibration seemed to have awakened the people in the Square, almost as a unified entity.

The loud boom sounded again. The feeling of excitement and anticipation was starting to grow within the Square, which was now about half-full. Then the loud boom sounded again . . . . and again . . . . until it adopted a rhythm. Sophia found herself whispering the words that had come to her from an earlier time:

'Trust instead the beating heart
Of the Greatest Unknown
You will ever know.'

Somehow she knew what it meant, and trust it she did. A smile came upon her face, and a sensation of lightness rose up through her body; she could feel the crowd's togetherness – its oneness – and at that moment she felt herself to be part of something much greater, something that just couldn't be explained, something akin to the Greatest Unknown.

As the rhythm of the sound gathered pace, it became clear that the sound was coming from the beating of a single drum. Then other drums started to sound at different intervals, so that there were various rhythms interweaving to create a complex tapestry of sounds. No one had appeared yet on the centre stage. In contrast, the Square was now completely full. Without knowing why, an interesting thought flashed across Sophia's mind; she wondered whether this was the Centre Point? Before she could follow this line of thinking, however, something happened in the Square: the loud booming sound of drums was suddenly silenced.

There were murmurs in the crowd, and a gradual stirring within a portion of the crowd over to Sophia's right. She got up on tip-toes, straining to see what was happening, but could not see anything. Instead, she felt the pressure of the crowd directly in front of her as it began to press backwards. And then as the crowd to her right began to part, Sophia caught a fleeting glimpse of the Sibyl. Sophia's heart rose, tears welled in her eyes – the effect was always the same. And as she glanced at other people's faces in the crowd, she realised that this was universal: somehow, the Sibyl touched all of their hearts instantly. They seemed able to open their hearts and to let the stones of cold-heartedness and hard-heartedness just fall away.

The Sibyl began to ascend the steps that led up to the stage. She was wearing long red robes, which flowed with grace and ease as she glided up onto the stage. She exuded the qualities of strength and elegance, of power and serenity, of determination and wisdom – it seemed to Sophia to be an endless combination of opposites that complemented each other. There seemed to be a harmonious union of such dual aspects - aspects that could be attributed to being either masculine or feminine in nature – that somehow enabled love and generosity to spontaneously flower from within the Sibyl. Sophia felt honoured to have shared time alone in the presence of one so great. And at this stage of Sophia's journey, the Sibyl was her hero.

The Sibyl stood motionless on the stage holding a scroll in her hand. She looked neither happy nor sad, and yet she was not expressionless either. Sophia just could not describe it . . . . . . and then she found the perfect word to describe how the Sibyl looked: It was a look of knowing. A look that said she understood the suffering and plight of all those who had come to the Land of the Shadows; that she was not there to pass judgement. No, her role was to guide through her wisdom, to heal through her love, and to lead through her strength. Sophia's eyes were drawn towards the sky and the ever present moon that resided over them. Its silvery glow seemed even brighter; a more than suitable spot-light for the Sibyl.

Then finally the Sibyl spoke:

'Welcome, my friends.' Her voice seemed to carry effortlessly across the Square, as she rotated to acknowledge all four corners. 'It is a great honour for me to stand here before you, knowing the pain and hardship you have endured in order to get to the Land of the Shadows. Some of you I have met along the way – others have come by alternative routes. But I welcome you all to this place of great learning and healing.'

She paused for a few moments, whilst the crowd remained suspended in silence. She then lifted the scroll she held in her hand, without attempting to open it. It seemed to be more like a conductor's wand or an angel's staff, indicating to the crowd that she was about to continue:

'In my hand I hold the essence of enlightenment, conveyed through the divine medium of words. I call upon you to think of your time here as an Incubation Period.'

As the Sibyl paused, Sophia let out a gasp. For she was regretting that she had not taken more time to study the Scroll in order to understand its message more clearly. But just then, as if to disperse such concerns, the Sibyl said:

'There is no need to rush. The true meaning of your time spent here will reveal itself eventually to each and every one of you. Neither you nor I can force the pace – for a river cannot be made to flow faster than the Laws of Nature will permit.'

The Sibyl stretched out her arms towards the crowd, revealing further the splendour of her essential nature enveloped in her gown.

'And now, my friends, we will begin our performance of "The Mirrors" . . .'

The drums began to sound again - invisible though they were to the crowd - and an actor suddenly appeared upon the stage. It was the young man whom Sophia had met earlier. He knelt down and stared at the floor of the stage, his face expressing the torment of his pain, whilst the Sibyl remained in the same position as before. The rhythm of the drums now followed a slow brooding pace, which seemed to have the effect of almost hypnotising the crowd. Sophia felt her eyes become heavy and her breathing become slower. She struggled to maintain concentration. But then she heard the commanding yet gentle tones of the Sibyl's voice, as she addressed the crowd once again:

'This play tells the story of a young man who is bereft because his beloved friend, his love, has gone away never to return. They had seen in each other, a powerful reflection: for each person was a mirror that reflected back to the other person parts of the Self that had been hidden up until then.'

The Sibyl turned gently to look towards the young man who had remained in exactly the same position, as if frozen in time. There was a hush over the Square. The drums had stopped beating, and the crowd seemed almost unable to breathe.

The Sibyl glided off the stage, this time so swiftly and silently that her exit seemed more like a disappearing act. And with her departure, Sophia was almost sure that the moon's light had dimmed.

"THE MIRRORS"

A PLAY

The young man took off his cap and clutched it in both hands. He lifted his head slightly but not to look at the crowd, for he was lost in his own world and seemed unaware of the presence of so many strangers.

Then, still kneeling, he began:

'The mirror is gone now.
You know-
The one you threw stones at,
Til it smashed to the floor!'

The young man's voice was filled with mournful sadness and futility. He let his cap fall to the floor as if to symbolise the fall of his own being. Then, slowly, he lifted himself up from the floor and stood on unsteady feet. Looking up, he began to address his "lost love" (though this was not represented by a physical being as such):

'But it is not your fault,
For why did I keep the mirror there for so long?
Knowing it was breaking,
Under the stress of your stare.'

The young man's voice was more pleading now, as he searched for illusive answers. He began to pace the floor of the stage:

'I have asked this of myself, many times and more.
I cannot blame you . . . .
For the stones, I mean.
For I gave them to you, didn't I?
What else could you do?

'The reflection was too sharp at times, wasn't it?
It threatened to cut you deep inside,
The joy and the sorrow were too closely entwined.'

He stopped pacing, and was now looking more animated and angry. Determined to make his point to his lost love, he said:

'So what happens now?!
Now that the mirror is gone?
There are many other mirrors, you say,
There are but many in your life today,
Yet why have you not smashed them?

'Is it that their reflection is not so sharp!
Not so clearly defined,
Just blurred and hazy images,
That are pleasant most of the time.'

The young man was suddenly silent, as if awaiting a reply that would either confirm or deny his perception of events. His hands were down by his side, and he appeared more vulnerable. When he spoke this time, it was in softer tones:

'What is so wrong with that, I hear you say,
Why should I be so unkind?
To imply that you should see a sharper mirror,
Knowing that I have my own mirror in mind.

'Yes – who am I indeed?!
To lay such arrogance at your door?
As if it is only I who can truly see you,
What were my motives, clean or impure?

'I have asked this of myself,
But at the time the glare was too bright
And I was blinded by the flash of light,
That came from mirrors held up to the sun.'

Slowly he looked up to the sky, and to the moon. His voice conveyed the longing and love he felt for what was now gone:
'Yet what a wondrous light it was . . . .
Can you blame me for wanting to bask in it,
For just a little longer?

To want to go out and play in the sun,
Separate yet together, together as One?'

Suddenly his head was hung down, and he dropped to his knees:

'But I fear we stayed out in the sun too long,
And developed blind spots.
For as the sun dimmed its light,
The mirror's reflection came into view,
And I could no longer be blinded,
Only bereft.

'Because that part of me,
Which in you I could see
Was no longer in view,
For the mirror was now gone.'

The young man's right hand swept across his face to wipe away the tears. For the first time he looked towards the crowd, before composing himself to speak to them:

'I now sit by a lake in an ancient forest.
The lake has become my mirror,
The only one I have,
Now that I am alone.
But what, alas, can it tell me?'

The resignation in his voice seemed to have already answered his question. The crowd wondered whether the play had ended, and were waiting for a cue from the young man. But he remained still.

Then out of the silence a voice made itself heard – though no one seemed to know from where it came – it seemed to come from nowhere and everywhere. The young man was startled, looking around him in search of the source of this elusive voice. The crowd did not know whether this was part of the actual performance, so real were its effects.

In loud, booming tones, the voice said:

'You are angry and bereft that your "love" took
  their mirror away!

'You have convinced yourself that you needed to see
  yourself reflected back to you.

'But that, my friend, is what you got!'

The young man was aghast at what he had heard. He waited to hear more but nothing came. He got to his feet and walked anxiously around the stage.

He cried out loud:

'WHAT DO YOU MEAN? PLEASE, TELL ME!'

He paced up and down repeating the same question until he was shouting up at the sky. But the "voice" did not reply.

All of a sudden the drums sounded, and a collective gasp from the crowd resonated back. Then a mist gradually descended upon the

Square, and with it a sense of unease spread through the crowd. One more booming drum-beat sounded, before in a split second the mist was gone and there was silence.

At that moment it seemed that the crowd breathed in unison. And then they realised that the young man had disappeared from the stage, and the play was over.

Chapter Eighteen
Awakening Dream

Sophia found her way back to her room very quickly. She did not wish to stay in the Square a moment longer. For the impact of the play was such that it had left her feeling a profound sense of confusion and sadness. In fact, she had found the whole experience in the Square to be more akin to that of a roller coaster ride; the highs of wonderment, of inspiration, and of divine wisdom; the lows of despair, of aloneness, and of fear. This was no doubt augmented and magnified by the shared experience of the many who had gathered in the Square with her. The mass of sounds, sights and emotions had bombarded her senses in all their limited human capacity, so that Sophia felt she might almost short circuit.

Now safely back in her room Sophia lay on her bed, the silent tranquillity all around her except in her head.

She closed her eyes and waited for sleep to come, deciding that after her rest she would have a bath and then go to find Emil. "Yes, he will know how to help me make sense of what is happening to me," Sophia thought to herself, as she drifted off to sleep.

Whilst she slept, she dreamt. So many moving pictures, depicting scenes from different stages of her journey thus far. But everything in the dream was confused and entangled so that the past appeared as the present, and Sophia was an adult in childhood scenes. It was as if different time entities had superimposed upon each other, resulting in a moving picture with no edits.

Yet there was one dream sequence Sophia experienced that was so vivid, that she later wrote it down as she remembered it:

"The Dream Sequence"

There are corridors . . . lots of corridors . . . . I'm walking, then running, looking for something that I know is there . . . . . a room. Yes, that's it! I have to get back to my room – a room just like the one in the Land of the Shadows. But I have to hurry . . . . "they" are waiting for me . . . . . to claim my prize! Not mine alone though – a shared prize – with all those I have travelled with. But I have to find my room . . . . . I don't know why, I just know I have to.

I come to a door on my right . . . . . yes, that looks like my room . . . . . I open it. No, something is not quite right . . . . . it looks the same, similar, but it's not mine. I close the door. I must hurry . . . . . the next door on the right . . . . yes, that's the one! I open it. There is someone in there . . . . . a woman . . . . she is lying in bed. But who is she? What is she doing in my room? The woman sits up. She is angry with me for intruding . . . . 'Get out!' she shouts. I must have gone into the wrong room. Yet I was so sure it was mine. I must leave this hostile environment . . . . this hostile woman . . . . but wait a minute! There is a towel at the end of the bed. It's my towel! This is my room. So what is this woman doing here? She's the one who has got the wrong room! She's the intruder! Yet the woman still wants me to leave. I have no time to resolve this situation . . . . . I have to hurry . . . . . the others are waiting for me.

I leave the room and run further down the corridor . . . . . perhaps this is a shortcut . . . . . but no, it leads to somewhere else. Time is running out and I don't know where this leads . . . . . . I must turn back and go the way I came . . . . . . I go back past the rooms – this time they are on the left – and finally I get back to where I started.

But where are the others? Have they gone without me? . . . . . .

After this dream, Sophia had woken up with a start. The stark silence of her room was so apparent that she felt uneasy at being alone. Suddenly she noticed something at the end of her bed – it was the towel that had been in her dream! Yet in her dream, she had been the one entering the room. Here, outside her dream, Sophia was the woman lying in bed.

'So, who was the woman that told me to get out?' Sophia said out loud. 'What does it all mean?' Sophia wracked her brains, not for the first time.

She would have welcomed a visit from Emil now. For her head and heart had already been reeling from all that she had experienced in the Square. And now she had more confusing images to deal with. Then Sophia had a thought – this time a clear thought – more an illumination:

'The play was about seeing a part of yourself – a hidden part of yourself – in someone else,' she said quietly. 'So . . . . was that hostile woman lying in bed – in my room – a hidden part of me? Like the Stranger?'

Sophia of course did not recognise the hostility of the woman as a part of herself – not consciously anyway. She did not want to see it either. She did not wish to meet the Stranger, whoever that was, but she knew at some point she had to. For the first time, Sophia had awakened to the fact that the Stranger might be a part of herself. And the familiar words of the wise old man of the forest came back to her, as if to reinforce her new insight:

'To be truly free, you have to face yourself.'

There was a knock at the door. Sophia jumped once again.

'Come in!' she gasped. The door opened to reveal the person she most wanted to see.

'Emil!' she jumped off the bed and ran over to hug him. 'I'm so glad to see you.'

'I heard your call,' he replied softly.

Sophia took what seemed like an age in telling Emil all about her adventures, experiences and dreams, and of the impact that they had had on her. She hardly stopped for breath so desperate was she to get everything off her chest. Emil sat attentive as always, though he looked more tired than usual, Sophia thought. Sometimes he seemed amused by Sophia's animated renditions, and sometimes he felt saddened by her emotional struggles. Nevertheless, he was always present, his focus never faltering for the time he was with her.

Emil loved to see the ongoing changes and developmental steps that Sophia made, and he delighted in sharing in her continual quest for the Truth. "Yes," he thought to himself, "she is indeed a courageous warrior." But more than this, Emil had watched her come back to life. He had seen the spirit of youth within her, reveal itself like never before. And he knew how important this was, not just for Sophia to live her future life with vitality and joy, but because he knew that she had yet to face a great unknown of her own: her Stranger - her Shadow - here in the Land of the Shadows.

Sophia fell into an exhausted silence, having surprised herself with all that she had expressed so freely to Emil. She had had so many other things she wanted to ask Emil, or clarify with him, yet she had said so much to him already. Finally Emil broke out of his silent watchfulness:

'My dear Sophia, you have achieved a great deal in a relatively short time. Remember that the limited human mind needs its own time to fully embrace new experiences and new learning. It will come . . . you will see. Trust, Sophia, trust.'

'Yes, I know – the Greatest Unknown,' she joined in harmoniously. 'Although it's still hard to totally let go. There is so much of my old life that still seems a part of me.'

She looked a little sad as if about to go into a reverie of the past. But she did not. 'You know, Emil, I wouldn't want to go back to the way things were even if I could. I know that my future is unknown, but I'm not as scared as I was. You see, I know now that I don't have to get everything right all the time – I don't have to be perfect. Now that's a cage if ever there was one! And it's not like I have ever got everything right – in fact, I don't really like people that do – but somewhere inside I have always given myself such a hard time for not being perfect. So much wasted energy, I can see that now.'

Sophia let out a deep sigh, and said, 'What was it all for? I've pushed myself to succeed in the Outside World, pushed my mind and body to its limits – beyond its limits. The truth is, Emil, that I never really took any notice of what my body was telling me – it was just there! Until of course it collapsed.'

'Like the Tower,' Emil interjected.

She looked at him and nodded knowingly. A tear began to roll down her cheek as she remembered her past life.

'I just wanted to belong,' she explained. 'To be the same as others, to do the same as others, to do things that would meet the approval of others – to impress them I guess. Then they would like me, would want to spend time with me.'

'And what happened Sophia?' asked Emil. 'Did you belong?'

'To some extent. I mean, I felt good at being "successful" – powerful even. The status and prestige fed my ego. But it wasn't just that – I did like helping others too.'

Emil was silent, conserving his energy for only utterances that were absolutely necessary, as he listened to Sophia's story.

'I gave out too much, I can see that now,' she continued. 'I can't believe that I didn't see it at the time. Perhaps I did but didn't take notice of it . . . . . too scared to change it . . . . . too caught up in the whirlwind of activities and events. "Better stick to what you know . . . . . . it's not that bad really." That's what I used to say to myself whenever I hankered after anything else. That's why I stayed so long in my Cage.'

Sophia stood up and walked slowly across to the other side of the room, her eye catching the Scroll that stuck out of her bag.

'I was so moved by that play in the Square,' she said. 'By the whole experience really . . . . the drums, the Sibyl, ... it was amazing. But more than anything,' she turned to face Emil, 'I felt a deep sense of belonging. It was only then that I truly knew what that feeling was like. And for a brief moment, suddenly everything made sense – as if a veil had been lifted from my eyes. That's the only way I can describe it.'

She went to sit back down on the edge of her bed. Emil leant forward and placed his hand on hers.

'You could see through the Veils of Illusion,' he whispered, at a tired but enlightened Sophia.

Then he stood up, still holding her hand, and said, 'I will leave you to rest now, for you have travelled a long way. But I will return soon, oh courageous warrior.'

Sophia tried to rest for a while on her bed but there was too much going on in her head. She felt restless. She even had a long soak in the bath to help relax her, yet instead she felt more energised. She needed to use up some of this energy, but in a fruitful way; in conversation perhaps, or in physical exploration. But she didn't know when Emil was next going to turn up – in any case, Sophia could not help but notice how tired Emil had looked. Somehow, he had not had the same sparkle in his eyes.

As she began to pace her room, Sophia was reminded of the time she had spent in her hotel room back in the Valley Town and how she had paced up and down, feeling like a caged animal - she grinned at the thought of it. She then smiled at the memory of Victor; how she had looked out of her hotel room window at the very same time that he was walking past.

'If he hadn't been walking by at that time,' Sophia said aloud to herself, 'I wonder what would have happened to me.'

For she was now starting to believe in the concept of "divine timing" – something that Emil had talked to her about. He would say that it was the only "clock" they used in the Land of the Shadows, and that the man-made clocks and calendars of the Outside World were of no use to them. At first Sophia had found this to be a most mysterious and magical concept – something nice to believe in, but a bit of a fantasy really. Yet in her own time and with no undue pressure from outside forces, she had come to understand that her initial response was just another example of the rather arrogant and vastly limited ego.

Sophia continued to pace her room. She began thinking about her journey with Emil to the Darkened Street, and the badly burnt man lying alone in that dark room. She had managed to block it from her mind but now the image resurfaced. Why had Emil taken her there? What was the significance that was meant for her? Was the badly burnt man supposed to represent something within her, like the "Mirrors" play had said? The same familiar words from long ago resurfaced yet again. Suddenly Sophia stopped pacing and said the words out loud:

'To be truly free, you have to face yourself.'

She knew she had to go back to the Darkened Street.

Sophia picked up her bag, making sure her canteen was filled with water and that she had some bread and biscuits in case she felt peckish, and then headed out of the front door.

Chapter Nineteen
Transformation

As Sophia walked along the main street, the idea of venturing into the Darkened Street on her own seemed to become more and more daunting. This was to be expected, she told herself. But when she reached the end of the main street, she decided instead to go and visit Jan. Whether or not Sophia was stalling she wasn't sure, but she felt it wouldn't do any harm. In any case, it had been quite a while since she had seen Jan, and she was curious as to how she was getting on.

She crossed the road, turned left and walked towards the bench that faced Jan's room. Taking a deep breath, she then walked over to Jan's front door and knocked softly in case Jan was asleep. After a few moments, the door slowly opened and there stood a tired looking Jan.

'Oh . . . hello,' said Sophia. 'I'm sorry if I disturbed you.'

'It's alright, I always look like this,' Jan quipped.

'I was just passing so I thought I'd come and say hello.'

'Oh,' Jan looked rather dazed. 'I'd ask you in, but to be honest I'm not really feeling up to it.'

'Look Jan, I can see that you're having a hard time. Believe me, I know! It's better to be honest. Really!'

'Yeah, thanks,' replied Jan, who was beginning to look a little tremulous. 'I must go now.'

'Okay,' Sophia smiled. 'Take care of yourself.'

Sophia could see that Jan was finding it difficult to tolerate any further display of vulnerability, and because of this she found herself feeling a deep sense of warmth towards Jan.

As Sophia started to move away from the doorway, Jan shut the door quickly behind her. Sophia walked back across the street to the bench and sat down. She felt sadness in her heart. But it was a kind of sadness that bore from it compassion; a wish to comfort and care for another living being. It was a sadness that drew one human being to another, rather than a sadness that led to isolation and withdrawal. Sophia realised that she had seen much of herself in Jan in those few moments, as they faced each other across the threshold of the doorway. It had been the sharpest mirror image Sophia had been able to see up until then of herself. The sadness and compassion she felt was not just for Jan she realised, but was also for herself. And perhaps it was for this reason that Sophia had been able to walk away from Jan.

'For there was a time,' she said softly to herself, 'when I would not have been able to walk away without trying to help.'

Sophia shook her head slowly, mostly in amazement at her own continuing transformation. Now she felt ready to step once more into the Darkened Street and to face whatever it was she had to face.

Once Sophia had stepped across the line between the silvery white light of the moon and the total absence of light in the Darkened

Street, she stood completely still. She tried to relax her body as best as she could, taking deep breaths and waiting for her eyes to adjust to the darkness. If she closed her eyes she had the sensation almost akin to that of weightlessness, of floating, as if this lightness in weight somehow served to counterbalance the darkness.

When Sophia opened her eyes she could still not see anything. Nor could she hear anything. In fact, there was nothing that stimulated any of her five basic senses. No, she would have to rely on higher senses – or deeper ones – to guide her, like intuition. Although this form of inner knowing was highly accurate, alas in Sophia it was still in its infancy.

It seemed like an age that she had been standing in the same position – and still nothing! Sophia decided to take a step forward . . . . then another . . . . . then another . . . . until suddenly she found herself walking with some assurance. If this was blind faith, Sophia thought to herself, then it was something she had never known before. And she started to feel strangely liberated.

'Trust!' she said aloud, as she continued her forward march. She then found herself repeating aloud the words that had come to her before on her journey:

'Tremble not within you,
For that which you do not know.
Trust instead the beating heart
Of the Greatest Unknown
You will ever know.'

She did not know where these words had come from – not now, and not before. They seemed to come from within her, yet also from somewhere else. She could not explain it. But she was beginning to believe it was another example of connecting with something much greater than herself; an all-knowing power that was all around her, but which she was also part of: the Greatest Unknown, as Sophia had come to know it.

Sophia had slowed down now, her pace no more than a gentle stroll. All that she was aware of was the sound of her footsteps on the sandy gravel, yet she still trusted that she was on the right track. She did start to wonder, however, why she hadn't seen the torch flame that she had seen previously with Emil. She decided to stop walking and rest for a while.

Sitting down on the spot where she stood, Sophia removed her bag from her shoulder. As she fumbled in her bag for her water canteen, she suddenly noticed a wavering light in the distance. She immediately got back up on to her feet again, picked up her bag and canteen, and started to walk towards it. As she approached it her heart began to pound. Was it a light that had been placed outside someone's room, like the badly burnt man? Sophia wondered. She could feel the growing anxiety inside her at the thought of meeting someone like the badly burnt man on her own. Yet she couldn't see any houses or buildings as such – only the flame of a torch.

She was now only a few yards away from it, when suddenly the flame moved. Sophia gasped. Frozen to the spot, she wondered what would happen next. The flame began to move towards her, and a woman's voice said:

'Blind your vision to distractions around,
Carry the torch of Truth with you.'

Sophia's throat now felt so tight that she could hardly swallow. 'Who is it?' she said, her voice barely louder than a whisper.

The flame was now stationary - about ten feet away from Sophia - but she could not see who was behind it.

The woman spoke again; 'Do you not remember me? I met you in the tunnels – I am the Flame Carrier.' Her voice was soft, shy almost.

'Oh my goodness!' Sophia was astounded. 'I'm sorry . . . of course I remember! How could I forget? You saved me when I was about to die. You showed me the way out of those awful tunnels.'

'They're not so bad really - when you get to know them as I do.'

'Maybe – but I don't ever want to go back there again!'

In the brief silence that followed, Sophia wondered whether the Flame Carrier had been offended by what she had said about the tunnels. After all, perhaps she spent most of her time in the tunnels. An awkward Sophia thought of what to say to the Flame Carrier.

'It's just that I was so frightened,' she sought to explain, 'so very frightened. I can't even find the words to describe how painful it was . . . .'

Sophia's voice tapered off to a whisper as she struggled to cope with the memory of that time. Closing her eyes, she lowered her head, about to ask the Flame Carrier a question – one that she was scared to hear the answer to.

'Do I have to go back to the tunnels? Is that how I get back to the Outside World – not that I want to go,' Sophia's voice was quiet, and trembled with the beginnings of her tears. Her breathing was clearly audible as she awaited the reply from the guardian of the tunnels. And when it came, it was with all the warmth and clarity that the flame she carried exuded.

'My dear,' began the Flame Carrier, 'the tunnels are not the only way back to the Outside World. I cannot tell you how you will find

217

your way back, only that should you need someone to light your way ahead I will be there. For the tunnels are my home.'

Sophia opened her eyes and lifted her head. There before her was a vision of profound beauty. Not one of majesty or of outward splendour like that of the Sibyl, but one that was more subtle and modest in its manifestation. Sophia could see the silhouette of the Flame Carrier's black robes, outlined by the brightest of yellow glows. She could not see the Flame Carrier's face, for this remained hidden behind the dazzling flame she held up in front of her.

Then the Flame Carrier held her torch out towards Sophia, and said:

'Carry this torch with you, Sophia. Be lost in the flame that fires up your heart. It is all you need to find your way.'

Sophia felt her heart deeply touched by these words, and by the offer of such a precious gift. She took a tentative step towards the Flame Carrier, and then another, until she stood only a few feet away from the torch. Yet what had happened in those few steps was quite remarkable. For the bright yellow glow that had outlined the Flame Carrier so beautifully, seemed to have disappeared leaving only the flame itself. Sophia could now see the fingers of the Flame Carrier enfolded around the torch handle. She reached out towards it, and gently placed her right hand over the Flame Carrier's hand, not wanting to lose this sacred moment. Suddenly, the torch was in Sophia's hand and she could not tell where the Flame Carrier was.

'Are you still there?' Sophia called out nervously in the dark. She stretched out her left hand hoping to touch the black robes. 'Hello . . . . can you hear me?' she called. 'Please say something!'

Sophia stepped forward, this time hoping that the flame would reveal something of the Flame Carrier. But it did not, and in her heart she knew that the Flame Carrier had already gone.

'But why did she give me her torch?' Sophia said, as she sat down on the ground cross-legged. She looked into the flame of the torch she held in both hands, feeling the warmth that emanated from it.

'Of course!' Sophia smiled widely. 'She doesn't need a torch with which to see. The darkness is her home – she carries a torch so that others can see!'

Looking out into the darkness beyond, Sophia said, 'Wherever you are, my unsung hero, I thank you.'

Sophia walked proudly with her torch, sensing the presence of the Flame Carrier embodied in the tangible gift she held in her hands. Ahead, she could see very little, but it did not seem to worry her as much.

'I can only see the darkness,' she said to herself. For, at this time, Sophia thought of the darkness as an entity outside of herself, rather than something that consumed her soul, as once it had.

When she eventually stopped walking, Sophia wondered why it was that she had been able to see more when Emil had been with her? And she started to wonder whether she would be able to find her way back to her own room. Yet although she was beginning to feel a little uneasy, she managed to counterbalance this growing fear by saying, 'Trust, Sophia, trust!' over and over again.

Onward she continued, determined to find something – anything – yet the more she walked, the less hopeful she was that she would encounter anything or anyone. She was getting tired and her arms ached from carrying the torch, so she decided to rest for a while.

Sophia knelt down on the ground and began to dig some earth up with her hands. Then, placing the torch handle in the hole, she packed the loose earth around the base of the torch until it held secure. Satisfied with the result, she off-loaded her bag and took out her canteen and sleeping bag. Very soon she was in her sleeping bag, having drunk some water, and was fast asleep beside the burning flame.

When Sophia woke, the flame was still burning brightly. But she didn't feel the warmth she had felt when she was in the Flame Carrier's presence. Indeed, she felt very lonely and isolated suddenly, wishing she could be in the company of trusted friends or even strangers.

'What am I going to do?' she asked aloud, her eyes fixed upon the flame.

Then sitting up, Sophia pulled her knees up to her chest and wrapped her arms tightly around her knees. As she fell into a rocking motion, tears began to roll down her face. She thought of Victor, and how he had befriended her when she was sitting alone by the roadside. How she wished he could be there now.

Sophia found herself thinking about others who had helped and befriended her on her journey: of Bob, who had helped her up the Mountain Road; of the Sibyl, who had held her and comforted her when she was on the edge of the Valley Town; of the wise old man, who had imparted stories of such wisdom; of Emil, who had given so much of himself to Sophia; of the Flame Carrier, who had led her out of the dark tunnels, and whose gift of fire and light Sophia now carried with her. Each of these people, and more, had imparted their individual gifts of unconditional friendship, love and wisdom, without asking for anything in return. Their gifts had manifested themselves in different forms and guises, yet to Sophia they came from the same place – the same Source. Theirs was a higher love, a higher wisdom, whose substance seemed almost divine. Sophia could see all too clearly now how different this was to that which the ego valued in the Outside World.

At that moment, her eyes still transfixed to the flame, Sophia felt the power of words come into her head – much like when she had been alone in the forest and had suddenly written "The Light". She delved into the bottom of her bag and retrieved her notepad and pencil. She had to write the words down before they disappeared from where they came:

"TRANSFORMATION"

How can you value what you have,
When all you see is that which you do not?
How can you value the good in someone,
When you focus instead on the bad?
You complain that others do not value you,
When you are only doing your best.
'Is nothing ever good enough?' you ask,
When perhaps you should ask this of yourself.

You feel deprived of something you cannot name,
As if the loss within you is somehow another's gain.

Yet you must believe there is enough to go around.
The Love of the Universe is a limitless Source.
You just have to know how to tap into it,
And you can if you try.

Sophia had not really listened to the words whilst she was writing them, and although she had written the words with her own hand she had an idea that they had come from somewhere else. They had not come from her head, not even from her heart. It felt as if she had been guided by an unknown force that was separate from her, yet also resided within her. She began to look at what she had written, and to read the words aloud. She could see that the words had formed a message that had specific meaning to her.

As Sophia lifted her head to gaze back into the flame, she felt strangely calmed. She felt different – as though she had undergone a kind of inner transformation; she felt she had tapped into an unknown source of life energy; she felt a powerful sense of connectedness with life itself.

'The beating heart of the Greatest Unknown,' she repeated aloud.

Sophia thought of the time she had spent in the forest; it was the first time she had connected so strongly with the forces of Nature, and it had somehow laid in her the first seeds of hope. The Outside World, for all its faults, was indeed home to the most wonderful sights, sounds and smells, which could arouse the most hardened of senses - it had been this form of life that had kept at least some part of Sophia alive at that time.

Yet here, beyond the Darkened Street, there was nothing like that to touch the senses. Once again, Sophia had had to try to get in touch with something beyond the basic senses she had previously relied upon, and in doing so she had found something deep within the core of her being, that had spoken to her in the darkness.

Looking down at her notepad, Sophia somehow knew that the love and wisdom that sprung forth from the words she had written, came from the same Source as the love and wisdom given to her by those people she now fondly remembered. She closed the notepad and carefully placed it back in her bag. She felt a new found sense of inner strength, which encouraged her to continue her journey.

Sophia got to her feet, rolled up her sleeping bag, put it into her bag and strapped it over her shoulders. For it was time, she decided, to go in search of the Stranger.

Chapter Twenty
In Search Of The Stranger

Sophia crouched down in order to lift the torch up and out of the ground. Placing both hands carefully around the handle of the torch, she was about to dislodge it when she noticed the feint outline of a row of houses. She couldn't believe it. She laughed aloud, bemused by her miraculous change of fortune, and at the wonders of the Greatest Unknown. Yet she knew now that such changes on the outside merely reflected the changes that had occurred inside her.

'That is what Emil would have said,' Sophia told herself, thinking how proud he would have been of her.

Sophia pulled the torch out of the ground and began to walk towards the houses. As she got closer to them, she saw that they were much the same as all the other houses she had seen in the Land of the Shadows; that it was only the people in them that were different. This being the case, there was no telling whether this row of houses was the same as the one where she had seen the badly burnt man. As she passed each closed door, a growing sense of trepidation began to descend upon her. She had not even been able to talk to Emil about her brief meeting with the badly burnt man, and yet now she could be standing on his very doorstep. Deep down Sophia felt guilty about having dismissed this wounded man from her mind. He had barely been able to move, and was dependent purely on the goodwill of people like Emil, yet Sophia had been afraid of befriending him. Only now was she able to admit to such feelings, and she felt ashamed.

She stopped walking for a while and wondered what to do next. She knew why she was there. She was there to meet a Stranger – her Shadow – and it was this that she wanted to run away from. But she also knew that she would only be running away from herself.

'There is a Stranger . . . . .' Sophia began to recite some words she had remembered from the Sibyl's Scroll, ' . . . . You do not know . . . . Yet must . . . . . Befriend the Stranger.'

These words served to propel Sophia further along her path, in the way that only words of wisdom can do. She began to look more closely at the doors of each house she passed; there were no numbers on the doors, or any other distinguishing features. She continued to walk slowly past each door, hoping that some kind of revealing sign would jump out at her, but the row of houses seemed to just go on and on. Sophia then made a decision: she would count up to ten more doors and if there was no obvious sign by then, she would enter the tenth house.

'One . . . . . two . . . . three,' she counted, when suddenly her eyes were drawn towards something shining further along. As she walked towards it, she continued to count each door she passed; 'Four . . . . five . . . . six . .,' without taking her eyes off the sparkling object. She was very near it now and her heart was pumping ferociously. She continued to count; 'Seven . . . . eight . . . . nine . . .' and then she stopped.

'Ten!' Sophia was standing outside the house from where the sparkling light emanated, and she was mesmerised.

The sparkling silver-white light seemed to come from some kind of object attached to the front door of the house. Sophia made her way towards it, and discovered that the sparkling object was in fact a large diamond-shaped clear crystal, more beautiful than anything she had seen in the Outside World. It was positioned where the door handle would usually be. Slowly reaching towards it with her left hand, the torch still held in her right hand, Sophia carefully touched the precious stone. The crystal's edges were finely cut yet silky smooth to the touch.

'It's perfect,' she whispered dreamily, lost in its magic. 'Why would something so beautiful be in hidden in a place like this?'

Suddenly, she felt the searing heat from the torch flame as it burnt her skin. Quickly removing her left hand from the crystal, she used it to steady the torch held in her right hand. The incident had served to jolt her back into the present moment, and to the reason why she was there: Sophia needed to open the door and go in. But where was the door handle? She looked at each corner of the door to see if there was a latch or lock of any kind, but there was nothing attached to the door except the crystal.

'The secret to opening this door must be in the crystal,' Sophia said to herself. So, touching the crystal once again – this time with her right hand – she gently pulled it towards her, then pushed it. Nothing. Then, she tried to turn it, clockwise, and without any effort the door clicked opened. She grinned as she thought of how people can often look for something more complicated in life, when sometimes things were actually much more simple.

Before her there lay a dark corridor, and as she prepared herself to step across the threshold into the unknown, Sophia said, 'Emil, I am being the courageous warrior you said I was. Wherever you are, please be with me.' Then she stepped into the dark corridor.

The atmosphere was heavy, the air musty and stale, as if no life had breathed within the confines of such a space for many years. Sophia decided to leave the front door open. As she walked slowly along the corridor, the air seemed to become even denser so that she found it harder to breathe; the flame she was carrying dwindled to almost half its original size. She saw a door to her right. Trying to remain as calm as possible, Sophia tried to steady her breathing so as not to use up too much oxygen. For she knew that she shared this precious oxygen with the torch flame, and that as long as the flame still burnt she would still breathe.

Tentatively, Sophia knocked on the door. There was no reply. She knocked again, this time louder, and the reply came.

'Hello! Who's there?' It was a man's voice. He sounded startled, though not defensive or unfriendly.

Sophia felt encouraged. 'My name is Sophia,' she said nervously, and then found herself adding, 'I've come to see you . . . well-er I'm not exactly sure why I'm here. You see, I was told something about meeting a Stranger . . . . well, that was what I understood from the Sibyl's Scroll. And . . . . well . . . I-'

'Come in! Come in!' the man's voice cried, with great enthusiasm.

The door suddenly opened. Sophia expected to see the man standing there, but this was not the case. For as far as she could make out, the man was sitting up in bed on the opposite side of the room. As she stepped into the room, the torch flame dimmed further and her breathing became more laboured.

'Come over here, Sophia,' the man beckoned. 'I can't see you there.'

Sophia began to walk towards him, her movements becoming increasingly difficult, as if she was walking through sludge. Each forward movement took a magnitude of effort and the torch in her right hand weighed down heavily. She moved her weaker left arm towards the torch handle with all of her might, managing to grasp the handle just as her right arm was about to give way. Her right and left hands now held the heavy torch so that it rested in a more centralised position, just in front of her chest.

Sophia stood motionless a few feet away from the bed. Yet she was unable to see the man because the torch flame blocked her view of him, and she felt powerless to move any further forward. Whatever the nature of the force opposing her movement, Sophia could no longer overcome it. It was equal to her, and as a result left her in a state of temporary inertia.

The man in bed responded to her struggle. 'Would you like to sit down?' he asked politely. 'There is a chair here – just next to the bed – you're standing right by it. You'll see it if you lower the torch.'

He had quite a youthful sounding voice, Sophia thought, and one that seemed to put her more at ease. She managed to lower the torch a little, enough to see the chair on her left. Then, she manoeuvred herself to a sitting position, the largely downward movement being easier to achieve. Sophia let out a sigh of relief, her knees now able to take the main weight of the torch.

'That's better,' said Sophia, almost out of breath. 'Thank you, ... I didn't know . . . . . how long I was . . . . . going to last out.'

'Well, I'm glad your legs didn't give way. We don't want the two of us to be immobile!' He sounded surprisingly cheerful.

'Yes, I can see that you're laid up in bed.'

'It's so good to have some company – at last!'

Sophia looked over at him. She could just about make out some of his features; he looked relatively young, she thought, perhaps in his thirties; he had long dark straggly hair; his face looked pale and drawn, but when he smiled it seemed to light up like a child. Sophia was beginning to wonder why she had dreaded this meeting so much.

'It's funny really,' she said, having recovered some of her breath, 'I thought that something awful might happen coming here – although I didn't know what exactly. Just that I automatically expected doom and gloom, something more macabre or more distressing. Like this badly burnt man I saw with Emil. I felt terrible for him, all alone in that state.'

'Yes, it can get terribly lonely here,' replied the man in bed. 'I wouldn't wish it on anyone. In many ways the loneliness is more difficult than anything.'

'Oh, I'm sorry,' Sophia suddenly felt embarrassed. 'That was really insensitive of me. I didn't mean to imply that things are better for you. I couldn't imagine being here on my own. But don't you see anyone else in the street?'

'From time to time I have visitors. I know Emil. He does what he can – he's a good man, but he can only give so much. The last time I saw him, he looked very tired. I wonder how long he will be able to continue doing his work.' He looked genuinely sad as he thought about Emil. But then he suddenly continued; 'As for my visiting others, well I'm afraid that that is a thing of the past. I am too weak and disabled to move now.'

He turned his head to face Sophia and smiled. 'That is why it is so nice to see you.'

Sophia could not help but feel flattered by this rather charming man. But she was also finding it increasing difficult to breathe, and her eyes were becoming heavy.

'I'm finding it difficult . . . . . to breathe,' she explained. 'I'm sorry . . . . but I don't think . . . . I can stay for too much longer.'

Sophia wanted to ask some questions however before she took her leave: 'Did you know . . . . I was coming to visit? Did . . . . Emil say anything . . . . . about me?'

'Oh, I am sorry about the poor air in here,' he responded politely. 'Alas it hasn't done me much good either over the years. I have watched the gradual deterioration in me.'

He paused for a few moments, as if wondering how to phrase his next response. 'In answer to your first question, Sophia: No, I did not know that you would arrive when you did. You see, I have always been waiting for you.'

Sophia felt a force compressing against her chest, so profoundly saddened was she on hearing his words. She felt a powerful throbbing in her throat, as though something was trying to force its way up through her neck. She clutched her throat with her left hand, whilst her companion continued with his heartfelt words:

'My time was running out, I knew that. And then I started to see more of Emil and wondered why. I would ask him when my "star" visitor would arrive, but he never answered me directly. All he would say was, "when the time is right, you will meet her." Of course I kept pleading with him to tell me, but he would not. He said he did not know. Yet I felt that the time was coming when you would finally arrive – particularly as I haven't seen much of Emil lately. It was as if he was withdrawing to make way for someone else. I do hope he is all right though . . .' his voice trailed off as he thought of their mutual friend and mentor.

Sophia, in her silence, felt overwhelmed by what she had heard from her new acquaintance. Was he really talking about her? She didn't recognise herself in his words – surely he was talking about someone else?

'Are you the Stranger?' she suddenly asked him.

'Do you mean the one in the "Incubation Period" verses, in the Sibyl's Scroll?'

'Yes! Do you know it?' Sophia was astonished.

'I was given it by the Sibyl. It's here somewhere,' he motioned to look for it, but instead stopped and turned to look at Sophia, whose head was hung downwards.

'Sophia,' he called to her. She slowly lifted her head to look at him, and then he continued; 'I can see that you have little energy left and that you need to go back outside into the street in order to breathe properly. But come back and see me, won't you?'

Sophia saw the longing in his blue eyes and managed to smile at him. Then, using her remaining reserves of energy, she lifted herself out of the chair and leant over towards the bed. She placed her left hand on the man's right shoulder in order to reassure him of her return, but suddenly let out a loud shriek. For nothing could have prepared her for what she saw under the glow of the flame's light: The man had the most horrific injuries imaginable; his right arm and both of his legs, from above the knee, were missing. What remained were pieces of bloody flesh and protruding bone, as though his limbs had been torn from his body with the ferocity of a lion devouring its prey.

Sophia's automatic response was to withdraw her hand. She stepped backwards, unable to look at the man's wounds any longer. She felt sick. She felt she had to get out; she could do nothing for him; his injuries were beyond repair; she had come too late. Sophia could hardly breathe now, and the flame had withered to little more than the light of a candle. She continued to step further and further backwards, towards the open door. The force that had opposed her earlier forward motion now seemed to aid her, for she could feel her momentum increase. As she approached the doorway the flame began to rekindle itself and her breathing became easier. Sophia wanted to just turn and run out into the street, yet she could not bring herself to just leave this poor dying man without saying something. He, who had remained silent, whilst all he could do was watch his visitor's horrified reaction.

Sophia hesitated at the open doorway of his room. When she finally spoke, what she said surprised even her: 'I'm s-sorry . . . . I will return . . . I-I p-promise.'

She turned to leave but suddenly checked herself. 'What is your name?' she called back into the room.

'Call me the Inertia Man,' came the sad reply.

Sophia quickly walked back along the corridor and out through the front door into the Darkened Street. The flame then burst back into life.

She ran and ran along the street feeling an immense sense of relief. Her body moved unhindered through the still air, no opposing force slowing her down. She felt in control; she was intact and was determined to remain that way. She would run and run until she could run no more, further and further away from the Inertia Man, her opposite. Away from his dying flesh and decaying body; from the lifeless room where nothing grew or prospered; away from inertia itself. As long as she kept moving, Sophia felt she would be conquering this inertia. For she was determined she would not be like him.

Sophia must have run for at least a mile without taking any notice of her surroundings. Soon she began to tire. Her feet dragged along the earth, kicking dust up into the air, until she started to choke. Her legs became heavier and she could feel them about to give way. Still she pushed her body forward, until her body finally refused and sent her sprawling to the ground. As she fell, the torch flew out of her hand.

Sophia spat the dirt from her mouth, whilst trying to gasp for air at the same time. She managed to push herself up on to her knees, feeling every ache and pain in her limbs. Then, somehow, she let out an almighty scream, 'NOoooooo . . . . .'

She was angry, very angry. She struggled to her feet and staggered over towards the torch, which was lying several feet away. But she did not pick up the torch, whose never-ending flame still burned. Instead, she saw some rocks and stones lying alongside it, and went straight over to them. Falling to her knees she placed both hands on one of the rocks and lifted it above her head. Then, with all the force of her anger, Sophia brought the rock crashing down to the ground, her hands gripping it as tightly as she could. She repeated the action again and again, shouting at times to release the frustrations from deep within her soul. And as she continued to beat the ground with her rock, a clear image suddenly came into her mind: It was the repetitive motion of axe against wood – it was the image of the Wood Chopper. Different tools perhaps, different materials, but underlying them was the same force of anger. Suddenly Sophia could see a clear aspect of herself in Jan, the Wood Chopper. She had seen through another veil, and it had revealed another painful truth.

Sophia let go of the rock. Her hands were blistered and sore, and sweat trickled down the sides of her face. Her heart pounded from over-exertion as she gasped for more air. She removed her bag from her shoulders, and tugged at it in desperation to get to the canteen of water. She felt such bliss as the water ran down her parched dusty throat. Now all she wanted to do was to sleep. But not by the roadside, lying on the hard stony ground, with a rock for a pillow. No, Sophia decided that she wanted a half-decent place in which to rest.

As tired as she was, Sophia felt now more than ever before that it was time for her to look for something better; to believe that she could have something better. It was time for her to consciously partake in the process of transformation; to listen to the words that she herself had written. She now remembered some of them, and spoke them out loud with some authority:

'You must believe there is enough to go around,
The Love of the Universe is a limitless Source.'

Picking up the heavy load of her body, her bag and her torch, Sophia went off in search of a place to rest.

As she began to walk she noticed that rocks and stones were lining the side of the street, rather than houses. Somewhere along the way, whilst Sophia had been running, the row of houses had ended and had been replaced by open space. Sophia's eyes felt sore from the dust and dirt, and from straining to see in the dark. She could not tell how far back from the road the open space extended, but she also did not want to venture away from the road itself.

'Surely it must lead somewhere,' she told herself, 'otherwise why would it be here?'

By now though, she knew she couldn't walk much further. All that seemed left for her to do, was to cry out for help in the hope that someone might hear her:

'HEEEEELP! . . . . . CAN ANYONE HEAR ME? . . . . . I NEED SOME HELP!'

She stopped and listened. It was so quiet. Then she noticed that the stones lining the right side of the road had stopped. Taking a closer look, she saw that more stones continued a little further up the road; that there was in fact a gap of about six or seven feet wide.

"Perhaps this is a side road," Sophia thought to herself, more in hope than anything else. But without a second thought, she had turned to her right and walked through the gap.

She carried on walking, as if guided by an unknown force, and a few moments later she saw something. At first she couldn't tell exactly what it was – just a large square structure of some kind – but as she got closer to it, she saw that the obscure shape was something rather familiar to her. Sophia had arrived outside an old barn.

'Thank you, God,' she whispered, as tears began to well in her tired eyes.

Wasting no time, she went over to the barn's double doors and tugged at the left door. It was stiff and creaked loudly, but it opened. Sophia stepped inside. Above her, she could make out several wooden beams, whilst on the ground there were all sorts of objects and boxes strewn across the floor. She walked a few steps forward until she was approximately halfway across the floor of the barn. Straight ahead of her, on the back wall of the barn, there was a window. Sophia walked towards it and then noticed that to the left of the window, in the corner of the barn, there lay a pile of straw. She could not believe it; this time, her cry for help had been answered. Sophia wanted to just collapse in a heap on the straw, but she knew that it would not be a good idea to keep the torch in the barn with her. Nor did she want to put its flame out. Instead she decided to place the torch somewhere outside the barn.

Once back outside the barn, Sophia quickly looked around her to see if there was an obvious place to put the torch. And there was! Near the entrance of the barn, to her right, Sophia saw a metal stand. It looked a bit like the metal holder she had seen holding a torch outside the badly burnt man's house. That one had been attached to the brick wall, whereas this one was fixed into the ground. Smiling to herself, Sophia placed the handle of her torch in the metal loop, and said 'thank you' once again.

Then she re-entered the barn, closing the creaky door behind her, and almost stumbled over the various objects in her path before she finally made it to the straw bed. Sophia dropped her bag on to the floor and duly collapsed in exhaustion, whereupon she slept for a long time.

Chapter Twenty One
The First Crescent

When Sophia awoke she saw the most amazing vision. At first she thought it was an illusion, or that she was still asleep and dreaming, such was its magnificence. She blinked several times and shook her head vigorously, but still the same vision lay before her: A few feet away, just by the window, there stood a round wooden table upon which lay a minor feast of food and drink. Although she could not see it clearly, Sophia was amazed that she could see as much as she did. For it seemed that there was indeed some form of light coming through the window, and it bathed the table in a soft silvery-purple glow.

Sophia was overcome by the magical sight. 'It's so beautiful,' she whispered to herself, not wanting to disturb the silent scene.

Slowly, she got to her feet and almost tiptoed over to the table. Her eyes shone with the delight of a child at what she saw placed upon it. There was a wonderful array of dishes and carafes; a variety of breads and cheeses, fruits and olives, dips and spreads, salads and sauces, water and wine. A wooden chair had been placed by the table and seemed to be waiting for Sophia to sit down. She obliged, but something seemed to stop her from delving into the culinary delights. Somehow, it just seemed too good to be true, or perhaps it was that Sophia believed it was too good to be true - for her. For she had been used to thinking that good things usually happened to other people, not to her.

Here she was, it would seem, facing another mirror; another truth about herself reflected in the abundance of good things placed on the table before her: that she could have good things in her life if only she allowed herself to. For the feast at her table was not meant for someone else, it was meant for Sophia – for who else was there?

'Is all this really for me?' Sophia asked, somewhat sadly. She was suddenly all too aware of how much she had deprived herself throughout her life, and it was indeed a painful realisation.

She could feel a solid lump form in her stomach, which started to cause her some discomfort. Placing both hands over her stomach, she grimaced in pain. It reminded her of the time when the Sibyl had asked her what she was finding difficult to "digest". Sophia asked this of herself now. She thought for a little while, and then answered herself out loud:

'My difficulty is accepting that good things can be mine. Like all this wonderful food!'

She was so hungry, yet it seemed that even her body could not accept the food that was being offered. Sophia did not want to be like this anymore. She remembered the words she had so very recently written down, and as she spoke them aloud she was strangely comforted by their sound and meaning:

'You must believe there is enough to go around,
The Love of the Universe is a limitless Source,

You just have to know how to tap into it,

And you can if you try.'

Sophia repeated these lines to herself several more times, and as the tears rolled down her face, she knew that for the first time in her life these tears were for her.

And when the tears had stopped, Sophia paused and dried her eyes. Then she poured the liquid from one of the carafes into a beaker, not knowing what she was pouring. Nevertheless, she took a big gulp without thinking about it. It was red wine, and it had the most wonderfully warming effect as she felt it flow down slowly into her body. Relaxing back in her chair, Sophia lifted her beaker of wine and said, 'Thank you, whoever brought this to me.'

She proceeded to taste something from each of the dishes. And when she had done this, she chose the ones she liked best and ate some more, until she could eat no more. Then she placed her hands on her stomach, sat back and laughed with joy.

'I'm so full,' she announced with pride. 'That was absolutely wonderful!'

Filled with renewed vigour, Sophia decided to move closer to the window and see what was outside; she wanted to know where the light was coming from. Pressing her head against the dirty window, her eyes were immediately drawn upwards whereupon she located the source of the silvery-purple glow.

'Wow, I don't believe it! How can this be?' she said in soft amazement.

For up above there was a scintillatingly bright crescent moon, as close in proximity as was the fully luminous moon that she had looked upon with Emil. Sophia decided she must go outside to see it more clearly. So, stumbling across the barn and its many scattered objects, she soon reached the front door and pushed it open. Bursting out of the barn, she caught a quick glimpse of the torch flame as she passed it. Then she stopped and looked up at the moonlit sky.

And it was under this crescent moon that Sophia felt transformed. Before she knew it, she was dancing around and around like a whirling dervish, her arms open and free, her head thrown back with joyous abandon. It was the closest she had ever felt to ecstasy, her heart beating in tune with the Universe, with that of the Greatest Unknown.

Once back in the barn Sophia rested on her bed of straw. She still couldn't quite believe her amazing change of fortune, but she was determined to revel in it for a while longer. She felt light-headed from the wine - or perhaps it was from the dancing – but there was no doubt that her spirits were higher than they had been for a long time. As she lay there, she wondered who might have slept there before her, and what had happened to them after they had left the security of the barn?

Eventually though, Sophia's thoughts came back to her own fate, and what lay ahead of her. For she knew in her heart that she was going to have to face something that filled her with dread, something that in her state of ecstasy she had managed to cut herself off from. But this time, unlike the other times on her journey, it was not the unknown she feared: it was someone she had come to know as the Inertia Man.

This unfortunate, but charming, man who lay in a dark room rotting away, said he had been waiting for Sophia. But who or what was he to Sophia? Was she meant to go back and take care of him?

'No, I can't! I can't,' she suddenly said aloud. 'Why should I? I don't want to! No, no, no . . .'

Sophia was starting to feel panicked at what she thought was being asked of her. Closing her eyes, she took some very deep breaths and managed to calm herself a little.

'Of course, it doesn't stop me from feeling a little guilty,' she told herself, now speaking in a more measured tone. 'I mean, all I have done is run as far away from him as possible. And it's not as if he even asked me for anything . . .' her voice trailed off as she realised what she had just said.

Reaching over for her bag, Sophia took out her notepad and pencil, and began to write something down. This had helped her in the past, when she was stuck or muddled in her thoughts and emotions, so perhaps it would help her now. In big capital letters, she wrote the word "INERTIA" on the top of a blank page, for that was the state she also felt in now, albeit for very different reasons to the poor Inertia Man. She wrote everything that came into her head, and when she had finished she did not even read it. Instead she closed the notepad and put it straight back into her bag. Then she lay back down again and closed her eyes.

'ARISE SOPHIA,' the booming voice crashed through the silence.

Sophia almost jumped out of her skin. Indeed she sat bolt upright, her heart pounding mercilessly as she stared in front of her.

'SIBYL!' she cried, with the excitement of a child being visited by their favourite person in the whole world.

Quickly getting to her feet, she ran to the Sibyl who was standing beyond the table by the window, and with open abandon ran straight into her arms. The Sibyl laughed fondly in response, seemingly delighted by such an uninhibited display of love.

Alas, the last time she had been alone with Sophia was when she had led her down the Twenty One Steps and into the tunnels. That had been one of the hardest things the Sibyl had ever done - to leave Sophia alone in such a dark lonely place knowing how frightened she would be. But the Sibyl had also known that this separation would ultimately be for Sophia's highest good. For it would lead her further along her journey, her individual path towards Wholeness and Truth; to become her true and complete Self, and therefore achieve ultimate freedom and enlightenment. The path that would enable Sophia to fulfil her deepest and innermost needs, her potential, her destiny. Of course, Sophia herself would not have understood this at that time. How could she? Instead, the Sibyl had to trust that Sophia would make it through to the next stage of her journey; that she would find the answers for herself; that she would eventually come to understand the reasons for her abandonment.

And now, in this warm embrace, the Sibyl's trust was being realised. 'My dear Sophia, how lovely it is to see you again.'

She stroked Sophia's hair as if carefully guarding a precious object. And in that moment, the very essence of love in its purest form bonded Sophia and the Sibyl together.

The sincerity of their embrace was very different from the embrace that had taken place on the hillside outside the Valley Town, where they had first met. Then, the Sibyl had encountered a very troubled, distressed and frightened young woman in Sophia, who although had been very courageous in her endeavours, was also looking to the Sibyl as someone to depend upon. At that stage of her journey, Sophia had come to recognise and acknowledge her own vulnerability, her concealed wounds, but she was still quite a way off from consciously accepting this as an important part of her self.

The Sibyl, in her wisdom, knew this internal, emotional, reflective, and nurturing side of one's self to be Feminine in nature - that it was one half of the duality of Masculine and Feminine energies that existed within everyone. Both therefore were equally vital aspects of existence, but it was the feminine aspect that had been repressed and denigrated for far too long. Alas, the Sibyl had seen evidence of this in so many people, not just Sophia: the cutting off of one's Feminine aspect. It had devastated the Sibyl in many ways. Worse still for her, was the myriad of people in the Outside World who spent their entire lives hidden behind their own Veils of Illusion; being slaves to external masters of the material world, never really getting to know their internal natures. This, the Sibyl knew, remained hidden to many people, to many souls, and as a result so too did the vast wonders of the Greatest Unknown. She had come to accept this sad state of affairs, frustrating as it was for one so enlightened. But she knew that she had to be patient and be content in guiding those who had already taken a glimpse into the landscape of their own internal selves and natures, in order to help them retrieve the lost treasures of their souls.

Sophia loosened her grip on the Sibyl and gently pulled away from their embrace. She felt energised from the embrace, from the Sibyl's energy, and could feel herself begin to blush a little.

'You look different, Sophia,' the Sibyl said, looking directly at her and smiling. 'More . . . . . yourself! Your true Self!'

'Really?' Sophia answered, pleasantly surprised. Then without waiting for a response, she said, 'Thank you.'

Sophia wanted to share so many things with the Sibyl now that she was here, but didn't know where to start. 'How did you find me?' she suddenly asked. 'How did you know I was here?'

The Sibyl was still smiling warmly at Sophia, having not averted her gaze for one moment. 'It was easy really,' she explained. 'For one thing, you called for help – quite a piercing cry too! And then of course you left your torch burning outside.'

'Yes, but how did you know it was mine?' Sophia persisted.

'Because everyone has their own unique flame – similar yes, but different. You see, the torch flame merely reflects the light of the inner soul.'

The Sibyl could see that the young woman standing before her looked suitably intrigued by what she had just heard, so she decided to continue:

'My dear Sophia, it is of no use to try to understand such things with the limited human mind - the ego; that only works in the Outside World. Here, we only deal with the internal world of humans – not the ego.' Then she held out her hand towards Sophia, saying, 'Come, let us go out into the moonlight.'

Sophia took her hand and followed her outside. In the relative brightness, she could see with more clarity the full majesty of the Sibyl. Once again she was wearing a flowing robe of finely crafted material, but this time the colour was that of warm orange. It seemed to Sophia that no matter how bleak the surroundings were, the Sibyl always managed to shine like a star – a bright guiding star. And now she guided Sophia further, beyond the barn, and eventually to some large stone slabs.

It had only taken them a few minutes to get there, and the closer they had got to the stones, the more awe-struck Sophia had become. The stone slabs varied in size but all were much bigger than the size of a person; some lay on their sides and others stood upright as they towered above Sophia and the Sibyl.

'Wow, this reminds me of Stonehenge!' Sophia said, letting go of the Sibyl's hand and starting to walk freely amongst the stones. 'What are they? Please tell me about them?'

'Perhaps I will tell you about them at another time,' the Sibyl smiled, 'but now is not the right time, Sophia.' She ushered the disappointed Sophia over to her. 'Come and sit beside me. We have much to talk about, and it is my duty to help you journey back to the Outside World.'

Quickly brought back to the central purpose of her journey, Sophia sometimes longed for diversions that brought with them joy and inspiration; and as she sat next to her wise mentor, Sophia told her of such wishes.

The Sibyl paused for a moment before offering a response. 'Joy and inspiration,' she eventually said. 'Yes, these are in themselves very healing energies. They bring life to the soul, they lift the heart, and they regenerate the body. Just as they did for you, Sophia, when you were dancing in the moonlight.'

'You saw me dancing?!'

'Yes, of course. And it was wonderful – your spirit was free!'

Sophia smiled as she realised that she quite liked the idea of someone with such integrity and wisdom, witnessing her actions without her knowing. For it felt like she had a guardian angel watching over her somehow, no doubt all part of the integral complex web of the Greatest Unknown.

The Sibyl, now a little more serious, began to address Sophia once more:

'You will have many opportunities for joy and love and inspiration, ahead of you Sophia. But it is also important to know when an activity is more a diversion, whose main purpose is to lead you to stray from your true path. For then, it is just a means of avoiding a difficult task or of facing a difficult truth.'

Sophia was looking down at the ground, her face no longer smiling. She said quietly, 'You mean my avoidance of the Inertia Man, don't you?'

'The Inertia Man?' the Sibyl sounded surprised.

'Yes, the man with no legs and no right arm – it was horrible.' Sophia still found it difficult to even think about him.

'The Inertia Man,' the Sibyl repeated. 'Yes, I can see why you would call him that.'

'He told me to call him that as I was leaving – it wasn't my idea!'

Suddenly the atmosphere had changed. There was a heaviness in the air that had replaced the recent talk of joy and inspiration. The two women sat in silence for a long while, both knowing that they had encountered something that Sophia needed to understand and resolve. Sophia's automatic and rather entrenched response to such a feat was to remain defiant in stance and behaviour, which only brought her back to the familiar but futile position of the isolated warrior. Sophia caught herself in the act this time, and decided to break out of this particular trap.

'I'm scared, Sibyl,' she found herself saying, her limbs starting to tremble in harmony with her words.

'That is why I am here,' the Sibyl said in a comforting voice. She put her arm around Sophia and went on; 'Go now to rest, and when you wake, eat. Then we will talk some more.'

They walked slowly back to the barn. Then, as the Sibyl was about to bid her farewell, Sophia suddenly stopped her.

'Wait! I have something I'd like you to read. I wrote it about my meeting with the Inertia Man. I haven't even read it myself yet . . . I just wrote and wrote without stopping . . . I seem to be doing that more these days. Anyway, I'll go and get it.'

A few moments later, Sophia emerged from the barn with a couple of pages she had ripped from her notepad, and handed them over to the Sibyl.

'Thank you,' replied the all-knowing Sibyl. Then she leant forward and kissed Sophia on the forehead, before disappearing gracefully into the distance.

Part Three
Transformation

Chapter Twenty Two
Amongst The Stones

After the sleeping and eating was done, Sophia decided to go back to the Stones. She thought of how things seemed much better now that the Sibyl was here. And there was certainly a spring in her step as she made her way to the Stones.

Ancient monuments had always fascinated Sophia, be they temples of worship adorned with magnificent statues, or the perfect geometry reflected in awe-inspiring structures such as the pyramids of Giza. Such monuments remained a source of mystery and intrigue to many in the Outside World, yet Sophia had often thought that the motivation and desire of the ancients to construct these wonders of the world, must have come from a deep sense of love and honour for the Divine. And in the relatively short space of time she had spent in the Land of the Shadows, Sophia had come to believe in something much greater and more enduring than the human-ego, whose main motivations were almost always those of personal gain.

As Sophia walked amongst the Stones, she somehow knew that the secrets hidden within them would only be revealed when the time was right; when mankind was sufficiently evolved and thus capable of receiving such knowledge. She touched one of the upright Stones which towered above her, letting the palm of her hand feel its awesome strength as it gently rested there. She grinned to herself as she thought of how modern-day man often viewed himself as more advanced than the ancients, when it seemed to Sophia that in many ways it was modern-day man who had to advance and catch up with the ancient ancestors! She thought of the parallels with her own journey; that she had only learnt truths about herself when she had been mentally and emotionally able to take them in. And when the Veils (which had hidden the truth from her eyes) had eventually lifted, they had indeed revealed many truths, some painful. Yet these were not punishments – Sophia could see that now – they were illuminations of part of the self: What she now knew to be the Shadow self.

She found a Stone on which to sit. She felt a tremendous sense of belonging, of acceptance, something she had not found in the Outside World. It was as if the energies of the ancients who had wondered here long ago still resonated, and that Sophia somehow felt in tune with them. Then she looked up at the crescent moon, which although reflected a dimmer light than that of the full moon, seemed sharper in its purpose. It seemed to give those who bathed in its light, a sharper sense of awareness and insight into hidden natures and mysteries. Most of all though, it brought into sharp focus that which Sophia had run away from; that which she had always run away from: her most vulnerable side – which in its nature was directly opposite to the hardness and strength of the fortifications it had remained hidden behind.

'Just like the Story of the Tower,' Sophia spoke softly and sadly. 'Just like the child under the sea, I have hidden away the truest part of me.'

Slowly getting up from her Stone, she walked a few steps into the open space before her. She also felt enclosed by the Stones, so that as she wandered within the open space, Sophia could almost feel a protective force of sorts – as though the ancient ancestors were keeping watch over her. She began to walk in a circle, looking almost trance-like, but she was far from that. Her mind was clear, her spirit light, and her heart full. Then quite suddenly, closing her eyes, Sophia fell to her knees. She laid her left hand upon her pained chest, and wept.

'I have left you alone and neglected, as no one should ever be,' Sophia cried. 'How are you to forgive me? How am I to forgive myself?' She put her head in her hands and let the tears flow.

A familiar voice sounded from beyond one of the Stones encircling Sophia: 'My dear, how sorrowful you are! Yet how brave you are indeed.'

It was the voice of her beloved Sibyl. And with these words Sophia allowed deep sobs from the depths of her soul to surface.

As the Sibyl looked upon the kneeling Sophia, she felt she was witnessing a scene reminiscent of the young man who had performed on stage in "THE MIRRORS" play. The intensity of the emotion was the same, but this setting was Sophia's centre stage. And it was for this reason that the Sibyl chose not to step forward into the arena. In her hand she held the pages that Sophia had given to her when they had last met. Indeed, the Sibyl had been very moved by the words she had read, and now she could see Sophia in front of her displaying emotions that closely resonated with the words written on the pages.

The Sibyl waited until Sophia had stopped crying, for she knew that the time was right for Sophia to hear these words, no matter how difficult this might be. The Sibyl began to speak in soft clear tones

so that Sophia would be able to hear the words that she herself had
written when she had first arrived at the barn:

'INERTIA'

'I could cry for you,
You with the rotten flesh
Limbs torn from their rightful place,
You who I can barely look at.

'I could shout at them
For not being better healers,
For waiting 'til the gangrene set in
Before tending to your wounds.

'Yet how is it that your spirit is not broken?
And you can sit so still with yourself?
And it is I, who am all a quiver,
As if sudden menace fills the air.

'What is this menace that runs through my veins?
As sure as the oxygen that fuels its flow,
Brings life to the limbs I have
But whose lifeless flesh makes for such a heavy load.

'You look into my eyes
And I look down,
For I fear that you may see inside
The wounds that I conceal.

'And for a while I am filled with shame
But also envy, strange as it may seem,

For you have no choice but to show
Your weakness and vulnerability,
Abhor these at your peril.

'Yet how abhorrent I find the fragile fragments
That reside in the deep vaults of my insides,
For if fully displayed, they would be but open wounds
For vultures to pick at,
And for others to scorn.

'So my choice instead is to scorn and reject
Such fragments so that others won't see,
And I am left fragmented on the inside
Whilst leaving my outsides intact.

'Lifeless flesh encasing a lifeless spirit,
Until I find the spirit to become whole.'

Neither Sophia nor the Sibyl knew what to say following these words, Sophia's words. Such raw honesty had stripped away any remaining layers of protection or pretence, leaving a naked being at its core. The Sibyl was now looking upon that naked being. Yet in that very core there existed the greatest thing in life: the spirit of Love. Without this, nothing could grow or flourish. This was never so clearly illustrated as in the last two lines of Sophia's heartfelt poem.

The Sibyl found herself repeating these lines out loud, as she now slowly glided into the arena and towards the still kneeling Sophia:

'Lifeless flesh encasing a lifeless spirit,
Until I find the spirit to become whole.'

Sophia lifted her tear-stained face to look up at the approaching Sibyl. How honoured she felt to be the sole focus of attention of such a magnificent being. But more than that, she could see how much the Sibyl was moved by her words; in all honesty Sophia had surprised herself by what she had written. It had come from somewhere deep within her soul, a place she did not normally have access to.

'And have you found your spirit, Sophia?' the Sibyl asked softly.

Then, in a single flowing movement, the Sibyl had sat down on the ground before Sophia. Sophia found it hard to look directly at the Sibyl when she was so close in proximity; she felt like a nervous child. It came as a great relief to Sophia, therefore, that the hidden aspects of herself were no longer hidden. This after all was the Land of the Shadows, and here was its Sibyl. It was only Sophia who had to face and then accept herself.

'The spirit to become whole,' Sophia repeated the last of her poem, without answering the Sibyl's question.

Sophia finally looked at the Sibyl, and then looked into her eyes: The eyes that could see so much. Suddenly it was like a thunderbolt striking at her heart. The face Sophia now looked upon seemed to glow with a light unseen in the Outside World. The Sibyl's eyes were a violet colour, but not a colour that one merely looked "at" – rather a colour that one looked "into", as if one could dive into an ocean of colour and dissolve into its very essence. And by doing so, one became part of it, and it became One. Sophia was hypnotised. She had lost track of herself as a separate physical entity to the world around her. Instead she was lost in the ecstasy of fusion of the spirit and the soul.

'I want to stay here forever,' she whispered to the Sibyl. 'I have never felt so complete as at this moment.'

'Then you have found your spirit?'

'Yes, I suppose I have.'

But suddenly Sophia felt a deep sense of sadness in her heart. How easy all this seemed to trigger such intense emotional states within her; from joyful ecstasy to heartfelt sadness in a matter of moments.

Yet these human emotions were a part of Sophia, and as such they needed to be accepted and embraced. They were an aspect of the Feminine Energy and just like most other aspects of the Feminine, like the ability to be open and receptive, they had been largely devalued in the Outside World. Sophia had learnt about such things from Emil and the Sibyl, but now she understood them more deeply. She understood that only when one had the ability to be receptive, could one allow the self to be open to the limitless source of Universal Love. Sophia had tapped into this spiritual energy; an energy that could flow like a river through the internal channels of the body, clearing away over the course of time the obstacles in its path. Sophia thought of each rock of emotional-hardness slowly being eroded, however long it took, until more love and light entered in.

For in the end, as the Sibyl knew only too well, the Love of the Universe was an energy whose power could not be held back. It existed at the core of every being, no matter how hidden or buried, but unlike the more transient and conditional nature of human love this Higher Love could not be destroyed. This knowledge and understanding had been with the Sibyl for many millennia, and it had kept her believing in her own mission:

To help those who entered the Land of the Shadows to meet and reclaim their lost selves; the lost parts of their souls, their lost powers, their lost light - and when this was done, to guide them back to the Outside World.

For as long as people, like Sophia, entered the Land of the Shadows, the Sibyl would be there. The Sibyl described each person's time there as an "Incubation Period", at the end of which each person would have been personally transformed in some way. It didn't matter how great or how small the degree of transformation was - the Land of the Shadows was not after all a place of competition. In the end, no matter how many lifetimes it took, the Sibyl knew that everyone would one day reach their Centre Point: the place where all hidden and unknown aspects of the self finally became known, and ultimate wholeness manifested as Unity. This Unity - this Oneness - was the greatest gift of all. But it was only worthy to those who knew its worth.

Sophia shook her head and looked up, feeling somewhat dizzy. She decided to get up and stretch her legs, having been in a kneeling position for some time. Once again she walked amongst the Stones, immersed in deep thought. Sometimes she stopped and leant against one of the Stones, as if this somehow helped her to process what was going on in her mind. Then, she carried on with her wandering, not once looking over at the Sibyl. Eventually Sophia stopped at a Stone that was lying on its side, and sat down. Her mood of sadness seemed to have lifted somewhat, and she was now ready to face the Sibyl, who was only a few feet away.

'You know, Sibyl, it was my spirit that found me,' she said, looking directly at the Sibyl. 'I think it has been trying to get my attention for a long time, but I was too frightened to listen to it. Too frightened of its powerful energy and where it would lead me. You see, I just wanted to fit in.' Sophia lowered her eyes to the ground before continuing; 'Then when I was in that lake – not long after I got out of the Cage – I fell asleep and had this profound dream. Even now, I wonder whether it was actually a dream because it was so vivid and real. Anyway, whatever it was, it served to give me a powerful message . . . . . . that my child spirit under the water could not remain quiet anymore . . . . . . that I would drown if I continued to ignore it . . . . . . and the rest is history, as they say.'

Sophia let out a deep sigh, whilst the Sibyl remained attentive and silent.

'I couldn't believe it when the "Inertia Man" had one of your Scrolls too!' Sophia chuckled. Then, looking over at the Sibyl again, she calmly said, 'So if he is the Stranger I need to befriend, why does he have the same message?'

'Because,' answered the Sibyl, as she lifted herself to her feet, 'you are also the Stranger that he needs to befriend.'

Sophia was stunned into silence. Every time she felt she had finally understood something, she almost instantly was met with something else that she had never considered. For she had never thought of herself in such terms; now suddenly she found herself wondering what the "Inertia Man" thought of her.

'Have you seen him?' Sophia asked the approaching Sibyl.

'Yes, I saw Edgar recently.'

'Edgar?!' exclaimed Sophia. 'That's his name?' Then more softly; 'I feel bad not finding out his real name, but the truth is that I didn't want to befriend him . . . . . I wonder though what he must think of me, rejecting him like that?'

'That is something you must ask him yourself, Sophia.'

'Yes, I know . . . . I must go to him.'

The Sibyl now held out the pages containing the "Inertia" verses towards Sophia. 'Thank you, Sophia, for sharing this gift with me. You do indeed have a special romance with the written word – as our friend Victor once said.'

Sophia smiled at the Sibyl, as she took the pages back into her possession and carefully folded them. Together they walked back towards the barn.

'By the way,' the Sibyl suddenly said, 'Edgar also writes.'

'Really?!' Sophia cried out in amazement. 'Wow, that's incredible!' She paused briefly, then added; 'Edgar . . . . yes, I like that name. It sounds rather grand.'

As they approached the entrance of the barn, Sophia turned and hugged the Sibyl. 'Thank you so much for being with me – for helping me. I'm not nearly so afraid now.'

The Sibyl smiled warmly, and as she began to take her leave she left Sophia with these parting words:

'Remember, Sophia, I am always at hand. Even when you are back in the Outside World, you can always find me, in the depths of your soul.'

Chapter Twenty Three
Old Acquaintances, New Understanding

When the time came for Sophia to leave the barn, she began to get ready to meet Edgar once again. She emptied her bag of its items and replaced these with some of the food from her table: bread, pieces of cheese, grapes, pears and a couple of pastries. Then she poured some red wine into her empty canteen, grinning as she did so, because she knew that this was more for her than for Edgar.

She made her way to the entrance of the barn, closing the creaky door behind her. The flame of her torch still burnt brightly as it rested in its metal holder. This pleased Sophia because she needed its light in order to find her way back to Edgar. Lifting her bag over her shoulders, she reached down and picked up the torch. Now she was ready to begin her journey.

She retraced her steps back to the main road, and then turned to her left. Very soon the light of the crescent moon disappeared. As she continued to retrace her steps along the gravel road, she thought of how differently she felt now compared to the time when she had run as fast as she could in the opposite direction. The principle thing that had changed for Sophia, was that she had learnt to ask for help from those she trusted, and to accept this wholeheartedly when it was given. And the more she had done so, the more gifts she had received when she least expected them.

These "gifts" came in many different forms and guises, and Sophia realised now more than ever how limited the meaning of this word was in the Outside World. For here in the land of darkness and subtle silvery light, Sophia's greatest gifts had come in the form of inner guidance, compassion and love. She smiled as she thought of both Emil and the Sibyl; she imagined them saying that these gifts formed part of the Feminine aspect, and that they were just a small sample from within the abundance of the Universe. Yes, Sophia had begun to understand such utterances, and now even saw them as truths. She was glad of it.

'All the gold and silver in the world, would be of little value to me now,' she said aloud, as she continued her forthright stride.

She thought of how much she had changed, transformed even, and wondered for a moment how she would "live" in the Outside World once she got back there. Perhaps for the first time, Sophia knew she would get there; she knew it to be her destiny. More than that, she could not say.

As she started to tire, she thought about stopping to rest for a while. To her right and left, there still seemed to be just large open spaces, which Sophia paid little mind to. She wanted to get to the row of houses, and was determined to keep going until she caught sight of them.

After what seemed like an age, she finally saw a building in the distance. 'YES!' she announced triumphantly. She was very pleased with herself.

When she arrived at the first house, on the left-hand side of the road, Sophia stopped and carefully propped her torch against the nearest rock. Then she heaved her bag from her tired shoulders and placed it on the ground. Gratefully, she sat down and let out a deep sigh of relief. She couldn't believe how far she had walked before; had she really run all that way after leaving Edgar?

'Poor Edgar. What must he think of me!' Sophia said, somewhat sadly.

Just then, a voice sounded in the dark; 'Is that you, Sophia?'

Sophia jolted forward, straining her eyes to make out where it was coming from. 'Who is it?' she said. 'Where are you? I can't see.'

'Hold your horses! Give the old girl a chance, won't you,' came the unmistakable reply.

'JAN!' Sophia scrambled to her feet. 'Where are you? I still can't see you.'

'That's because you need your eyes looking at!' Jan then came into view from the other side of the road, carrying a torch.

Sophia wondered why she hadn't been able to see Jan's flame before, but didn't ponder for long on this particular mystery. She was just delighted to see her old acquaintance again. She walked towards the approaching Jan, whose face was beaming like never before; she too seemed genuinely delighted to see Sophia again.

'I can't believe it!' Sophia exclaimed. 'It's so good to see you.'

'Same here.'

And with this, they both burst out laughing.

The two women sat by the roadside chatting and laughing for the first time. Their paths had crossed fleetingly before on three occasions, but none of these could be described in any way as joyous. Neither Jan nor Sophia knew each other well, yet there existed something unspoken and unnamed, which instinctively drew them together for certain periods of time. Each seemed silently intrigued by something in the other, but neither could stay long enough to find out what it was. The same unconscious force that drew them together, seemed to also pull them apart; it was as if the reflection each woman saw in the other's mirror was too "sharp"

And thus it seemed that the pause in their light-hearted banter intuitively led them to talk about one such play entitled, "The Mirrors". For both Jan and Sophia had been present in the crowded Square, when a young man performed with heart and soul on a circular stage under the full moon.

'Oh, I didn't know you were there too,' said Sophia. 'What did you think of it?'

'Very good,' Jan replied, not wanting to give too much away. 'How about you?'

Clearly, Jan wished to deflect the subject matter back to Sophia, who by now had come to realise that her companion had greater difficulty than she in talking about anything that touched on a more emotional level.

'I really felt for him,' Sophia said, 'the man on the stage. He seemed so sad and alone. I guess I could identify with him, even though I'm not sure I understood the whole thing. I was going to ask Emil about it, because he used to talk about "mirrors" quite a lot, but I never got to see him again.'

Sophia's voice trailed off as she thought of her beloved Emil, the most gentle of men - whom she felt she might never see again.

'Yes,' agreed Jan, this time more sympathetically, 'Emil was a good man. By the way, he knew that you had made your way into the Darkened Street.'

'Did he?!' said a surprised Sophia. 'You mean you saw him? When? What did he say?'

'Not much,' came the almost dismissive reply. Then: 'He was very tired. But he said something about you being a courageous warrior . . . . . oh, and that he would miss you.'

'NOT MUCH?!' Sophia retaliated. She was more than a little perturbed by the nature of Jan's response. 'What do you mean "not much"? That's a huge amount! It means so much to me to hear news of Emil. How can you be so cut and dried about it?'

'Don't have a go at me!' Jan said, hardly raising her voice a decibel. 'You're the one who left.'

Sophia was suddenly stunned into silence. She felt stung by the words of criticism, which had come her way from this rather curious woman sitting beside her. Burning anger rose up within Sophia, whilst she struggled to know what to do with it. She quickly got to her feet, feeling the need to put some distance between her and Jan, and was determined not to lose control. For somehow, Sophia intuitively knew that the more Jan remained the dispassionate one, the more she would feel the angry emotional one. There was an imbalance of energy – emotional energy – existing between them, which sorely needed to be redressed.

'Balance in everything, balance is everything!' Sophia whispered softly to herself, as she almost disappeared into the darkness on the other side of the street. She inhaled several deep breaths, trying to calm herself. Then she stopped, turned round and began to walk back towards Jan.

'There's something I've wanted to ask you for quite some time now,' Sophia's voice was suddenly stronger and more assertive, as though she had found a power from within. 'When I saw you on the edge of the forest, why did you leave and not come back?'

Jan's posture remained fairly still, but perhaps the first rumblings of discomfort were beginning to surface, for she picked up some nearby stones and started to fumble and fidget with them.

'Something came up,' Jan offered, in response to Sophia's question.

Sophia stood several feet away, looking directly at the seated Jan. She was determined to get a more meaningful response, or reaction, from Jan. How quickly it seemed their laughter had turned into hostility.

'WHAT came up?' Sophia persisted.

'What does it matter? I got caught up with something, that's all.' Jan started to toss the stones she was holding, one by one, onto the ground in front of her.

'I'll tell you why it matters!' Sophia walked over to her torch, whilst Jan apprehensively looked on. She was not used to being confronted, and she wondered what Sophia was about to say. 'It matters because I spent so long on my own, hiding away in the forest, too frightened to come out, too frightened to face another human being! But I knew I couldn't stay there forever – so when I heard the sound of your chopping away at wood, I managed to finally leave my hideaway. If you only knew the strength it took to overcome my fears, to approach you and befriend you. And you told me that you would be coming back the next day . . . . . I waited and waited . . . . . I believed you!' Sophia's voice was loud, as she conveyed her sense of anger and injustice.

Then unexpectedly Jan said, 'And I let you down.'

266

'YES! You let me down. And I want to know why? It's not good enough saying, "something came up"!'

Sophia stood defiantly, looking down at the now visibly uncomfortable Jan. The tables, it seemed, had turned: the timid, vulnerable Sophia who had approached the Wood Chopper on the edge of the forest, was now the foreboding and forceful Jan of that time. Jan conversely was now more vulnerable. Each had become their opposite. And it surprised both of them.

The power that Sophia felt at that moment was unlike anything she had felt before. For this was not simply part of an outward display - this was from somewhere deep within her core. An inner force or power that had lain dormant for many a year, waiting for the right time to rise to the surface and unleash itself in all its glory! Sophia was not used to feeling this powerful, and she was wondering why Jan was not rising to the challenge. Where was the feisty axe-woman, whose mere physical presence was once so intimidating? Yet hadn't Sophia, even back then, seen a glimpse of the vulnerability that lay hidden behind her powerful outward persona?

'Alright!' Jan looked nervously up at Sophia. 'I meant to come back. I could see how vulnerable you were but . . . . . b-but I-I,' there was a long pause before she could utter the truth, 'but I didn't want to.'

Sophia, for all her display of strength, felt deeply wounded by these words. Her arms suddenly dropped down by her sides. In stunned silence, she bent down to pick up her torch from the ground. Its comforting effect took hold almost immediately, the warmth of its flame taking off the chill that had so swiftly spread through her body. The fire of her torch would be Sophia's strength, her power, whilst her body recovered and regained its balance.

267

Jan shifted awkwardly, juggling stones from hand to hand. She was trying to find a way to soften the blow she had just dealt Sophia, it not having been her intention to cut Sophia down so bluntly. Jan felt, however, that she had to tell the truth – her truth – no matter how painful the effects were on others; she felt it was her duty now to be true to herself. She had not wanted to be so brutally honest with Sophia – and would not have been, if it had not been for the fact that Sophia had insisted on knowing the truth. Back in the Outside World, Jan had often spared other people's feelings, never letting others down, and always on hand to help when called upon.

Jan now stopped juggling the stones in her hands, and decided to tell Sophia some of her story. She told Sophia about how she had not only weathered most storms that had come her way back in the Outside World, but she had also deflected whatever stones and arrows had come in other people's way. Such was Jan's aversion to seeing others in pain. But one day an arrow struck Jan so deeply, that she found she could not recover from the inflicted wound. Instead she retreated to the edge of the forest, away from the Outside World, so that no-one could see her weakened state. In doing so, however, she knew that she would be letting down all those people who had relied on her before. She thought that if she stayed in the forest for a little while, she would regain her strength and then go back to her old life in the Outside World.

'But a strange thing happened,' Jan continued. 'The longer I stayed away from my old life, the more I realised how much it had taken out of me. How much other people had taken from me – how much I had allowed them to! That's when I became angry. And the more my strength returned, the more angry I became – at others, at myself, at the world, at everything.'

Sophia had been listening attentively. 'So was that why you were chopping so much wood? Because you were so angry?' she asked Jan.

Jan nodded. 'More than angry though. I was raging! I couldn't believe there was so much rage in there! That's why when you came along, looking so timid and fragile, I didn't know how to deal with it. You reminded me of all the people I was trying to run away from – the people who relied on me.'

By now Sophia had sat down a few feet away from Jan. 'And that's why you didn't come back?' Sophia said. 'I think I can understand that. I would probably have done the same myself. The only thing I don't get is why you didn't just tell me this at the time.'

Jan, who now seemed to have regained some of old form, looked at Sophia at the same time raising her eyebrows in surprise. 'Oh yeah?! Just like you did with your injured chap back there? The one you were supposed to go back to.'

'What?' Sophia was now the surprised one. 'Do you mean the "Inertia Man" . . . I mean, Edgar?

'Well, I don't know what his name is but the door was wide open, so I went in. Pretty horrific really.'

Sophia looked down on the ground. 'What did he say?' she asked softly.

'He asked if I'd seen you. I said that I hadn't seen you for some time. That's when he said, that you told him you would go back to see him – but you hadn't. He looked pretty disappointed, so I said that I would pass the message on if I saw you. That's why I wasn't so surprised when I did see you.'

'Yes, I can see that now,' Sophia said, thoughtfully. 'So, what you're saying is that we've both done the same thing – rejected those who have appeared weak and vulnerable – rather than help them.'

'That's what I reckon,' replied Jan. 'And of course we feel guilty, but not half as much as the anger we feel.'

'What do you mean?' Sophia looked up, intrigued to know more.

Jan began to throw stones one at a time across the street, as if demonstrating some of what she felt. 'Well don't tell me that you haven't felt angry with your life – being the great martyr, always running around for others. You wouldn't have come down here if your life was all sweet and roses, would you?'

Jan had, it seemed, fully regained her flippant style of delivery, which had the effect of ruffling Sophia's feathers once more.

'Do you mind not talking to me like that!' Sophia counteracted, looking directly at Jan.

Jan stopped throwing stones, and met Sophia's stare with a smile; 'Well, I must say, you've got a bit more spirit in you!'

Sophia liked the way Jan could take what she gave. She realised how liberating it was to be able to express feelings of anger directly to someone, without fear of reprisals or fear of damaging them. This was something Sophia had often feared - so misunderstood was the expression of anger in the Outside World. Too often she felt that it was confused with aggression; too often it was labelled in a derogatory fashion, as part of the "hysterical" nature of women, of their over-emotionalism. It seemed to Sophia that human nature was often being divided into either/or categories: of masculine rationality and logic, or feminine "irrational" emotion and intuition. Yet what she could never understand was that if men were supposed to be more rational and less "hysterical", why were most violent and aggressive acts committed by men? Sophia had often felt a sense of injustice and unfairness at what she saw as the suppression of the female voice.

'You know something,' Sophia suddenly announced, 'you're right! I have found my spirit – to express what I really feel. I used to worry so much about how I looked to others. Now, I'm learning to be myself. And yes, I have been angry with my life; angry that I've had to compromise myself so much for others; angry at living in that Cage for so long.' Sophia picked up a stone and threw it as far as she could.

After a brief silence, Sophia asked Jan; 'What happened to your axe? Did you leave it in the forest?'

'No, I've still got it.' Jan took the small rucksack she was wearing off her back, and opened it. Carefully, she lifted out the axe with both hands, as if it was her most treasured possession. 'Here she is.'

'Why do you carry it around with you?' asked Sophia.

'Never know when I might need it.'

'What do you mean? Why should you need it?'

'You're too trusting, you,' Jan snapped back.

'You're making me nervous, Jan. What are you trying to say?'

Sophia had never met anyone whom she liked so much one moment, but was wary of the next. This continual vacillation between poles disconcerted her, but somehow she was finding a way to stay as centred as she could. She was managing to keep her rocking boat afloat, by sitting in the middle of it!

Jan, on the other hand, was having to confront her own motivations and actions, which she realised had not been challenged before. Usually others felt too intimidated by her, so that she continued on her way unabated, aware of her own power and its potential to manipulate, and even destroy. Yet, how she had wished at times for someone wise and strong, to know of her struggle: the struggle to restrain such negative inner forces.

Jan placed the axe on the ground between her and her challenger. She began to roll up her left sleeve, then reached for her torch with her right hand. Holding the light over her left arm, she showed Sophia the underside of her bare arm. Sophia leant forward to see that Jan's arm was covered in scars and burns.

Trying not to seem too shocked, but failing, Sophia's eyes suddenly filled with tears. 'What have you done, Jan?'

Jan quickly withdrew her arm, and answered as best as she could, and with surprising honesty: 'See? I carry this axe, not so much to protect me from others, but to protect others from me! I have to smash things – wood, objects, anything that I can get my hands on. That's the only way I can get some of this rage and hate out. But sometimes it's not enough. Sometimes I have to hurt myself instead . . . . . to feel the fire slowly burn through my skin, until I can't take it anymore . . . . . until it has overpowered me and I have to succumb to its power . . . . . .'

Jan appeared to be almost in an eerie trance, with a smile on her face and her eyes glazed. But she was far from happy, and she was far from a place of peace. Sophia had to bring her back:

'JAN!' She took hold of Jan's upper arms and shook them, as once Emil had done for Sophia. 'It's all right, I'm here. Come back! JAN! Come back!' Sophia shouted with determined authority, until finally . . . .

Jan's eyes adjusted to her present surroundings. She looked down at her arms, still in Sophia's grasp, and seemed moved by this comforting gesture. Her eyes, for the first time she could remember, moistened. Alas, it was not difficult to see the incredible discomfort Jan felt, as a result of lowering her guard. Suddenly, Sophia was being the wise and strong person that Jan had longed for, yet would never allow herself to admit to anyone.

'Jan, don't you see how courageous we both are? To venture alone into such darkness and to face the unknown, takes quite a lot of guts you know.'

Jan slowly withdrew her arms without saying anything. Sophia shifted her position awkwardly, then said; 'Would you like something to drink?'

'Do you have anything strong?' Jan quipped.

'Yes, as a matter of fact I do,' Sophia chuckled, getting up and walking over to her bag.

Sophia came back with her canteen of red wine and two beakers. She handed a beaker to Jan, and then poured the wine. The two women raised their beakers, said 'Cheers,' and then gratefully drank the contents.

'Jan?' Sophia asked softly. 'What did you do with all that wood?'

Jan burst out laughing. 'You're quite funny you, aren't you?'

'Thanks.' Sophia was genuinely pleased to be considered funny.

'Well, I made quite a lot of campfires – the campsite consisting of one! Yours truly.' Jan pointed at herself. 'It was nice though, to look at the flames and to listen to the crackling sounds. I ended up seeing all these shapes in the fire-' she suddenly straightened up and looked at Sophia. 'A chap called Bob turned up one day. He'd seen the smoke from a distance, you see.' Jan suddenly started laughing; 'Poor thing! There I was, with my axe raised above my head, telling him to scarper or else he wouldn't be able to!'

'My goodness!' exclaimed Sophia. 'Did you really say that? Poor Bob. I know he was a bit funny, but he did help me a lot. In fact, if it wasn't for him I wouldn't have made it up that Mountain Road.'

'Yeah, yeah, I know. Don't worry yourself – things turned out all right in the end. But there was no way I was going up that Mountain Road – I told him that in no uncertain terms.' Jan paused. 'Anyway, where were we with the wood? Oh yeah – I had a couple of knives with me, so that I didn't have to carry the axe all the time when I went for my walks in the forest. Then I started getting bored with doing the same things everyday, and as you said before, I had all this wood. So one day, I began carving the blocks of wood into different shapes with my knives. Most of those went straight onto the campfire, but at least it gave me something to focus on. And I was also directing some of my pent-up energy into creating something – quite a revelation for me, I can tell you.'

'That's brilliant!' Sophia joined in. 'Do you know, I discovered that I could write verses when I directed my pent-up energy into that.'

'Go on, then. Let's have a look.'

'You're joking! I couldn't possibly.'

'Charming, I must say,' Jan seemed a little offended. 'Do you think I can't read or something? Or is it that I'm not as "cultured" as you would like?'

'No, of course not. I didn't mean it like that.'

Except Sophia wasn't sure what she had meant, particularly as she had only too happily given the Sibyl her most intense piece of writing. What, indeed, was her resistance to sharing this part of herself with Jan? There ensued a rather awkward silence between Jan and Sophia for a few moments, whilst Sophia pondered on this.

'Okay then,' Sophia suddenly announced. 'But only if you show me something that you've made.'

'Oh it's like that, is it?' Jan replied more playfully. 'I'll show you mine if you show me yours!'

Sophia started giggling like a child. 'Well, I suppose it is a bit like that. You must admit, it is a bit exposing, isn't it?'

'Yeah, I know what you mean.' Jan thought for a moment, and then said, 'I'll tell you what – the next time we meet, it's a deal!'

'But how do you know when we'll next meet?' Sophia said, more serious now.

'I don't.'

Jan's blunt reply had the effect of suddenly reminding Sophia of her current mission, which she had temporarily forgotten about, perhaps all too easily: She had to see Edgar. Yes, she was having a pleasant time with Jan, and felt she could go on drinking and chatting, but she knew deep down that it was now becoming a diversion from her main goal.

Sophia got to her feet, walked over to her bag and picked it up. Turning to face Jan, she said, 'I must go and see Edgar.'

'Yeah, I know. Good luck,' Jan's reply seemed genuine in its sentiment.

'What are you going to do?'

'Don't fret about me. You've got enough on your plate as it is. I'll be alright.'

Jan looked up at the hesitant figure of Sophia, and gesturing with her hands, said, 'GO ON! Get to that poor man. I'll see you when I see you, yeah?'

Sophia picked up her torch. 'Thanks, Jan.'

'What for? It's me that should be thanking you,' Jan held aloft her empty beaker.

But underlying this gesture, Jan knew that her earlier display of vulnerability was the most "naked" she had allowed herself to be with another human being. Sophia had enabled a concealed part of

Jan to be set free; to illuminate its existence in order that it could be healed.

As Sophia set off on her way, something made her stop and turn back. An image had come into her head, as clearly as a moving picture projected onto a dark screen: The final scene of "The Mirrors" play - the young man kneeling on the stage, despairing that his beloved had abandoned him and thus had taken his mirror away. How was he now to "see" himself? he had wondered aloud, until a loud voice came to him and told him that he was in fact already seeing his reflected self.

'Jan!' Sophia called. 'What did you make of that last scene in the play? You know – when that loud voice came over, and the young man didn't know what it meant.'

Jan was still sitting by the roadside, with her axe in the ground in front of her. 'The way I see it is that he got back what he was giving out – rejection, abandonment, etcetera.'

'Really?' Sophia was amazed at the sharpness of Jan's perception.

Jan seemed to have the ability to cut away all that was superficial and irrelevant, and get to the crux of the matter. It was easy to see how some people would be put off by her blunt no-messing attitude, but the more Sophia engaged with her the more she admired and respected her directness. And the more receptive Sophia was, the more she gained from such interactions.

'You know Jan, your perception is really sharp.'

'Yeah, as sharp as this blade,' Jan lifted up her axe and grinned.

'But the man in the play didn't seem like someone who rejected others – as a rule I mean. That's what I don't understand.'

'That's because it wasn't necessarily "others" he was rejecting,' Jan clarified. 'He had rejected himself . . . . . like us!'

Jan got to her feet, immediately feeling the effects of the wine. 'I need to go and have a lie down. See you, Sophia.'

Picking up her belongings, Jan wandered off tiredly across to the other side of the road and beyond. Sophia in turn slowly made her way towards the house where the abandoned Edgar lay.

Chapter Twenty Four
The Meeting Of Opposites

Sophia stood outside the door with the crystal handle. It was closed. She placed her hand upon the crystal with the intention of opening the door, only to withdraw her hand at the last moment. Once again it seemed as if two opposing forces within her were battling for supremacy, but were so evenly matched that they all but cancelled each other out. As she stood immersed in her battle of wills, Sophia suddenly found herself slightly amused by the scenario.

'Here we have two forms of inertia,' she said softly to herself. 'One lying on his bed in a dark room, and one standing outside on the doorstep. A fine pair we are!'

But what was completely different about their two situations, was that one had choice whilst the other did not. As long as Sophia chose to stay outside, Edgar would continue to fester in the dark. But he would also continue to exist for as long as Sophia existed. Sophia realised for the first time that it was she who held the power. Words from the Sibyl's Scroll suddenly came into her head:

"Befriend the Stranger,

And his power ceases to be . . . .

. . . . . know his power to be yours . . ."

Sophia turned the crystal, and the door opened. Immediately a voice called out in the dark; 'Hello! Who is it?'

Sophia walked along the short corridor to the open door on her right. 'It's me. Sophia.'

'Oh how marvellous! Please . . . come in. Sit down, won't you.'

Sophia marvelled at Edgar's joyous welcome; she felt she did not deserve it. Yet such negativity was of no use to either of them now. "I will try to be as open and receptive as Edgar is," she told herself, as she stood in the open doorway. Then, she stepped forward into the darkened room. She could not yet see Edgar, for the flame of her torch had dwindled as it had done before. Her breathing once again became more laboured, and her movements more heavy.

'Edgar,' she said, 'is there anywhere I can put this torch, so that it doesn't go out or burn anything?'

'Yes, yes, of course,' he replied eagerly. 'There is a metal torch holder on the wall behind you. Just by the door . . . . . can you see it?'

Sophia found it easily and wondered why she had not seen it before. Once she had placed her torch in the holder, she turned back round in the direction of Edgar. 'Thanks, that's better. My arm was starting to ache.' Then realising what she had said, she quickly added; 'Sorry, Edgar, that was very thoughtless of me.'

'Do not worry, Sophia. I am just grateful that you have returned.'

There was something in the way that Edgar spoke, which made Sophia feel like a queen; the genuineness with which he conveyed his feelings for her, was something that Sophia found hard to believe. Yet she did undoubtedly believe him.

Sophia stood for a while, somewhere between the doorway and the bed on which Edgar lay, and gradually her breathing adjusted to the reduced levels of oxygen in the room. The torch flame was also a little stronger, now that it was situated near the open doorway, and soon Sophia was able to make out some of the lay-out of the room. She could see the outline of Edgar sitting up in bed, with what looked like writing materials; pens, pencils, journals, and scrolls. The chair, on which she had sat before, was still situated next to Edgar's bed as if waiting for her return.

'Edgar, do you mind if I move that chair over here?' Sophia asked politely. 'It's just that I can breathe a bit better here, because I'm nearer the doorway.'

She could just make out his smile. 'I do understand, you know,' Edgar replied reassuringly. 'Please sit wherever you wish, Sophia.'

'Thank you.' She removed her bag and placed it on the floor, where she was standing. Then she walked slowly towards the chair. As before, her breathing became more laboured and her movement more stilted. Even so, she did not feel quite so stuck, or rooted to the spot. She managed to pick up the wooden chair, conscious that she had not yet made eye-contact with Edgar. She could sense him looking at her, and she knew that she was avoiding the act of reciprocation. It was true that Sophia did not want to see his horrific injuries, or tend to his wounds; and she did not want to patronise Edgar by trying to conceal this side of her nature. For he already knew this.

Sophia carried the chair over to where her bag lay. She sat down, panting a little from the exertion of her efforts, and now faced Edgar from a distance. 'I brought some things for you,' she said, as she leant forward to open her bag, 'food and drink.'

'Oh how lovely. Perhaps I could indulge myself once you are gone. That way, it gives me something to look forward to.'

Once again Sophia could make out his smile, but this time she also saw that he had a beard, which for some reason she had not noticed before. The silence that ensued was an awkward one for Sophia, yet she resisted filling it. She was feeling tired from her long walk – and perhaps from the wine too!

Edgar noticed this. 'Did you come a long way to get here?' he asked, thoughtfully.

'Yes, it was quite a way. I've been staying in an old barn, a couple of miles up the road.' She paused for a moment before adding, 'I'm sorry I stayed away for so long.'

'The main thing is that you came back.'

Sophia wondered how he could remain so peaceful and still. 'Why aren't you more angry, Edgar?' she suddenly asked spontaneously. 'How can you be so forgiving?'

'Because you are here.'

Edgar seemed to have a natural ability of silencing Sophia. She did not feel blocked or obstructed in any way, but rather was lulled into a thoughtful contemplative silence. He had an economy of words which conveyed a great deal, without detracting from the point at hand; and although intense in his focus, he never forced the situation. Not for the first time on this journey, Sophia was left wanting to know more. Now she mulled over Edgar's answer, because although she had thought she knew what he meant, she didn't really.

'Do you mean that you were angry before . . . . but you aren't now . . . . because I'm here?'

Edgar smiled knowingly. 'Exactly, Sophia. You know me better than I thought!'

Edgar watched Sophia closely, such was his level of intrigue and joy at the presence of his Feminine counterpart. He had waited for so long to be found and to be befriended by Sophia, that he did not now want to scare her off! In truth, it was Edgar who at this moment was more nervous, for he knew that Sophia could get up and walk away whenever she chose. He, in contrast, could not move anywhere unless she helped him. Therefore, he would try by means of communication and expression to befriend Sophia; to woo her in a sense, so that she wanted to be with him rather than felt she had to.

Edgar could see how tired she was, as he watched her heavy eyelids force themselves to remain open. With her torch flame glowing behind her, Edgar was filled with a sense of awe and admiration for this young woman. To him, Sophia was a hero, because she had journeyed such a long way from the Outside World into unknown territory, which was darker than she could have ever dreamt. Yet she had persevered nonetheless, and here she was: Edgar's hero.

By now, Sophia's eyes had closed and her head was hung down against her chest. This pleased Edgar because he considered it to be a sign of her growing trust in him. He smiled contentedly. As Sophia's head gradually lolled backwards, so that the light fell directly upon her face, Edgar noticed several dirty marks on her cheeks and forehead. He chuckled with fondness to himself, at which point Sophia's head suddenly lolled forward. She woke up with a start, wondering where she was. Looking around her, she eventually came to realise where she was, except now she noticed something that she hadn't been able to see before. Directly opposite her, on the other side of the room, there was a fireplace; a hearth.

She leant forward, her eyes squinting, and tried to get a better look. 'Edgar, I didn't know you had a fireplace,' she said, with sudden newness of life. She wanted to go over to it, but knew that the levels of oxygen would not carry her there.

'Yes, I'd almost forgotten it was there myself. When I first arrived here, it was burning with the most beautiful of essences – the incense of sandalwood almost numbed my senses. It wasn't so bad back then – when the Outside World was more connected with the mysteries of the darker world; when the world ruled by the moon, was equal to that ruled by the sun.' He looked directly at Sophia. 'When the Feminine and Masculine energies were in perfect balance. But that was long ago . . . .'

Sophia could somehow see the sadness in Edgar's eyes. His words about the sun and the moon, Masculine and Feminine, had strongly resonated with those of Emil and the Sibyl. She wanted to ask Edgar more about these things, but she began to feel sleepy again and was struggling to keep awake.

'We are both tired, Sophia,' Edgar's delivery was more serious now. 'We need to restore our wavering energy levels, so that we can help each other to move out of this darkness.' He noticed that Sophia had shifted to a more upright position, so decided to continue, the tone of his voice ever more serious: 'I have watched many things perish in this land of darkness. You have already seen some of them, but there was much more – it is not important now to tell you about them.'

Sophia thought about the ancient slabs of stone that she had encountered with the Sibyl, and how she had wanted to know more about them. Yet the Sibyl had said to her then, what Edgar now said to her.

'What is the point,' Edgar reinforced, 'of telling you about ancient wisdom and rituals that have been driven into this darkness until they have all but completely been lost to the Outside World?'

Edgar's anger was now clearly evident, and it was starting to ruffle Sophia's feathers. She tried to think of something meaningful to say in response, but it was Edgar's voice that needed to be heard:

'Look at this rotten body!' he suddenly cried. 'I have been the leper, the untouchable, the discarded . . .,' his voice began to break as he continued to express his agony. 'Yet once I had much to give. I write these words,' he lifted up a journal with his left hand, 'but what's the use!' he threw it back on to the bed, 'when they do not see the light of day?'

Edgar's left hand rested upon his forehead, and then went down over his eyes. Sophia knew that he was crying. Suddenly, without hesitation, she got up and went to him. She touched his head gently before leaning down to whisper in his ears, the words he would have traded in for a multitude of his own creations; 'I'm sorry, Edgar. I'm so sorry.'

And so it was that Sophia came to spend much more time in the company of Edgar. Because of her breathing difficulties she slept in the corridor, wrapped in blankets that had been stored in a cupboard in Edgar's room. In fact, as Sophia brought more love and light into the room, she began to discover more and more things that had been hidden to her before.

Some items were quite beautiful. Sophia was particularly fond of the writing bureau, which stood against the wall opposite Edgar's bed. Like a spirited child, she loved to open all the drawers and compartments, as if trying to find hidden treasures or lost secrets. Edgar would look on, sometimes smiling with fondness, sometimes laughing with joy; for Sophia had brought life back into his home. And in time, Sophia seemed to acclimatise to the lower levels of oxygen in the room, much like a climber would in high altitudes.

On one occasion, whilst exploring Edgar's room, Sophia noticed some material hanging from the wall opposite the bed. It was made of quite a rich material, like velvet, and was dark in colour although there seemed to be a pattern woven into it. Sophia turned to address Edgar; 'What's this material hanging here for, Edgar?'

There was no reply. A little worried, she went over to the bed to see if he was all right. She discovered that he was sound asleep, his face the most peaceful she had seen. But then she had never looked at Edgar's face properly before. Usually there was a brief meeting of their eyes from a distance, before Sophia turned her own eyes away. She was all too aware of doing this, and although she consciously tried not to, she was alas unsuccessful. Edgar, for his part, often felt the strength of his own gaze towards Sophia, but could not seem to avert his eyes for fear that she would suddenly disappear from view.

Yet now, Edgar slept peacefully under Sophia's gaze. He was holding a journal in his left hand, and Sophia was struck by how beautiful his hand was. She longed to see some of his writings, but had not felt it "right" to ask him. Somehow they seemed sacred to Edgar; creations which had kept his spirit alive through all of the darkness. She did not wish to dishonour him either, by prematurely or secretly viewing his life's work.

Sophia's eyes had not yet looked over towards the right side of his upper body. Edgar would normally have kept it covered up with a blanket when Sophia was in the room, but now whilst he lay sleeping the blanket had dropped from his right shoulder. Sophia could not bring herself to look, despite feeling ashamed, and instead closed her eyes. Turning around, she sat down near the bottom of the bed where she remained in silence for some time. She was thinking of some of the lines she had written about Edgar's wounds, in her "Inertia" piece, and began to softly whisper them under her breath:

'I could cry for you,
You with the rotting flesh,
Limbs torn from their rightful place,
You who I can barely look at.'

At that moment, Sophia suddenly knew that what she was also finding so painful to face was a part of herself: The weak, ugly, vile and useless side of herself; the side that was so strikingly displayed in Edgar. This was the Stranger – her Shadow side – that Sophia had not wished to face for much of her life. She had wanted this to remain hidden from the Outside World, and ultimately from herself, and Edgar had known that only too well. But now, finally, there was a meeting of these opposites; the dual aspects of her nature.

Sophia felt Edgar's hand touch hers. Her eyes instantly filled with tears, as she heard his reassuring voice say; 'It's all right, Sophia. You are helping me just by being here.' Then, he shook her left arm with some urgency. 'Look! Sophia, look!'

Sophia turned to face him, wiping her eyes with her right hand. Edgar was pointing to his right shoulder. This time she looked, and what she saw astonished her. Skin had grown so that it now completely covered the flesh of Edgar's upper arm; there were no open wounds to be seen.

'It's a miracle!' Sophia said, in whispered tones.

She was now unable to avert her eyes from this physical transformation. Her jaw had dropped open and remained so, whilst Edgar gleefully revelled in the delights of his fully healed – albeit part-formed – limb.

'I'm so happy for you, Edgar,' Sophia moved up along the side of the bed a little to embrace him.

'Thank you, Sophia. Thank you.' Edgar was stroking her shoulder-length hair, and then kissed her forehead.

Edgar could feel a new found sense of vitality take hold, and he knew that it was only a matter of time before victory would be theirs.

'We're going to make it, Sophia,' he said, gripping her tightly. 'We're going to make it.'

Chapter Twenty Five
The Sharing Of Attributes And Virtues

'Tell me about the Outside World,' Edgar asked Sophia on one occasion.

She smiled warmly, as her thoughts scanned through the many images contained within her memory bank. 'Well, I guess what I miss most is the sun,' Sophia eventually replied. 'On a lovely summer's day where I live, it can transform everything. It's as though people themselves lighten up, and become sunnier in nature. Then there are the seasons, which I love; in autumn there are carpets of leaves all over the ground, and wonderful colours – browns, greens, golds. My favourite time though is spring, when everything in the plant and animal kingdom that has been in hibernation, suddenly comes back to life. You start to see the first buds – it's wonderful really.' She paused for a little while, then continued; 'But you know what – I've only realised how wonderful these things are since being on this journey. Always the way, I suppose.' She looked at Edgar and shrugged her shoulders.

'So why is that?' Edgar asked, in all seriousness.

'Oh, I suppose it's because humans get so caught up in themselves – or in others,' Sophia's mood began to dampen a little. 'And that's something I don't miss.'

'Go on,' Edgar insisted.

Sophia was beginning to feel slightly unnerved, as she realised that Edgar was quizzing her for specific details. He seemed to want answers.

For Edgar though, to know what it had been like for Sophia in the Outside World, was to know more about his own part in her life. Directness and sharp focus, with all their inherent forcefulness, were attributes that Edgar had once possessed in abundance. Though not always welcomed by others, they were none-the-less absolutely necessary at times to get things moving; to get results. This had been Edgar's energy – the Masculine energy – which Sophia had used often to good effect in the Outside World. This Masculine energy was part of Sophia. Edgar knew, of course, that the Feminine attributes of softness and receptivity, the attributes of listening and of more gentle persuasion, were altogether more effective at times. But these had not been his forte.

In his need to be noticed and acknowledged, Edgar's Masculine energy had forced its way into Sophia's consciousness for much of her life. And how successful he had been! For he had managed to find expression in the Outside World by using the Masculine attributes of power, competitiveness, and rational intellect; indeed these were to become the victors in Sophia's young life. Certainly, Edgar had been more or less content with this state of affairs for a while, and had presumed that this was also the case with Sophia.

For she had accumulated a fair amount of material possessions, as well as achieving a number of impressive goals. Even when she had floundered or struggled, Edgar had made sure that she knew of his power and steely determination to win through, to soldier on, to not be defeated. "Yes," he had often told himself, "I have served her well. She should be happy with my efforts."

So now, he wanted to know what life had been like for Sophia. 'Please, tell me,' Edgar insisted, 'what it was like for you in the Outside World.'

'Well, I suppose some things were good,' Sophia said, rather sadly. 'But it was pretty tough and competitive at times. There seemed to be so little time to just relax – to just be. I was always on the go, never enough time in the day to get things done. And because the people I mixed with were quite similar in that respect, we were always talking about how busy we were.' She stopped and smiled sadly at Edgar. 'But you know, I was always too frightened of failure – whatever that means! You see, in the Outside World – the one I know anyway – success and failure are measured in ways such as, how much money you have and what you look like. Attributes like honour, or integrity, are not really valued. In fact, you'd probably be considered a bit odd if you talked in terms of those sort of things.'

Edgar was listening intently, and now asked Sophia, 'Why were you so frightened of failure?'

She thought for a while before answering. 'I suppose it all comes down to rejection. In the Outside World, we all want to be noticed, liked, admired . . . . . . you see, Edgar, the whole of the society or culture seems to work like that. So if you manage to achieve "success", then that is considered good by the society's rules and values. And so you get more attention, and feel more liked and admired . . . . And it works the other way with failure.'

'So, does no-one have the courage to fail – or to admit their failings? Isn't that a little arrogant and small-minded?'

'Oh yes, of course it is. But underneath it all, is fear again – though most people would never admit it. Fear that others will look down on them, or reject them. So much so, that people usually blame others when things go wrong. Most of the time, if a person were to put their hands up and admit their failings, or wrong doings, they would feel the wrath of others very quickly upon them. There are of course situations – usually within loving relationships – where this doesn't happen, but generally speaking this is the case.'

'But it is an illusion, is it not?' Edgar seemed genuinely surprised by what he had heard.

Sophia nodded in agreement, for now she knew this only too well of her previous life in the Outside World.

'You know, Sophia,' Edgar suddenly shared, 'I understand now why you allowed my power, my energy, to be so prevalent in your life. For it seems from what you are saying, that the Masculine energy has been directing affairs in the Outside World to such an extent that to "succeed" in that environment, one has to be powerful and outward-directed. To play the game, so to speak.'

'Yes,' Sophia answered in a soft thoughtful voice. 'And to lose your soul.'

Edgar could see that Sophia's spirits were dropping, and that this was not helping either of them in their ultimate goal: To unite their energies and to emerge renewed and whole. Edgar decided to change the course of the proceedings. Edgar leant forward and picked up one of the scrolls lying on his bed. Quickly opening it, he gestured to Sophia to come closer.

'Look Sophia! Remember the words of the Sibyl's Scroll – "The Incubation Period" – it says at the bottom . . . . . .

Know his power to be yours
Instead.
And slowly will it propel you
Back to the Outside World
Where your living can be done.

'Don't you see? It doesn't have to be the same for you anymore! Because we will be working together – in harmony. I may not have the strength I had before, as you can see,' Edgar looked down at his body, 'but I am still here for you. The Feminine energy, however, will be restored to its rightful place. In balance, we shall go forth into the Outside World . . . . . You, Sophia, will call on me when you need the power of action, and I on you when nurturing is needed. We will listen to the murmuring of our soul, and follow our destiny!'

Sophia was by now laughing heartily at the increasingly vocal Edgar.

'What?' asked a bemused Edgar.

'Oh, you're so sweet, Edgar. I do love you.'

Sophia and Edgar continued to converse freely with each other about their different adventures as well as their trials and tribulations. Most significantly, Edgar was now able to spend some time out of his bed, and with Sophia's help, to sit in a chair. Sometimes, Sophia insisted on moving him in his chair to the entrance of his home. There was, of course, nothing much to see there, but it was all part of Sophia and Edgar's developing strength of union. Sophia would make regular trips to the well that Edgar had told her of; it was a relatively short distance behind the row of houses, and Sophia would usually bring back two buckets of water. One bucket would be used for personal hygiene, and the other for drinking.

On one particular occasion though, Sophia brought back two buckets of water for an altogether different use: She had decided to do some cleaning in Edgar's room.

'Good luck!' Edgar laughed. 'But I'm not sure it's worth it. There must be layers upon layers of dirt and grime.'

'Be quiet,' asserted Sophia. 'I know what I'm doing – call it woman's intuition!'

Edgar smiled warmly at her, intrigued as to what she was up to. He sat outside on his chair, which now leant against the wall of his house, and began to write in one of his journals. He had not really been able to write anything of substance since the time he had spent in The Place of Souls – but that was another story; one he would soon disclose to Sophia. Now, however, he would try to write again and see what happened.

As he sat out in the Darkened Street, Edgar could breath more easily. The wounds on his legs, once so appalling, had healed up. He still covered up the stumps above his knees with a blanket, although he often wondered whether this was more for him than Sophia. In the end, he decided that it was probably a bit of both. At this moment, though, Edgar felt a deep sense of inner contentment; Sophia was more than he had ever dreamt of. Their friendship was now so harmonious and balanced, that together he knew they could achieve a magnitude of dreams. Their unified energies could, he was sure, bring new life back to the Outside World. It made Edgar think of a chemical equation, which led to a wondrous yet powerful reaction.

'Take two specific and separate entities or elements,' he said out loud. 'Put them together, and watch a powerful reaction take place: an end-product is formed, which is now one entity.'

But what excited and fascinated Edgar more than anything, was that the original entities would be transformed forever. They would no longer be what they were before; a transformation would have taken place.

That was how he saw the growing union between himself and Sophia. A newly inspired Edgar felt a surge of enlightened energy fill him up, and he suddenly found himself writing about the journey to come. The verses were written with such swiftness, that he couldn't wait to show them to Sophia.

'SOPHIA!' he shouted. 'Come quickly. I have something to show you!'

'Just a minute!' Sophia called back from inside Edgar's room. 'I'm in the middle of something.'

'What are you doing in there? It can't be that important – there isn't much of interest in there!'

Sophia took offence to this, and responded accordingly. 'Do you mind, Edgar! What I am doing here is just as important as what you are doing out there.'

Although Edgar's almost childlike enthusiasm was a little deflated, it was not long before he bounced back – this time with a different approach. 'Yes, yes, you are right Sophia. In fact, I am most intrigued to know what you are doing in there. When you come out, we can share in each other's secrets.'

Edgar proceeded to sit in silence for a while, listening to the occasional sounds of activity coming from his room. At one stage, it sounded as though Sophia was reorganising the furniture. 'Surely she can't be doing spring cleaning,' Edgar wondered to himself. Then he heard a soft thud, followed by a bout of coughing. In the next instant, Sophia came scurrying out of the house in a fit of coughing and spluttering. She was covered from head to toe in dirt and dust.

'What on earth are you doing?' enquired a startled Edgar. 'I thought we were going to be leaving here at some point, not making it cleaner to live in!'

'Oh be quiet, Edgar!' snapped Sophia, by now snivelling and sneezing from all the dust particles.

On turning to face Edgar, he let out a tremendous roar of laughter.

'What's so funny?' asked a rather annoyed Sophia.

'YOU!' Edgar was pointing at Sophia's face, which was streaked with so much dirt, that the whites of her eyes stood out like beacons.

'Honestly, Edgar. You are such a child!'

'ME? Look at you! You look more like a child – and one who has been up to all sorts of mischief!'

Sophia looked down at her hands and clothes. Letting out a deep sigh, she conceded, 'Oh alright. I suppose I must look quite a sight. I'm glad you find it so funny!'

'Healing through joy, Sophia,' Edgar chuckled. 'Healing through joy.'

Sophia managed a smile. 'I did, however, uncover some hidden treasure in your room,' she said, as she made her way back into the house.

Edgar, now more quiet and serious, waited for the mystery to be revealed.

'HERE!' Sophia announced. She was standing on the threshold of the front doorway holding, with both hands outstretched before her, a sword. It was still encased in its scabbard, so that when Sophia began to slowly pull out the sword, there was almost at once a sparkle of silvery light that emanated from its blade. It was indeed a majestic sight. Sophia had never held a sword in her hands and was surprised by its heaviness. She imagined herself at that moment to be one of the Knights of the Round Table, pursuing with pride and humility the noble causes of King Arthur's reign. She imagined herself riding on a white horse, whose power and loyalty assured that it would stay with Sophia no matter how arduous the journey. Her white horse would carry Sophia back to her land and people - after she had slain the dragon that had threatened to cast darkness on her people.

Yes, Sophia was truly transfixed by the majesty of the sword that she now held; it was as though it could evoke the most grand and vivid imaginings, through touch alone; as though ancient memories revealed themselves through the will and desire of the person who lovingly held the ancient sword. Whatever it was, Sophia let herself be carried along in the spirit of it all. She stepped across the threshold and placed the scabbard on the ground before her. Edgar watched her in silent awe, as she raised the sword with both hands. Sophia was now imagining herself to be Queen Guinevere, about to welcome the noble knights home from their long journeys. In this role, she knew she could trust in the knights' integrity, their honour and their chivalry, and that all whom they encountered along their way would be treated with respect and regard. She knew that they would carry the name of the land and people that they represented with love and pride, and not with hate or the selfish pursuit of power. Such virtues were indeed hard to find in most humans, hence the special place that was reserved in the hearts and minds of the people for the courageous knights.

Sophia, in her role as queen, turned to face the seated Edgar. In her incongruous attire blackened with dirt and dust, she stood up straight and proud, her eyes shining like gemstones, and began to address Edgar.

'Sir Edgar,' she announced. 'I honour you, in whom courage and virtue abound.' She did not know where the words had come from, just that they had come to her naturally.

As she placed the tip of the outstretched blade upon Edgar's right shoulder, he lifted his head up to her. His face was streaked with tears, his left hand still clutching his pen and journal. Sophia carefully raised the sword above his head, and then slowly brought it down again until it was resting upon his left shoulder. Then, one last time, she brought the sword back over Edgar's head on to his right shoulder, before withdrawing it. Never had she seen Edgar so silent and deep in thought, his head now hung slightly. The sword now weighed heavy in Sophia's hands, so that she felt ready to place it back in its scabbard.

'Thank you,' Edgar said in a quiet voice.

Sophia looked at his sad deep blue eyes, and they filled her with love and compassion. Suddenly she did not know what to say. Instead she smiled, and then placed Edgar's sheathed sword on the ground by his chair. She was suddenly taken by surprise when Edgar started to chuckle.

Looking up at Sophia, whose face and hair were covered in a blanket of dust, he said, 'And you are indeed the most majestic and beautiful queen that I have had the pleasure to be honoured by!'

Sophia responded by taking a bow, and duly replied, 'Thank you, Sir Edgar.'

They smiled warmly at each other, before Sophia reverted to a more familiar role; 'And now I'm going to clean myself up a bit – which will probably take me some considerable time looking at the state of me.'

Sophia went to retrieve her torch from its holder, and then headed off to the nearby well. As she went, Edgar called after her, 'When you get back, I'll read you my poem. I wrote it for you!'

'Yes, of course,' she shouted back. 'I look forward to it.'

Chapter Twenty Six
The Story Of Edgar

As Edgar waited for Sophia to return from the well, he wondered how she had known about his sword. Over the years, Edgar himself had forgotten that it was there, hidden within the recesses of the hearth in his room. "Perhaps she didn't know what she was looking for?" Edgar thought to himself. "Perhaps she just knew that something of significance lay hidden there?" In the end, whatever the truth was, he marvelled at Sophia's insight and determination.

Edgar looked down at his sword, which lay on the ground by his chair. In many ways it brought with it memories of sadness; a tangible reminder of the power and strength that Edgar once had. For Edgar had indeed been a noble man, as Sophia's recent "knighting" re-enactment had so vividly demonstrated. Then, over the years, through the force of his Masculine energy Edgar had fought to ensure that Sophia would be a "noble" woman in the Outside World. He after all represented the Masculine side of Sophia. So, armed with sword and sharpness of mind, Edgar had sought to help Sophia reign supreme over others when the situation warranted. This did not mean to dominate others for one's own gain, but rather to stand up for the good of the cause. He had helped Sophia to defend herself emotionally and physically, by keeping others at bay and by fighting off the negativity of destructive forces.

Then, as Sophia came to know this Masculine energy so well over the years, she began to call upon it - even when he needed to rest and recover from his battle scars and injuries. But how could Edgar let her down? How could he tell her that he had no more energy to give, when he had fought so hard for her to know of his energy? How could he let her see him in such a state of weakness and inertia?

Eventually Edgar came to realise that his days were numbered, as he was forced to take refuge in the Darkened Street. Emil and the Sibyl had kept him company in his darkest hours, but they could not return him to his previous state of being. Nor was it their desire to do so. No, their main purpose was to keep Edgar alive for as long as was humanly possible, in the hope that Sophia would rediscover her own Feminine energy and attributes, which had been unwittingly pushed aside by Edgar. The main Feminine attribute that Sophia needed to tune into was: receptivity. If she could do this – look inward and listen to her inner voice – then she would begin the most important journey of her life. She would release herself from the limited world she had been living in; she would liberate herself from the Cage of her "ego" mind.

It was during the time that Edgar had resided in the Darkened Street, that he began to witness the Feminine aspect in all its glory. For he saw the gifts of inner wisdom and gentleness in the guise of the healer, Emil. He learnt about the mysteries and magic of the ancient moon cultures, of peaceful communities and goddess rituals, and of other dimensional realms that existed beyond the 3-dimensional Outside World. He learnt about love, about the emotional body, and about the Feminine energy of creation: this fertility had boundless potentiality, so long as it was protected and nurtured. In the Outside World, it manifested as the abundant forests and flowers; the rivers and springs that flowed upon Mother Earth's beautiful body; the plants and crops that regularly offered up themselves for the nourishment of others; and the offspring of a multitude of animals. It was the energy of life itself.

In the days before Edgar had lost the use of his legs, he had regularly ventured out of his room and was often drawn towards the sound of singing and music. So pure and tender was the sound, that Edgar could not describe it in words, despite his many attempts with pen and paper to do so. High-pitched tones arising from flute and vocal chords, intermixed with lower frequency vibrations of drumbeat; and the vibrations of these sounds seemed to resonate through Edgar's entire body. He had followed the direction of the sounds, at first listening with his ears, but soon listening with his whole body. As each foot touched the ground, Edgar felt a gentle vibration of energy travel upwards. It felt like a tiny current of electricity. He could not have known then that at this very same time, Sophia was following the rhythmic sound of the Wood Chopper's axe, which would finally lead her out of the forest. Sophia in turn was not aware at that time that she was beginning to tune in to the "callings" of Edgar. Slowly but surely, Sophia and Edgar were being drawn together.

Edgar remembered how he had walked some distance from behind the row of houses in the Darkened Street, in pursuit of the source of the sounds. He could sense he was getting nearer, as his path began to take a downward slant. He felt as if he was travelling deeper into the Earth's body, the sound vibrations getting stronger and stronger. But Edgar had begun to struggle, and in his growing weakness he began to stumble over rocks that he could barely see.

Yet still he was determined to reach the source of the sounds. As he stumbled and fell heavily, he gashed his right leg on a sharp rock. He could feel the blood ooze from his leg, and tried to stem the flow with his hands, but eventually he was no longer able to feel the lower part of his leg. Yet in his pain, Edgar had still heard the angelic sounds around him, and could feel them rising up through his abdomen and torso. He knew he wasn't far away. He had to make it somehow – it was his only hope. So, he dragged himself with all his might along the rocky ground, his right leg by now a dead weight. This was to be Edgar's greatest test for salvation:

For the ground beneath him began to give way, and Edgar could no longer hold on to his position. He remembered how he had started to slip, and how he had tried desperately to hold on by digging his fingers as deep as he could into the earth. But the force of the downward movement was too great. Edgar had been terrified, as in the darkness his body began to roll down the earthy descent. And on the way down, his already badly wounded body had collided with rocks and other hard surfaces, which mercilessly tore away more bits of his flesh. Edgar had prayed that his end would be quick.

And then he remembered reaching the bottom. Somehow he was still conscious. His eyes were closed and his head pounded, but he could not feel the rest of his body. Edgar in truth had not been sure at the time whether he was alive or dead. He remembered trying to open his eyes but they were so swollen and painful that he gave up. It was then that he heard the angelic sounds of singing. They were the same sounds he had heard before, only clearer. Edgar somehow managed to force his eyes open for a brief moment, and through the pain he saw glistening pools of water and female figures playing stringed instruments.

And all this, under the light of a brilliant half-moon, had led Edgar to whisper; 'Perhaps I am dead, and this is heaven.' The salt tears that welled up in his eyes stung painfully, and it was not long after that that he had lost consciousness . . . .

. . . . When Edgar had opened his eyes again, he was not aware of any pain. He felt a strange kind of peace that he had not known before.

'Have I finally reached heaven in the bowels of Mother Earth?' he remembered saying.

Alas, when he had glanced down at his battered and bruised body he quickly realised that he was in fact still alive. Edgar remembered letting out an almighty scream. It was not so much the despair of still being alive, but more the discovery of the state of his once strong and muscular body. His upper body rested on the gently sloping banks of the pools, whilst his lower body was immersed in the turquoise coloured water. Edgar could still remember how warm and comforting the water was, as it wrapped itself around his limbs. But it was also the clearest and purest water he had ever seen, so that when he had looked down he could see with horrific clarity the true extent of his injuries. For just above his knees, there lay the tattered remains of bloodied flesh and bone. Yet Edgar could feel no pain. It seemed that this heavenly water had soothed away his pain, and that this was the only reason for Edgar's salvation; he could not have survived his injuries otherwise.

Then as Edgar had closed his eyes and laid back his head in exhaustion, he listened more intently to the musical sounds around him. The singing was as sweet as could be; the high-pitched sounds of pipes and flutes played on; the drumbeats carried a continuous rhythm. Somehow in this most deteriorated and deadened of bodily states, he had felt at his most peaceful and blissful. How such opposites could unite in this way, Edgar was at a loss. The Masculine energy of rational, analytical power – which had been one of Edgar's fortes – was simply redundant in trying to solve such a mystery. Yet he remembered thinking how gladly he would have laid down any weapon in order to surrender to the beauty of this feminine energy, which clearly ruled in that place of sacred sounds.

Now, as Edgar waited for Sophia to return from the well, more memories of that time came flooding back to him. Indeed this was the first time that Edgar had allowed himself to remember back to that time when he had known the beauty of Divine love. And as specific memories came to him, so too did his longing for that earlier time. Edgar was suddenly overcome with emotion. Tears began to roll down his face, as he began to relive that time in his heart and mind.

This is how he remembered it:

'Welcome to the Place of Souls, Edgar.' The voice was one of authority and warmth.

Edgar could not see where the voice came from. He felt sleepy, yet his thoughts were very clear. He was thinking about the union of opposites again; the wonderful combination of authority and warmth in the voice he had just heard. "The authority, which seeks to respect and honour one's own sacred space," Edgar thought to himself, "and the warmth, which shows an openness to share that same space."

Edgar then began to whisper his thoughts aloud: 'Masculine and Feminine energies existing in harmony . . . . . equal and opposite . . . . . strength and gentleness . . . . . . the union of opposites.' It was simply a revelation to him, and he could not help but smile.

At that moment he saw a type of silvery mist coming towards him from the opposite bank. The singing had now stopped, and so had the playing of the pipes and flutes. There remained a single drumbeat, which Edgar felt resonating within the chambers of his heart. The silver mist had now almost reached Edgar, who could do nothing but remain where he was. The mist began to encircle him, a swirling mass of energy descending upon him. In surrender, he closed his eyes and let go. Suddenly he felt lighter, uplifted, and he felt a tremendous sense of love in his heart. This came from within him. Yet it was also from somewhere or something outside of him: This essence of pure love was part of him, yet he was also part of "It".

Edgar felt a kind of inner transformation, and when he opened his eyes he saw the most magnificent of beings. She was wearing robes of gold and her hair sprinkled with gold dust; her eyes were the biggest and darkest he had ever seen, her smile the most loving. Edgar was so overcome that he wept with joy, and when he had stopped weeping, he was suddenly overcome with tiredness. As he struggled to keep his eyes open, he managed to find the energy to speak;

'Who are you?' he asked politely.

'I am the Sibyl.'

Edgar strained his eyes to get a clearer image of her face, for he did not recognise her. The Sibyl could see the confusion on his face, and so said, 'Yes, it's true Edgar. You already know me.'

'But I don't recognise you. You look different.'

'It is you, Edgar, who sees differently,' she explained. 'You have opened yourself to your heart and soul, and now see through these instead. This is the greatest gift you can have.'

Closing his eyes, Edgar drifted off to sleep once again, safe in the knowledge that he would be taken care of in this most benevolent and sacred of places. And when Edgar awoke, it was to the sound of singing. This time, however, he could also hear the sound of running water. Yet when he opened his eyes, he could only see a dark rocky ceiling. Eventually he realised that he was lying on his back at the entrance of a cave; for he had been moved out of the pools and on to dry ground. His head felt fuzzy, as if he was heavily hung over. He could feel something covering him from the waist down – a blanket or quilt of some kind.

With all his might, Edgar managed to heave himself up on to his elbows, and was suddenly awe-struck by the setting that lay before him. For the entrance of the cave looked out towards a pool of silvery water with many streams gently running to it and from it. He could see female figures in the pool of water – one floating silently, another gaily singing from her heart. Then over to his left, a woman crouched down to fill her urn with water from a flowing stream. Everything seemed to flow effortlessly and continuously; everything seemed to be in perfect balance and harmony.

Suddenly feeling a sharp pain in his lower body, Edgar winced and slowly lowered himself back to the ground. A woman wearing a sarong placed some water beside him; Edgar recognised her as the woman who had been filling her urn with water from the stream.

'Do not worry,' the woman said kindly, 'you are safe here. We will help you as much as we can to get stronger, though your injuries are quite severe.'

She knelt down to help Edgar drink some water. 'Thank you,' he said sincerely. 'You are most kind.'

The woman smiled warmly before making her way back to the stream. 'How blissful a place this is,' Edgar spoke softly to himself. 'I could stay here forever.'

'What is your name?' a man's voice suddenly echoed from somewhere behind him.

Edgar was startled by it. He twisted his head round to his left, from where the voice seemed to be coming. 'Who's there?' he said. He saw something shift in the darkness of the cave. Although he was not afraid as such, he could not help but feel a certain sense of uneasiness because of his helpless physical state. Edgar had to stay put, no matter what, and he had no way of knowing who or what was in the darkness of the cave behind him.

Then out of the darkness crawled a figure who was also undoubtedly in a great deal of pain and discomfort. The man was clothed in very loose white garments from head to toe, so that Edgar could not see his face underneath the large hood. The man's hands, which gripped the floor of the cave, were the only parts visible. It was then that Edgar realised the predicament of this man and why he had no reason to fear him. The scars and burns that covered the skin of the man's hands and wrists, showed Edgar with resounding clarity that both men had shared a similar fate. And now, it seemed they were at the same stage of their individual journeys: that of rebirth and regeneration.

Seeing this hooded man exert so much effort to move no further than a few inches at a time, left Edgar feeling an enormous sense of helplessness. 'I am sorry that I am unable to help you,' he offered. The man had stopped crawling and was now lying prostrate a few yards to Edgar's left. 'But you see,' Edgar continued, 'I can't move. I have no legs.'

'I know,' replied the breathless man. 'I saw the women bring you in.'

There was a brief silence before both men started laughing. And as each man heard the other's laughter, the infectious nature of the sound grew. They laughed and laughed until it hurt, yet it was the greatest feeling they had had for a long, long time. When they could laugh no more, it was the hooded man who spoke first:

'My friend, you are helping me just by being here.' He paused for breath and then said, 'My name is Tomas.'

Edgar liked the deep rich sound of his voice. 'I am happy to meet you Tomas. My name is Edgar. How long have you been here?'

'I don't know. But what does it matter anyway?' he sounded happily philosophical. 'I am here for as long as I need to be here. They have taught me well!'

Chapter Twenty Seven
The Place Of Souls

So Tomas and Edgar rested, and let their minds and bodies heal as much as they could in the Place of Souls. And the sacred women who inhabited this place, deep in the heart of Mother Earth, gave freely of their love and kindness to help in the healing process. This they did for any troubled or lost soul who came to them. For in this place of beauty and truth, there existed a universal pool of love from which all souls could be filled and refilled. It was a limitless source that could be tapped into at any time, to nourish hearts and souls for evermore. This was a place of no egos, for the soul was the true source of a person's life. The ego existed only in the Outside World.

It was in this place that Edgar came to understand many things about the soul and the ego. He knew that the main purpose of the ego was to bring gains no matter what the cost to the individual – material, emotional, or psychological gains – and to increase that person's sense of importance. Edgar mulled over such ideas in his mind many, many times. Although it was very hard for him to accept, he finally conceded to the truth about himself: that he too, through his Masculine energy, had sought to have a dominant role in Sophia's life, by and large for his own gain. This was not to say that his actions had never benefited Sophia - or others through her, in the Outside World - but underlying all of this, was Edgar's own need for recognition and power.

He had also learnt that only those whose lives were no longer directed by their ego-self could enter the Place of Souls. Only those who had dropped their ego by the wayside would know of the true Life Force which guided them; a force that served for the ultimate benefit of all on Mother Earth, even if this was not always apparent.

Edgar knew now with his heart and soul that he was meant to put down his sword. He no longer needed to give his power and protection to Sophia in the way he had. He needed instead to express his Masculine energy through other actions. He needed Sophia to develop her connection with her Feminine energy; to be receptive to the creative and nurturing energy of the Feminine. And he needed Sophia to forgive him for the dominant role he had played in her life. But all these things would have to wait until Edgar finally met directly with Sophia.

One day whilst he was lying next to a flowing stream Edgar felt a strong need to talk with the Sibyl, whom he had not seen since he first arrived. He needed to ask her about Sophia, for he felt intuitively that the time was approaching when he would meet Sophia. He did not know where this would occur or how this would come about, just that it would. But where was the Sibyl?

Edgar waited until the woman with the urn came to the stream, as she regularly did. He decided he would ask her about the Sibyl.

'Excuse me,' he called out politely. 'Do you know when the Sibyl will be here next?'

'She is very busy with her duties,' the woman replied. 'Do you wish to speak to her?

'Yes! Yes,' Edgar almost pleaded. 'Please can you tell me how I can get to see her.'

'You have already asked to speak to her. She has heard your call. You only have to wait until she returns your call.' The woman went about her business, but sensing Edgar's desperation she turned to him before leaving the stream, and said, 'Don't worry, Edgar. She will return. She always does.'

Then off she went, her urn resting upon her right shoulder.

'Thank you,' Edgar called after her, before returning to his own thoughts.

He became transfixed with the half-moon above. He thought about how he could only see half of the moon yet still knew that it was a whole entity; so that just because a person could not see something, it did not mean that it did not exist. Half of the moon was concealed from the light of the sun, and Edgar knew that in essence he too was half of a whole entity. He was the part of Sophia that was in many ways hidden from the Outside World, the dark unknown part of her that Sophia concealed from herself. Edgar was the Stranger she was yet to meet, and together they made up the whole. One half could not exist without the other. They were counterparts; they were two sides of the same coin.

It was at this point that Edgar first started to write. He felt inspired by something deep inside himself, as if he had touched his own soul. The setting around him too provided the most perfect example of harmonious living, where Feminine energy led the way. This harmony had been largely unknown to Edgar in his previous existence, where battle for supremacy ruled the day. But then, those were the days when the ego dominated; when the main concern was that of who appeared "above the water". Until of course Edgar eventually became so weak and could no longer forge ahead. But those days had gone, and with them so had his ego self. Yet it was only with this "death" that Edgar was able to make way for the beauty and mystery of the spirit of the soul. It lived as part of a world deeper than the sea and higher than the sky, a limitless domain of wonder and magic. Edgar had touched this domain. He was beginning to understand that it was part of him and that he was part of it. And so there was precious little to concern himself with, when such a Divine force was in control. All he had to do was surrender to it, and to let it guide him.

Edgar laughed with joy as he looked at the heavenly views around him. He felt at peace. But soon this peace was interrupted by thoughts of Sophia. For he wondered where she was? Would she somehow be able to connect with this spiritual place that Edgar had found? For it was hers also. Edgar began to wonder whether there was any way in which he could help her? That was when he put pen to paper, opening his heart and releasing his thoughts in the hope that Sophia might hear him. And somehow, the words flowed with divine rhythm upon the page:

THE GREATEST UNKNOWN

How do we live in the presence of time?
Not the future, not the past
Just the here and now.
Experience the moment for the exactness it brings,
Feel it touch you and feel it exist.
Blind your vision to distractions around
Carry the torch of truth with you
Be lost in the flame that fires up the heart,
Where a thousand dancing ladies dance to its beat.

And tremble not within you
For that which you do not know,
Trust instead the beating heart
Of the Greatest Unknown
You will ever know.

And such was the nature of Edgar to joyously display his newly accessed talents and abilities, that it wasn't long before a variety of scrolls were circulating around the community in the Place of Souls. It was not an attempt on his part to preach to the converted, rather a gesture of his gratitude for the love he had received from this sacred place; for the healing which had come from this purest of energies; for the subsequent transformation he had experienced, which had brought him in contact with the Divine Feminine energy and the gift of creativity. Edgar knew that his gift for the written word came from the Divine Source, so that his eagerness to share this with others was his way of giving back what he had received. The manifestation of this creative energy, however, came with Edgar's own unique style of expression.

One of the recipients of Edgar's written creations was Tomas, who still tended to spend most of his time in the darkness of the cave.

'It is very good, Edgar. You have found your calling, my friend,' said Tomas on one occasion, when he had brought himself to the entrance of the cave.

'Thank you,' replied a jovial Edgar. 'Your opinion means a lot to me.'

But there was another topic of conversation that Edgar wished to address with Tomas, and now was his chance to do so:

'Tomas, there is something I have been meaning to ask you,' he began tentatively, his manner more measured and less jovial. Then looking directly at the dark features of Tomas's face, Edgar said, 'Why do you spend so much time in the darkness of the cave? There is friendship, music, wisdom, moonlight, and so much more here by the water's edge. Surely this can help you more than lying on your own in the dark?'

Tomas lifted his dark brown eyes to look directly into his friend's eyes. He smiled warmly at Edgar, whose exuberance and sharpness he both loved and admired. Tomas did not take offence at his questions or presumptions in the least, because he knew that Edgar only sought the truth. He saw that Edgar was not afraid to ask or to talk about those things that most others shied away from; that he sought to clear away confusion and to be rid of the superfluous. Edgar's gift was the Masculine energy of analysis, of logical argument and meaningful action. How could Tomas not love and admire this in his friend? So Tomas would now try to answer Edgar's questions as truthfully as he could:

'In the past I was more like you, my friend. Remember, I have been here in the Place of Souls much longer than you.'

Tomas paused, slowly turning away from Edgar to look into the clear crystal water beyond. Yet it was clear to Edgar that there was much pain still.

Tomas then continued; 'For so long – many lifetimes, you understand – I did not listen to anyone. I scaled the heights, whilst others perished. It did not occur to me that I should be any other way! For if I were to lose my power, surely others would be waiting to take my place. "Why not me, then?" I said to myself. That is what God intended for me, I believed.' Tomas looked back at Edgar, who was listening intently, and then said, 'Maybe that is true, eh? I don't know . . . . . . it doesn't matter. It is like your poem . . . . . . what does it say . . . . . something about the "here and now", eh? And "blind your vision to distractions around", eh?'

Edgar nodded in agreement, but stayed silent.

'So that is what I do deep in the cave, my friend. This is my time to redress the balance, no?' Tomas was becoming more emotional, his arms now gesturing to emphasise his message of truth. 'To listen, listen, listen! To listen to my heart and soul . . . . . I never knew they existed until I came here–' his voice started to break.

Edgar leant across to touch his shoulder. 'I don't know what you did in the past, Tomas, but I dare say we have all done things we feel guilty about. That is why we are here, isn't it? Here, we are all part of the same community, the same family of souls. Now is the time to go forward. As you said, listen to our hearts and souls; listen to our own truths, follow our own destiny.'

'To trust the Greatest Unknown,' Tomas finished off.

'Yes!' Edgar tapped his shoulder in a gesture of comradeship.

The two comrades celebrated their friendship by drinking to their futures with glasses of the purest water. They would often sing songs they had learnt from the women, and would teach each other songs they had brought with them. And with the joy of song and laughter, Tomas and Edgar had tapped into the source of Universal energy, which would further heal their wounds.

In time, the open wounds of Edgar's amputated legs had healed, so that clean healthy skin now covered the flesh and bone just above his knees. He would often cast off his blanket and manoeuvre his body to the water's edge, using his upper body strength. He never lost sight, however, that his underlying goal was to achieve union with Sophia. But he knew that he must be patient and wait until the Sibyl heeded his call.

Similarly, Tomas had by now found the will to spend some of his time outside the cave with his friend. Slowly, the badly burnt skin over his body began to open out a little so that there was more flexibility in his movement, and this movement did not carry with it as much pain.

Tomas was generally more bashful in his demeanour than his friend Edgar. So it was more his style to talk privately with one of the women about his thoughts and ideas, rather than to share these with the wider community. Tomas was so grateful to the women for not rejecting him, that he continued to seek their counsel in virtually everything. He was indeed a man consumed by gratitude, which at times restricted his own movement and growth, but it suited him to be this way at this time as he felt he was making up for his past. It was not until the arrival of Edgar in the Place of Souls that Tomas began to make some bigger changes.

He had heard about Sophia from Edgar, and about how he planned to seek union with her. Tomas was filled with admiration for his friend's determination to achieve this, even though Edgar had no idea how he was going to do it. Somehow Edgar seemed to just know that he would, and of course this resonated in the words of his poems.

'Trust,' he would say to Tomas, 'Trust the Greatest Unknown.'

And so it was, that Tomas too began to be more open to trusting in something much greater than himself. Soon, Tomas was asking the women around him if they knew who his Feminine side was:

'Who is she who walks upon Mother Earth for me?' he asked on several separate occasions. 'I do not even know her name!' If they knew of her, they did not tell Tomas. And soon he stopped asking.

Then, one day when he was resting in the cave, he saw a chunk of wood. Moving over to it, he touched the wood with both hands, feeling its texture and strength, the roughness of its outer skin, the smoothness of its solid interior. He found himself marvelling at this most modest of natural creations, as if he was holding a mound of precious stones in his hands. 'But how did it get here?' he asked aloud, in tones of amazement. He was even more amazed at the response he received:

'All of the earth's treasures come from the womb of Mother Earth, Tomas,' echoed the voice of the majestic Sibyl, from deep within the cave.

The block of wood fell from Tomas's hands, as he gazed upon the silver robes. 'Sibyl, Sibyl! How I have waited to see you again.' The tears fell freely upon his face.

Once she had approached Tomas, the Sibyl took his hands in hers and spoke to him more softly. 'I know Tomas, I know you have been waiting. And at last the time is here. Take this piece of wood with you, outside the cave, and you will soon learn to carve. The women will share this gift with you now that your hands are supple enough.'

'But what is her name, Sibyl?' Tomas pleaded. 'I keep asking but they won't tell me. Who is the woman I must meet?'

'Her name is Jan,' the Sibyl let go of Tomas's hands gently, and then picked up the block of wood. 'This is from her, although she doesn't yet know it!'

'Really!' Tomas took the wood from the Sibyl in wonderment. 'Does she know about me? When will I get to meet her?'

'That is up to you Tomas,' the Sibyl smiled warmly, before retreating into the cave. 'I must go now. There is much to do.'

'Please! Please don't go yet,' Tomas called after her, 'Sibyl! Sibyl!' But all he could hear was the echoes of his own voice.

Yet Tomas had gained much from his encounter with the Sibyl, and now it was up to him. As the rejuvenated Tomas exited the cave, he did so with new found determination to learn his craft and to meet his Feminine counterpart, Jan.

In the shallow silky-smooth waters of the Place of Souls, Edgar bathed his healing body. He felt stronger now, although he knew he would never regain the physical strength he once had. Yet he had gained much more than he ever had before, and all he could think about now was letting Sophia know of such wonders as these. "If she knew what existed here she would never fear again," he thought.

Edgar's writing had dried up, so rather than persist he tried to relax his mind and body, and be at one with his surroundings. He could hear a single flute playing, which intrigued him because it sounded very different to the ones he usually heard playing in the Place of Souls; this sound was more raw, more innocent, like a child learning to play a new instrument. Edgar smiled to himself as he continued to listen intently.

'You look very pleased with yourself, Edgar.' The unmistakable tones of the Sibyl sounded from behind him.

Edgar immediately shifted his body round in the pool. 'Sibyl! At last you have come to see me!' He could hardly contain his excitement.

The Sibyl sat down by the edge of the pool in one graceful flowing motion, this time robed in mystical violet. 'The time has come,' she announced, with more seriousness in her manner.

Edgar held his breath, all the while keeping his eyes fixed on the Sibyl's face. He trusted her totally as he had never trusted anyone before. He trusted her word and knew that she was telling him it was time to leave. Suddenly remembering to breathe, Edgar said:

'You know, I have been waiting and waiting for you to come and tell me this, yet now that you have I only feel sadness and fear.' For the first time he averted his gaze from her.

'Yes I know, Edgar,' the Sibyl replied with compassion. 'I also know that you have much courage and love in your heart, which you must put to use for the good of the whole. If you stay here, how can the Outside World benefit from your input? How can transformation in the Outside World occur?'

But Edgar could not find it in him to be anything other than down-hearted. He felt more like a child at this moment than a man of courage. A solitary tear fell from his face into the pool below, generating circles around it until it finally dissipated altogether into the body of water. 'I'm sorry, Sibyl. I didn't expect to feel like this.'

Edgar felt the Sibyl touch his right arm and gently lift his hand up above the water. Opening his palm, the Sibyl placed an object into his hand. 'Edgar, I want you to take this with you from the Place of Souls. It will help you to unite with Sophia, and will help you both from then on and beyond, in the Outside World.'

Edgar looked down at the clear sparkling crystal that lay in the palm of his hand. 'It's beautiful,' he whispered softly, as if already cast under its spell. 'Thank you . . . . . I will treasure it with all my heart.'

When he finally managed to look up from the crystal, Edgar realised that the Sibyl had already departed. He grinned to himself, albeit a little sadly, knowing that that was the way of the Sibyl – the mysterious, magical and wise Sibyl.

Suddenly, another familiar voice called to him: 'My friend!' It was Tomas, shouting from the other side of the pool.

Edgar looked up to see the rejuvenated Tomas, standing with crutches. He could hardly believe the transformation.

'Hello, Tomas,' Edgar called back enthusiastically. 'Where on earth have you been?'

'I have something to show you, my friend.' Tomas was holding an object in his hand, which looked to Edgar like a pipe or flute.

Edgar laughed heartily, and said, 'Yes, and I have something to show you also!'

Chapter Twenty Eight
Sophia Returns From The Well

Whilst Edgar was reliving all these memories in the Darkened Street, he had dozed off in his chair outside his house.

Suddenly he was jolted out of his deep sleep by the rapturous behaviour of Sophia. She was shaking him from his sleep in her impatient excitement to tell him of her latest adventure. The energy of her child spirit could not be quelled, and it was this that would ultimately lead them out of the Darkened Street.

'Goodness me!' Edgar exclaimed. 'What is it, Sophia? You nearly made me fall out of my chair!'

'Sorry, Edgar,' Sophia said, trying to calm herself a little. 'It's just that I've found a stream . . . a river . . . . when I went down to the well . . . . and the moon! Edgar, I saw the moon!'

Edgar was suddenly wide awake, his eyes not veering away from Sophia's. He wanted to know more. He wanted to know everything.

A more composed Sophia continued: 'There I was, at the well, trying to get all the muck off me and change out of my dirty clothes. It was difficult, I can tell you, but then – I don't know what it was really

– but something made me want to explore further. To go beyond the well. Of course I didn't know where I was going, but these days I'm getting much better at following my intuition.' She paused for a moment whilst Edgar nodded in agreement. 'Anyway, I kept walking as if being propelled by some invisible force and then suddenly, there was light! It was magic, Edgar. Up in the sky, a half moon! Well, I've seen a full moon and a crescent moon here in the Land of the Shadows, and now a half moon. It was so beautiful, and it seemed to make the sky around it look a sort of lovely purply-bluey-'

'Violet?'

'Yes, that's it, violet. But, there I was, so transfixed by this sudden appearance of the moon that by the time I looked back down again I saw a silvery stream of water in the distance. I couldn't believe it! I just had to go further, towards the stream. It was further away than I thought, and by the time I got there I had to lie down, I was that tired!

'Anyway, it was much bigger than a stream – it was a river with quite a strong current. After I had rested for a while, I washed myself in the water. It had the most amazing feel to it – like velvet, or perhaps more like mercury – and it made me tingle all over.'

'Yes, come to think of it, you do look rather different,' Edgar said. 'Your face is glistening.'

Sophia touched her cheeks. 'Is it?' she said, suddenly feeling a little shy. Then, she went and placed herself on the ground next to Edgar's chair, her back leaning against the wall of the house. She felt a wave of tiredness come over her, as she finally came down from her euphoric heights.

Edgar remained silent. For he already knew about the river which lay beyond the well. It was how he and Tomas had journeyed back from the Place of Souls. But that was a story he had yet to tell Sophia, and it could wait for another time. Edgar for now was lost once again in his own thoughts about a time and place that he held dear to his heart: a place of silvery pools of healing and love, of angelic songs and sacred sounds, of true friendship and solace, and of the blissful peace that existed in simply "being" . . . . . .

It was through knowing the Feminine energy of receptivity, which had allowed Edgar to sense his soul; the true essence of his being. Yet this he had achieved only when he had begun his search for Sophia, his female counterpart. Edgar had learnt when he was in the Place of Souls that only in a receptive state – when Masculine energy was put aside – could he make a true and lasting connection with Sophia. The Sibyl had told Edgar that once he had done this, Sophia would find him; then through their union they would achieve wholeness, and their soul and spirit would live and flourish through them. Edgar remembered back to the time when he had had to leave the Place of Souls, and how difficult it had been for him to leave there despite his wishes to find Sophia.

He had not yet told Sophia of the time he had spent in the Place of Souls. How could he tell her that he had wished to stay there forever? How could he say that in truth he had only left there because he had to? For the Sibyl had instructed Edgar in her kind but firm way, of his rightful destiny:

'You must go back, Edgar,' she had said to him. 'It is your chosen destiny in this lifetime.'

Edgar had pleaded with her like a child, but still she would say: 'There is no more need for you to stay here. You must use your new found wisdom and divine energy for the betterment of the Outside World. This you will do through your union with Sophia.'

The Sibyl had elaborated no further to Edgar, before she took her leave. He remembered crying himself to sleep whilst wrapped tightly in his blanket, not even wanting his friend Tomas to be with him. Edgar never got to know exactly what had happened after that, except that when he woke he was no longer lying at the entrance of the cave but was in his bed back in the Darkened Street, nursing yet another horrific injury – this time the loss of his right arm.

Then later, when Emil had visited him, Edgar learnt that he had been brought back on a boat which travelled between the Place of Souls and the Darkened Street. But Edgar had never seen the river in all the time he had resided in the Darkened Street, so that he never quite believed it existed. In fact, he had sometimes questioned whether he had ever been to the Place of Souls, or whether it had all been a dream; that perhaps the darkness and silence of his room had started to play tricks on his mind. Whatever it was, Edgar had slowly blocked from his conscious mind all memory of the Place of Souls. Until now, that is . . . .

Now, sitting on his chair outside his house, Sophia seated on the ground next to him, so many memories had come flooding back. And as they washed over him, they brought with them the full force of emotions that had been kept at bay. At that moment, Edgar felt the warm touch of Sophia's hand on his, and so he released from within him the pain and love that had been locked up inside his saturated heart.

When finally the tears had subsided, it was Sophia's turn to reflect upon a painful parting. This memory she decided to share with Edgar:

'Did the Sibyl ever tell you about my first meeting with her?' asked Sophia.

'No,' replied Edgar, 'but I'd love to hear about it.'

'Well, I had just climbed the Mountain Road with a chap called Bob. He was a rather strange man really, but he helped me a lot,'

Sophia smiled at the memory of him. 'Anyway, I was in a bit of a state really – so desperate and scared of everything. Bob had left you see, and I was so exhausted with the struggle of it all. But then this magnificent woman appeared . . . . like someone who had stepped out of another age . . . . and she befriended me. I was totally awestruck! She was like a goddess – a knight in shining armour so to speak – who had come to protect me and take care of me. Well, that's how I saw her.'

Sophia suddenly looked a little embarrassed by what she had just said, but Edgar was eager to hear more. 'Go on!' he urged.

'Well, for that brief time I don't think I've ever felt so safe and so loved. I can't explain it but I just felt like I didn't need to worry about anything ever again.'

'Yes,' Edgar said dreamily, 'I know exactly what you mean.'

'You do?'

'Yes, I'll tell you about it later. But I want you to finish your story first.'

'All right,' Sophia agreed, and then continued: 'She told me she was the Sibyl of the Land of the Shadows. And then, on the other side of the valley to where we were standing, I saw all these separate shadows which darkened the hill. She told me that not everyone could see them, but that each of the shadows belonged to a person. It was amazing really.'

'What happened next?'

'I can't remember exactly,' Sophia suddenly sounded more subdued. 'Just that she left me alone by the roadside, and I felt so pained.'

It was now Edgar's turn to hold Sophia's hand.

'But you know, Edgar,' she said, looking up at him in his chair, 'I understand now why all that has happened has happened. I've learnt

so much about myself, about life itself and what really matters . . . . .
. and that we all have a Shadow side . . . . or a Stranger, as the Sibyl
would say, and that we have to face ourselves in the end. I'm so glad
I've met you, Edgar . . . . . and that I didn't give up when there were
so many times that I nearly did.'

'Yes, I too, Sophia, I too. But tell me, what happened to you after
the Sibyl left you in the valley?'

'Well, I remember sitting on the side of the road that led into the
Valley Town, feeling so angry and distraught – probably lots of other
things too! I'd had enough and didn't know what to do . . . . and
then I found myself writing.'

'Really?' Edgar was most surprised.

'Yes, I thought you knew,' Sophia was a little surprised herself.

'No. How would I know such a thing?' Edgar enquired.

'I don't know really. I thought that perhaps the Sibyl had said
something.'

'I'm afraid that I felt too angry and dejected by the Sibyl,'
explained Edgar honestly, 'to be in a position to listen to anything.
The poor Sibyl has so much to contend with really.'

Sophia nodded in agreement, amazed to hear how similar Edgar's
reactions and feelings were to her own.

Edgar suddenly said with great enthusiasm, 'I'd like to see some
of your writing. What did you write whilst sitting on the roadside?'

'I wrote something called: "Where did you go?"' Sophia answered
thoughtfully. Then she started to laugh, partly out of embarrassment,
as she recalled other memories from that time. 'Oh Edgar, I met this
lovely man called Victor and I was so rude to him. He didn't deserve
that.'

'A bit like the way I treated the Sibyl,' added Edgar.

'Actually, Victor and the Sibyl seemed to know each other really well. It was like they worked in unison, to help people like me journey from the Outside World of materialism and physical form, to the Inner World of intuition and creativity.'

'Yes, very good,' Edgar seemed genuinely impressed. 'The duality of inner and outer worlds, of the spiritual and the physical, of Feminine and Masculine. And the ultimate goal of uniting these opposites: to go beyond the world of duality and into the world of Oneness.'

Sophia looked up at Edgar in his dreamy state, and smiled. 'I love the way you speak,' she said warmly.

'Thank you,' Edgar blushed.

Sophia suddenly noticed Edgar's journal and pen lying on the ground. They had fallen from his lap whilst he was sleeping. Leaning over towards them, Sophia picked the journal up.

'I've just remembered, Edgar,' she said excitedly. 'You were going to read me the poem you had written. Is it in here?' Sophia began to open the journal.

'No, wait!' cried Edgar. His earlier wish to show Sophia his works seemed to now be replaced with a self-consciousness that Sophia had not seen before.

'It's all right, Edgar,' she said reassuringly. 'I won't look at it if you don't want me too.'

Closing the journal, she handed it over to Edgar who clutched it awkwardly.

'What's the matter?' asked Sophia. 'I've not seen you like this.'

'I don't know!' Edgar retorted. 'I'm sorry. I just feel a little embarrassed, that's all. Did you read any of it?'

'Hardly! I didn't get the chance, did I? I only saw the title – which I liked incidentally.'

'Did you? Like it, I mean?'

'Yes, I did Edgar,' Sophia said firmly. 'And I'd like to read some more, if you'd let me.'

'What's the title, then?'

'Oh really, Edgar! This is silly.'

'Yes, I know. But please,' he insisted, 'just say the title and then I'll read out the rest.'

'Okay then,' Sophia took a deep breath, and then shifted her position on the ground so that she was facing Edgar. She cleared her throat, straightened her back, and then announced in a loud voice:

'"THE HORSE AND THE HERO"'

Edgar opened his journal a little nervously, and began to read aloud:

'She rode and rode on the back of her horse
As if either or both had wings,
That would carry them through the mists of the night
And over the hills and on with their plight.

'The stallion that flew with the wind for its name,
As free as the wind and as light as a flame,
The wildness of nature to clutch on the breeze
Yet slip through her hands, as the spirit is free.

'And she, the one with the flame coloured mane
Rose with majesty unto the land of her reign,
Land of mists and magic and myth
Beset in beauty transcending Earth's plane.

'Onward they rode deep into the night
With stars to guide them 'til dark became light,
Then through the Gateway of Power they took flight
For nothing could halt such a magnitude of might.

'Whilst the draw of destiny and lure of the Divine
Held in its elements the transcripts of time,
Their forward leap broke through the hidden Veil
And the Horse and the Hero had touched the Holy Grail.'

There was a brief silence before Sophia began to clap enthusiastically. 'That was brilliant, Edgar. What an adventure!'

Edgar grinned shyly, and then confessed, 'You, Sophia, are the Hero.'

'Me?!' Sophia was genuinely surprised by the high esteem in which she was held. 'I don't know what to say . . . . . I mean, it's the loveliest thing that anyone has ever said to me.'

'Then I am glad it was I,' replied the ever noble Edgar.

Sophia took his hand and kissed it. 'Thank you, Sir Edgar.'

'Here, take it!' Edgar held out his journal to her.

'No, Edgar. I can't possibly take your written works,' she said, pushing the book away.

'Please, Sophia, I want you to have it.'

There was something in his voice which conveyed to Sophia a sense of urgency. It made her feel uneasy. Not because she didn't wish to have Edgar's writings, but because there was something rather final about the way in which Edgar spoke. In fact, if she was truly honest with herself, she would say that ever since she had returned from the well with news of the river and the moon, Edgar had somehow seemed different.

Sophia took the journal from Edgar's hand. 'What is it, Edgar?' she asked. 'There is something wrong. I know it.'

Edgar looked at her, concerned that she was worried. 'No, Sophia. There is nothing wrong,' he smiled warmly. 'It is just the opposite, everything is exactly right, everything is perfect. Just trust me, Sophia. Trust the Greatest Unknown.'

Sophia smiled back at him, feeling a little reassured but knowing that something had changed – or was about to change.

Chapter Twenty Nine
'Your Chariot Awaits, Madame!'

Sophia and Edgar no longer spent time in Edgar's house, neither to talk nor to sleep. Instead they slept on blankets outside in the Darkened Street. Ever since Sophia had gone on her cleaning spree and discovered Edgar's sword, so much dust and dirt had been disturbed and re-distributed around the room that it seemed even less habitable than before. But although this was the initial reason for moving out, it merely masked a more fundamental reason: That both Edgar and Sophia knew the time was coming for them to leave the Darkened Street altogether. And where once it had provided them with a sense of security and protection, now it felt more like a prison.

Sophia wanted to move to the river; she wanted Edgar to see the moon. Edgar, for his part, knew they had to find a way of getting to the river but could not comprehend how he was going to make the journey. He could not even remember how he had once made it back from the river to the Darkened Street on his return from the Place of

Souls. Somehow, Edgar had to listen to his own words and to trust the Greatest Unknown.

Sophia, by now, had journeyed to the river on more than a couple of occasions, partly because she found it so beautiful there, but also to make sure that it was still there! She would often try to come up with a means of getting Edgar to the river, but could not. She wished she had more physical strength so as to carry him there, but she also knew that this type of wishful thinking was futile. Then she suddenly thought about Jan, and how much more feasible it would be to get Edgar to the river if she was there to help. Sophia was indeed surprised that she had not seen Jan again in the Darkened Street, and wondered where she might be.

On one occasion whilst sitting by the river and looking up at the half moon, Sophia suddenly felt inspired to go in search of Jan. She remembered that one of the lessons she had learnt on this journey was to ask for help when she needed it rather than to continue to struggle alone. This, Sophia felt, was such a time.

As she made her way back from the river, she decided that she would tell Edgar of her plan:

'But what if you get lost?' Edgar asked her, on first hearing the news. 'We will then be in a worse state than ever!'

'No Edgar, that won't happen,' Sophia seemed unusually confident of her chances. 'You see, I'm going back to the old barn. I know exactly where that is, and I've got this strange feeling that Jan might be there. Anyway, even if she isn't I'll just come straight back.'

Edgar was quiet, thinking that it was perhaps worth a try, but still a little worried about losing her.

'It's no use, Edgar. You can't stop me – I'm on a mission now!' Sophia was almost triumphant.

Edgar couldn't help but smile at her. 'Be careful, won't you Sophia?'

She went over to him and kissed him softly on his forehead. Holding his face in her hands, she tried to reassure him, as he had previously done for her. 'You have to trust me now, Edgar. And the Greatest Unknown.'

Edgar nodded, his deep blue eyes beginning to moisten. 'You are my Hero, after all,' he whispered softly.

He then watched Sophia stride along the Darkened Street with her bag strapped across her back, until she disappeared from view.

Along the way back to the barn, Sophia suddenly realised that she was not carrying her torch. When once it had been the single most important thing to accompany her through the darkness, now it seemed to no longer be needed. She thought of the Flame Carrier, and their last encounter in the Darkened Street. 'Thank you, Flame Carrier, for helping me find my way,' Sophia said aloud.

She smiled to herself at the knowledge that she was now being guided by her own light.

When Sophia finally arrived at the barn, suddenly all the memories of her time spent there came flooding back to her. It had been a wonderful place of sanctuary; a place of rest and protection when she had felt lost and weary. She laughed at the memory of dancing and twirling around under the crescent moon.

'That's a point,' Sophia said looking up to the sky. 'Where is the crescent moon?'

At that point, the heavy barn door creaked open, and Sophia's head immediately shot downward to see who or what was there.

'Thought I heard something,' said a voice from just behind the barn door.

'JAN!' exclaimed Sophia in delight. 'How brilliant it is to see you!'

'Yeah, same here.'

Jan stepped outside the barn, but before she had the chance to close the door behind her, Sophia had encircled her in a heartfelt embrace. There was no doubt that even with her more natural style of emotional restraint, Jan was genuinely pleased to be the recipient of such expressive behaviour. And in her own imitable style, Jan reciprocated by tapping Sophia's back with her right hand.

'By the way,' Jan began to explain, 'the crescent moon is on the other side of the barn. You can see it through the window from inside.' Withdrawing from the embrace, Jan motioned to go back through the barn door.

'Yes, yes, of course,' Sophia replied, following Jan into the barn. 'I used to look up at the crescent moon from my bed of straw.'

Once inside the barn, Sophia was immediately struck by the transformation that had taken place in a space that was once so cluttered and encumbered with all sorts of strewn objects. She followed Jan as she walked in a virtually straight line across the barn floor, with no need to step over objects or to be careful not to trip over things. Sophia was so amazed by how neat and orderly the barn was, that she stopped halfway across the barn to survey the area around her. It looked much more spacious, she thought to herself.

'Jan, this is amazing! It was such a mess when I was here.'

'Well, I had to keep myself busy somehow, didn't I?' Jan was sitting on a chair by the window. 'Besides, you know me and wood! Most of the stuff in here was made of wood, so I couldn't resist chopping some of it up.'

'And using it for firewood?' Sophia enquired.

'Some of it, yeah,' Jan laughed. 'But you'll be pleased to know that some of the items looked quite useful – so I didn't break those up! Actually, I fixed them.'

Sophia walked across to the window where Jan sat, and then could see once more the silver-violet sickle shape of the moon. Out of the corner of her eye, she saw more clearly Jan's face; she still looked a little gaunt and there was more grey in her hair, but her eyes seemed to have softened. She looked sad, Sophia thought to herself, but also somehow more peaceful.

'You're looking different,' Jan suddenly said. 'Not the scrawny little thing you were before.'

Sophia was taken aback by Jan's blunt observation, particularly bearing in mind her own observations about Jan. 'Goodness me, you don't mince your words, do you?!'

Sophia looked directly at Jan, only to see even more clearly the vulnerability in Jan's face. Sophia decided to pull up a chair and sit down opposite her.

'You know, Jan, you don't have to be so tough all the time. I know you are hurting inside,' Sophia spoke gently, knowing that she was taking a risk in being so honest.

At first Jan did not respond, and as they sat in silence together Sophia could feel herself tense up in anticipation of a potential angry outburst. It did not come.

Instead, Jan's eyes darted nervously in different directions, her jaw muscles visibly tightening as she struggled to maintain composure. Sophia found herself reaching across to touch Jan's hands, which were clasped firmly together, and said, 'I am your friend, Jan.'

No longer able to hold back her pain, Jan gripped Sophia's outstretched hand and let the burning tears flow.

Before Jan had fallen to sleep on the wooden bed she had constructed, Sophia assured her that she would still be there when Jan awoke. Although this was a genuine gesture of support by Sophia, it was also one which would hopefully serve another purpose. For Sophia did not wish to lose sight of her own mission: to ask Jan for help in transporting Edgar to the river. Yet as Sophia sat by the window, looking over at her sleeping friend, she questioned the point of this. The reality of the situation as she could see it was that Jan was now weaker than before - both physically and emotionally. Like Sophia, it seemed that the rigours of her past life had taken their toll. 'Not that that's such a bad thing,' Sophia said softly to herself.

Sophia got up quietly from her chair, and walked slowly along one side the barn. In one corner, there was a pile of wooden objects that had been stripped down to their individual parts; wood of different shapes and sizes, some painted over but most of them bare. Over in another corner of the barn, there were objects that seemed to be in the process of construction, though Sophia could not tell what they were. Then, a little further on, there were some completed products. Sophia went over to what looked like a pair of crutches. As carefully as possible, she lifted them up and brought them out into the open space in the centre of the barn. Placing a crutch under each arm, she tested them out for their weight-bearing ability before proceeding to move, with one leg raised, over to the barn door. Then, turning around, Sophia moved swiftly with the aid of the crutches, back across the barn floor and over to the window.

As she sat back down on her chair, Sophia marvelled at the sheer organisation and practical skills of her friend. "She's a true crafts-woman," Sophia thought to herself, "whose medium is wood." Indeed she was in awe of the way Jan could break things down and reconstruct them into more useful objects; to create a new form of life out of something which ceased to be of use. It was at that point that Sophia began to wonder if there was anything within the piles of stock that might be the answer to Sophia and Edgar's problem.

A groggy and slightly disorientated Jan sat on the edge of her bed for several minutes, before realising that there was someone else in the barn.

'Oh, ... you're still here,' she said wearily, as she spotted Sophia by the window.

'Yes, I said I would be,' replied an alert Sophia, immediately taking some water over for Jan to drink.

'Thanks,' Jan took the water gratefully.

Sophia walked back to the window, and waited a while until Jan had come round a little. Then, she expressed her admiration for Jan's skills, holding up one of the crutches in her hand.

'Where did you get that from?!' Jan retorted. 'I hope you haven't damaged it!'

Feeling rather humiliated by Jan's reaction, Sophia picked up both crutches and went to put them back in their original place. She could feel the anger rise up within her, until it burnt her cheeks. 'Right! I think I'll head off now,' Sophia said, marching over to her bag.

'Look – I'm sorry. Okay?' Jan was sitting on her bed, with her head in her hands.

'What is it, Jan?! Why are you so angry?' Sophia was standing by the window, hands on hips, looking directly at Jan.

Taking a deep breath, then letting out a deep sigh, Jan said, 'Tell you the truth . . . . . I don't know.' She paused briefly, before continuing along a different route. 'What am I saying? Of course I know why I'm angry . . . . . I don't want to face that man again. That-,' she broke off.

'That what?' Sophia pursued gently but firmly.

Jan got to her feet without answering. She walked across to the crutches and picked them up. 'That badly burnt man who can hardly walk! What do you think these are for?' She was now looking in the direction of Sophia, her face showing the fear that lay beneath the anger. 'I finished making these ages ago, and yet I manage to find so many other things to do – anything to avoid going back there again!'

On hearing these words, Sophia realised that she was looking at a mirror of herself in Jan – except that this was how Sophia used to be. And if everything happened at exactly the "right" time – the Divine timing that Emil had spoken of – then perhaps the reason for Sophia being with Jan at this particular time, was to help Jan make it through this barrier of fear: to overcome her own inertia. Sophia suddenly understood with amazing clarity that she had to try to follow in the footsteps of the Sibyl, so as to help Jan move forward along her path, as once the Sibyl had helped Sophia. This was the true love of friendship.

Sophia sat down by the window, and spoke to Jan about her own experiences and difficulties in trying to face the Stranger, but also about the untold rewards of inner peace and strength that she had eventually found. She spoke of how the Sibyl had helped her, and of the desperate words she had written in her notepad to express her feelings of shame and disgust. 'I called the poem "Inertia",' Sophia explained.

'Hang on,' Jan intercepted, 'I'm sure I saw a notepad here.' She got up from her wooden bed and pulled it out from against the barn wall. After a few moments of searching, she found something. 'Here's a sleeping bag – I don't know if it's yours?'

'Yes! Yes . . . . I can't believe I didn't remember leaving it here! Or my notepad!'

Sophia got up and walked over to where Jan was. She picked up the sleeping bag with a depth of affection that took her by surprise. Holding the material against her, her eyes moistened with tears as she thought of how much of a comfort it had been to her in the past. 'My security blanket,' she whispered.

'Here's your notepad,' Jan said, holding it aloft. 'Oh, and there's a tin-opener somewhere too.'

Sophia smiled warmly, grateful to Jan for having kept her belongings safe. She was about to take the notepad from Jan, when Sophia suddenly changed her mind.

'No, it belongs here. You see, I've overcome my inertia now . . . . I found my spirit to become whole.'

'What?' Jan looked understandably confused.

Sophia silently walked back to the window, deep in thought. Gazing up at the bright crescent moon, she thought of the time she had spent amongst the ancient Stones with the Sibyl. She had sat in the centre of the Stones, whilst the Sibyl had reflected back to her the words from her "Inertia" poem - the words that described the other side of Sophia; and at that point she had finally faced herself. It was painful at the time, that there was no doubt, but it had led her through the process of transformation and this, in essence, was the ultimate goal of Sophia's journey:

"To truly be free, you have to face yourself," Sophia whispered softly.

Yet it was only coming back to the barn that had brought this realisation to the fore. Sophia marvelled once again at the never-ending unconscious reasons for things happening in the way that they did.

'It's funny,' she said, turning her head away from the moon to face Jan, 'but I initially came back here hoping to find you so that I could ask you for help – practical help.'

'Oh?' Jan was intrigued.

'Yes, to help me carry Edgar – I think I called him the "Inertia Man" when I saw you last – down to the river. But now I see that there were other reasons for me being here.'

Jan was looking at Sophia with an expression of confusion.

'Look, it doesn't matter about that,' Sophia said, realising that her new insights were not necessarily helpful to impart on Jan. 'I would like you to have the words I wrote here, they might be of help to you. Let them be gifts.' Then, suddenly grinning, she added, 'Besides, I remember us making a deal.'

'What?'

'Me showing you something I had written, if you showed me something you had made from wood.'

'Oh yes, I remember now,' Jan managed a smile.

There was a brief pause before Jan got to her feet and started to make her way towards the door of the barn. 'Come with me,' she called out. 'I've got something to show you.'

Once outside the barn, Sophia followed Jan as she turned left and then left again, so that they could now see the crescent moon. Sophia stood looking up at the moon she had come to adore.

'No, not that!' Jan's command swiftly brought Sophia's gaze back down to earth. 'This!' Jan was pointing at a wooden cart by the side of the barn. 'Your chariot awaits, Madame,' announced Jan, as she performed an elaborate bow.

'I don't believe it!' Sophia gasped. Her eyes were as wide as saucers. 'You're absolutely amazing, Jan!'

Sophia went over to the cart and studied it with the same degree of wonderment as she had the moon. Her hands gently brushed across the wheels as if careful not to place any undue pressure which could bring about its demise. The floor of the cart came up to Sophia's waist, which meant that with any luck she would be able to pull it along by herself.

She looked at Jan and said, 'I don't know how to thank you. How did you learn how to do all this?'

Jan pulled a funny face. 'Well, without wishing to dampen your admiration of me, I have to confess that it wasn't me. I just found it here the other day.'

'Really! You mean it's been here all the time.'

'I guess so – just that you didn't see it.'

Sophia started to laugh in amazement. 'Well, thanks then for seeing it. You know me and my eyesight!'

'Yeah,' Jan laughed, 'I do.'

Chapter Thirty
Unified Forces

Jan went over to the cart and stood between the two wooden levers attached to the front. They came up to just above waist-height. She took hold of one of the levers, and then gestured to Sophia to join her; 'Seeing as we don't have a horse at hand, we'll have to do the honours.'

Sophia all too willingly obliged and took hold of the other lever. Together they pulled the cart out to the front of the barn.

'Hold on a sec,' Jan suddenly said, as she hurried back into the barn. It seemed that she had discovered a new lease of life.

Meanwhile, Sophia tried to grip on to both of the levers as tightly as she could, and attempt to pull the cart along by herself. She managed to pull it a few feet, before stopping and then heaving again. Another few feet, and then she stopped again.

'Damn!' Sophia cursed, unable to believe how difficult it was to move the cart.

'What's all the puffing and blowing?' Jan appeared, somewhat amused by what she saw.

'Oh stop it!' Sophia answered in frustration. 'It's not a laughing matter, you know.'

'I think you'll find that it is,' Jan quipped. She was holding the pair of crutches and the notepad, which she took over and placed in the cart. 'You're funny, you,' Jan continued, undeterred.

'Oh? And why is that?'

'Well, you didn't think that you would be able to pull this thing all the way back to the Darkened Street by yourself, did you?'

'Yes, as a matter of fact, I did,' Sophia remained indignant. 'Anyway, I don't see why you find me so funny!'

Jan was laughing, in complete contrast to how Sophia had first found her. 'I'm sorry,' Jan said rather unconvincingly, trying to conceal her urge to laugh. 'It's just that you look so serious.'

'Well, excuse me,' replied Sophia, still unable to see the funny side of things, 'but you looked pretty serious not so long ago.'

At that point, Jan's urge to laugh gradually dissipated. When she spoke next, she was more serious. 'Yeah, I know. I suppose I need to thank you for cheering me up. It's been a long time.'

There was a pause until the two women found a more balanced and equal level of emotion.

'Okay, Sophia,' Jan said assertively. 'Are you ready?'

'You mean, you're coming too?' Sophia was genuinely surprised.

'What did you think? It's the only way we're going to overcome this particular inertia, as you call it!' Jan nodded in the direction of the cart.

Sophia found herself grinning at Jan's choice of words. But more than this, Sophia was touched by her friend's insistence in helping her. 'Thank you so much,' she said humbly.

'Don't mention it,' Jan immediately replied. 'Besides, you're helping me too. Who knows how long I would have stayed hidden away in this barn! Come on – before I change my mind!'

'Okay, but hold on a minute. I've left some things in the barn.' Sophia ran off into the barn, and emerged a short while later with her bag. 'I couldn't forget my sleeping-bag this time, could I?' she smiled broadly, as she tossed the bag into the cart and took hold of the spare lever.

Then off they went into the darkness, pulling their chariot behind them.

On the journey back to the Darkened Street, Jan and Sophia talked about many things; including the time each had spent in the forest. Sophia learnt how Jan had lived amongst the ash trees, whose strong and durable wood was good for the burning of warm fires as well as in the construction of weight-bearing objects. Indeed the cart they were now pulling was made from ash wood, as were the crutches that lay within it. Sophia was intrigued by her friend's knowledge of trees and her ability to make use of their specific qualities. She decided to ask Jan how she had learnt all of this, and was even more surprised by the answer she received.

'Well, remember that chap Bob?' Jan began. 'Being a sort of forest ranger, he used to patrol the area from time to time, making sure that I didn't chop down too many trees!' She laughed as she remembered that time with some fondness. 'You know, I think he was quite scared of me. I can see him now . . . . hovering in the distance . . . not sure whether to risk coming over or not . . . . and there was me, chopping away with my axe . . . . pretending I hadn't seen him.'

'So what happened next?' Sophia asked eagerly. 'Did he come over eventually?'

'No, not whilst I was chopping,' laughed Jan, sounding almost pleased with herself. 'He turned up one night though, when I was burning a camp fire. I guess I did get a bit carried away.'

'What do you mean?'

'Well, the fire was raging wasn't it? I'm surprised you didn't see it – or smell it!'

'Yes, so am I,' agreed Sophia. 'But I'm guessing that Bob did?'

'Yeah – that's when he finally overcame his nervousness and came over to tell me off!' Jan was still amused by her recollections. 'But I must give him his due, he did his job well. He loved the forests and didn't want to see them destroyed – and that's what I needed really: to be told where to draw the line!'

'Pushing the boundaries, eh,' Sophia said, knowingly.

'Oh yes,' replied Jan, with more openness and honesty than Sophia had ever seen.

Both women retreated into their own silence, it seemed in unison, whilst they continued to pull their cart behind them.

Within Sophia's silent thought, she found herself remembering when she had reached her own limits on her way up the Mountain Road; a most harrowing experience, which she had not yet shared with Jan. Even now, she decided not to do so, but instead felt immense gratitude for the help that Bob had once given to her. For he had stopped Sophia from going beyond the line, which almost certainly would have led to her death. He had made sure that she got to the top of the Mountain Road, a feat that Sophia had not necessarily been thankful for at the time. Yet now, she was able to look back and know from the depths of her soul, that it had been her destiny to survive.

Sophia looked over at her friend who was, and had been, travelling a parallel journey to her own, and smiled. 'So Bob taught you about trees, and wood?' Sophia said.

Jan nodded. 'His favourite trees were ash, so he taught me how to make practical objects out of ash wood – I guess we were quite similar like that. He told me about other trees in the forest too, but I've forgotten most of it. I think the part of the forest where you were, was elm.'

'Really! How interesting. You see, I'm useless when it comes to trees, even though I love them.'

'Yeah, I know what you mean,' agreed Jan. 'Anyhow, I remember him saying something about the trunks of elms being different shapes – not just straight. Oh, and something about them having this large canopy of branches and leaves.'

'Yes, well that sounds about right,' replied a fascinated Sophia. 'That is how I remember them. I felt so protected by them – particularly as I didn't want much light at the time.'

'Bob brought some elm wood over to me actually,' recalled Jan. 'He showed me how I could make a raft out of it. He said the wood was good to use in water, which was very handy seeing as I was determined not to go up that Mountain Road.'

Sophia was so amazed by her friend's revelation that she suddenly stopped pulling the cart. 'You mean you went on a raft?!'

'That's right,' answered Jan, grateful to have stopped. 'There was a river on my side of the forest. That's how I got to the Land of the Shadows – quite a journey, I can tell you!'

Sophia was stunned. 'I can't believe it! I had no idea that you could get there by that route. In fact, I never knew there was a river!'

Jan pulled herself up on to the back of the cart for a rest. She suddenly felt exhausted from her efforts. Sophia, still bemused by what she had just heard, followed suit. Seeing her bemused expression, Jan directed a pertinent question at her:

'Would it have made any difference if you had known?'

Sophia thought for a while before answering. 'The truth is, I don't know. But maybe I would have liked the choice.' She was looking rather down-hearted.

'Like me, you mean?' came the sharp yet astute response from Jan. 'Have you thought that maybe I needed another option!'

Sophia looked at Jan, who sounded a little annoyed with her. 'What do you mean?' Sophia asked, tentatively.

'I mean,' stressed Jan, 'that I am petrified of heights – don't ask me why – and I had tried several times before, to go up that damned Mountain Road – only to run back down again! How do you think I felt when I knew that you had reached the top? I had been in the forest for so long and couldn't find a way out.' Jan's lips were quivering, and suddenly Sophia felt very foolish.

'I'm sorry, Jan. I didn't know.' Then in the ensuing silence, Sophia softly said, 'Please forgive me.'

Jan fidgeted awkwardly before getting down off the cart. 'Come on, silly,' she called to Sophia. 'Let's get this thing going.'

The rest of their journey was uneventful but not unpleasant. The two women were eager to get to their destination, and so focused solely on the road ahead. All that could be heard was the sound of the wooden wheels turning on the gravel underfoot, so much so that it had an almost hypnotic effect.

'I think I'm starting to hear things,' Sophia suddenly said. 'I've got a kind of high-pitched sound ringing in my ears.'

A few moments later, Jan replied, 'You're not hearing things, old girl. What you're hearing is a flute. Look!'

Sophia had to wait another few moments before she could see what Jan was referring to. Although a somewhat blurred image, she saw a tall figure standing in loose white clothing, playing a flute. At first Sophia wondered whether she was seeing an angel. That was until Jan spoke:

'It's Tomas!' she said, almost in disbelief. 'And he's serenading Edgar.'

Sophia did not have to wait too long before she too could see with clarity a tall black man in white – whom she had once referred to as the badly burnt man – facing the seated Edgar, whose sword lay on the ground between them. She smiled with her heart at this most beautiful of images.

And so for the first time, there was a meeting of the four; a coming together of those who had once feared each other with varying degrees of magnitude.

Sophia and Jan had each journeyed independently into the Land of the Shadows with a courage that neither had believed they possessed. For theirs was an inner courage, not often valued in the Outside World, and therefore mostly hidden from view. Sometimes, Sophia wondered why the Land of the Shadows was not more hellish – like the dark evil Underworld she had often read about in books. Once, she asked Edgar about this, to which he replied:

'My dear Sophia, that is the greatest misconception of all: Alas, the evil you speak of already exists in the Outside World.'

Yet as difficult as it was, Sophia knew she would have to journey back to the Outside World; the Incubation Period that she had been going through, was now coming to an end. On more than one occasion, she had told Edgar of her wish to stay in the Land of the Shadows, but he would only say that it was her duty to go back; that with her new found wisdom and understanding she could better serve the Outside World:

'And in your own transformation,' Edgar would say, 'you can help transform the Outside World.'

'But what about you, Edgar?' Sophia had replied. 'You'll be with me too, won't you?'

'Oh yes, Sophia. If you are the Hero, than I am the Horse that propels you! We are the Horse and the Hero!'

Part Four
Gateway To Freedom

Chapter Thirty One
The Power Of Four

When the time came for the four to go down to the river, a general feeling of melancholy began to descend upon them. There seemed to be an unspoken consensus between them that said they were about to end a significant chapter in their lives and in doing so would have to say goodbye to what they had come to know. Many nostalgic memories were contained within this magical underworld of Shadows and Souls, but these memories now had to be left as memories. For however difficult it might be to leave this familiar world behind, it would enable Sophia and Edgar, Jan and Tomas, to step into a new chapter; one which would hold untold adventures and mysteries that needed to be lived.

As the four sat on the ground outside Edgar's room and quietly contemplated their impending departure, Tomas suddenly asked Edgar about a poem he had written when they were in the Place of Souls.

'I remember being inspired by it,' Tomas said, in his rich deep voice, 'and I think now we could all do with some inspiration, no?'

Sophia's ears pricked up at the thought of hearing more of Edgar's words. She looked over eagerly at him, without saying anything. Edgar's spirits seemed to lift almost at once, the fair skin upon his cheeks glowing a soft red.

'Which one was it?' Edgar asked Tomas.

'I can't remember exactly, but it was quite short . . . . good for my poor brain,' Tomas laughed.

Sophia looked from one man to the other, sensing deeply their love for each other.

'Was it "The Greatest Unknown"?' Edgar asked his friend.

'Yes! Yes, that was it,' Tomas answered enthusiastically.

'But I'm sure I know that one too!' Sophia said in astonishment.

By now, Jan was feeling rather sidelined by the unfolding discussion. 'Well I definitely don't know it,' she said, nonchalantly.

Edgar, however, was busy wondering how Sophia might have come across his poem. His thoughts were to be short-lived though, when Tomas intervened to give a much-needed sense of direction to the proceedings:

'No matter, my friends. Please Edgar, speak the words for us now - before we depart from here and step into the unknown.'

'Yes,' Sophia nodded in agreement. 'Go on, Edgar.'

Jan remained silent.

Edgar was a little embarrassed by all the attention that was being placed on him, although he couldn't help but like it. He shifted his position on the ground so that he was sitting as upright as possible. Then he closed his eyes, inhaled a deep breath, and began:

'How do we live in the presence of time?
Not the future, not the past,

Just the here and now.

Experience the moment for the exactness it brings,

Feel it touch you and feel it exist.

Blind your vision to distractions around,

Carry the torch of truth with you,

Be lost in the flame that fires up the heart,

Where a thousand dancing ladies dance to its beat.'

At this point, Sophia and Tomas decided to join in to speak the last five lines:

'And tremble not within you,

For that which you do not know,

Trust instead the beating heart

Of the Greatest Unknown

You will ever know.'

Sophia and Tomas lapsed into a bout of raucous applause, whilst Edgar's reddened face broke into the widest of smiles. Jan remained on the outside of things, looking upon the others with a degree of suppressed disdain.

Sophia was the first of the four to speak. Moving closer to Edgar, she said, 'Those words kept coming to me at different times along my journey. In fact, it was those words that kept me going when I was about to give up.' She looked up at him, her eyes glistening. 'Thank you, Edgar.'

Edgar smiled back at her, feeling blessed in the knowledge that his attempts to reach Sophia whilst he had rested in the Place of Souls, had been successful after all.

Tomas turned to face Jan, whose face was directed downwards at her knees. 'And how about you, Jan?' he asked. 'What kept you going?'

Jan seemed startled by his question and didn't know where to look. 'Don't know,' she answered abruptly. 'I just did.'

Her response had the effect of silencing the rest of the group, whose brief euphoria was cut short. It seemed as though this one person somehow exerted a more powerful effect on the group than did the other three; as if Jan had raised her axe and with one decisive strike had cut off the life force of the group! It was becoming clear to all that a significant imbalance existed within this group of four, and that at this precise moment they were unable to move forward.

Sophia and Edgar glanced a knowing look at each other, whereas Tomas appeared unusually awkward, fidgeting with the flute he held in his hands. There was no doubt that Tomas was upset by Jan's response, and he didn't know how to deal with it. Sophia was trying hard not to jump in and rescue the situation, for she knew by now that this would only be an attempt at concealing an underlying truth which needed to somehow surface. Instead, Sophia made a decision to confront the matter head-on:

'Jan,' she called out, 'why don't you just be honest and say what's bothering you!'

It was now Edgar and Tomas's turn to glance at each other. Jan glared at Sophia, which conveyed her feelings of anger more succinctly than anything else could. She did not answer Sophia's probing question, but this did not seem to put Sophia off. In fact, Sophia no longer seemed to feel intimidated or over-powered by Jan's anger, for she was all too aware that underneath Jan's hard defence lay a softer and more vulnerable opposite. Sophia proceeded as before:

'Look Jan, we're all in this together whether you like it or not. And let me tell you, we've all suffered our fair share of grief!' Sophia was starting to feel more angry than she had expected herself to feel. 'After all that we've been through, don't you think we owe it to each other to be honest?'

'Yes, Jan,' Tomas agreed, rather nervously. 'You can be honest about your feelings with us.'

Jan looked even more angry now as she got up off the ground. 'Honest, you say!' she shouted. 'How are you all being honest?!'

The other three looked startled by Jan's accusatory outburst.

'What do you mean?' Sophia asked, genuinely confused.

'What I mean,' replied Jan, in a steely measured way, 'is that we've all been making plans to get out of here, but no-one has given so much as a thought to how or where Emil is.' Then she turned to face Tomas directly for the first time. 'And in answer to your question, it was Emil who kept me going when I was determined to die. If it wasn't for him, I would not have even met you! I would not be here now.'

So in her eventual display of honesty, the root cause of Jan's anger was suddenly made clear to Sophia, Edgar, and Tomas. She was angry with herself and the others for forgetting Emil. But what became more apparent to them was their own part in this; it was not that any one of them was unthinking or ungrateful in their nature – no, what surprised each of them was that despite this, they had indeed "forgotten" someone who had given them so much.

No one was more aware of this than Sophia, who got up from the ground and slowly wandered off by herself along the Darkened Street. Suddenly she could not believe how selfish she had been; she had always thanked Emil and shown her appreciation, but she had often wondered in her heart whether he was becoming unwell. Edgar had often thought about this too – for he had said to Sophia that he had not seen Emil for a while, and that Emil had been looking very tired.

Sophia walked further along the Darkened Street until she came to the place where she had once encountered Jan; the place where they had chatted and drunk wine; when Jan had brought word of Emil – saying that he had spoken of Sophia as a courageous warrior. Sophia remembered saying something to Jan like, "I hope he's all right". The only other thing she remembered was being annoyed with Jan for not telling her sooner about Emil's message.

Then Sophia stopped walking. For she suddenly remembered Jan's response to her at the time: "Don't have a go at me! You're the one who left!" What had she meant by that, Sophia wondered? Had Emil been unwell when Sophia had first decided some time ago to venture alone into the Darkened Street?

'Why didn't I go back to say goodbye to him?' she asked herself aloud. For all these questions now seemed to trouble her greatly, when previously they had not.

Sophia began to wander back along the Darkened Street towards the rest of the group.

As she approached them, she saw that they too were deep in their own thoughts, their consciences weighing down heavily upon each of them, it seemed. Edgar looked up when he heard Sophia's footsteps. He smiled warmly at her, though this did not disguise the sadness in his clear blue eyes. Sophia smiled back at him before kneeling down in the space between Edgar and Jan.

'Jan,' she said softly, but assertively. 'You are right in what you say about Emil. He helped me so much, that in my heart I will always be indebted to him.'

Sophia could feel her voice breaking, and so stopped speaking for a moment. Jan briefly glanced up at her, whilst Edgar and Tomas sat in full attention. Then, Sophia continued her story:

'At the time I entered the Darkened Street alone, I had every intention of returning to my room, back there in the half-light. I hadn't seen Emil for quite some time, so I assumed that he was just busy. The truth is that I didn't want to burden him unnecessarily. I felt it was time for me to try to do things on my own . . . . . not to be too dependent on him. Then, later on, when I thought he might be becoming unwell, I guess I avoided finding out more . . . . just in case it was something I didn't want to hear-,' she broke off, unable to continue her confession.

Instead it was Edgar who spoke. 'I too did not want to hear. I told myself that he was just tired and that he would recover once he had rested. But in truth I needed him too much, so I decided that he had to be all right.'

'You are talking about him as if he is no longer with us!' Tomas suddenly said, in a loud voice. Then turning to address Jan directly, he said, 'Well? Is he . . . no longer with us, I mean?'

Jan lifted her head to see all eyes focused upon her. And whilst the others waited for her answer, they could not breathe.

'I don't know,' Jan finally said. 'All I know is that he was pretty ill, even though he tried to hide it from me.'

'When was this?' gasped Sophia.

'The last time he came to see me in my room,' explained Jan. 'You had already gone into the Darkened Street – somehow Emil knew – and he started talking about me going there too.'

'Go on!' Sophia urged.

Jan looked visibly shaky now and had begun to sweat.

'What is it, Jan?' Tomas asked with some concern. 'Talk to us. We are here to help each other.'

This seemed to help Jan overcome the invisible obstacle that appeared to be placed in her path. She answered nervously; 'The truth is . . . I told him I wasn't interested in going anywhere – certainly not in the dark. And n-not with him,' she looked down at the ground in embarrassment. 'He looked a bit taken aback – just the reaction I'm good at provoking I guess. He told me it was up to me . . . . that he was only there to help . . . . and that he would visit me again.'

'And did he?' the other three asked in unison.

'Yes, he always kept his word,' Jan answered, the others nodding in agreement. 'But there was something different about him. He looked pale and had lost weight. He'd also lost that sparkle in his eyes. Anyway, I said I thought he looked a bit under the weather, and he just smiled but didn't answer. Then when he said goodbye to me . . . . he had tears in his eyes. You know, like it was more final,' Jan's voice was much softer now, as she struggled to talk about her last memories of Emil. 'And then I watched him through the window . . . . . . the way he was walking, more a kind of shuffle really, his head bowed . . . . . . he looked as if he was putting all his strength into just standing. I thought for a moment that he was going to collapse, but he turned the corner . . . . and I didn't see him again.'

In the emotional silence that followed, Sophia's mind went back to a much earlier time on her journey: to the Story of the Tower. She wondered how much of that sad story was now reflected in their beloved Emil? For he had been a tower of strength and enduring love to them all; yet when he had begun to collapse, no one had been there to break his fall, or to give back some of the love that he had given out. Emil had helped to bring them together, whilst he had fallen apart.

None of the four said anymore on the subject of Emil. Each carried his of her own thoughts and feelings within them, and didn't try to find excuses or explanations to rid themselves of their feelings of guilt or remorse. But in the end, it was this very acknowledgement itself that enabled the group to go forth in search of their destiny.

Chapter Thirty Two
Forgotten Treasures

J an and Sophia lifted Edgar on to the wooden cart, along with several blankets. Sophia placed his sword and scabbard carefully by his side, and then her bag containing her scrolls, journals, canteen and sleeping bag. Tomas was busy trying out his wooden crutches and was clearly delighted with them. His flute was hung on a string around his neck, as it had been ever since he had left the Place of Souls. It was his most precious possession; it was his only possession.

Tomas stood still for a moment and looked over at Edgar seated in the cart. He noticed that something was missing; 'My friend, where is your special blanket? Surely you cannot leave without it?'

Sophia, who was leaning against the wall of Edgar's house, stood up straight. She was intrigued to know more about this "special blanket" that Tomas spoke of, and she wondered why Edgar had not told her about it before.

Edgar, however, brushed it aside. 'Oh, I'd forgotten about that,' he replied. 'I have not seen it for such a long time.'

'What?!' Tomas said, incredulously. 'Surely you don't expect me to believe that! Why, in the Place of Souls it was your most treasured possession.'

Edgar merely shrugged his shoulders. The astounded Tomas stared at Edgar, unable to believe his friend's dispassionate attitude. Sophia remained silent, but secretly had her own ideas about the missing blanket. She left the two men, and wandered unnoticed back into Edgar's house for the last time.

Sophia walked over to the wall facing Edgar's bed. She had remembered coming across some thick velvety material, which had been hanging against the wall; and when she had asked Edgar about it at the time, he hadn't answered her. But now she was sure that this material was Edgar's special blanket; a once treasured possession that for some reason Edgar no longer wanted anything to do with. This did not deter Sophia from the task at hand, and with a couple of firm tugs she managed to detach the material from the wall. What also came down with it, however, was a cloud of thick dust which had her coughing and spluttering, not for the first time.

'What on earth is going on in there?' called Jan, from the corridor. 'I thought we were getting ready to leave.'

The two women would have crashed into each other as Sophia came hurrying out of Edgar's room blanket in hand, had it not been for Jan quickly jumping out of the way! She, too, began coughing through the trail of dust that followed Sophia down the corridor and out through the front door. As they both exited the house, they could see the startled looks on the faces of the men. Tomas let out a most hearty laugh at the sight of the spirited Sophia crumpling into a heap on the ground next to the blanket.

'Sophia, how marvellous! Well done,' he cried, hobbling over to her as quickly as his crutches would take him.

Edgar, however, did not share his friend's enthusiasm. 'Why must you insist on raking things up from the past?!' he said angrily, looking directly at Sophia. 'I didn't ask you to, did I?'

Sophia was taken aback by Edgar's anger, so much so that she couldn't bring herself to speak.

Jan, once again, merely looked on at the proceedings from "outside" the main circle. As she stood by the doorway of Edgar's house, she thought of how she sometimes wished that she could be more on the "inside", and feel more a part of the group. Yet, if she was honest with herself, Jan could see that even wanting and wishing for this was in itself a big step forward from the angry isolated Wood Chopper she had once been. She grinned to herself in recognition of this, before her mind reverted back to the scene taking place before her:

Sophia, still upset by Edgar's angry outburst, was sitting silently on the ground, her head hung low. Tomas hobbled a few paces towards Edgar, and for the first time an angry encounter took place between the two comrades.

'I don't understand you!' shouted Tomas, pointing one of his crutches at Edgar. 'Why are you being so pig-headed? Look at you, sitting up there like a king, looking down on us – sending out orders to people who are trying to help you!'

'Aahh, so that is it!' Edgar retorted. 'You still want to be "ruler" after all! Despite what you told me in the Place of Souls, you haven't got it all out of your system yet, have you? Have you?!'

Tomas was visibly wounded by Edgar's cutting words, and said, 'That is not fair, and you know it! What I told you then in the cave was very hard for me . . . . . . how can you be so cruel?' Tomas retreated into the darkness of the street, saying softly under his breath, 'I thought you were my friend.'

Sophia got up from the ground without saying a word, and followed Tomas into the darkness until they were out of sight. Jan watched eagerly to see how Edgar would react to the others' rejection of his behaviour; for she had been so used before to being in that position herself. For the first time, Jan could see herself clearly mirrored in someone else: Edgar. And as she watched him sitting there alone, trying to stifle his anger whilst more vulnerable feelings threatened to come to the surface, Jan no longer felt she belonged to the outside of the circle.

Jan stepped forward from the open doorway and entered the circle. Suddenly Edgar realised she was there, and without thinking, lifted his sword out of its scabbard that was lying beside him. He pointed it towards Jan, daring her to approach further; his eyes burned with a rage that she had only ever known in herself. Seeing this fiery rage in Edgar, however, did not scare Jan, for she understood it. Rather, she pitied him. She knew that beyond the sharpness of the sword's blade, lay a weakened man who was terrified. It seemed to Jan that, momentarily, Edgar had lost touch with logic and reason; all that he had written about – his trust in the Greatest Unknown – had deserted him, so that there was now only a shell, filled with fear and nothing else. Edgar could not find his way back, it seemed, and Jan at that moment knew it was up to her to help him.

She lifted up both hands in a gesture of peace and surrender, whilst Edgar's outstretched sword trembled in his hand. His face was twitching, his eyes looked on in madness, and Jan wondered what it was that he was "seeing". Slowly and carefully she took a step towards him.

'It's all right, Edgar,' she said, calmly and firmly. 'No one is going to hurt you – do you hear me? No one is going to hurt you. You are safe.'

A new look registered on Edgar's face; it was a look of confusion, as if he was drifting from one state of consciousness to another. Jan took another step towards him. She felt she had to find a way to get Edgar to reconnect with her, and his current surroundings – the 'here and now' as Edgar would call it. "That's it!" she suddenly thought to herself. "His poem. I must recite some lines from his poem."

Jan's level of eye-contact with other people generally had never been that good, but she now ensured that she maintained constant eye-contact with him. Looking into the deep blue pools of Edgar's eyes, she spoke with more tenderness than she had ever known:

'Stay with me, Edgar. You can do it, I know you can! You are a good man, a kind man.'

She paused before taking another step forward, and then began to recite Edgar's poem:

'How can we live in the presence of time?
Not the future, not the past,
Just the here and now.
Experience the moment for the exactness it brings,
Feel it touch you and feel it exist.
Blind your vision to distractions around,
Carry the torch of truth with you . . . . .'

. . . . . Jan could not remember anymore – indeed she was amazed that she had remembered so much! She was trying to think of something else to say, when she noticed that the look on Edgar's face had changed. Somehow, his eyes seemed to have locked back into the present moment, and there was a look of recognition on his face.

Edgar could now see the familiar face of Jan looking directly at him. Next he saw the sword in his hand, the tip of which was almost touching Jan. In a split second he flung the sword to his left, and with such ferocity that it rebounded off the wall of his house and landed a few feet away from Jan. Yet Jan remained standing firmly in the same spot, unflinching. She held out her hand towards Edgar, whose own hand was still trembling. Sweat trickled down his troubled face, as he began to wonder what had happened to him: How had he almost lost complete control?

Edgar looked at the woman standing in front of him. She had, up until now, been a rather distant figure to him, yet here she stood holding out her hand to him in friendship. He did not feel he deserved it, but he was not about to reject it. So, leaning forward, he stretched out his hand and clasped Jan's right hand. The expression on his face was full of gratitude. There was no need for the spoken word.

Whilst Edgar and Jan waited for their counterparts to return, Edgar asked Jan if she could take his sword away; he had made up his mind not to take it with him. Of course he knew that Sophia would be upset by this decision, because she saw in it the symbolism of honour and nobility. Although Edgar understood this, for him the sword had come to represent too much of his past; a time when he had had to use it in the pursuit of salvation and victory. There were indeed many nostalgic memories, none greater than the comradeship that had bound him with other men, but there had also been too much bloodshed; too much loss, too much pain. In fact, the sword had almost become Edgar's right arm, until that too had been lost to him.

But all of this was in the past, and that was where it needed to stay. Edgar knew that his destiny now was to accompany Sophia back to the Outside World, this time without his armour. Deep in the heart of his soul, Edgar knew that the time had come for the Feminine force to lead the way; not at the expense of the Masculine force, but working in complete harmony with it.

Jan complied with Edgar's request and hid the sword in a place that only she knew. Then, walking back to where Edgar was, she picked up the "special blanket" which lay crumpled on the ground. 'Do you want me to get rid of this too?' she asked.

Although Edgar had been angry with Sophia for unearthing the blanket in the first place, he now looked upon it a little differently; he wondered whether this was purely because it was about to be taken away from him? Edgar needed to make a decision: Was it time to discard something that had once brought him so much comfort? Of course Jan was not aware of its past role or significance to Edgar; to her it was just a blanket - something that at this moment was hindering their progress. Yet it was this very neutrality that Edgar needed, in order that he make his own decision: A decision unhindered by the emotions of others.

'Well?' Jan was still patiently holding up the blanket. 'Have you decided yet? I feel like I'm holding the Golden Fleece!'

Edgar couldn't help but chuckle. 'I can see why Sophia likes you so much,' he said. 'But you are right of course. I do need to make up my mind.'

He reached out his hand to Jan, gesturing for her to bring the blanket to him. As he touched the rich texture of the material, all his memories from the Place of Souls came flooding back.

'You know, Jan,' he said softly, 'this is like the Golden Fleece to me. It comes from a place and time unlike any other. And one in which there is love and wisdom beyond the realms of human understanding or comprehension.'

Jan noticed that tears had welled up in his eyes. 'Is that why you didn't want Sophia to remind you of it?' she asked him. 'Too painful a reminder?'

Edgar looked at Jan, a tear falling down his cheek. He nodded and said, 'It was so hard for me to leave there, that when I came back to the Darkened Street I did not want anything to remind me of it again. I just wanted to wipe it from my mind.'

'I can understand that,' Jan agreed, thinking of her own past.

'Yes, but why am I still behaving like a sulky child? I have friends around me now, and I have come to know the wonderful Sophia: She has journeyed for so long in the near darkness, away from the sunlight of the Outside World, to find me and be with me! I must not drag her down . . . . I need to follow her now.'

Suddenly, Edgar took the blanket from Jan and kissed it. He then placed it around the lower part of his body, before smiling warmly at Jan. 'It seems I have decided!' he announced. 'Thank you, Jan, thank you.'

Jan returned the smile, patting Edgar on the shoulder before turning and walking towards the door of Edgar's house. Once she had reached the doorstep, she shouted back her own feelings of gratitude to Edgar. For it had been with his help, and through their recent interactions, that she had finally been able to make the transition from being outside the circle to inside it. And it was because of this that Jan had made the biggest step of her journey so far: She had been able to bury her axe in the place where Edgar's sword now lay.

But now there was something else that occupied Jan's mind, something that had been a source of intrigue to her ever since she had arrived at Edgar's house: the crystal door handle. She remembered Sophia describing its beauty, and how it had drawn her to Edgar in the first place. But why was it here, she wondered? Did it belong to

Edgar, or was it just part of the house? Jan crouched down in the doorway and began to examine the crystal more closely. She touched its smooth surfaces and its perfectly crafted edges, and for the first time she felt herself succumb to its gentle yet powerful charms.

'Beautiful, isn't it?' Edgar shouted over.

Jan was so surprised that she lost her balance and fell backwards.

'Oops, sorry!' Edgar said, with a touch of humour in his voice. He waited for Jan to pick herself up from the floor, before continuing in a more serious manner; 'You couldn't do one last thing for me, Jan, could you? I would be most grateful, and indeed indebted, to you.' For Edgar's mind had now been directed to another forgotten treasure.

'Go on, then,' Jan answered.

'The crystal. It was a gift to me from the Sibyl, but was placed there on the door in order to help Sophia find me. It was Emil's idea, in fact, and a very good one at that! But now I need to take it with me.' Edgar paused briefly, and then made his request to Jan; 'What I wanted to ask you is, could you try to remove it for me? Particularly given your skill with crafts?'

'Enough of the flattery,' Jan replied, amused by Edgar's charm. 'Leave it to me, I'll see what I can do. Anyway, it will give me something to do until the other two decide to return.'

'Thank you so much, Jan. I am truly grateful to you.'

Before getting to work, Jan laughed and said to Edgar; 'And I, too, can see why Sophia likes you so much!'

Chapter Thirty Three
Down To The River

Before finally leaving the Darkened Street behind, Edgar made his peace with Sophia and Tomas. It hadn't taken long - perhaps a few moments at most - for the image of Edgar wrapped in his special blanket was enough to soften the hardest of hearts. Indeed when Sophia had seen this image, she ran over to Edgar and embraced him in the most maternal and nurturing of ways. Edgar in turn apologised to Sophia with all the noble sincerity that only he could express. Then, noticing that Tomas was waiting in the wings, Edgar called him over, not by using his name but by referring to him as his friend. The two men made their peace, and no more was said.

Then the four began their journey down to the river; Sophia and Jan pulled the cart with Edgar sitting in it, and Tomas walked alongside them using his crutches. It was a slow and tiring journey for all. Tomas in particular found the going difficult as he was only used to walking a few steps at a time; although the crutches were invaluable to him, he realised that his expectations of himself far outweighed his ability. Tomas was a tall man, whose long limbs seemed to go on forever. It meant that he had more weight than most to carry around. His right leg was the one that caused him most pain, the burnt scar tissue so extensive that it was almost impossible for him to straighten. And because he had to make frequent stops, he kept apologising to the others for holding them up. Edgar in turn expressed his own feelings of guilt for being such a burden, in having to be carried by the two women. Meanwhile, Jan and Sophia simply felt a sense of sorrow for the physical suffering of their male counterparts.

The group made a lengthy stop at the well, where they rested and refreshed themselves. Sophia knew that it would not be long before they caught sight of their destination, for she knew the journey well. She could hardly contain her excitement at the prospect of being by the river once more, yet she waited until the others were ready to go rather than to force the pace herself.

When the four did continue on their way, it was only a matter of minutes before their eyes gazed upon the river. They all let out a collective gasp of delight. Even Jan who was not known for her emotional expressiveness could not help but be enchanted by such a splendid sight. From a distance, the water seemed to flow like mercury, making not a sound. The light in which it bathed was that of the moon, but with one marked difference: it was a gleaming crescent of pure golden light. The silver of the flowing water under the gold of the shining moon was a picture to behold, and would stay in the minds of those whose honour it was to see it, forever.

Sophia, who was always reminded of Emil when she saw the moon, thought of him now; she could hear his utterances about the sun and the moon, about Masculine and Feminine in perfect balance.

Somehow, such sentiments seemed to be poignantly and precisely portrayed in the image now before them.

And so, the group completed their journey to the river in silence, not once taking their eyes off this divine vision of beauty. No one dared to speak, for fear that their trivial utterances would break the spell that had been cast upon their hearts and minds. Then at the river's edge, it was possible to hear the soft sound of the gently flowing water, as though it whispered ancient secrets from a divine source. The light airy sounds which floated on the gentle breeze seemed to almost serenade the romantic scene.

Edgar, who was now lying on the ground wrapped in his special blanket, looked over at his friend Tomas. He smiled at the sight of seeing Tomas now seated in the cart, playing a sweet tune on his beloved flute. Edgar lay back his head and closed his eyes.

Jan had rolled up her sleeves and proceeded to take off her shoes and socks. Carefully, she dipped her toes into the river to test the water and, encouraged by the warmth of its texture, proceeded to submerge both her feet. Her main intention was to bathe her arms in the soothing liquid in order to reach for the healing properties that Tomas had spoken to her of in the past. Looking down at her arms, Jan could see the history of her pain and suffering, but now in a different light: somehow in this soft gentle light, she became more receptive to her innermost feelings. No longer did she feel the sense of detachment that she usually felt when she saw the self-inflicted scars. The precious water seemed to wash away the years of torment and abuse so that Jan could now see through the veils which had hidden her unexpressed emotions for so long. No, not the anger and fear that had directed the course of her life so significantly, but rather the soft and deep feelings of sorrow and love that lay closer to her heart. As she looked down upon the damaged skin of her arms, Jan began to cry for the first time. The river, in turn, absorbed her tears into its body and carried them effortlessly away. And in their place, familiar words of wisdom found their way into Jan's consciousness, and she spoke them softly:

' . . . . then you will know
the time of healing to have truly begun,
and slowly will it propel you
to venture back into the Outside World,
where your living can be done.'

Jan leant back and sat down on the banks of the magical river, with her feet still in the water. She began to feel a wonderful sense of inner peace. Closing her eyes, she was able to feel the sensation of pure unconditional love, from this most gentle yet powerful source. She felt loved. It was as if her heart had finally opened and in came the purest essence of love. It felt like a miracle to Jan, a blessing.

For in her lifetime, the seeds of love had never been nurtured or allowed to grow; only an empty space had existed, which had been gradually filled with the seeds of destruction, until nothing but the smallest sparks of light remained. It would have been so easy for this spark of light to cease existing altogether, to be snuffed out in a split second. And most of the time Jan had wondered why it wouldn't just go out; why it wouldn't just die and put her out of her misery once and for all. But somehow she kept going, and only now in this present moment, did she understand why; why she had journeyed for so long, over so many obstacles, through bleak terrain and such dark nights of the soul. This, she felt, was her true home. This was where she had come from, and she had finally found her way back. The veils had been lifted from her eyes. Jan could see the beauty of life itself, here in the heart of Mother Earth.

Looking into the water's face of ever-flowing compassion, she wondered why there were not more people gathered in this place? After all, so much healing was needed in the Outside World; so many suffering souls still wandered the Earth's plane in search of salvation. As she continued to gaze into the water, Jan's eyes became fixed on one particular spot, and her mind became more still. Gradually all her thoughts and concerns about people in the Outside World began to drift away, leaving her mind empty and clear. Without realising it, Jan had reached the still centre of her true Self. Buried beneath all the doubts, fears, insecurities, anger, and general baggage which she had carried around in her lifetime, lay the most precious treasure of all: Love. It was this universal energy of Love that always followed peace of mind and heart. And now that Jan could truly feel this, she became aware of its Divine nature and its ability to permeate anything and everything.

She could feel her limbs begin to tingle and a general feeling of well-being come over her, as if a warm blanket was being wrapped around her by the most loving of hands. In essence, Jan was experiencing a communion with the Divine Source of Life itself; a source of which she was a part, and would never disconnect from again. Jan's heart filled with joy as never before. She became more fully aware of the love and joy that already existed around her in that very moment: She could hear Tomas playing his flute, yet now it sounded sweeter to her ears; she could hear Edgar laughing heartily at intervals when Tomas played a wrong note, and the special nature of their friendship made her smile.

Jan wondered where Sophia was? Perhaps she had gone for a walk in the moonlight? Jan had never known anyone to be so entranced by the moon as Sophia – except for Emil of course – and she had come to see Sophia and Emil as quite alike in many ways. Perhaps the thing that struck Jan as most similar was the way in which they had both kept trying to befriend her – despite Jan's many rebuffs and overt discouragement of their friendship. She hadn't told either of them, but it was their friendship above all else that had kept her going. She had never thanked them, somehow seeing this as an acknowledgement of her own neediness and dependency on them. But Jan had come to realise the futility of this stance, just as Sophia had done on her journey, and now more than ever she felt much more compassion towards Sophia and Emil.

Suddenly Jan wanted to express her gratitude in some way. But it was too late to do so with Emil, and this still troubled Jan, for she had never shown any warmth or real friendship towards him. How could she ever make it up to him? How could she ever right this wrong? Maybe never, she told herself, but she felt she had to try anyway.

'Wherever you are, Emil,' Jan spoke softly to the flowing water, 'I hope you can hear me. I want to say "sorry" for how I treated you, when you were only trying to help me. I was scared . . . . . . I've always been scared. But I guess you already knew that.'

She stopped for a few moments, as her emotions threatened to rise up and choke her. When they had subsided, she leant forward and splashed her face with the refreshing water.

'But I'm not scared anymore, Emil,' she continued. 'And I'm ready to go back to the Outside World. Thank you for everything . . . . . I'll never forget you.'

Jan felt strangely liberated. Far from feeling weakened by her acknowledgements, she felt a rising inner strength within her which came from facing her personal truths. She was about to stand up and take her leave from the river, when the most amazing of gifts presented itself to her: silvery-purple lights suddenly appeared on the surface of the water in front of her and proceeded to dance upon the water. Jan gasped, as the dancing lights slowly settled to form the face of Emil. She kept squeezing her eyelids shut and then opening them again to see if she was imagining things, but to her amazement Emil's face was still there looking at her. Then he smiled his warm smile, and spoke:

'I heard your call, Jan. Thank you for your kind words. But do not be too hard on yourself; remember, we can only do what we are able to do. That is all. You, too, are a courageous warrior – a spiritual warrior – and you must continue along this path when you are back in the Outside World. You have much to offer, and others who have forgotten their way home will learn from you.

'Tell them of this Divine Love you have found, and of the following words, which I now leave you with:

... You must believe there is enough to go around,
The love of the Universe is a limitless Source.
You just have to know how to tap into it,
And you can if you try ....'

And with this, Emil's smiling face slowly dissolved into the river.

A speechless Jan tried to get to her feet but could not. Her quivering legs gave way beneath her, and as she stumbled to the ground she started to laugh hysterically. Tomas immediately stopped playing his flute, and Edgar lifted his head up off the ground, both startled by the figure of Jan rolling on the ground and laughing.

'What's happened?!' shouted a concerned Tomas.

'A miracle!' Jan shouted back with glee.

Chapter Thirty Four
By The Silver Birch

Sophia walked for quite a distance along the river's edge, her adventurous child spirit inspiring her to search and explore; it seemed that it had never really gone away. Although she had been walking in the direction of the flowing water, Sophia had not realised the gentle yet upward sloping nature of the earth underfoot. It was only now when she stopped to rest that she looked back and saw the lower ground in the distance where her brethren rested.

Sophia sat cross-legged on the ground and watched the ever-flowing silvery river, as it made its way from its source deep within the core of Mother Earth, up towards the outer regions of the Earth's plane. She wondered how far the journey was, and whether she and her brethen would end up travelling upon the water and be carried by the river back up to the Outside World? But how could they sail without a boat or raft? Or would a boat suddenly appear from somewhere, and ferry them to where they needed to go?

'Questions, questions, and more questions,' Sophia sighed a deep sigh.

For she was tired of questioning that which she did not know. In fact, she was just plain tired. She knew her mind and body needed to rest, so she decided to do just that: 'And everything else can take care of itself.'

So with no more hesitation, she lay down and went to sleep in the arms of Mother Earth.

When Sophia awoke, it took her a few moments to realise where she was. She didn't know how long she had been sleeping. It felt like it could have been for hours, but perhaps it was only minutes. What she noticed more than anything was how warm she felt; how comforted and loved she felt without any effort on her part. And all Sophia had to do was to receive. She felt as though she was floating on a warm gentle sea, with no feelings of fear present, just safe and secure as she had never felt before.

Sophia's eyes were still closed whilst she indulged in the dreamy delights of this Divine Love. A broad smile swept across her face, and she felt like laughing out loud with profound joy. But instead she opened her eyes, and saw that her body was wrapped in the finest softest material.

'The time has come, Sophia,' said the knowing voice of the Sibyl suddenly, 'to cast off your old self – the one which has lived in a world of restriction and limitation – and to venture back to the Outside World, renewed and whole.'

Sophia was now sitting bolt upright, holding the beautiful shawl to her neck. Before her, the dazzling gold that emanated from the Sibyl's robe rendered Sophia speechless. The Sibyl looked different each time Sophia saw her; her glowing attire took on an array of different colours and materials, each strikingly beautiful to all who cast their eyes upon her. But there were other differences too; the colour, length and style of her hair was always different, and sometimes she wore elaborate head-dresses which covered her hair completely. And then there were the most striking differences of all: the colour of the Sibyl's skin and eyes changed on each occasion. Sometimes her skin was milky white, sometimes olive, sometimes brown. Her eyes were green, or brown, sometimes even gold. Yet there was never any mistaking that this was the Sibyl, of the Land of the Shadows.

The Sibyl held out her hand to Sophia. Responding immediately, Sophia took the outstretched hand and was lifted up on to her feet. The Sibyl then silently beckoned Sophia to follow her further along the water's edge. Sophia quickly threw the shawl over her shoulders and followed in the footsteps of the Sibyl. Soon Sophia would see something that she had not seen in a long time:

Standing proudly before them was a tree. Sophia could not believe it and was eager to go over and touch it, yet she hesitated. Somehow it looked much more delicate than the strong sturdy trees she had lived amongst in the ancient forest.

'Yes, you are right to be careful with her,' said the Sibyl, reassuringly.

'She's beautiful,' Sophia responded, mesmerised by the silver coloured bark of the tree under the moonlight.

'She is a silver birch, but I call her the moon-tree.'

Sophia nodded in agreement. 'Yes, I can see why. It is a perfect description.'

The Sibyl walked over to the slender trunk of the tree and gently touched the silver bark, the gold of her gown contrasting most beautifully with it. Suddenly, Sophia felt deeply blessed by being granted such a vision, and she told herself there and then that wherever she went in the future, she would carry this divine image with her.

'There were once many ancient rituals performed,' the Sibyl began, 'where the Feminine principle in the form of the goddess was worshipped and revered.' Her eyes suddenly looked sad and faraway, as she reflected on a more glorious past that was no more.

Sophia had not seen the Sibyl display such vulnerability before, but she was not uncomfortable with it. In fact, it made Sophia realise how far she had come on this journey; for earlier on in her journey, she would have been unable to cope with the vulnerability of those that she relied on to help her: Sophia was the vulnerable one, therefore others had to be strong. But now she was stronger, so that others – even the majestic Sibyl – did not have to be strong all the time. Sophia could see that dual aspects such as; strength and weakness, hardness and softness, Masculine and Feminine - could exist together, in the same person. She felt that there was more balance somehow, and her mind could not help but think of Emil.

The Sibyl began to speak once again, but this time her words seemed to almost synchronise with Sophia's thoughts: 'All is not lost, Sophia. Far from it! The time for a more balanced humanity is approaching – when the Feminine force will rise once again to co-exist in equality and harmony with the Masculine.'

The Sibyl then became increasingly animated in her gestures, as if about to address an audience of followers: 'And as that begins to happen, all will come to know once more the beauty of this Universe, and the Divine peace and love that exists at the heart of each and everyone.'

Yet the Sibyl was also aware of the need to reconnect with Sophia more directly and personally, so as to help her to find her own purpose in this grand design. 'Do you like trees, Sophia?' the Sibyl said, looking into Sophia's eyes.

'Yes, very much. In fact, I realise now how much I miss them – I relied on them so much for comfort and food when I was living in the forest.' Sophia paused for a moment before adding; 'But I've never seen a tree as lovely as this.'

The Sibyl smiled a beaming smile, her eyes lighting up to project a golden glow. 'She is more delicate than most trees, but she is also strong. The secret is balance – and trees are masters of balance.'

It was now Sophia's turn to smile broadly. 'Yes, Emil used to talk about balance. I remember him saying: Balance in everything, balance is everything.'

'Yes, yes,' agreed the Sibyl, enthusiastically. 'Fine words. Emil was indeed a fine teacher.'

Sophia was suddenly struck very deeply by these words, for they came from someone who knew Emil, and who had spoken of him in the past tense. But Sophia felt she had to know the truth about Emil before she could ever walk freely in the Outside World. Now was her chance to find out:

'Where is Emil?' Sophia asked. She inhaled a deep breath whilst awaiting the reply.

'I wondered when you would ask,' the Sibyl smiled warmly, as she walked over to Sophia. 'And I am very glad that you have. Sometimes we do not ask when we fear the answer. But there is no need to fear in this case, Sophia, for Emil is in the most wonderful of places.'

'Y-you m-mean he's dead, don't you?' Suddenly Sophia became very distressed; 'I-I never even g-got to say goodbye to him.' She hung her head down to the ground in shame.

A few silent moments passed before the Sibyl placed her hand under Sophia's chin, and raised it with gentle firmness until Sophia was looking directly into her eyes. The colour of the Sibyl's eyes had now changed into the deepest blue of the deepest ocean, and Sophia could not help but feel herself drift towards the great expanse of their source. She felt herself surrender to its flow, and could feel herself in the same vast ocean of life as the Sibyl. In this briefest of moments, Sophia experienced the ultimate reality of Oneness; she experienced her own connection and connectedness with the rest of life. She did not just believe it, but knew it beyond all rational explanation; there was no separation between the many life forms, everything was part of the same big whole.

Sophia felt that all the Veils of Illusion had been lifted from her eyes, so that everything suddenly seemed so clear: Everything that existed in the Outside World was merely a physical manifestation of the Life Force that lay behind it. This Life Force, or Universal Energy, was ever present and indestructible, so that whatever happened to the physical form, status, or the ego – be it illness or death – the underlying Life Force would never die.

Gradually the intensity and vividness of Sophia's experience in that moment diminished, until a more familiar one took its place: she could feel her feet more firmly on the ground, and she once again felt the physical sensation of the Sibyl's touch. The deep blue of the Sibyl's eyes had become a more earthy brown, and Sophia came slowly back down to earth.

'So you see, Sophia,' the Sibyl explained, 'you do not have to worry about Emil. He has done his life's work many times over and has finally returned home.' Then she smiled and said, 'I am sure however that he will visit you whenever he can, and in whatever way he can.'

Still feeling slightly drunk with ecstasy, Sophia smiled the broadest of smiles. Then with the spontaneous nature of the child spirit, she embraced the Sibyl so tightly that even the noble Sibyl felt a little overcome with emotion. She stroked Sophia's hair as they shared these precious moments together.

'There are some things you must know, Sophia, before you return to the Outside World,' there was now a sense of urgency in the Sibyl's voice, as she gently withdrew herself from the embrace. 'We do not have long. The others will be worried about you.'

Sophia knew that she was right and that Edgar in particular would be worried about where she had got to. She was now ready to hear more of the Sibyl's words of wisdom.

'On this West Road that you have travelled,' the Sibyl began, 'you have journeyed to a place where the sun forever sets. In the darkness, it is that which is hidden that rules. Here, as you know, the moon is the great celestial teacher which reflects back to us all that we do not normally see in our nature. She is the silver multi-dimensional mirror in the sky. She allows all who travel into the darkness the opportunity to know the mysteries of one's own true nature, and in doing so we are no longer imprisoned by such unconscious forces, as you yourself once were.

'But more than this, Sophia, the West Road of darkness holds the mysteries and teachings of all that has gone before; all that our ancient ancestors knew and experienced. It holds our past in all its glory, and all its tragedy. I am telling you this, Sophia, because now that you have freed yourself from the limitations of the ego-mind - that has long taken prominence in the Outside World – you are much more open to receiving such ancient knowledge. Remember, this is the ultimate power of the Feminine aspect: to be receptive, to be intuitive, to listen with all the senses open. Then, the wisdom of the Divine, the Universe, the Greatest Unknown, will be available to all who value and respect the Feminine.'

As the Sibyl paused, she saw that Sophia's eyes were big and bright, and that her face looked like the face of a child who had been listening with wonder to a fairytale; and of course believed it to be true as most children do.

The Sibyl gestured to the silver birch, and then continued with her own true story: 'Like this beautiful tree, Sophia, you must learn to live in balance. When you are back in the Outside World, you may find yourself caught up in the day-to-day routines and problems, which then take you away from your inner nature, your true Self. When this happens, you must find time and space to root yourself, to be still and silent. The more you do this, the more natural it will be until it becomes second nature.

'Remember the lesson of the tree: It remains firmly connected to Mother Earth from which it receives nourishment and support, yet it also stretches out to the sun and sky, and gives to all who are in need of its gifts; its branches to the birds, its flowers to the bees, its fruits to us . . . . . the list goes on. If you remember this, Sophia, you too will be balanced perfectly between this inner world and the Outside World. You too will know peace and harmony, from which will flow love.

'And now I must tell you how to get back to the Outside World.'

The Sibyl looked directly at Sophia, seeing at once the look of apprehension in her eyes. Yet the Sibyl knew that there was little point in prolonging the inevitable; the sooner Sophia focused on her next step, the sooner her resistance would melt away.

'First, you must go back to the others,' the Sibyl explained, 'but you must not tell them of our meeting; for each has a different path to follow, and it would not help them at this crucial time to know about your own experience. Edgar, in truth, will already know. He is after all, closely attuned with you.

'Then, when all are asleep, you must bid your farewell to Tomas and to Jan. You can do this in whatever way you see fit, whatever feels right to you – but you must do it. Then, you will wake Edgar from his sleep and tell him that it is time to cross the river.'

Sophia listened intently to every word. She wanted to make sure that she understood all the instructions being given to her. But she could not help but be shocked by the revelation that she and Edgar were to cross the river, rather than to sail along it as she had originally assumed. And although the Sibyl could see the look of surprise on Sophia's face, she decided to continue unheeded with her message:

'Before you enter the river, Edgar will give you an object – a very special object, from the Place of Souls – which you are to accept from him. Keep this object safe, Sophia, for it will prove to be of great importance to you in the coming years. All you need to know now is that it will help you to stay in close contact with this world: The world of forgotten wisdom and ancient mysteries.

'And lastly, Sophia, you must carry Edgar into the river. There is no other way.'

On hearing this, Sophia's jaw dropped open. But before she could say anything in protest, the Sibyl spoke again:

'Do not expend your energy worrying about this, Sophia, you will be able to do this despite your fears. Once you have walked a few steps into the river, Edgar will be lifted by the water and the burden of his weight will be taken from your hands. This immersion of yourself and Edgar in water is an important and beautiful ritual, which symbolises the sacred union between the Masculine and Feminine aspects within you. You will emerge, Sophia, on the other side of the river, renewed and whole – and ready to take your first steps through the Gateway of Freedom.

In the intense silence that followed, Sophia looked nervous and unsure of what was required of her. But more than this, she was finally facing the moment that she always knew she would one day have to face. She was about to leave the familiar safety of the Land of the Shadows, and embark on an unknown journey into the now unfamiliar Outside World.

The Sibyl placed her hands upon Sophia's brave shoulders, and almost immediately tears welled up in Sophia's eyes. As the Sibyl watched the tears tumble upon Sophia's flushed cheeks, she softly said, 'I know it is hard for you to leave here, Sophia, but your time now is better served in the brightness of the sun. That is your destiny, that is your future. It will not be long before you see and feel the magnificent beauty of Nature once again, and the wondrous creations of Mother Earth. You are meant to be a part of that also, as are all children of the Earth, and to follow your own creativity and inspiration so that you will bring forth the fruits that will help make the Outside World a better place for everyone.'

'B-but w-what happens w-when I cross the river?' Sophia asked, tearfully.

The Sibyl smiled sweetly, and said, 'Do not think about that now. All will become clear when you reach there. Trust me, Sophia.'

'O-o-okay,' Sophia nodded.

The Sibyl leant forward and kissed Sophia's forehead. 'Hurry now, Sophia, time is precious.'

'Goodbye, Sibyl.' Sophia looked up at the Sibyl with tear-stained eyes. 'I love you,' she said.

Then Sophia quickly took her leave, scuttling off down the gentle slope of the river bank towards the others.

Chapter Thirty Five
Communion

As she neared her destination, Sophia was suddenly heartened by the image she saw of her comrades. The three were seated around a glowing fire, their voices dimly audible as they shared the communion of friendship. The sadness that had filled Sophia so recently on departing from the Sibyl, had seemingly dissipated and had been replaced by a feeling of warmth and love. She could hear the sound of their different voices, but the most animated of these was Jan's, and she could not believe it. In fact, Sophia realised all too clearly how she had never heard Jan laugh before - a chuckle perhaps or a look of amusement on her face, but never a wholehearted belly laugh!

'Whatever has happened in my absence, it's been quite remarkable!' Sophia thought to herself. 'And a joy to behold.'

Tomas was the first one to notice the reappearance of Sophia in the distance. He frantically waved his long arms in her direction as if to get her attention, which amused Sophia no end because she was hardly likely to miss the fire burning! Yet she loved his enthusiasm for life and his honest expression of emotions. Indeed Sophia had seen this aspect of Tomas in its most revealing light when they had both been upset by Edgar's behaviour in the Darkened Street:

She remembered being touched by Tomas's genuine feelings of love and respect for Edgar, and his openness in sharing this most feminine of energies. If she was to think of words to describe Tomas, it would be to say that he was a generous soul; he gave with an open heart, whether it be in his encouragement or praise of another, or in celebrating the joy of another. Sophia could see, however, that this meant he would feel more hurt when his openness was not welcomed by those less open than he. She had therefore not been surprised when Tomas had told her about his difficulties in communicating with Jan. Yet, as they both knew, this was exactly the task set for each of those who entered the Land of the Shadows: to befriend their Stranger, their Shadow side.

Looking upon the nature of Tomas's and Jan's interaction, as Sophia did now, she could only marvel at the transformation that had taken place. She decided then and there to share in their joy.

Jan stood up to greet the approaching Sophia. 'Welcome back, oh happy wanderer!' Jan said, in the most jovial of tones.

'Yes,' agreed Tomas. 'Won't you join us by the fire?'

Smiling broadly, Sophia suddenly realised how much she loved these people. She had made sure that the shawl from the Sibyl was wrapped up in a bundle under her arm, so as to try to make it look more like an ordinary blanket. She found a spot to sit in, aware that Edgar had not said a word.

'What a lovely warm fire,' Sophia said, as she stretched out her hands towards the flames. 'Did you do it?' Sophia directed her question at Jan.

'Who else?' Jan answered.

'But where did you get the wood?' Sophia was intrigued.

'She is a most resourceful woman,' enthused Tomas. 'She put some blocks of wood in the cart before we left the Darkened Street – under the blankets!'

'So that's why the cart was so heavy!' exclaimed Sophia, in a light-hearted manner. 'And I thought it was just me feeling tired – that or Edgar was heavier than I thought!'

'Yeah, well, I didn't want anyone to talk me out of it, did I?' Jan said matter-of-factly.

Sophia leant over towards Jan, seated on her right, and nudged her on the arm in jest. 'Well, I'm glad you didn't get talked out of it. This is wonderful, Jan.'

'Here, here,' Tomas agreed, 'and I think it is time to celebrate - to drink and be merry!'

'I don't think Edgar's in the mood,' interjected Jan, highlighting his silence at last.

Sophia felt bad that she had not acknowledged him first. She glanced over at Edgar to see that he was gazing into the fire, appearing neither sad nor angry, just detached.

'Edgar, what's the matter?' Sophia called across the flames, but he did not answer. Sophia found herself becoming angry with him; 'EDGAR! TALK TO ME!'

Edgar could not help but be jolted out of his strange reverie. He looked up at Sophia in surprise.

'You have to tell me what is happening with you, Edgar,' Sophia pleaded and demanded simultaneously, 'otherwise we won't make it. We have to keep communicating with each other.'

Finally Edgar spoke; 'Like you communicated with me?' he said, with quiet dispassion. 'You just disappeared. I was sitting here . . . . useless . . . . worrying about what had happened to you. That's why

The Veils of Illusion

Jan started up the fire – in case you were lost and could not find your way back. Some of the wood she even broken off from the cart itself-' Edgar broke off, not so much in anger, but in the emotion that was making its way up to the surface.

Sophia felt an overwhelming wave of emotion begin to sweep over her too. She tried to make amends in the best way she could; 'I'm so sorry, Edgar . . . . . I am sorry to all of you . . . . . and I thank you from the bottom of my heart for . . . . caring about me.' She looked over at Edgar, her voice beginning to break, and said, 'Edgar, please forgive me for leaving you . . . . . a-and trust me w-when I t-tell you that from this m-moment I will never l-leave you again.'

Edgar's deep blue eyes filled with tears and he brought his left hand up to cover them. Sophia got up and went to him.

Then Jan got up, but instead walked over to the now broken down cart. What she brought back with her to the group defied all rational explanation, but it was the perfect gift of celebration to them all: For as the others looked on speechless, Jan placed four beakers on the ground by the fire and presented the group with what looked to be a bottle of wine.

'This is what I discovered after I'd lit the fire,' she explained. 'It was under all the blocks of wood in the cart – and I can assure you that it wasn't there when I put the wood in the cart!'

The other three shook their heads in disbelief, Tomas even more so as he thought about the pun he had made "to drink and be merry".

'Well, I for one,' announced an animated Jan, 'am getting to rather like these miracles! And I don't know about the rest of you, but I'm rather partial to a glass of vino! So I say that we accept this bottle gratefully and gracefully - and drink to its source!'

'Here, here,' agreed Tomas once again.

'What does it say on the label?' asked the ever inquisitive Sophia.

Jan glanced at the hand written label. 'Very poetic words, I must say: "WINE FROM THE MOON TREE".'

Sophia gasped, but was conscious of the Sibyl's instructions not to talk about their meeting by the silver birch. Jan looked at Sophia curiously, without saying anything. Edgar, however, looked at Sophia more thoughtfully, which made her wonder whether he knew more than he let on, like the Sibyl had said.

'I just think it's amazing,' Sophia said, enthusiastically. 'I mean, what a wonderful image – a moon tree!'

'Yes, indeed it is,' agreed Tomas. 'So let us all try this wine from the moon tree!'

A relieved Jan proceeded to pour the wine into each of the four beakers, and it soon became obvious that it was quite different to the wine that they were more familiar with. The moon tree wine was much lighter and paler in colour; a cross between lilac and orange.

Then, each of the four raised their beakers and made a toast: 'To Mother Earth,' they chanted in unison, before taking their first sips.

They all agreed that the wine was sweeter and more subtle in taste, but at that moment it was the best wine they had ever tasted!

Chapter Thirty Six
The River Crossing

After the joy of laughter, song, and merriment had filled them, and the last flames of the fire had died out, each of the four took a blanket in their hand and a space on the ground. It was time to sleep.

Not wishing to draw unwanted attention to herself, Sophia wrapped herself in an ordinary blanket as she lay down beside Edgar. She closed her eyes, her mind heavy with the knowledge of what she had to do, and she went over in her head the instructions she had been given by the Sibyl. She felt uncomfortable with not being honest with the others, and was tempted to just go to sleep as a temporary means of avoidance. Indeed, she did find herself dropping off to sleep on more than one occasion. But in the end it was Edgar who shared Sophia's burden; he called softly to her whilst she slept. Sophia opened her eyes to find herself looking into Edgar's eyes.

'Sophia,' he whispered. 'We must go.'

Suddenly faced with her own avoidance and resistance, Sophia began nodding frantically. She sat up and looked over at Tomas and Jan, who were snoring away happily.

'How can I say goodbye to them?' she said quietly. Then, looking at Edgar, she said, 'How can we say goodbye to them?'

'In the best way we know how,' Edgar replied, thoughtfully. 'By leaving the gift of the written word.'

Edgar watched Sophia's face as it changed from a look of confusion to one of clarity and focus. He smiled to himself as Sophia reached over to her bag and retrieved a pencil and a notepad.

'Thanks, Edgar,' she whispered, before getting up as quietly as she could and going over to the river's edge.

There she sat, gazing at the gentle flow of the water, pencil in hand and empty page upon her lap.

After a while, she looked over to the other side of the river, screwing her eyes up in an attempt to see what was over there. Yet despite the bright yellow light of the crescent moon above, Sophia could not see anything beyond the river. She looked back down at the empty page and wrote: 'Dear Jan'. She could think of nothing else to write, nothing that seemed adequate. She decided to close her eyes instead and try to empty her mind of all its thoughts. She asked for help from the Greatest Unknown, the Universe, the Divine Source . . . . and then she waited in the silence of her mind until the words came to her:

Dear Jan,

Should I see you again, my friend,
Standing by the roadside,
I would offer you a ride
To journey as far as you would like,

Or as near as you could abide.

For though we are not on the same road,

Our paths, I'm sure, will cross from time to time.

Sophia signed the bottom of the page, "With my love, Sophia", before quietly tearing it from the notepad.

She felt a pang of sadness at the prospect of leaving, but knew this was no time to dwell on such things.

Quickly she kissed the page and got up from the ground, her only aim now to leave it next to Jan without waking her up. This, Sophia succeeded in doing with one minor hiccup: the page needed some kind of paperweight to hold it down. She looked around her for an object that could do the job, when her eyes suddenly fell upon something perfect: next to the ashes of the fire lay the four empty beakers. Carefully creeping over to them, Sophia picked one up at random, making sure that it was dry before creeping back over to Jan. Jan's loud snoring made Sophia grin, but she made sure she didn't laugh as she leant down and placed the beaker upon the written page. For a few moments she gazed at Jan's face; the tired lines under her eyes and on her forehead displayed the former hardness of her life. Yet now, Jan looked peaceful, her face almost smiling whilst she slept as if to reflect the promise of a more pleasing life ahead.

When Sophia returned to Edgar, she found that he too was now asleep. She was about to wake him when she noticed a shining object in his hand. Gently prising open his fingers, Sophia saw the beautiful crystal that she had first seen on the door of Edgar's house. Suddenly she remembered what the Sibyl had said at the Moon Tree: that Edgar would give her a special object from the Place of Souls, before they entered the river. 'So, this is that special object,' Sophia whispered, feeling as if a crown had been placed upon her head. For she had never imagined such a wonderful gift coming her way.

Sophia watched Edgar as he slept. Despite all of his traumas and hardships, his face now looked like that of a young boy. His hair was wavy and long, brown interspersed with grey; his nose was small and rather dainty, Sophia thought, and his skin pale and smooth. Reaching out her hand, she gently stroked his face and his hair, until gradually he woke up.

'Sophia,' he whispered. 'At first I thought you were the Sibyl.'

Sophia smiled warmly at him, flattered by his words. But now it was her turn to hurry along the proceedings. 'We must go now, Edgar. Is there anything you wish to leave Tomas before we go?'

Edgar nodded straight away. 'Yes, yes. I have decided to leave my special blanket with him.'

'Are you sure?'

'Yes,' Edgar quietly insisted, 'there is no question. Could you go over to him, and place it carefully over him – I want him to wake up as I did in the Place of Souls.'

'Okay.'

Sophia wasted no more time. She lifted the blanket off Edgar and proceeded to follow his instructions. Tomas was also snoring, although more lightly than Jan, and he did not stir when Sophia placed the blanket over him. She noticed that his dark face seemed to shine in the moonlight, as though his inner flame never dimmed, no matter what the time of day or night was.

When she returned to Edgar, Sophia could see his reddened face struggling to hold back the tears. He was sitting up, looking towards the river; for as the Sibyl had said, Edgar knew that they had to get to the other side.

Edgar had waited so long for this moment and now that it had arrived he wasn't sure how to deal with it. Greatly unexpected to him, there was a feeling of resistance which now gripped him. He, who had once been a scribe of such words of wisdom, was now being called upon to surpass this resistance and to walk freely into the unknown. Edgar felt this to be another test of character, and one that if he didn't pass would let Sophia down in the most unimaginable way. Perhaps even greater than this, he would be laying to waste all the future contributions that he and Sophia could make in the Outside World; all that they had learnt, and all who had taught them. Edgar knew he owed it as much to himself, as he did to Sophia or anyone else, to see this journey through to the end.

As he sat there, he thought of the words he knew off by heart, the ones he had once asked Sophia to believe in. Now he needed to believe in his own words, and so he whispered aloud those familiar words in an attempt to help himself:

'And tremble not within you
For that which you do not know.
Trust instead the beating heart
Of the Greatest Unknown
You will ever know.'

Taking a deep breath, Edgar started to feel a little more balanced, a little less scared. He turned to look at Sophia and found that she was only a few feet away. She had been watching him, waiting for him to be ready. It seemed that she had decided to take her bag, which was strapped securely across her back, despite the inevitable soaking it would receive once in the river. Edgar's smile beckoned Sophia to him, and once she had knelt beside him, he placed the crystal in one of her hands. Sophia felt the original coldness of its touch to have transformed into comforting heat, its feel to be silky smooth, and its size and shape to somehow perfectly fit into the palm of her hand.

'Thank you, Edgar,' she said softly. 'You will always be with me now.'

Edgar felt a surprising sense of relief as he handed the crystal to Sophia, as if it was she who the crystal really belonged to and that Edgar had merely been keeping it safe for her.

'You know, Sophia, I feel strangely lighter.' He started to chuckle but then quickly placed his hand over his mouth so as not to wake the others.

'I'm glad to hear it,' Sophia whispered, whilst she looked for a safe place on her body to put the crystal, 'because I'm going to have to carry you across the river, Edgar!'

Before Edgar had the chance to respond, Sophia manoeuvred herself into a squatting position, took hold of Edgar's left arm and wrapped it around her neck. With one of her arms under Edgar's thighs and the other arm across his back, Sophia told him to hold on tight whilst, at the count of three, she heaved him up and off the ground. Her legs began to tremble like a young foal, as she staggered towards the river's edge. She couldn't yet feel the water under her feet and was all too aware of the nervous look on Edgar's face. Her back and shoulders ached as Edgar gripped on to her more tightly, yet Sophia was determined to make it to the river. She, like Edgar, saw this as their final test of character on this journey of the West Road, and she was not about to fall at the last hurdle.

Then, as the first drops of sweat began to trickle down her forehead, Sophia felt her right foot make its first step into the river. The water felt cool and refreshing, giving her a welcome surge of energy which rose up through one foot and then the other. 'We've m-made it,' panted an exhausted Sophia.

Edgar loosened his grip a little and kissed Sophia on the cheek. 'My Hero,' he said loudly.

'Shhh,' responded Sophia, worried that the others would wake up.

Wading heavily through the silky flow of water, Sophia was relieved to find that the ground underfoot was remarkably smooth. Deeper and deeper she persevered, until the water eventually reached up to her thighs. No longer did she feel able to carry Edgar's weight and so letting out a cry they both lunged forward into the body of the river and disappeared below the surface.

As the water pulled her down, Sophia managed to catch a glimpse of Edgar drifting past her. She tried to reach out for him, but the touch of his body seemed to elude her. The bag strapped tightly across Sophia's back was not only weighing her down but was also restricting her movement. She tugged frantically at the rope in an attempt to loosen it and pull the bag up over her head. The bag contained her only possessions, her most prized possessions. Wrapped as securely as possible within her sleeping bag were her writing journals, Edgar's poems, the Sibyl's Scroll and her beautiful shawl. But now Sophia realised that she had to let them go; they would mean nothing without Edgar. She knew she had to save him, to bring him back up to the surface to be with her.

Somehow, Sophia managed to free herself from her bag and immediately set about making her way to Edgar. The water was crystalline, the purest she had ever seen, and she could see Edgar lying at the bottom of the river. His body was motionless but his eyes were open as he looked upwards to the surface. Sophia swam towards him and when she reached him she saw that he was smiling at her. she wasted no time however in putting her arms around his waist and lifting him off the bottom. She knew time was running out for both of them.

As her body turned round to face the surface of the water, Sophia understood the reason for Edgar's smile: for the Light of the most heavenly rays streamed down through the water until it touched her body. It wasn't long before she could feel the warmth and vibrant energy of the Light as it infiltrated every cell of her body. Edgar's hand was now in hers and together they floated upwards towards the source of the Light, each suddenly feeling unconcerned about the outcome. For instantly they knew that they were being cradled in the arms of the Divine Light. They were being lifted up above the level of earthly struggles, and were being given more than just a glimpse through the last of the Veils of Illusion. This glorious burst of Light which now illuminated both Sophia and Edgar, was the Source of Life itself; and in its glory each knew with their heart and soul that they too were a part of this miracle of Creation.

As they were lifted higher and higher, becoming lighter and lighter, they felt no separateness between themselves and the Divine Light. They were connected in Oneness, and it brought with it such Joy, Power and Love, from which neither Edgar nor Sophia would ever wish to part. Their light bodies seemed to soar to unimaginable heights, so that they had no concept or perception of themselves as separate physical beings. Sophia and Edgar had now merged into one entity - a Higher, more enlightened, Self; it contained the Feminine aspects of Sophia and the Masculine aspects of Edgar in perfect harmony. This was a sacred union between two opposite aspects of human nature, creating wholeness through which the natural Life Force could flow.

Sophia was about to break through the surface of the water, to be reborn in newness of life; her lower self of physical form remained intact, but it was now at one with her Higher Self of spirit form.

Chapter Thirty Seven
The Sacred Union Of Opposites

Sophia gasped for air as she broke through the surface of the water. Although she felt light-headed and dizzy, the over-riding feeling was one of ecstatic liberation. And before she had the chance to catch her breath, Sophia could not help but become entranced by the night sky above. For the sky was filled with so many stars that the brightness shone like a dazzling aurora; a spectacle of night-lights put on show by the Divine, with the sole purpose of manifesting its Glory in the most exquisite of styles. Sophia lay her head back against the cushion of the water, her eyes as wide as saucers and her arms stretched out on either side. She had little awareness of her physical body, quite contented to be lost in the delights of the higher realms.

As she floated peacefully upon the water, she suddenly heard a voice sounding from afar; a voice which sounded strangely familiar to Sophia but one which she could not place. It called her name. Sophia lifted up her head so that her ears were now above the surface of the water. Almost immediately she heard the man's voice again, except this time it seemed much closer. He called her name over and over; 'Sophia! Sophia!', his voice soft yet insistent.

She felt confused, her head still light and hazy as she looked around her. The brightness of the stars upon which Sophia had gazed for quite some time, seemed to have left her temporarily blinded. The voice seemed to come from ground level, thought Sophia; from the same level as her physical body. It was as if she was being called on to come down from the lofty dimensions of her Higher Self, now that she had spent some time there, and to reconnect with the lower planes of physical reality.

The voice called again, this time louder; 'Sophia! This way! I am over here!'

Although her vision was still somewhat distorted, Sophia looked in the general direction of the voice. She could just about make out something in white. It seemed to be moving from left to right, then back again. Sophia made herself focus as much as she could on this vague image, following its movement from sided to side, until eventually it stopped. Whatever it was, it was now only about a hundred yards away from Sophia, so that when the voice called out again she was sure that it came from this figure in white. As she tried to move towards it, Sophia was struck by how stiff her limbs had become. The water seemed to have permeated through the cells of her skin, and her lack of physical movement had caused a substantial lowering of her body temperature. It seemed now that Sophia had reconnected with her physical self, she was beginning to fully experience the sensation of physical pain. Suddenly she felt so very cold.

The man's voice served as a source of encouragement at that moment, urging her to persevere and to find her strength once more.

'Sophia!' he called. 'You are almost there. Just a few more yards to the shore.'

In response, Sophia raised her heavy trembling arms, one at a time, and kicked out her legs in an attempt to swim. She knew now that there was solid ground nearby, and that she wouldn't have to stay much longer in the water. Just one more thrust forward, then another, then another . . . .

'Here, let me take your hand,' said the man in white, as he knelt down by the bank of the river.

Sophia could now feel the solid ground of the river bed beneath her feet, its foundation providing her with the security that only the element of earth could bring. Standing up, her shoulders lifted above the water, she saw the hand outstretched towards her. It seemed to beckon her towards it, and to the promise of better things. Yet each stride she took felt like her last, her cold exhausted body urging her to stop. Sophia's own will battled in turn to overcome the frailties of her body, as it had done many times before, for she saw that the helping hand was only a few feet away . . . . . .

The warmth of his firm hand-grip was the first thing that registered in Sophia's tired mind and body, as it pulled her upward and out of the water. Then collapsing to the ground, she felt a blanket being wrapped around her.

'Well done, my child!' said the man with the familiar voice. 'You have crossed to the other side of the river, though I must say you did give me a bit of a fright at one point!'

Sophia looked up to see the face of the wise old man of the forest; the kind sad face she had last seen when he had left her contemplating the "Story of the Tower". Yet now his eyes looked brighter and seemed to sparkle amongst the array of stars in the night sky. Indeed he could hardly contain his delight at seeing Sophia again. She in turn could not believe the never-ending surprises that seemed to meet her at every step of the way.

'This was how we first met,' he said, as he busied himself with sticks and other pieces of wood. 'You came out of the water, shivering and shaking, and I brought you a blanket and a mug of hot broth to warm you. Then we sat round a fire, which I am making now, for I am sure you would welcome that.'

Sophia nodded gratefully. 'T-thank y-you,' she smiled through her chattering teeth, somewhat amused by the old man's bounding energy.

'But you must rest, my child, and I'll call you once the fire is burning.'

Sophia closed her eyes and thought back to the time that the wise old man had referred to. How could she forget it? Her experience in the lake, when she had fallen asleep underneath the sunny sky, and dreamt the most vivid of dreams; Sophia had been left confused and bewildered by the profound nature and "message" of the dream. And then there was the Story of the Tower, recited to her by the wise old man amongst the scattered remnants of stone. Sophia remembered feeling so frustrated when not being told in more specific and straightforward terms the meanings of certain stories or words of wisdom; when not being given direct answers to her many questions. She knew now of course that if she had been told of what lay ahead, she would probably not have wanted to take another step. Yet it had also been the most amazing of journeys, Sophia thought to herself, as she lay wrapped tightly in her blanket:

"An internal journey of intrigue, wonder and mystery – and it was this very man, this wise old man whose name I don't even know, who first taught me about the existence and meaning of duality."

Sophia had not understood this at first, but over the course of her journey she began to recognise the concept of duality, as it manifested itself in different ways:

"The ego of the Outside World, and the Shadow of the Inner World," continued Sophia, in her thoughts. "The Masculine and the Feminine; the light and the darkness; the hidden and the seen; the sun and the moon; the receptive and the expressive; the stillness and the action . . . . . one could go on and on."

As she lay by the side of the flowing river, Sophia smiled at the realisation that these were no longer just concepts held in her intellectual mind, but were very much an integral part of her now. She did not have to think about how to apply these concepts to herself anymore, because she instinctively and wholeheartedly knew them to be such a fundamental part of her own makeup and of the world around her. Now she had truly come to know the dual aspects of her own nature: That of her physical self and of her divine spiritual self; her lower self and her Higher Self. Sophia had emerged from the river reborn. She felt renewed and whole.

'Congratulations on completing the West Road,' the wise old man said, placing a basket of bread and a mug of hot broth by her side. 'You have, as they say, completed the cycle.'

Sophia sat up slowly and thanked him. She found herself grinning from ear to ear, feeling uncharacteristically pleased with herself. Then she gratefully delved into the nourishing food the wise old man had given her.

When she had finished eating and drinking, she got to her feet and walked carefully over to the roaring fire, her blanket still wrapped around her. Her legs ached and felt very fragile, and she longed to feel the warmth of the fire. She found a suitable spot and sat down cross-legged, only to yelp out loud as soon as her bottom touched the ground. The old man, who had been sitting peacefully up until then, almost jumped out of his skin!

'Goodness me, child! What on earth is the matter?' he cried, clutching his chest.

Sophia was busy fumbling beneath her blanket, trying to root out the source of her discomfort. 'I just sat on something sharp – a stone or something. Sorry, I didn't mean to startle you!'

Her elder companion and guardian was still trying to recover from his sudden jolt, taking in deep breaths and trying to centre himself. But no sooner did he appear to have done so, when there was a shriek of excitement from Sophia which unbalanced him once again.

'Look! Look!' she cried, holding the object of discomfort aloft. 'I can't believe it! It's the crystal from the Sibyl . . . Edgar's crystal. I'd forgotten all about it!'

The wise old man had been about to protest against Sophia's unexpected outbursts, but instead stared in stunned silence at the sparkling object in Sophia's hand. 'From the core of Mother Earth,' he said, dreamily. 'How wonderful.'

'Yes, I can't believe I forgot about it. I suppose I just got taken over by so many other things.'

'Like crossing the river with Edgar,' the wise old man agreed, never taking his eyes off the crystal.

'Would you like to have a proper look at it?' Sophia asked, as she made a gesture to get up.

'That would be lovely,' the wise old man nodded.

Sophia went over to him and placed the crystal in his hand, all too aware of the look of wonderment in his face. Suddenly he seemed like a young boy who had just received the gift he had most wanted in the world!

'You have brought untold pleasure to an old man, Sophia,' he said lovingly, as he gently caressed the diamond shaped crystal.

Sophia saw his eyes begin to fill with tears, as they had done when he had looked upon the field strewn with the stone fragments of the Tower, when they had first met. This time however, they were tears of joy. And when he had wiped the fallen tears from his face, he suddenly burst into uncontained laughter. Getting to his feet, the wise old man began to dance and skip around the fire, as if his body was being propelled by the force of his own Divine spirit. He laughed and looked up to the night sky, holding the crystal aloft, whilst Sophia could only stand and watch. She was both amused and amazed, though she did not fully understand the extent of his ecstasy.

Yet this image reminded Sophia of herself, when she had danced her spiral dance of ecstasy outside the barn. Thinking back to that time, she could not entirely comprehend the reasons for her own immense joy then, but at the time she was overcome by feelings of renewed hope, inspired by the sight of the crescent moon and the Sibyl. She now knew that true understanding or empathy could only occur if one could place themselves in the context of another's situation.

After he had settled back down into a state of peaceful equilibrium, the wise old man took Sophia's hand and gently placed the crystal back in her palm. Folding her fingers around the crystal, he said:

'Though you do not know its significance yet, Sophia, you must look after this precious stone as if it were your greatest treasure. It has been many ages since I last saw it, and I had come to believe that it was lost forever. Now it has been entrusted to you, my child, and when the time is right you will understand its true value and its true meaning.

'For now, all you need to know is that it will help you to attune yourself with the Divine Energy, to link the world of Spirit and Higher Wisdom with the world of matter and physical reality.'

Sophia remained silent as she tried to comprehend what was being said. She could not quite believe that she held in her hand an object of such importance. She valued the crystal for her own personal reasons; as a gift, a beautiful momento from those who had touched her and whom she had loved on her journey along the West Road. Yet now she felt slightly unnerved by the crystal; privileged and esteemed on the one hand, but burdened with the prospect of responsibility on the other.

The wise old man was aware of Sophia's silent burden and so decided to address it, not directly but by using the art of storytelling. 'Come, Sophia. Sit with me by the fire,' he beckoned. 'I want you to tell me a story.'

A puzzled Sophia complied with his request, all the while gripping the crystal tightly in her right hand for fear of losing it.

'Tell me about your river crossing,' he urged her. 'Every detail is important.'

Sophia began:

'I carried Edgar in my arms. The first few steps were easier than I thought – Edgar didn't seem that heavy to begin with. But as I entered the river, and it was more difficult to move forward, I began to feel the burden of his weight. You see, I also had a bag strapped to my back – the one you gave me all that time ago. I was sweating and I wondered if I was going to make it, but I didn't want to worry Edgar-' she began to smile as she remembered something; 'He called me his Hero . . . . he had called me that before, you see, and had written this wonderful poem called "The Horse and the Hero". It was in my bag

409

along with other writings and scrolls – things that meant a lot to me.' Sophia looked sad as she recalled these losses.

'So you were faced with having to sacrifice one thing for another.'

The wise old man's statement startled Sophia, for she realised that he already knew her story. 'Yes,' she said softly, 'but you already know my story.'

The wise old man smiled lovingly at her, and said, 'That is true, my child, but it is you who needs to understand the lessons of your own journey – of your own story.'

After a brief silence, Sophia spoke; 'I suppose I have wondered about what happened in the river . . . . Before I entered the river it seemed so important to me to take the scrolls and journals . . . . . and the shawl the Sibyl gave me by the moon tree . . . . . . to have them with me in the Outside World, something tangible I suppose. But when it came to it . . . . when I saw Edgar's motionless body lying at the bottom of the river . . . . . well, there was no choice in the matter. I could do without those tangible objects, no matter how precious they were . . . . . . But I could not do without Edgar . . . . He is part of me.'

'A sacrifice of the lesser, for the greater,' said her learned companion.

'Yes! Yes, that's it exactly,' responded a now animated Sophia. 'Much greater, in fact! And when I had let go of the bag and all its objects, I realised how much it had been restricting me . . . . . preventing me from moving freely in the water. If I hadn't let go of that bag, I wouldn't have reached Edgar . . . . . . and I wouldn't have known the greatness that mine and Edgar's union would bring . . . . So much glorious Light! So much Love!'

'Peace? Serenity?' enquired the wise old man.

'Oh yes, definitely! I was . . . . in communion with the Divine . . . . I know that now.'

A natural silence followed as both looked into the flames of the fire. Then, Sophia looked over at her elder companion, eager to get his full attention again. 'More than anything though,' she began, 'I felt the power of inspiration. I felt I could do anything! I was fearless – and I have never felt like that before.'

The wise old man looked directly at Sophia with smiling eyes.

'That was my Higher Self, wasn't it?' Sophia asked him. She wasn't surprised however when he did not reply. 'My spirit Self,' she continued. 'But then I had to come back down to earth, as they say. I don't ever want to lose my connection though – with the Divine Source. Not when I'm in the Outside World.'

'I am glad to hear you say that, my child. After all, you have worked so hard and gone through so much to arrive at this state of being. The sacred union that you underwent with Edgar represented the union of the Masculine and Feminine aspects within you, yourself. This is the ultimate union because in its resultant wholeness, it gives birth to a new self – one in which you can feel the true connection with your Higher Self, or spirit Self as you have said. And with this new sense of being comes the realisation that we, each and everyone of us, are part of the Divine light. You, Sophia, have seen through the last Veil of Illusion. You have seen with clarity, however briefly, the truth of your own nature. For in the still Centre, the opposites of duality have disappeared-'

'The Centre Point!' exclaimed Sophia, interrupting her mentor mid-flow. But the wise old man was more amused by such healthy spontaneity than offended in any way, and he waited for her to continue:

'I remember you saying something about reaching the Centre Point . . . . . Yes, yes, "to truly be free, you have to face yourself" . . . . and when I asked you how, you said that I had to reach the Centre Point . . . . . but that I would know where it was when I got there.' Sophia got up and walked slowly around the fire. 'So . . . . I know that I have reached there now . . . . but . . . . .' she let out a deep sigh, 'I still don't know where it is!'

The wise old man then burst out laughing, slapping his thigh, whilst Sophia simply stared at him in amazement! It was not long, however, before the infectious nature of his laughter had gripped her too. And as she began to giggle, she saw that his eyes had filled with tears of laughter and that he was overcome with hysterics. He held his sides as the tears rolled down his face, and Sophia had almost forgotten about what she had been saying before. Instead she thought of how wonderfully different this time spent with the wise old man was compared to their last meeting.

When he had regained his composure he looked over at Sophia, who was now in a seated position, and noticed how calm and centred she was. 'I hope you are not offended, my child?' he said, with true sincerity. 'It's just that I suddenly saw how serious you were in your determination to know where the Centre Point was, and in the end it does not really matter: You have found your true Centre – in your balance and wholeness – and it is here that you are connected with the Divine. That is all that matters. Enjoy it! Celebrate yourself, Sophia! Getting stuck in your head will not bring enlightenment.'

Sophia smiled over at him. Tilting her head back, she gazed once again at the star-studded sky. Had the night sky always been like this, she wondered, or had she just noticed it now? She then noticed that something was missing: 'Where's the moon?' she immediately enquired.

'Ah, yes,' he replied. 'I am glad you have noticed. For the dark phase of the moon is upon us.'

'How long does that last? Not too long, I hope. I spent so long in the Darkened Street.'

Sophia seemed to be too closely in touch with her own fears; fears that came from holding on to memories of the past; fears that would block her progress if she stayed too attached to them. Yet as was the nature of the Universe, the Greatest Unknown, Sophia was being presented with an opportunity to face these fears and to clear away these obstructions in her path.

The wise old man looked sympathetically at her, before saying, 'And you fear that you will be back there again? In the Darkened Street?'

Sophia looked over at the river, but just like before she could not see anything beyond the water. 'I don't know really,' she sighed deeply. 'When I think about it, I don't really believe that I'll end up back there – not that it was all bad anyway. In fact, looking back I wouldn't change anything because I realise now that I had to go through it, to come out the other side. And I've learnt so much about myself and about life, that I feel a different person now. Not like the woman I dreamt about in the lake, who only worried about what she looked like to others; because inside, I was so alone . . . . . . ' Her voice trailed off as she remembered the emptiness of her past life.

'How do you feel about that woman now?' asked her mentor.

Sophia's head was hung down, but she raised it to answer his question. 'I feel very sorry for her. Not pity, just sadness.'

'Compassion?' asked the wise old man.

'Yes, I suppose it is compassion.'

In the silence that ensued, there was peace. The peace that comes from no longer fighting; from just accepting that which is and has been – the past and the present.

Eventually, the wise old man returned to the subject of the dark moon:

'Use this time, Sophia, when the moon is hidden from the Earth's view, to retreat and rest. To reflect and absorb all that you have learnt and experienced on the West Road. Use the natural virtues of woman to go within, and be receptive to your own inner wisdom. Acknowledge the feelings and the fears that may come to the surface, and accept them for what they are. Only then can you truly let go, and allow the gifts of peace and harmony to flow into the Centre of your Being. For when this happens, it does not really matter what chaos or confusion occurs around you. Your true power lies within.

'These lessons you must practise and reinforce within yourself at this time, as you prepare to step through the Gateway that leads you back to the Outside World.'

He stood up and picked up his staff, the fire having all but burnt away. 'Follow me, Sophia. I will take you to your place of retreat. There are warm clothes and refreshments there, which will aid you in your quest for rest and regeneration.'

Sophia did not hesitate in proceeding to follow him, and she made sure that the crystal remained tightly in her grip. She suddenly realised how tired she was, and the thought of rest and retreat sounded undecidedly blissful.

Chapter Thirty Eight
The Gateway Of Freedom

As Sophia followed her learned guide, it became apparent to her that they were on the edge of a forest. Feelings of excitement welled up inside her as it dawned on her that she had finally left the Land of the Shadows; she had passed through a place where darkness ruled both day and night - and she was now in a place where the sun shone by day and it was only dark at night.

Sophia felt a deep feeling of love surge within her when she realised and saw the many examples of life on Mother Earth itself; life displayed in the beauty and glory of Creation. She saw it in the strength and endurance that was inherent in the trunks of the trees; she heard it in the many sounds of the night forest. In fact, she was sure she could make out leaves on the branches of the trees, which made her wonder what time of year it was. "Perhaps it's spring?" Sophia thought to herself, excitedly.

She felt the chill of the night air, although this was no doubt made more piercing because of the dampness which still lingered in her clothes. Clutching her blanket more tightly to her, she followed in the footsteps of the wise old man until finally they reached their intended destination. They were now standing in front of a small wooden hut hidden between the trees. It was no bigger than ten foot by eight, with a tiny window on one side.

The wise old man then turned to Sophia, and said, 'I will leave you now to make yourself comfortable. Tonight is the first night of the dark moon – there are three dark nights this month. You must stay here until the new moon appears; that is when the new cycle of the moon commences and brings its new energies to us on Mother Earth.'

Sophia nodded. She did not feel afraid of being alone for she knew that it was only for a short while, and she knew in essence, deep down, that she was never really alone. 'Thank you,' she said. 'Do you know, I don't even know your name?'

'My dear,' he smiled, 'I have been known by many different names over many different lifetimes. It is of no matter.'

'But I have to call you something,' Sophia insisted politely.

'Then what would you have call me?'

Sophia thought for a few moments, aware of the crystal in her hand. Her dark eyes began to sparkle and her face suddenly broke into a luminous smile. 'I know!' she announced triumphantly. 'I will call you Merlin . . . . Merlin the Wise! What do you think? I mean, is that alright with you?'

The wise old man could hardly contain his pleasure at Sophia's chosen name for him. In fact, Sophia had not seen him quite so full of joy as on this first evening of their reunion. And as if to join in on the joyful proceedings, the happy high-pitched harmonious sounds of birds singing began. They both burst out laughing like little children.

'Oh it's so wonderful to hear the sounds of Nature once again,' Sophia twirled round, her arms outstretched.

The wise old man nodded knowingly. 'And it seems as though spring has come early this year.'

'I thought I could see leaves on the trees,' Sophia enthused.

'Ah! Now those are evergreen trees,' he corrected.

'Really? I hardly know anything about trees, except that I love them and I would like to learn more about them!'

'Well, this is an ancient yew forest, although there are quite a few elder trees about – they are much smaller of course, and they make me feel more at home!'

Sophia smiled compassionately at him. She loved learning from this man she called Merlin.

'I'll be on my way now,' he said. 'I must confess, Sophia, that I feel rather tired.'

'Yes, me too.' Sophia went over to him and hugged him. 'Thank you, Merlin,' she said. 'For everything.'

A little overcome by this gesture, the wise old man – now called Merlin - patted her hair. And when Sophia stood back, she saw such tears of love in his eyes.

'Rest well, my child,' he said. 'Then return to the fire, which I will burn on the first night of the new moon.'

He took his leave, but after a few steps he stopped and turned round. 'Oh, I forgot to tell you. When the light of the dawn appears tomorrow, it will be too strong for your eyes. Remember to place a blanket over the window. You have to accustom yourself gradually to the powerful light of the sun.'

For the first two days of her retreat, Sophia had hardly been able to awaken from her deep slumber. She had remembered to cover the window before changing out of her damp clothes and had snuggled up contentedly under several woollen blankets. The force of the wind had at times been considerably strong, causing the window and door of the hut to rattle on their hinges, whilst the branches of the many surrounding yew trees had swayed and swished in their relentless struggle to cling to life. Yet Sophia had somehow felt so safe and secure, so warm and protected in her new little hideaway, that she had slept and slept like an animal in hibernation. Even when the sun had shone against the window, forcing some of its rays through the blanket curtain, and the birds had chirped loudly in neighbouring trees, Sophia had still not awakened from her sleep. At times she had opened her heavy eyelids, had blinked and sighed, only then to return to the delights of dream-time. She rested peacefully in her cocoon that was hiding her temporarily before it would release her back into the Outside World.

Indeed, it was only when the third day of her retreat had arrived that Sophia finally arose from this slumber: The butterfly was now ready to emerge from its cocoon.

Sophia was almost sure that tonight was the night of the new moon, yet as she lay on her straw mat under woollen blankets, she wondered whether she would be able to see the moon's slim crescent. For the sky had been covered all day in a thick layer of dark cloud and it showed no sign of lifting.

In many ways, though, this lack of direct sunlight had come as a blessing in disguise for Sophia, because it had enabled her to venture outside of the hut during daylight. Indeed it was the first time since she had left the Valley Town all that time ago, to descend the 21 Steps into darkness, that Sophia had seen daylight; her eyes needed time to adjust to this increased level of light just as the wise old man Merlin had said. With this in mind, she had covered her head with a large piece of light fabric, which she had found amongst the piles of clothes and blankets placed in the hut. It was just possible for Sophia to see through this fabric. At the time, she couldn't help but laugh at herself when she emerged from the hut covered almost from head to toe under what looked like a sheet! She had then found her way down to the river where she had sat listening to the flow of the water and the serenading songs of birds. Having spent most of the day by the river, Sophia had returned to the hut at dusk feeling strangely invigorated. A constant smile adorned her face and there was nothing she could do about it!

She was not sure how long she had sat in the now dark hut – perhaps two hours, maybe three. The wind had died down only to be replaced by the sound of falling rain. Sophia found the tapping of each raindrop against the rooftop to be so delicious that it motivated her to get up off the floor again and go outside.

She lifted her face up to the night sky, welcoming the cool rain upon her skin and hair. She breathed in deeply the wonderful aromas that only the forest rain could bring and laughed out loud into the night air. Then, opening her arms to all life, Sophia danced and twirled around and around as she had done outside the barn in the Land of the Shadows. Back then, it had been her first sighting of the crescent moon which had sent Sophia into rapturous delight. But now, more than ever before, it was the feeling of being truly free.

By the time she had re-entered the hut, the rain was falling much more heavily. Sophia was drenched, but she did not care. She felt alive, charged up with natural energy, her heart pounding with a joyful beat. Sophia swore she could feel the very cells of her body vibrate and dance to the same rhythmic beat. Her skin and her bones seemed to come alive as they too joined in the Dance of Life. She felt a little dizzy, certainly overwhelmed by this powerful Life Force flowing through her, and so she decided to go and lie down on her bed and wait until the dizziness had passed.

Soon she began to feel exhausted. It seemed to Sophia as though the power of these internal energies was almost too much for her mind and body to take, and she began to worry again. She worried about her relative physical weakness, about her inability to see the new moon and what would happen if she didn't see it . . . . and then she stopped. She stopped worrying. She surrendered, she let go. She told herself that if there was one thing she had learnt on the West Road, it was to trust; to trust the Divine, the Universe, Life itself – or as Edgar called it, the Greatest Unknown.

'I've learnt to trust at much worse times than this!' Sophia said out loud. 'Things will turn out the way they are meant to.'

In essence, she just accepted her situation, as it was.

Suddenly, there was a loud knock at the door.

'Sophia! Are you in there?' called the voice. Sophia jumped up at once. 'Merlin!' she cried, rushing to open the door.

Standing outside was the wise old man, cloaked in a purple cape and holding a glass lantern in his right hand. His hair and beard seemed to glisten in the rain and his eyes were not so much blue as a light violet. Struck by the vision in front of her, Sophia wondered how it was that he was not drenched by the heavy rain.

'Wow, you look amazing!' she said, unconsciously touching her own wet hair with her hand.

'It is always nice for an elder to hear such compliments. Thank you, my dear.'

As he stepped into the hut, the lantern seemed to light up every corner of the room. Sophia's face, too, lit up to reveal a magical child-like glow. He placed the lantern in the centre of the room and then lit a white candle which he had brought with him. Securing it into a golden candlestick holder, he placed it in the corner of the room farthest away from the door. Next, he placed two silver goblets on the floor and a small carafe between them. All these items seemed to come from behind Merlin's cape!

'Sit down, my child,' he beckoned to Sophia. 'I trust that you are rejuvenated after your rest?'

'Yes, very much,' agreed Sophia, as she sat down on one side of the candle.

Her elder sat opposite her, on the other side of the candle, before proceeding to fill the two goblets with the elixir from the carafe. It was a clear liquid which Sophia took to be water. He lifted up one of the goblets, and called for Sophia to do the same. As they raised their goblets, the wise old man made a tribute to Sophia:

'Let us acknowledge and celebrate this time of transition and transformation as you, Sophia, approach the Gateway of Freedom.'

They both drank to this sentiment, and Sophia was pleasantly surprised by the sweet nature of the water.

'Mmm, this is delicious,' she said. 'What is it?'

'I am glad you like it. It is the purest water flavoured with the aroma of elderflowers. Such an ancient tradition, and one of the many gifts given to us by the elder tree.'

'The trees give so much to us, don't they?' Sophia said, thoughtfully.

But her mind was also on the words that the wise old man had spoken previously. For Sophia knew that this was as much a farewell drink as it was a celebratory one; that any change, any new freedom in life, any new start, also brought with it a farewell to the old.

'I'll miss you,' she said, suddenly feeling rather sad. 'But I know I must go. I have to follow my destiny . . . . . my Soul, my Higher Self.'

Looking up at her older companion, Sophia smiled. For a memory had just come to her; 'Edgar said something to me that I'll always remember: "If you are the Hero, than I am the Horse that propels you." You see, he wrote a poem called, "The Horse and the Hero". I only remember bits of it, but even that helps me . . . . let me see . . . . oh yes, "On through the Gateway of Power they took flight".' Then she softly said, 'Edgar is with me now.'

'Yes, indeed,' nodded her companion. 'He is the Masculine aspect of you. He is your will, your power. And he will propel you to reach your true life goals, if you let your Feminine aspect lead the way. For this Feminine aspect of you is attuned to your inner nature; your intuitive, receptive and creative side. If you do this, Sophia, your life will be naturally abundant and harmonious. This is all that the Universe ultimately wants for us. And at the same time the Outside World becomes a much brighter place to live in.'

Sophia felt a warm glow build up inside her as she listened to his words of wisdom and encouragement. Then she asked, 'Is there an actual gateway, Merlin?'

He chuckled when he heard his adopted name again. 'Yes, there is,' he replied. 'And you might be surprised to hear that it was once known as the Gateway of Power.'

'Really?!'

'Everything is connected after all,' he explained. 'But the name has changed now, because of the unhealthy connotations that have been attributed by mankind to the word "power". Where once it meant "to be in one's own power," or "to have power over one's own nature" – it has now come to imply having power over another. It has become a tool of the ego, which serves no one truthfully. In the Outside World, power has come to mean the opposite of freedom, for it suppresses and oppresses one's true nature.' The wise old man paused for a moment, then continued:

'Yet to know one's own nature, to have faced your Shadow and to have befriended it – as you have done Sophia – leads to wholeness, and opens up the channels to the Divine Self. This is your Divine and unique individual power, Sophia, and it is the only true and eternal power. It leads to freedom from all earthly and mortal limitations.'

Then Sophia suddenly remembered something that the wise old man had said to her at the beginning of her journey. 'To truly be free, you have to face yourself!' she announced.

'Yes, yes! Exactly,' he laughed heartily.

When the candle had burnt down, the wise old man told Sophia that it was time for him to depart. But before he took his leave, he pointed her in the direction of the Gateway. Sophia could not believe it when he said that it was only a few hundred yards behind the hut! After they had embraced and had bid each other farewell, Sophia stood tearfully at the entrance of the hut and watched the wise old man, Merlin, slowly disappear into the forest. In his hand he carried his still brightly burning lantern to guide his way. Yet although Sophia felt saddened by his departure, there was no doubt that she also felt a sense of excitement at the thought of what the future could bring her; and of what she could bring to the future!

The rain was still coming down rather heavily as Sophia remained standing in the open doorway. The fresh crisp aroma in the night forest air seemed to somehow heighten her senses. 'I've been away from the delights of Mother Earth for so long,' she sighed. Then, beginning to feel a little chilly, she went back inside the hut and closed the door behind her.

Sophia was in total darkness now that there was no lantern or candle to light the hut. Nevertheless, she managed to make her way across to the window fairly swiftly, where she proceeded to pull down the blanket that had been acting as a curtain. She had decided that as soon as daylight appeared at her window, she would get up and make her way to the Gateway.

As she lay on her straw mat, Sophia's mind seemed to be so alert, with a hundred different thoughts going through her head all at the same time; the past, the present, and the future all rolled into one. Sophia was sure that she would not be able to sleep in this state. Yet to her surprise, once she had closed her eyes it wasn't long before sleep had descended upon her.

It was just after sunrise when Sophia's eyes began to open. The light streaming through the window was even brighter at this early hour than it had been at noon the previous day. Sophia got up immediately and went across to the window, squinting all the way. She saw that the sky was a vibrant blue.

'The sun! Oh, how I've missed you!' she said excitedly, before dashing outside.

It was indeed a beautiful spring day; a more beautiful day she could not remember. Sophia felt so happy, ecstatic almost. Her eyes hurt from the piercing sunlight, but it was not just the sun that was bright; it seemed that everything around her was in vivid technicolour!

'I don't remember it like this,' she said softly, in amazement. Then, remembering words she had been told when in the Land of the Shadows, she added with a smile, 'No, it is I who sees things differently.'

Sophia turned to head back to the door of the hut, when suddenly she caught sight of something beyond it . . . .

She could see two stone pillars, almost as tall as the trunks of the ancient yew trees, and across the top of the pillars lay another large oblong stone.

'The Gateway of Freedom!' gasped Sophia.

Without any further hesitation, she set about getting ready to go there – although she didn't really have anything to take with her except the crystal, which she made sure was safely tucked away somewhere on her person. Yet when Sophia went to close the door of the hut, she noticed something sparkling towards the back of the hut. She walked back into the hut and saw that it was one of the silver goblets that Merlin had brought with him. She wondered why it was there, and whether it would be alright to take it with her, as a memento? Then she noticed a small rucksack a few feet away from the silver goblet – it looked almost identical to the bag that she had carried throughout her journey. Sophia reached over for it and quickly opened it. She could not believe what she discovered: The shawl that the Sibyl had given to her by the moon tree! With ecstatic joyfulness, Sophia pulled the shawl out of the bag, only to find her old sleeping bag underneath it.

'I don't believe it! How on earth did it get here?!' she squealed with delight. 'It was buried at the bottom of the river!'

She wasted no time in pulling the sleeping bag out and then unzipping it. She wanted to see if those things she had placed inside her sleeping bag before she had entered the river, were still there. She was not disappointed. In fact, Sophia was overcome with emotion when she saw the precious items from the Land of the Shadows – items she thought she would never see again. The Sibyl's Scroll, Edgar's journals, and Sophia's notepad were all lying there before her, as dry as a bone!

'Thank you! Thank you!' Sophia repeated over and over, in her overwhelming wish to express her feelings of gratitude to the Divine Source, to the Greatest Unknown. 'And thank you, Merlin!'

Shaking her head in disbelief, Sophia carefully placed all the items back into the rucksack. Then she picked up the gleaming silver goblet, still wondering whether to take it with her, and held it for a while.

'It's almost like holding the Grail Cup!' she said, smiling.

Yet this very utterance seemed to serve as a decision maker; for Sophia had suddenly made up her mind in that instance not to take the silver goblet. Instead, she gently placed it back upon the spot where it was originally. Then she got to her feet, strapped her ever so familiar bag across her back, and headed off out of the hut for the last time.

As she got closer and closer to the Gateway, Sophia's heart sped up with excitement and anticipation. And then she was there: Standing before the two large stone pillars. She could see that the stone itself had been heavily worn down, weathered by the passing of time; much of it was now covered with forest growth and moss. What struck her though was that the newly risen sun seemed to be shining directly through the Gateway; Sophia knew she was facing directly east.

She stepped forward through the Gateway, towards the rising sun, and towards her destiny.

Sophia was at once surprised by the contrasting landscape in front of her; fields of lush green grass now replaced the ancient yew forest which stood behind her. She walked straight ahead, in an eastward direction, taking in the sights and sounds around her. After a while, she decided to relax and settle down upon the carpet of green grass beneath her feet; indeed she was surprised by how dry the grass was, considering the heavy rainfall of the night before! Lying back, she rested her head on her bag and closed her eyes. It was not long, however, before Sophia felt a "presence" of some kind.

Immediately, she opened her eyes and was startled by the sight before her: A white horse. Sophia sat up quickly, not taking her eyes off the magnificent creature to her left for one moment. The horse was only a few feet away from her and it was also looking directly back at Sophia! Very carefully, Sophia got to her feet and almost tip-toed over to the horse. Reaching up slowly, she began to stroke its long neck and mane. The horse was already saddled up, complete with reins.

'The Horse and the Hero!' Sophia whispered, thinking lovingly of Edgar.

Just then, the horse seemed to reply with a grunting sound. Sophia laughed heartily. 'You know,' she informed her four legged companion, 'it's been years since I rode a horse.'

Nevertheless, she went over to collect her bag and once it was securely strapped to her back, she returned to the horse and rather tentatively placed her left foot into the stirrup. She attempted to heave herself up on to the saddle, but it didn't work first time. In fact it took three goes for Sophia to succeed. Once she did succeed, Sophia had next to no time to contemplate her next move for the horse had galloped off towards the rising sun, and all Sophia could do was to hold on as tight as she could to the reins.

'Steady on, Edgar!' she cried out, addressing the horse by its proper name . . . . . . 'There's no need to overdo it!'

The horse galloped onwards and onwards and Sophia's laughter could be heard as it was carried upon the breeze, her heart rising to meet it. Joyfully, Sophia called up to the heavens:

'I am the hero, and you Edgar are the horse! We are . . . . .

427

"THE HORSE AND THE HERO":

She rode and rode on the back of her horse
As if either or both had wings,
That would carry them through the mists of the night
And over the hills and on with their plight.

The stallion that flew with the wind for its name,
As free as the wind and as light as a flame,
The wildness of nature to clutch on the breeze
Yet slip through her hands, as the spirit is free.

And she, the one with the flame-coloured mane,
Rose with majesty unto the land of her reign,
Land of mists and magic and myths
Beset in beauty transcending Earth's plane.

Onward they rode deep into the night
With stars to guide them 'til dark became light,
Then through the Gateway of Power they took flight
For nothing could halt such a magnitude of might.

Whilst the draw of destiny and lure of the Divine
Held in its elements the transcripts of time,
Their forward leap broke through the hidden Veil
And the Horse and the Hero had touched the Holy Grail.

About The Author

Maria Pelengaris was born in London's Drury Lane. Her mother is English and her father Greek Cypriot. She lived through the 1974 war in Cyprus which saw the division of the island. Returning to the UK Maria attended the London School of Economics where she graduated in 1984 with a mathematics and business degree. For a time Maria worked in the city at the height of Thatcherism, then in 1987 Maria went off travelling all over Western Asia and the Middle-East. During this time Maria discovered her love for writing poetry and prose. On her return, she embarked upon a new career in the NHS, working with people suffering from difficulties with mental health issues. The next twelve years saw Maria work at St. Bartholomew's hospital and in Hackney where she became a Senior Charge Nurse running a busy in-patient ward for women. She ran an out-patient unit specialising in group-work and counselling. Maria is also a trained "CAT" counsellor (Cognitive Analytic Therapy). At the end of the 1990's feeling somewhat burnt-out Maria took time off. During this time she experienced a profound 'spiritual calling' – her world felt shaken-up to such an extent that her old ways seemed like they counted for little. She was forced to rely on something else - a connection with the soul. She needed to connect with mind, body, spirit on a deeper level. Maria began writing 'The Veils of Illusion'. She is now a trained Reiki healer and sometimes works with crystal and chakra balancing. She enjoys workshops and reading about St. Germain and Merlin, Mary Magdalene and The Divine Feminine Energy, Gnosticism, and The Christ Energy. Other interests include reading about mythology and mysticism, holism, and on a very pragmatic Earth level Maria is training as a professional driving instructor.

Printed in the United Kingdom
by Lightning Source UK Ltd.
110077UKS00001B/163-255

9 781420 884869